GUARDED ADDICTION

BY

L. ANN

GUARDED ADDICTION

Copyright © 2021 by L. Ann.

All rights reserved.

No part of this book may be used or reproduced in any manner whatsoever without written permission except in the case of brief quotations embodied in critical articles or reviews.

This book is a work of fiction. Names, characters, businesses, organisations, places, events and incidents either are the product of the author's imagination or are used fictitiously. Any resemblance to actual persons, living or dead, events, or locales is entirely coincidental.

Cover design by A.T. Cover Designs

Interior Formatting by Crow Fiction Designs

Edited by Margot Mostert

First Edition: April 2021

ISBN: 979-8738370052

L.Ann Online -

www.lannauthor.com

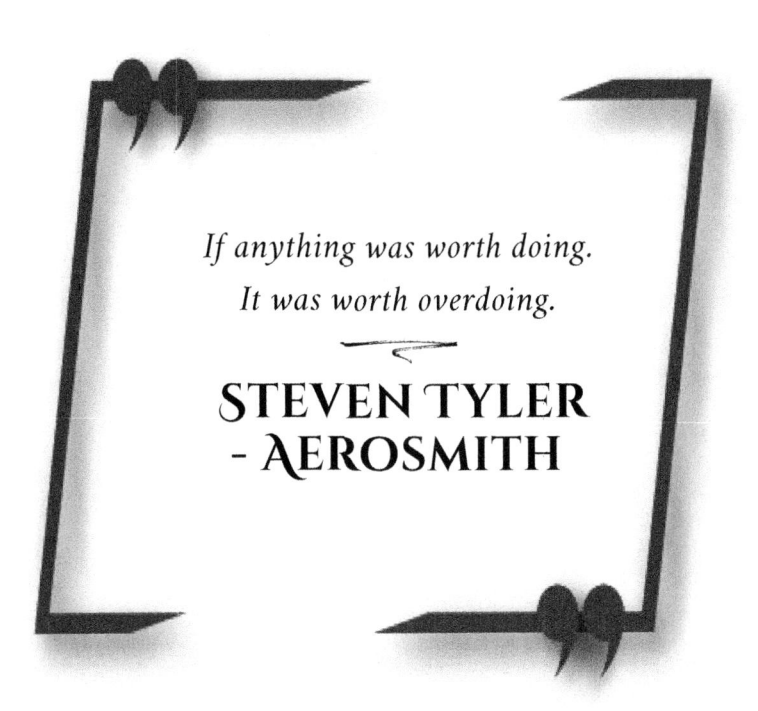

If anything was worth doing.
It was worth overdoing.

STEVEN TYLER
- AEROSMITH

After
10 Years

Dedication

To the real Siobhan, who let me borrow her name. This one is for everyone who has embraced my broken rock band. You're all nuts and I love you for it!

PLAYLIST

Paparazzi - Kim Dracula
Cherub Rock - Smashing Pumpkins
Happy People - Deal Casino
The Lovecats - The Cure
Dark Necessities - Red Hot Chili Peppers
Don't Look Back In Anger - Oasis
Run Away - Lacey
Cherry Pie - Warrant
Nothing To Say - Galactic Cowboys
Wolf In Sheep's Clothing - Set It Off
All To Myself - Marianas Trench
Lonely Dance - Set It Off
Think I'm Crazy - Two Feet
Middle Finger - Bohnes
Novacaine - The Unlikely Candidates
Crazy - Aerosmith
Bad Habit - The Kooks
Beautiful Mistake - Maroon 5
Drugs and Candy - All Time Low
Wolf - Highly Suspect
IDFC - Blackbear
Head Like A Hole - Nine Inch Nails
Drugs - Eden
It Won't Last - Blacktop Mojo
Never Enough - Two Feet
Snow White - Dennis Lloyd
I Remember Way Too Much - Mod Sun
Nine In The Afternoon - Panic! At The Disco
Madness - Muse
I Don't Like The Drugs - Marilyn Manson
Secrets - OneRepublic
Cry Baby - Missio

Girlfriend - Badflower
Happy Pills - Weathers
In Chains - Shaman's Harvest
Monsters - Shinedown
Easy To Lie - Forest Blakk
You - Two Feet
Fighting In The Car - Joe P
Foolish - Boy Epic
Leave Me Alone - I Don't Know How But They Found Me
Trouble - Cage The Elephant
Bad Things - Jace Everett
Bad Girl - Avril Lavigne ft Marilyn Manson
Do It For Me - Rosenfeld
Where Is My Mind - Milky Chance
I Don't Love You - My Chemical Romance
Keeping Me Alive - Jonathan Roy
Cotton Candy - YungBlud
My Name Is Human - Highly Suspect
I Want My Life Back Now - The Wrecks
Could You Be Mine - Billy Raffoul
Hear Me Now - Bad Wolves
You're Mine - Disturbed
20 Dollar Nosebleed - Fall Out Boy
Whole Lotta Love - Hollywood Vampires
Habits (Stay High) - Tove Lo
Power - Isak Danielson
Bang - AJR
If I get High - Nothing But Thieves
Under The Bridge - Red Hot Chili Peppers
Angels and Demons - Jxdn
I Kissed A Girl - Twenty One Two
Beautiful Way - You Me At Six
Snap Out Of it - Arctic Monkeys
Semi-Charmed Life - Third Eye Blind
Let The Band Play - Badflower

GUARDED ADDICTION

PROLOGUE

PAPARAZZI - KIM DRACULA

SOMEWHERE IN LA

"I'm standing outside the police station where there are reports coming in that Dex Cooper and Luca Tallorico from the rock band, Forgotten Legacy, have been arrested this morning on suspicion of murder. No news has been released so far on who the victim could be, but the band's manager, Karl Daniels, along with Matthew Carmichael and Jared Kilroy of Carmichael and Sons, were also seen entering the station half an hour ago.

"Everyone knows that the band has had a troubled year—with Gabe Mercer and his fiancée being attacked and almost killed by his bodyguard. In a surprising turn of events, it led to the arrest and incarceration of Meredith Walker for her part in Harper Jackson's kidnapping.

"Seth Hawkins has also had a share of the limelight recently for his relationship with the much younger Riley Temple. As most of you know, it was at Ms. Temple's graduation where Dex Cooper overdosed a few months ago, which resulted in him being sent to the prestigious Red Wood Complex Rehabilitation Center, where he was asked to leave after a few short weeks for reasons unknown.

"Dex Cooper has a troubled history with drug and alcohol abuse and, although rumors suggest he has been clean for a while now, it does raise the question ... has this arrest come about due to a relapse?

"His relationship with the band's drummer has always been questionable, leaving people wondering if there was more to it than just that of bandmates and friends. They have a reputation for sharing women, and although no one has ever come forward to share those stories, they have been seen leaving nightclubs or restaurants together with a single woman more often than not.

"Any one of these things could have a connection to the rumors of murder circulating. Sadly, right now, all we can do is wait for more information to be released."

Karl Daniels switched off the television with a noise of disgust and turned to survey the room. "What happened to innocent until proven guilty?" he asked of no one in particular.

"Just another day in the life of Forgotten Legacy." His friend and co-owner of NFG Records, Marley Stone, said dryly from across the room. "I can't stay long. Those reporters catching me here will turn that circus out there into a bigger nightmare than it already is."

"You didn't have to come, anyway."

"Our flagship band, barring Black Rosary, has not one but *two* of its members arrested for murder and you think I'm not going to be here to find out what the story is?" Marley snorted. "You should know better than that."

CHAPTER 1

CHERUB ROCK - SMASHING PUMPKINS

Dex
PRESENT

It's funny how life works. When I was ten years old, my old man told me I should get used to seeing bars in front of my window because I'd end up dead or in prison by the time I was eighteen. Ironic coming from him, since he was between stays himself when he said it, and it was only a few short weeks later when he went back inside again.

Here I was almost twenty years later, the world at my feet, a bank account my dad would have salivated over, and a house which would have been on his list of targets. Women threw themselves at me. So did men—fruitlessly, since I didn't swing that way. They always assumed I did because Luca and I liked to play together, occasionally.

I've traveled the world, been to countries I doubt my dad has ever heard of. We even have a private jet available for our use. Okay, so the jet belonged to the entire band, but I owned a quarter of it, so it still counted, although we only used it for tours and not for short trips

- the expense of running it cost more than a plane ticket.

The point I'm making is that I *didn't* end up in prison—although it *was* touch and go for a while there—and I proved my father wrong on a regular basis because I wasn't *dead* yet either. But standing in a hotel room in the center of cold, wet London, I questioned whether our band had hit its peak and were now on the downward slide into obscurity. After all, when you hit the top, the only way was down ... right?

I stood at the window of the hotel room, hands shoved deep inside the pockets of my jeans and flicked my tongue piercing against my teeth while I listened to the men arguing behind me. The discussion washed over me, each of them rehashing the same points over and over until I wanted to grind my teeth in frustration.

When the conversation finally swung back around to whether or not Forgotten Legacy was over, I spun around.

"For fuck's sake!" At my snarled words, the rest of the guys fell silent and three sets of eyes fell on me. "He's not quitting the band. He's fucking coming back home with us."

"I'm right here," Luca pointed out. "I can speak for myself."

"Then when *are* you coming home?" I knew it would be Gabe who'd take the lead and demand an answer.

"When I'm ready."

"It's been two months," our lead singer pointed out through gritted teeth.

"Is there a time limit on how long I need?"

"No." Gabe's hand raked through his hair, and I knew he was

trying to control his own frustration with our drummer. "Look man, I get it, but we have obligations. Come *home*. We'll hit the studio and get back to work. We have an album's worth of music ready to go. We just need to finish it off."

Luca snorted. "Hire a session musician. You don't need me to lay down the drums, you can get anyone to do that."

Gabe scowled, and it was obvious he was on the verge of saying something *everyone* would come to regret. I saw the battle wage in his eyes, and prayed that common sense won the war and he was able to keep his patience.

"What the fuck? *You're* Forgotten Legacy's drummer, not some no-name session musician!"

I breathed out a silent sigh of relief.

"So get a *name*, then. Deryn will stand in." Luca mentioned Black Rosary's drummer.

"What the fuck is wrong with you?" Gabe roared, and I realized my relief had been premature. "I fucking give up." He threw his hands up in disgust. "You talk to him." He stalked out of the suite and slammed the door behind him.

"Luc," Seth said into the silence.

"I know," Luca cut in before he could say anything more. "Believe me, I *know*."

"Then you also know that we need you. *Not* a session musician, not a friend to cover for you. We need *you*," Seth said quietly. He reached out to pat his shoulder then turned to follow Gabe.

Luca glanced at me, and I looked back at him.

"Let's hear it," he grunted.

"I don't have anything more to add that hasn't already been said," I told him. "It's time to come home."

"And then *what?* We can't play happy fucking families, D."

"We've *never* played happy families. But we *are* a family, you got that part right. And you know what? Families *fight*, Luc. Even ones that aren't as fucked up as ours. The difference is we *chose* to be family. We picked our brothers. Now will you please fucking drag your ass out of this pity party and come home?" I played my trump card. "All this stress makes me want to go and get high."

He glared at me, and I smiled. I knew he had no argument against what I'd said. Forgotten Legacy *wasn't* simply a band made up of four guys who'd met at school. It was made up of four boys who had lived through hell as kids and bonded together over it. We *were* family and we could spill each other's blood a thousand times over, yet still be there when we were needed.

Luca huffed a sigh. "Fine."

My smile broadened and I reached into my jacket pocket, took out an envelope and handed it to him.

"What's this?"

"We're booked to go home tonight. That's your ticket. You have an hour to pack."

"An hour?"

"We have tickets for a first-class flight. We've been here two weeks, Luc. Gabe's right. It's time to get back into the game. We've managed to keep this whole mess out of the papers, but you know the longer you're out of the country, the more they'll sniff around. And once they decide you've left the band and report it, all hell will break loose."

He dropped onto the couch with a heavy sigh. "That's the problem, D. I'm not sure I *want* to go back to it."

"What the fuck are you talking about?" I scowled at him.

"What's it done for us? *Really*? Gabe lost Harper for years. Lexi wouldn't have ..." His voice broke and he swallowed, looking away.

"Don't go down that path. Lexi would have killed herself a long time ago without the money and resources Seth had. She was fucking selfish," I snapped.

Luca's eyes flashed and he surged to his feet, fingers clenching into fists. "She wasn't selfish. She was *sick*."

I tipped my chin up and let my lip curl into a smirk. "Want to hit me, Luc? Go right ahead. Do it. You know I'm right. Take it from someone who's been at rock bottom. Doing what she did, the way she did it? *That* was fucking selfish and one more shout for attention from her brother that she didn't need. She saw Seth was interested in Riley and couldn't handle the thought of not having his undivided attention. There's no doubt the girl had issues, yeah she was sick, but doing that at the time she chose ... I'm sorry, man, but that was done for maximum fall out."

"You don't know what you're talking about," he growled.

"I know enough. Now fucking sort your shit out and come home."

I walked into the bedroom as I spoke and hauled his suitcase out of the wardrobe. Throwing it onto the bed, I started packing his clothes.

"What are you doing?" Luca followed me and leaned against the doorframe, arms folded across his chest.

"An *hour*, Luc. Then we hit the air. I thought I was messy, but what the fuck have you been doing? Buying clothes instead of washing the ones you have?" I picked up a t-shirt that still had its sales tag on. "The London Eye?" I shook my head, laughing. "Fuck's sake."

He shrugged. "I did the tourist thing."

"You did the tourist thing," I repeated flatly. "While the band burns, *you* did the tourist thing?"

"You have no room to talk. How many times have you flatlined because you can't leave the fucking drugs alone?"

"It's been six months since I touched anything harder than a diet Coke, Scout's honor." I lifted my hand in the Scout's salute.

He snorted an unwilling laugh. "You were never a Boy Scout."

"I also have very little honor, but it's the truth. Karl makes me take a drug test every week."

"Sure, and we both know you can get around that if you really wanted to get high."

I continued stuffing his clothes into the suitcase and didn't respond. He wasn't wrong. If I wanted a fix, I could get one easily enough and still pass the drug test. I might lie to everyone else, but I wouldn't lie to Luca. I would omit things, but I wouldn't outright *lie*. We'd been through too much together.

After watching me for a few minutes, he walked into the room and shoved me to one side. "Get out of the way, I'll do it. You're making a fucking mess."

I stepped back. "Good. I need to go and sort my own shit out. I'll see you at the airport."

Luca didn't turn up for the flight. Ten minutes before we were due to take off, my cell rang. His name popped up on the screen. I connected the call and put him onto speaker phone.

"Sorry. I'm not going to make it. I'll get the next available flight out." Muffled shouts and sirens could be heard in the background, above the noise of a car engine.

I waited for Gabe to tear into him, but our lead singer merely shook his head and returned his attention back to his own cell.

"What happened?" I asked.

"Got stuck in traffic. There was a crash and the cab had to take a detour. It's added extra time to the journey. Don't delay the flight. Go back home. I promise I'll be on the next available flight." He cut the call before I could reply.

Fucking asshole.

A shadow fell across me and I glanced up at the flight attendant who appeared silently beside me.

"Can I get you anything?" she asked, her smile so white her dentist must have been proud.

"Diet Coke for me," I told her, knowing if I asked for the tequila I badly wanted, I'd get a lecture from one of my bandmates.

I hadn't quit drinking, but I knew I'd get a ton of questions asking how many I'd already had.

"Coffee," Gabe grunted without looking up.

"Coming right up!" She spun and almost bounced her way down the aisle.

I smothered a laugh.

"Think she's new?" I said in response to Seth's questioning look. "She's trying too hard."

"Don't they all?" He tipped his head back against the headrest and closed his eyes. "But give it an hour or two, and I have no doubt she'll be more than happy to bounce on your dick."

I smirked. Seth was right. She *would* want to do that—I was the only available rock star on board but, unfortunately for her, she'd end the flight in disappointment. While her hair *was* a nice shade of red, she wasn't the redhead I intended to have bouncing on my dick when I got home.

Guarded Addiction

CHAPTER 2

HAPPY PEOPLE - DEAL CASINO

Siobhan

PRESENT

"Everyone wants to fuck the lead singer, Harp." I waved the cherry sucker at the television where we could see Gabe and Seth on the screen. "You've just got to realize that this particular lead singer isn't interested in fucking anyone other than *you*."

I popped the sucker back into my mouth, watching as Harper's gaze bounced from me to the crowd on television, jostling each other to get closer to Gabe and Seth. Both men seemed at ease, signing papers thrust into their faces, posing for photos—Gabe sporting a charming smile, while Seth's expression appeared relaxed. But anyone who really knew either of them could see the faint hints of tension—the way Gabe's smile didn't reach his eyes, or how Seth avoided the touches and kisses with seemingly innocent head turns or hand gestures.

The footage was from a movie premiere a few months before Gabe crashed his way back into Harper's life, part of a montage detailing the rise of the rock band known as Forgotten Legacy.

Harper rose to her feet and turned off the television. "I *know* he doesn't," she said quietly as she returned to her position on the couch. "But seeing how they're treated. Like they *belong* to the fans. It's different seeing it on television or reading about it. But being there and *watching* it happen? I don't like how it makes me feel."

We were sitting in my apartment—the one that Harper used to share with me—having yet another girls' night while the guys of Forgotten Legacy were in London trying to talk Luca into coming home. Gabe had wanted Harper to go along with him. She argued that since the whole kidnapping incident, followed by their bass guitarist's overdose, and then the tour which had been cut short by Lexi's death, she'd barely had a moment to breathe. She needed some time to slow down and adjust to the lifestyle she'd been thrust into. Reluctantly, he'd agreed, but that didn't stop him from blowing up her cell with calls and texts almost non-stop.

Two bottles of wine and we were at the stage where we weren't *quite* drunk, but we weren't exactly sober either.

"But are you happy?" I pointed my sucker at her and Harper scowled at it.

"How can you eat those things and drink wine at the same time?"

I gave an exaggerated lick of it and smirked at her eye roll. "Answer my question."

"Of course I'm happy."

I leaned forward to top off our glasses, handed one to her and leaned back against the cushions. "You don't sound it."

"No, I am! Having Gabe back in my life is *everything* I wanted.

I guess I'm finding it hard adjusting to all the ..."

"Fame? Groupies?" Sipping my drink, I eyed her over the rim of the glass. "You know it's going to get even worse once they bring Luca back and release their new album?"

Harper grimaced but didn't reply. I set my glass down, dropping my sucker into it, and reached out to take her hands.

"Has something happened? You trust Gabe, don't you? Do you think he's done something while he's been in London?"

"No, he's not going to cheat on me." Her voice was firm. "That's not the problem. I *know* he's all in with me."

"Then what is it?"

She gave me a helpless look. "What if *I* can't handle it, Von? What if I end up losing him because I can't deal with it all? Every time we go out together, he's mobbed by fans. The paparazzi photographs our every move. It's like living in a goldfish bowl."

"You really think Gabe is going to let you walk away from him? That man gives new meaning to the word *obsessed*. He *loves* you, Harper. *You*. Not any of those girls out there trying to get into his pants. And if you think he's going to let that go any time soon, you're in for a huge shock. Didn't that big deal he made on stage when he proposed tell you that?" I scooped my glass back up, licked the wine off my sucker and tossed it into the trash can. "You've got time to get used to it. They have no new tours planned any time soon."

"Karl is already talking about a headline tour to go with the new album. He wants to squash the rumors about any internal fighting before they get off the ground."

"Well, you'll be on tour with them, won't you? I doubt it'll be like the last one." I didn't want to think about that period of time. I knew if I let myself, something would show on my face and Harper would notice. I wasn't ready to answer the questions she'd ask me.

"Gabe would want me to go," she was saying. "But, I don't know, Von. After the last one..."

I waited. She chewed on her bottom lip, an obvious tell I recognized.

"You could come with us again, couldn't you?"

"You want me to come on tour with the band because you're scared of being the only girl on the bus... *again?*" I snorted a laugh. "What do you think is going to happen to you? It's not like it'll suddenly turn into a one-girl-and-four-hot-men wet dream. *That* only happens in books." I paused to unwrap a fresh sucker and swirled it around my mouth, before adding thoughtfully, "Plus, Gabe would kill anyone if they tried to climb into bed with you."

Harper went red. "I didn't even *think* about that! Why would that be the first thing you go to?"

"I don't know Harper. Why is *your* go-to for everything somebody being murdered?" I raised an eyebrow, smiling. "We all have our thing. Maybe fantasies about sex with multiple hot men was mine." My smile faded. "Although, I have to be honest, in reality I think one dick at a time is more than enough for me to deal with. But a girl needs her dreams, right?"

Harper took a sip of wine. "You joke about it, but would you? If the opportunity ever presented itself?"

I gave the question the serious attention the wine in my system felt it needed. I could be honest with Harper and tell her the opportunity *had* presented itself, but for all her open-mindedness and the public displays she let Gabe get away with, I didn't think it was something she would understand, so I shook my head and gave her a truth I'd discovered.

"No, I think sharing could potentially ruin a relationship, at least for me. Would it be nice to have all that attention focused on me? Sure, but could you imagine the headache juggling all those male egos? I'd rather find one guy who knows how to use his dick …" I paused for a mouthful of wine, and sent my best friend a grin, "and his tongue. That would make me very happy." Another sip of wine and I cocked my brow at Harper. "Hell, show me a man who can make me come so hard I see stars, and I'd lock him down tight."

Harper laughed. "Maybe you'll find him if you come on tour with us again."

I screwed my face up and gave a derisive laugh. "And maybe hell will freeze over."

"What happened to your mission to experience the ultimate orgasm?"

"Ohhh!" I pointed a finger at Harper. "I see how it is. Using my quest to get your own way."

"It's a *quest* now?"

"To find the elusive perfect orgasm? Of course! It ranks up

there with discovering unicorns are real."

Harper flopped back against the cushions, giggling. "The two aren't necessarily exclusive. *Your* unicorn could be a hot man who can give you multiple orgasms." She gave an expansive wave of her hand, sloshing wine over the rim of her glass. "I know, for a *fact*, they're out there."

"Oh you do, do you?" I purred, raising an eyebrow. "Gabe lives up to the rumors, huh? Well, I suppose if *you* can find one of these mythical beasts, then surely there must be more of them out there." I already *knew* there was, but I also knew they came with so many issues that I wasn't certain it was worth the effort.

"Please, Von?" Harper caught my hand, the one *not* holding the wineglass and returned to her main topic. "I grew up with these guys. I *know* how disgusting they can be. I'll need another woman there otherwise I'll lose my mind."

I snickered into my glass. "Well, when you put it that way..."

Harper relaxed when she realized I was agreeing to join her on a tour that may or may not happen, and the evening continued to pass in a blur of girly chatter and drinking.

A little after midnight, our conversation had wound down to short bursts of chatter interspersed with sleepy yawns and I was going to suggest we both get some sleep when there was a quiet tap on the door. Frowning, because it was late and neither of us were expecting anyone, I rose to my feet and peered through the peephole. I was surprised to find Gabe standing just beyond it, looking tired, under Remy's watchful eye. I eased the door open and smiled at Harper's shriek of delight when she spotted him.

"I thought you weren't going to be home until tomorrow!"

My friend threw herself at her rock star boyfriend and planted a wet kiss on the corner of his mouth. One dark eyebrow hiked up and he shot a glance at me. I shrugged.

"I told her to pace herself. Wine *always* goes to her head." I sent him a grin. "You're welcome. You'll be in for a great night."

Gabe Mercer, famous lead singer and frontman of the rock band Forgotten Legacy, snorted a laugh, and swung his tipsy, and clearly-elated-to-see-him girlfriend up into his arms.

"Pretty sure she'll be snoring before we reach the car. Thanks for looking after her," he threw at me over his shoulder, and strode out, kicking the door shut behind him.

The silence of the apartment was heavy once he and Harper left and, yawning, I rose to my feet to seek out my bed. As I was drifting off to sleep, my cell vibrated on the nightstand. Snatching it up, my first thought was that Harper had forgotten something. But the message that greeted me made me frown and blink at the screen, sure I was misreading it.

ROCK STAR - I'm home. You alone?

I stared at the message. The right thing to do was not to reply at all *or* say I *wasn't* alone, because I was *sure* if I said anything else, he'd be at my door soon after he received it. And, where he was concerned, my willpower was weak. And yet, I didn't do either of those things.

ME - Why wouldn't I be? What do you want?

Nothing came through for a couple of minutes and I wondered if, by replying, I'd given him what he wanted and he wasn't going to bother answering me, but then a new reply popped up.

ROCK STAR - I fucked up, Red. Someone passed me a gram of coke on the way out of the airport.

I sat upright, all irritation at him contacting me gone.

ME - Did you use it?

I held my breath, waiting for his reply. It felt like a lifetime before it came through.

ROCK STAR - Not yet.

This was *bad*.

Guarded Addiction

CHAPTER 3

THE LOVECATS - THE CURE

Dex

AGE 22

I pulled the ball cap low over my eyes and stepped onto the train. I *could* have called for a car to pick me up, but I wasn't like Gabe or Seth. Because they were the frontmen of the band, they were more recognizable. Our recent explosion onto the professional music scene didn't make me feel like I needed the protection of bodyguards and private cars, it made me want the opposite—anonymity. Having a suited bodyguard hulking around, shadowing my every move would draw attention to me and I didn't want that. Alone, unless I made a point of attracting attention, only the most obsessed fans of the band who had followed us during the early days would notice my presence. I was the bass player, not the singer or lead guitarist. And people only saw what they expected to see. Finding a member of one of the hottest upcoming local rock bands on public transport ranked up there with finding an alien from Mars walking down the street—it wasn't gonna happen. And hell, if it was good enough for Keanu

Reeves, it was good enough for me.

Anyway, I wanted some time to myself. The crazy train we'd signed up for when we put our names on the NFG Records contract had been on a constant high-speed journey for months. I needed space to breathe, to hear myself think, and this was the only way I was going to get it.

All of us had spent years using public transport before we had more money than we could spend, and the rest of the band *hated* it. It reminded them of the years we struggled and what we might have to go back to if our first album flopped. But me? I could move around the Metro with my eyes closed, hopping from train to train, station to station. Being among the hustle of people leaving work, hearing random snatches of conversation as they passed, ears glued to cells, or their focus on the person with them, gave me a feeling of … not contentment, exactly, but some kind of normalcy we didn't get in our daily lives anymore as new almost-celebrities.

I braced myself as the train pulled out of the station, knowing people were going to shift and sway in time with the motion—and *that's* when I spotted her. Well, more accurately, I spotted her *hair*. I recognized her as being someone Harper knew, how well I wasn't sure. But I'd definitely seen them together, during my brief stalker-like check-ins on Gabe's childhood sweetheart's well-being.

She stood midway down the train car, one hand wrapped around a pole to anchor her in place, while the other clutched her cell against her ear. I watched as she spoke furiously, eyes narrowed and, in my imagination, spitting angry sparks. Something woke inside me. I couldn't pinpoint what it was, exactly. All I knew was that I needed to get closer, to feel the heat of the anger pouring off her.

With murmured apologies, I pushed my way through the bodies crammed inside the train car and moved toward her. She hadn't noticed me, but then why would she? I'd never spoken or approached Harper when they were together. In fact, I hadn't spoken to Harper since the night Gabe unceremoniously threw her out of the house we shared.

I managed to step right up behind her, and wrapped my hand above hers on the pole while I eavesdropped on her conversation. She didn't pay any attention to me, her focus on the argument she was having and staying upright on the crowded train.

"I *know*! You'll get it," she was hissing in a low voice to whoever was on the other end of the call.

Someone moved behind me, forcing me to take a step closer and she automatically shifted to the side, still not looking to see who was encroaching on her space.

"I'm *not* struggling." She made the claim through gritted teeth and I dipped my head, trying to hear the person on the other end of the line. "What do you *want*, David?"

If I concentrated, I could just make out the voice.

"I wanted to make sure you were okay."

"Why wouldn't I be?" she asked.

"Young woman, alone. It's not the safest area."

"*You* own the building. You could *make* it safer," she pointed out.

The fine hairs on the back of my neck rose up at what I was hearing. I didn't like the sound of where this conversation was going.

"*It's not cheap to maintain the building. There are overheads.*" I heard the guy on the other end of the line say.

"Sure. Look, I have to go. You'll get your rent tomorrow." The redhead in front of me sounded tired.

"*If you need some extra time ...*"

"Thanks, but no. I can't afford your interest payments." Her reply was sharp.

My eyes narrowed. The discomfort in her voice told me my gut instinct was right. I didn't even consider my action when I reached out and plucked her cell from her hand.

"Hi. David, right?" I said, and leaned away when she tried to snatch her cell back. "This is Dex, Red's fiancé." I didn't know her name, so I had to improvise and that hair was so fucking *red*.

"*Fiancé?*" The guy at the other end almost screeched. "She never told me she was engaged."

"We were trying to keep it quiet. Look," I let go of the pole to plant my palm against my new soon-to-be wife's shoulder and held her out of reach while she attempted to retrieve her phone from my grip. "She didn't want to tell you this, but the reason money is tight right now is because she's been saving for our wedding."

"*What?*" The word came at me in stereo—both the mysterious David and the redhead saying it at the same time.

"Yeah." I grinned down at the raging spitfire in front of me, who was trying her hardest to reach her cell. "We're getting married. But we have to keep it quiet because her family doesn't approve, you understand? We're sneaking off to Vegas for the wedding as soon as we can afford it. Then we're gonna get outta town for a while. So I'd really appreciate it if you could ease up on the pressure, okay? We'll get the rent paid."

"Yes, of course! She should have told me." The guy sounded way more subdued now that he wasn't talking to her.

"Thanks. I'll let her know." I cut the call and held out the cell.

"What the *hell* do you think you're doing?" she whisper-snarled, snatching her phone from my palm.

I smiled, ignoring her outrage. "You're welcome, Red. Now you've got time to pay your rent."

"I think I'm going to put that money toward your *funeral*!" She made a grab for the pole as the train slowed to a stop at Glendale Station to let people off.

The surge of people aiming for the door knocked against her and she stumbled forward. I caught her before she face-planted the floor.

"The one thing I hate about the Metro is the inability of people to watch what they're fucking doing," I said with a sigh, and wrapped an arm around her waist to keep her upright.

"Why were you eavesdropping on my conversation, anyway?"

"You seemed angry, and I needed a little excitement in my day. It's been so boring lately. I might as well be dead."

She scowled at me. "Why would you say something like that?"

"Aww, Red. Would you miss me?"

"I don't *know* you."

I gave her a look of mock horror. "You're marrying someone you hardly know? We can't have that. Ask me anything. I'm an open book. My life is your pleasure."

She shook her head. "I'm not marrying you. Stop saying that."

"*What?* But the wedding is all arranged. We can't back out now. Think of the children!" I canted my head. "Don't tell me you haven't bought a dress yet?"

"Of course I haven't. Are you always this annoying?" She tried to step back and put some space between us, but there were too many people crammed into the carriage.

I tightened my grip on her waist. "I don't think you should get a white dress. Get red."

"*Red?* That would clash with my hair. Are you crazy? I can't wear red!" She blurted the words out before realizing what she had said, and I snorted a laugh when she glared at me.

"Red," I repeated. "It's my favorite color. Red for my Red." I twirled a lock of her hair around one finger. "Red dress and a ruby engagement ring. We should go shopping. There's a fantastic jeweler I know in Vegas."

"Have you completely lost your mind? We're *not* getting married."

I kept my face expressionless and my voice serious when I looked down at her. "But we have to, Red. We've told your creepy landlord now. In fact, he's going to want evidence of the fiancé you've been hiding." I tugged the lock of hair I held, holding back a grin at her look of bemusement. "Damn, I didn't think of that. One second." I pulled my cell out from my back pocket and opened the camera app. "Smile, baby," I told her, angled the camera to take a selfie, then planted a kiss on her surprised lips, simultaneously hitting the button to snap a photograph.

The train jerked forward, and she stumbled against me, her hands lifting to steady herself against my chest. I lifted my head, parting my mouth from hers reluctantly and licked my lips—the flavor of cherries exploded on my tongue—and I turned my head to look at the photograph I'd taken.

It looked genuine—like we were comfortably intimate and having fun while we were out together. I knew her landlord would swallow it hook, line, and sinker.

"See," I told her. "Check that out." I turned the screen toward her. "If you give me your number, I'll send it to you."

She didn't even look at it. Instead, she glowered at me, but didn't remove her hands from where they held onto my shirt as the train rocked.

"Where are you going?" she asked, instead.

"Home. I live in Burbank." I cocked my head. "Didn't you already know that?"

"Why the hell would I know where you live?" she asked in clear exasperation.

I shrugged. "No idea. Just thought you'd know. You should... since we're getting married and all."

"For God's sake!" she hissed. "We're *not* getting married. I'll have to tell David we broke up."

"Why? All you have to do is play the role of my doting fiancée until we get married." I flashed her a grin. "We can get divorced on the honeymoon. Didn't work out. Too bad, so sad." I gave an exaggerated sigh. "The sex was great, living together was impossible. I simply couldn't deal with your slovenly behavior."

"*My* behavior?" Gorgeous green eyes flashed fire at me. "I think it'll be closer to I couldn't deal with you constantly flirting with other women all the time and sneaking off to cheat with them."

I frowned. Interesting perspective to take for someone who seemed so vivacious and full of confidence.

"Why would I be looking at other women if you were with me, love? Have you looked in the mirror lately?"

She rolled her eyes. "Guys who look like you ... they play the field. Anyway, looks aren't everything. Makeup masks a multitude of sins."

My grin turned into a leer. "Speaking of sins. Maybe we should practice some ... just in case David wants to meet me before the wedding."

"Why the fuck would he want to meet you? He didn't even know you existed until five minutes ago!" The outrage in her tone made me chuckle.

"My point exactly. This guy's been your landlord for how long? Surely he's invested enough in his tenants to know who you're marrying?"

"Are you *always* like this?"

"Like what?"

"Insane and annoying."

I considered it for a second, then nodded. "Yeah, probably. Hard to say, really. I'm not always sober enough to notice."

Her expression turned serious, and she took a step back again. When her back hit another passenger, she twisted her head to mumble an apology, and then turned back to me.

"Let go of me. My stop is coming up."

"Burbank? We have another few minutes before we reach it."

"I'm not going to Burbank, I'm going to Glendale."

"Sweetheart, we've already left that stop."

"*What?*" She twisted in my arms to find a window. Not that she would be able to see anything outside, since we were underground.

"What's in Glendale?" I asked curiously.

"My grandmother lives there. I travel out to see her on the weekends."

"That's sweet." She shot me a look to see if I was mocking her. I wasn't, but she had no idea of my history and how unusual it would be for me to spend time with most of my family willingly.

"She lives in an assisted living facility and doesn't get out much," she offered slowly, "my mom and dad don't live in LA, so that leaves me."

"You're an only child?"

She nodded.

"Me too. See, we've got something in common. Our marriage

is saved. Jesus be praised!"

As hoped, she laughed. "I *can't* tell David I'm getting married, it's crazy. There's no way he'll buy it."

"Sure you can," I argued. "It's not going to hurt anyone. And it's not like anyone else needs to find out. I've already laid down the groundwork for why we've kept it quiet. We're saving to tie the knot in Vegas."

"And what happens when we don't get married?"

"It didn't work out. We drifted apart. We never said *when* we were going to do it. Tell him the thought of living together was too much to deal with. You caught me cheating. Whatever you need to say, I'll back it."

"You're talking like you're actually going to meet my landlord," she pointed out.

"I *should*. It'll drive the story home. He sounds like a creep and, yeah okay, so it's corny as fuck because I only just met you, but I really don't like the thought of you being in a position where he can take advantage of you."

She blinked up at me, her face showing her puzzlement over my words. "You don't even know me."

I gave her a slow smile. "My name's Dex, and I'm your future husband."

Guarded Addiction

CHAPTER 4

DARK NECESSITIES - RED HOT CHILI PEPPERS

Dex
PRESENT

It was fucking stupid. *I* was fucking stupid.

I hadn't even thought about what I was doing when I was walking through the airport. A hand brushed against mine, and I had the little packet between my fingers before I even realized what was happening. I pocketed it and carried on following the rest of the band out and into the waiting car.

I didn't give it a second thought when we reached NFG Records and went our separate ways. Diesel—my latest bodyguard/driver/babysitter, who'd taken over from Jason a couple of weeks ago—was waiting for me with the car, and we traveled back to my place in Burbank in relative silence. I didn't know him well enough yet to make idle conversation.

It wasn't until I stripped out of my clothes to shower and the little package fell out of my pocket and onto the tiled floor that it really hit me.

A little package of freebase cocaine. Something I hadn't seen for months. I had drugs in my possession and no one knew.

I showered, but my thoughts kept going back to it. I should flush it, get rid of the temptation.

I was sober.

I was *clean*.

But, truthfully? I wished I wasn't. Because being sober meant there was nothing to stop the thoughts and memories roiling around my mind. No barrier to stave off the nightmares, which had me waking up in a cold sweat, throat hoarse from the screams echoing around my room. It left me no excuse to hide away from the world. Without them, I had to face everything and everyone head on and deal with the shit life threw at me.

I rested my head against the tiles.

Fuck.

I wanted to get high so bad; it scared me. And the person at the airport? It *had* to be someone who knew I enjoyed smoking cocaine sometimes—which is why they handed me the solid freebase cube instead of powder.

Why hadn't I looked to see who it was? Was it someone from the usual entourage that surrounded us when we went anywhere as a band? Bodyguards, personal assistants, groupies, hangers-on—any one of them could have slipped it to me. If that was the case, then there was someone inside our small circle who I couldn't trust, and I ... I didn't like how that felt.

I cut off the water and stood, breathing deeply with my eyes closed, while I summoned up the willpower *not* to unbox my gear and get high.

I had to flush it. I *had* to.

But I didn't. I picked it up from the floor and put it in the medicine cabinet.

An hour passed, and then another, while the knowledge I had cocaine close by spun around in my mind. I was in my game room, playing a solo game of pool. The distraction wasn't working. The thought of that little packet in my bathroom was burning like fire in my veins and I knew if I didn't do *something*, I wasn't going to be able to stay away from it.

In a last-ditch attempt to redirect my thoughts, I pulled out my cell and fired off a text to the one person who I *knew* could keep me from using it. When she asked me if I'd used the coke, I faltered.

I hadn't ... but fuck, I wanted to. Did I tell her that? Did I tell her the truth? Or did I lie?

CHERRY PIE - You still with me, Rock Star?

I felt myself smile at her nickname. I could visualize the gleam in her eye when she said it, teasing and goading me at the same time.

ME - I'm here. I haven't used it. But I want to, Red. Fuck, I really want to.

My cell lit up a second later with an incoming call. I wavered. I hadn't spoken to her since the night of Lexi's death in Paris. I sucked in a breath and connected the call.

"Where did you get it?" That soft voice which did things to

my libido sounded down the line.

"Someone slipped it to me at the airport."

"Who?"

I sighed. "I don't know, Red. I didn't see their face."

"You know if you use it and Karl finds out, you're screwed."

"I know."

"Are you drinking?"

I glanced over at the half-full bottle of beer. "Not enough to be a concern. Why?"

"You could... come over." I could hear the hesitancy in her voice.

I chuckled. "Do you have any idea how many dealers I'd need to pass to get to your place?"

Siobhan's sigh was soft. "Dex ..." I heard rustling, then footsteps. "Okay, I'll call a cab and come to you."

"You don't need to do that."

"And if I don't? What then? Will you get high?"

I couldn't answer that without lying, so I said nothing.

"I'm coming over." Her voice was firmer. "Don't do anything stupid." She cut the call.

I tossed my cell onto the couch and picked up my pool cue. It would take her at least an hour to get here. Until then, I had to keep my focus away from the freebase cocaine in my bathroom.

I was upstairs standing outside the bathroom, arguing with myself about whether I was going to go inside or not, when she buzzed at the intercom for me to unlock the gates to my house. I unpeeled my fingers from the doorknob and headed back down. The control panel was in the kitchen, but the alarm for it ran through speakers around the entire house. It took me a couple of minutes to get there, but once I did, I leaned on the button to unlock the gates and watched through the camera as she paid for the cab and walked through.

I saw the driver lean out of the window and say something to her, which caused her to turn back to him. She shook her head and waved a hand toward the driveway, then smiled and began to walk toward the house. The cab driver didn't pull away until after the gates had closed on her figure and she was no longer visible.

I met her at the door, opening it right as she lifted a hand to knock, and we stared at each other.

Paris had been the last time I'd laid eyes on her. She left the country with Harper and Gabe, saying she wanted to be with her friend as she grieved the death of a woman she'd known since childhood. The entire band had known Lexi. Seth had brought her with him often to our practice sessions, where she would curl up and flip through magazines, loudly complain about the noise and generally make a nuisance of herself. She wasn't quiet like Harper, who had been content to sit and watch Gabe with stars in her eyes. But Lexi was family, like Harper was, and so we put up with her attitude.

We all knew a little of what Seth and Lexi had lived through, although not as much as Gabe did. Seth and Gabe were closer to each other, the way I was closer to Luca. We all had our baggage, our trauma, but Lexi masked it better than any of us had realized. Her death was a shock to us all—and it ricocheted through the entire band like a tsunami, leaving us all scrambling and reeling from the resulting chaos. More so than when Gabe had unceremoniously dumped Harper and cut her out of our lives.

But we both knew *that* wasn't the real reason Siobhan had left Paris. It had just been a convenient excuse to run away without looking like that's what she was doing.

A warm hand on my cheek drew me out of the memories and I blinked, refocusing on the redhead in front of me.

"Dex?"

I didn't speak, my eyes tracking over her face and pausing on her lips. Reaching out with one hand, I wrapped a lock of her hair around one finger and used it to tug her toward me.

She resisted, her fine brows pulling together into a scowl. "I'm not sleeping with you, Dex."

I shrugged. "Whatever," I said, leaned forward and kissed her.

Her sharp intake of breath was the only warning I received before she wrenched her mouth from mine and stepped back.

"I *said* I'm not sleeping with you!" she snapped.

"I was trying to tongue-fuck you, not *fuck*-fuck you." I reached for her again, and she ducked under my arm and walked past me. I dropped my hand and rolled my eyes. "Killjoy," I muttered.

"Where is it?" she demanded, glancing over her shoulder at me as she moved through the hallway.

"The joy you killed? Right here in my pants," I quipped.

Siobhan stopped in her tracks and spun slowly to face me. "You're not funny, Dexter. Where is it?" She repeated the question, pulling her cell from the back pocket of her jeans and waving it at me. "I can always call Harper and get her to bring Gabe over, and you can tell *him* you've got drugs in the house."

I shook my head. "I thought you would be on *my* side."

"I'm on the side that keeps you clean and sober. Are you going to tell me where you put it?"

I considered refusing. *Why the fuck should I tell her?* And then it hit me what I was doing. Hiding my stash, keeping it so I could use it. Everything I'd spent the past god-knew how many months trying to *stop* doing.

"Upstairs bathroom," I muttered.

She changed direction and brushed past me as she moved toward the staircase. I followed close behind her, admiring her ass as she ascended the stairs.

"Why did you take it?"

"Huh?" I dragged my eyes from her ass and up to where she'd turned her head slightly to talk to me. "I didn't really think about it. It happened too fast. Something touched my fingers and I took it."

"Who was it?"

"Dunno, love." I sounded a lot more flippant than I felt. "I didn't see them."

"But clearly it was someone the band's security didn't feel they needed to stop getting close to you. Who was with you?" She paused by a door and looked at me, silently asking if it was the bathroom. At my nod, she opened the door and walked in.

"Medicine cabinet," I said in response to her glance around the room and ignored her question.

My fingers clenched, nails biting into my palms when she opened the cabinet and found the little packet tucked behind the tube of toothpaste. I found myself biting my lip to stop from demanding she put it back.

Siobhan crossed to the toilet and tore open the packet. "Why didn't you get rid of it?"

"I…" I paused to clear my throat. "I couldn't." I closed my eyes and swallowed when the toilet flushed.

"Is there any more?"

"No." My voice was little more than a whisper. I could feel sweat breaking out on my forehead, my mouth was dry and I felt breathless.

"Dex?" Her hands touched my cheeks. "Look at me."

I forced my eyes to open and met green ones, dark with concern.

"I'm fine," I assured her as best I could.

I *wasn't* fine. I was craving a fix so bad, I could almost taste it, but I plastered a smile onto my face, masking the hunger I felt.

"You're not fine," she denied. "If you were, you wouldn't have called me. You wouldn't have hidden that packet in the cabinet. You definitely wouldn't be standing here shaking."

"I *said* I'm fine." I licked my lips and turned away to leave the room.

"You're so far from fine, it's scaring me." The words were spoken so quietly, I wasn't sure I was supposed to hear them. "Do you need to go to a meeting?"

"I've been back in the country for five minutes, Red. The only thing I need to do is sleep."

"And you couldn't because you knew *that*," she waved a hand toward the toilet, "was here." Reaching up, she turned my face so she could press a kiss to my jaw. The first time she'd willingly touched me since South Carolina. "You might not realize it, but you've done something huge tonight, Rock Star."

Rock Star—how long had it been since I heard her call me that out loud?

"How'd you figure that?" I asked.

"You could have given in to the temptation and used it. No one would have known, not until your next drug test. You could have kept it hidden and said nothing. But you didn't. You asked for help."

I bent my head so I could breathe in the scent of cherries that always enveloped her. "I wanted to use it though, Red. I *still* want to." I glanced across the room. "I wanted to take it away from you."

"I know, but you *didn't*. It's a win, Dex. A huge one." Her fingers stroked across my jaw. "Do you want me to find a meeting? It's LA, there's bound to be one going on somewhere."

I shook my head. "No, I'll be okay. I have one in a couple of days."

"Sure?" She had her cell in her hand.

I plucked it from her fingers, pulling myself back together and presenting her with the cocky rock star everyone was used to seeing. "Don't need one. Not when I have my guardian angel here to keep me on the straight and boring." I turned to the door.

"Come and play pool with me."

Guarded Addiction

CHAPTER 5

DON'T LOOK BACK IN ANGER - OASIS

Siobhan

PRESENT

I followed Dex down to his game room where a half-played game of pool was in progress.

"Was someone else here?" I asked, looking around, and he shook his head.

"No, I was playing against myself."

Even though I was still slightly tipsy from the wine I'd shared with Harper, and *really* wanted to go to sleep, I knew Dex needed someone to be with him right now. It seemed he'd chosen *me* to be that person—which was a surprise considering how we'd left things after South Carolina.

"Set up a new game then, Rock Star." The relieved smile he flashed at me made the sleep loss I was going to suffer worth it.

He set up the game and we took turns—neither really trying to win or follow any rules, just hitting the balls into pockets. We played in silence for almost thirty minutes before Dex spoke.

"Thank you." His voice was low and gruff, and he kept his

head turned away, focused on the pool table as he took his shot.

I didn't reply, noting the tension in his frame, the slight crease between his brows which could have been him paying attention to the game or a sign of stress. Propping my pool cue against the side of the table, I moved up behind him. As he straightened from taking his shot, I wrapped my arms around his waist and rested my head against his back. He didn't speak or move, and we stood quietly for a minute. I felt him relax and he patted my hand where it rested against his stomach.

"C'mon, let's go get a drink." He tugged my hands apart and stepped out of my embrace, turning to face me. "Or…" he quirked a brow, lips curling up.

I rolled my eyes. Dex's smile grew wider.

"That's not a no."

"It's definitely a no, Dexter," I said primly. "Make me coffee."

He huffed, but didn't argue and led the way out of the game room and down the hallway to his kitchen. I looked around curiously. I'd never been inside his LA home and, over the years since I'd first met him, and then spending so much time with him on tour, I had to admit to being curious about where he lived.

Photographs covered the walls of the hallway—the band, other bands, friends, people I assumed were family since I could see a passing resemblance in some of the faces.

"Through here." He led me into a large kitchen and waved a hand toward one of the bar stools set against a long black marble breakfast bar.

I climbed up onto it and settled back to watch as he moved around the room. On one of the countertops was a large complicated-looking coffee maker and Dex spent a couple of minutes fiddling with the settings, before placing a cup beneath it and pushing a button. The machine flared into life, the familiar noises and smell of coffee being brewed filling the room.

"Cream and sugar, right?" he asked.

"Please." I stifled a yawn, glancing at the wall clock. Almost three AM. Thank goodness it was Saturday and I didn't have to go to work. "So, how's Luca?"

"He'll be fine. He's on his way home now. Somehow he managed to miss our flight. Once we get back into the studio, everything will go back to normal." He paused and cocked a brow, blue eyes glinting. "Or are you interested for another reason?"

I fought not to blush. "No. How about you?"

"What about me?" He handed me my drink.

"Won't going back to normal be hard for you? Your *normal* includes getting high or drunk as often as possible."

He shrugged. "I got through a three-month tour without touching a single drug."

"Except in South Carolina," I pointed out quietly.

"I still didn't actually take anything." He leaned back, propping his elbows on the worktop behind him, and crossed one ankle over the other, eyeing me across the room.

"Only because I was there to stop you." I took a sip of coffee. "I won't always be available, Dex."

"Planning on going somewhere?"

"You know what I mean."

"I know that you're the reason I was going to get high."

"Don't blame me for your own lack of willpower."

Straightening, he prowled across the room toward me. "Not sure I understand what you mean. You made a promise to me." He came to a stop in front of me.

"So did you, and you broke it less than two days later, or have you forgotten that?"

"Hard to forget the biggest mistake of my life."

"And yet you seemed to carry on perfectly well."

"*Seemed* being the key word there, Red. What's your excuse?"

"I don't need an excuse," I said. I didn't want to have this argument with him again. "What we did ... *everything* we did ... was a mistake. Something to distract us from the world. We both knew it didn't mean anything. We were young and stupid."

"Were we?" He reached out to twist a lock of my hair around his finger. "Because I'm pretty sure it meant a lot to us both at the time."

"You remember it wrong."

He knew I was lying. It was right there in the smile he gave me, but I couldn't afford to let myself fall into this man's games again. I couldn't become attached to him. *More* attached than I already was. He was an addict, unreliable. He liked to play games. Games that were dangerous to my mental health. But like he looked to drugs for a high, I knew I could get high off *him*, if I let myself.

He'd entered my world—larger than life, brash, confident in

his attraction—and turned my life upside down. Just as quickly, what had been building between us had detonated like a bomb. The fallout had been far-reaching—for me, anyway—and I had been left believing I would never set eyes on him again.

Then Gabe exploded back into Harper's life...

CHAPTER 6

RUN AWAY - LACEY

Siobhan

NINE MONTHS AGO - CLUB DAMNATION

I first met Harper when she was nineteen and I was twenty. We both started working with the same company within a few days of each other and went through the orientation training together. We clicked almost immediately. There had been an air of fragility about her and after a while she admitted she'd recently had her heart broken. It was clear that she still felt raw and the subject was one she didn't want to talk about, so I didn't push and we never mentioned it again.

She didn't have much of a social life, her mother was ill and between work and caring for her it left very little time for anything else. We also ended up working different shifts, so after the first few months at work, we didn't get to spend a lot of time together. We would sometimes see each other at the main office for the cleaning company we worked for and grab lunch together, but over time, even that became rare.

A couple of years later, I was looking for a roommate. My

rent had increased and was reaching a point where I was finding it difficult to juggle my finances. Harper's mom had just died—although I didn't know it at the time—and since the lease on her mom's apartment was running out and she couldn't afford to keep it, she was looking for somewhere cheaper to live. She'd found my ad pinned to her front door after coming home from work one evening, and I opened my door to find her standing there, with the ad clutched in her hand and desperation on her face.

After she got over the shock of finding out it was *my* apartment, I'd hustled her inside and she moved in a couple of days later. At no point in the four years we lived together did she mention that the guy who had broken her heart was Gabe Mercer—famous rock star and bad boy singer of Forgotten Legacy. There hadn't been any reason to bring him up since he was no longer a part of her life.

So, when I first saw the interview Gabe did with the LA Inquisitor at the beginning of his quest to bring Harper back to his life, I admit I was shocked. And then she admitted they had been childhood friends, and *he* was the guy who had broken her heart. She went on to tell me what had happened between them, how he had treated her after sleeping with her.

My initial thought was that I needed to support and protect her—either by keeping him away from her or listening while she debated on whether she wanted to trust him again. I'd seen how devastated she had been, the aftermath of the destruction he'd left with his callous treatment of her, so it was a difficult decision for her to make.

I hadn't taken much notice of the band itself, other than knowing their name. Music wasn't really my scene, and most of the bands Harper talked about—because she *lived* for music—I barely recognized. But we *had* been to a concert of theirs. I'd won tickets through a competition I didn't remember entering and, of course, I'd taken Harper with me. It would have been the perfect time for her to mention her previous friendship with Gabe, but she didn't, and I really couldn't hold that against her since I was keeping my own secrets.

After Harper explained her history with Gabe to me, I did a little covert research of my own, because I didn't want my friend getting hurt again. And *that's* when I discovered that the Dexter Cooper from my past was a member of one of the biggest, hottest rock bands in the world. It had taken every single ounce of acting skill—I didn't know I possessed—to stop any reaction other than polite interest from showing on my face whenever she talked about the other band members.

I mean, what were the odds?

I studied my reflection in the mirror. This was a mistake, I knew it deep within my soul, but I had no excuse I could give Harper to avoid going to see Forgotten Legacy perform a surprise gig at Club Damnation. Not without raising any suspicion.

I was worrying over nothing, right? What were the chances of being recognized? I thought they were pretty slim. It was a long time ago, we'd both changed, and Dex had been high more often than not. I had *never* connected the Dex Cooper from my past with the tattooed, pierced, and troubled bass guitarist from Forgotten Legacy. Even though I'd known he had a taste for smoking weed back then, he always had a ready smile and a big heart—*nothing* that matched what I'd read about the bass player.

Smoothing my hands down over the silky figure-hugging dress I'd chosen, I slid my feet into my heeled strappy sandals, detoured to the kitchen to pour two glasses of wine and went in search of Harper.

"Are you ready?" I asked.

My lavender-haired friend turned to greet me, her lips pursing as she took in my outfit. "God, it's disgusting how good you look," she said, and I laughed.

"This from the woman who is dating one of the sexiest men in rock music?" I sat on the edge of her bed and offered her a glass of wine. "Tell me ... is he as wild in the sack as rumors suggest?" Harper choked on her mouthful of wine and I gaped. "Oh my gosh, he is!" I set my glass on the floor. "I need to know all about it, Harper. It's best-friend code. You have to share all the nasty, dirty details!"

She shook her head at me. "Not going to happen."

I chuckled. "At least tell me he's *good*."

Harper laughed into her glass, cheeks red. "Oh, he's *very* good."

I raised my own glass in a toast and smiled. "I'm so proud of you. Now drink up. Our ride will be here soon."

I spent the entire journey to Damnation trying to think up a way to avoid meeting the band, but it was impossible to find a way to do it that wouldn't upset Harper, who was almost bouncing with excitement in the seat beside me. The closer we got, the more anxious I became.

Our driver, Miles—Gabe's bodyguard, Harper explained—opened the door and escorted us inside, past the heaving mass of people lining up around the block. Movement caught my eye and I turned my head as a blond bartender waved at Harper.

"Who's *that?*" I whispered.

"Bran ... Brax? I don't remember his name," Harper replied.

Could that be my excuse to stay in the main bar?

"I might just sashay on over and say hi," I said, injecting a flirtatious tone into my voice.

Harper caught my hand, stopping me. "Oh no, you're coming with me to meet the rest of the band."

I dug my heels into the carpet. "I didn't agree to that. I don't want to meet the men I may have lusted over from a distance. The reality is *never* as good as the fantasy."

"Von!" Harper protested. She twisted to search out Miles, who was waiting a few steps away. "Tell her!"

Miles inclined his head. "You're both to go up to the VIP suite. Come along, ladies."

And before I could protest, he'd pressed a hand to the small of my back and urged me forward and up the stairs.

Gabe stole Harper away almost the second we walked through the door and I found myself standing alone. My eyes darted around the room, looking for somewhere I could hide. I was heading toward a dark corner when a hand closed over my arm.

"Well, fuck me. If it isn't the sweetest cherry pie I've ever tasted."

I stopped breathing.

"I always said you'd look good in red," that low, deep voice continued. "Did they have to pour you into that dress?"

I didn't reply. I was pretty sure I wouldn't be able to. My mouth had completely dried up, my mind shut down. So much for not being recognized.

Why had I worn red? Had I done it subconsciously, knowing it was his favorite color?

"Nothing to say?" he continued. "How long has it been? Turn around so I can look at you."

I took a breath and slowly turned to face the man I'd last seen convulsing in the street outside my apartment while EMT's fought to stabilize him enough to get him to the nearest hospital.

His eyes, a brilliant shade of blue, were unreadable. I licked my lips nervously and I could have sworn I saw him smile. He placed a hand beside my head and gazed down at me.

"Dex," Harper called and his head turned from mine to my friend. "You play nice."

"I always play nice, babe," he replied and glanced at me. "Better look like you're not about to run out of the door, Red," he murmured.

Pasting a smile onto my face, I curled my fingers over his bicep and rose up to peer at Harper over the top of his arm. "I'm a big girl, Harper," I said and winked.

Thankfully, Gabe distracted her and I released my hold on Dex's arm and took a step backwards.

"You look good, Red," he told me. His head dipped and he inhaled. "And you still smell like cherries."

CHAPTER 7

CHERRY PIE - WARRANT

Dex
PRESENT

"You remember it wrong."

She spat the words at me, her green eyes almost blinding me with their intensity while she glared at me.

I smiled. "Is that right, *Cherry Pie?*" I emphasized the nickname I'd given her and saw it hit the mark.

She flinched, coffee sloshing over the rim of her cup. I took it from her before she burned herself and placed it on top of the breakfast bar.

"See, Red, the way I remember it is we had a good time. You promised to stay with me, and then before I knew it you gave up, didn't even fight to stay with me."

"You're missing out the part where you sneaked away to get high and I found you face down in the dirt on the verge of dying from an overdose from the drug problem I didn't know you had!"

She tried to keep her tone matter of fact, but she couldn't hide how she felt. Her eyes gave away every emotion, and right now they were spitting fire at me.

"I know. I was there. Doesn't mean I had a problem. All it means is I wasn't paying attention." And there I was... *lying* again.

She shoved at my shoulder, forcing me to take a step backwards and hopped off the stool, shaking her head. "Denial is one of the symptoms, you know."

"I'm not denying anything, Red. I liked to have a little fun now and then, that's all. Taking something to increase the intensity didn't mean I had an uncontrollable addiction." I knew it was bullshit the moment I said it, but maybe if I repeated it often enough, it would become the truth.

"How many times have you nearly died?" she demanded.

"How many times did you want to crawl into my bed and fuck me while we were on tour?" I countered.

Her gaze shuttered.

"That's what I thought. Are *you* addicted to sex? Do you need to get counseling for that?"

"I don't use sex to make me feel better about myself."

I snorted. "Don't you?"

"I'm not easy, Dex."

"I never said you were easy, Cherry Pie." I cursed inwardly for letting the endearment slip off my tongue for a second time. "I said you were using sex to make yourself feel better."

"You know nothing about me!"

"I know *enough*." And I did. I knew a lot more than she realized.

"I'm calling a cab and going home. I came here to help you,

not to be attacked." She pulled her cell out from her pocket as she spoke and unlocked it.

"Like fuck." I took it from her and lifted it above my head.

The redheaded spitfire was more than a foot shorter than me, barely reaching my shoulder in her bare feet, and we both knew she couldn't reach it. Not unless she climbed me like a tree which, thinking on it, I gave serious consideration to suggesting. One look at the fury on her face warned me it would be a really bad idea.

She shoved at me again. "I'm not playing around, Dexter. Give me my cell."

"I'm not playing either. I don't want you to leave." I tossed her cell onto the table behind me and caught her wrists when she made a lunge for it. "Oh no, you don't."

"Will you stop touching me!" she snapped, attempting to break free of my grip.

"I remember a time when you liked me restricting your hands."

"Well, people change." Cheeks red, she wrenched free and stalked past me to snatch up her cell.

I didn't stop her, watching in silence while she found the number for a local cab firm and dialed.

"Don't leave, Siobhan," I said quietly when the call connected. "Stay."

"*Hello?*" The person at the other end of the line said when Siobhan didn't speak.

"Give me one good reason why I should stay," she said, refusing to look at me.

"Because if you leave, I'll be alone in the house and there's a high chance I'll take a drive downtown and pick something up." I didn't even need time to think before answering her.

"That's blackmail."

I gave a shrug she couldn't see. "It's the truth." The sad part was I was using it as an excuse to get my way, but the second the words left my lips, I knew it was the truth. Her being here, fighting with me, distracted me from the constant hunger burning like poison through my veins.

"*Hello!*" The voice screeched down the line again.

"I'm not having sex with you."

I think she'd forgotten all about the call she had made.

"I know. I'll respect your decision." I reached out and cut the call, took the cell from her hand and pocketed it. Turning her back around to face me, I pressed two fingers beneath her chin and tipped her head up. "That doesn't mean I'm not going to kiss you, though," I whispered, and covered her lips with mine before she could respond.

The flavor of cherries exploded on my tongue when I licked across her lips before delving inside. She didn't stop me, her lips parting at my invasion and allowed my tongue slip inside to stroke against hers.

Her hands lifted to rest on my shoulders, and I thought she was going to push me away, break the contact, but she didn't. Instead, she stepped closer, into my body, and wound her arms around my neck. I followed her lead, wrapping an arm around her waist to hold her close, and brought my other hand up so I could cup her jaw and tilt her face to a better angle so I could deepen the kiss.

She didn't resist, and I kept my eyes open for long enough to see hers drift closed. Her hands slid into my hair, and her nails scraped over my scalp. I smiled against her mouth.

There she was. My Cherry Pie.

I lifted my head just enough to separate our lips. "Want to go upstairs?"

Her eyes fluttered open. "I'm not—"

"I know," I said over her. "But we can fool around. Hell, you can tie me up if you don't trust me."

I saw the spark of interest in her eyes before she lowered her lashes and I hid a grin. Like I said, I knew her better than she realized. Probably better than she knew herself in some ways. Pressing another kiss to her lips, I caught her hand and led her from the room.

Chapter 8

NOTHING TO SAY - GALACTIC COWBOYS

Siobhan

PRESENT

What was I doing?

You're not sleeping with him. You said so. Twice!

He needs someone. If I don't distract him, he might get high again.

That doesn't mean you should fuck him. He's not your responsibility. Having sex with him again is a disaster waiting to happen.

The argument went on in my head as I followed Dex upstairs. I'd already said I wasn't going to have sex with him, so I had no business walking through the door of his bedroom and then turning to curl my fingers into the soft material of his shirt and tugging it over his head.

And yet, that's exactly what I did.

Dex didn't argue or stop me. Why would he? He'd made it clear from the outset that his end game was to get me into his bedroom. And, honestly, it wasn't that I was *against* having sex with him—far from it. Sex with Dex Cooper was an experience every woman should have at least once in their lives. The problem I had was the fear that he was using sex as a means of controlling his need to get high.

That and the last time we had sex, it had been angry and bordering on violent … and I'd never been so turned on in all my life.

I threw his t-shirt to one side and smoothed one hand down his chest, following that dark happy trail down to the waistband of his sweats.

"Sit down," I instructed.

He strode across the room and sank down onto the mattress. I stepped between his legs and rested my hands on his shoulders. Dex said nothing, but his blue eyes were intent on me. His skin was warm beneath my palms as I moved them down his arms to his elbows and then back up again, over his throat, to cup his jaw. He allowed me to tip his head back and continue my exploration. I traced the outline of his lips with one finger, the sharp cheekbones, his dark eyebrows, and then down his nose.

"What are you doing, Red?" His voice was a low rumble.

"Comparing you now to how you looked back then."

His head canted, brows pulling together. "Oh?"

"There was none of this." I flicked his eyebrow piercing, the one in his nose and then finally, the one in his lip.

Something flickered in his eyes, gone before it was really there, and then his lips tilted into a smirk and he poked his tongue out, displaying the bar piercing his tongue. "But you know I can perform magic with this one."

"Is that why you got it?"

"What other reason is there?"

There wasn't much I could say to that. His hands rested on my hips and I leaned away to study him. "You should sleep."

"I'm still on London time. It's early evening there." His hands squeezed my waist. "Daytime sex is the best sex."

"It's nearly four in the morning."

"Not in London." His fingers found their way beneath the hem of my shirt and I shivered at the light touch. "But you're not going to have sex with me ... are you, Red?" Cool air washed over my skin as he lifted my shirt, baring my stomach and pressed a kiss to the top of the tattoo peeking out from the waistband of my jeans.

I tangled my hand in his hair and pulled his mouth off me. His eyes laughed up at me and I shook my head.

"Just a little taste, Cherry Pie," he teased. "One ... small ... bite?" He licked his lips and slowly peeled my top upwards.

I could have stopped him, but I held still, one hand still in his hair, the other resting on his shoulder, and let him bare my breasts. I was braless—having rushed out without doing much other than dragging on jeans and a shirt in my haste to reach him before he succumbed to the temptation of getting high.

His tongue swept over his lips again and he leaned forward to hook his little finger into the hoop piercing my nipple.

"Don't." My protest came a second too late.

He gave the hoop a gentle tug and watched as my nipple

immediately hardened.

"Put your hands behind your back," he told me. When I didn't move, he grunted. "I *won't* fuck you, not even when you beg me … and you *will* beg me, Cherry Pie. You said no sex, so no sex it is. But you didn't veto foreplay."

"I'm not playing your games."

"There is no game."

"You can lie to yourself all you like, but don't lie to me. There's *always* a game." I tugged my top back down and forced myself to step backwards out of his reach. "You should sleep."

"And where will you be?"

"In one of the spare rooms." I had to get out of the room before I caved and let him do things to me that I'd regret come morning. He might be a drug addict, but I had my own addiction and it came in the form of the tattooed and pierced man in front of me.

I backed toward the door, half-expecting him to stop me, but he didn't move from his position on the bed, blue eyes watching as I walked away.

"Goodnight, Dex," I said softly, opened the door and walked out.

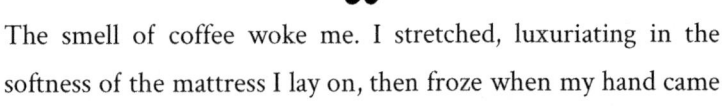

The smell of coffee woke me. I stretched, luxuriating in the softness of the mattress I lay on, then froze when my hand came into contact with something warm. My eyes snapped open and focused on a pair of blue eyes close to mine.

"Morning, Cherry Pie." I could almost feel that deep rumble vibrating through me.

He was lying on top of the sheets beside me, head propped up on one hand as he sipped coffee from a mug with Forgotten Legacy's logo on the front.

"What are you doing in here?" I asked, pushing my hair away from my face.

"Harper's been blowing up your cell for the past hour."

That woke me up. I sat up, clutching the sheet to my chest. "Did you answer?"

Dex snorted, his eyes dipping down to where my breasts were covered by the sheet. "Do you think I have a death wish? No, I didn't answer. You left your cell in the kitchen last night."

I hadn't. He'd taken it from me, but I didn't argue. He bounced up off the bed and I scowled at him. "What time is it?"

"Nine."

I groaned and flopped back against the pillows. I hadn't even had three hours sleep. After walking out of his bedroom and searching out a guest room with a bed in it, I'd spent most of my time tossing and turning.

Listening for footsteps.

Part of me had expected Dex to show up and try and get into bed with me, but he hadn't, and eventually I must have drifted off to sleep.

"Come on, Red. Get your ass up," Dex broke the silence. "Luca is gonna be here soon, so unless you want him to find you here…"

"*How* soon?" I demanded. "Do I have time to shower and call a cab?"

"You have time to shower, have breakfast, and *then* call a cab. He'll be here around eleven." He turned and walked toward the door. "I've left you a clean shirt and towel in the bathroom," he said and disappeared out of the bedroom.

I climbed out of the bed slowly, wrapped myself in one of the sheets, grabbed my jeans from where I'd dropped them and scurried out of the bedroom and into the bathroom. As promised, there was a towel and shirt folded neatly on top of a free-standing cabinet. I twisted the lock on the door, not that I thought Dex would try to come in while I was showering but out of habit, and stepped into the glass shower cubicle.

There was an array of buttons and knobs on the wall and I stared at them, trying to figure out which one would make the shower work. After some trial and error, which resulted in me discovering he had the kind of shower that acted like rainfall, I finally managed to get it working the way I wanted, and hurriedly washed, dried, and dressed.

The shirt he left for me was red and had the Forgotten Legacy logo emblazoned across the front. I pulled it over my head. It smelled like him—woodsy and exotic. I didn't *want* his scent on my skin, but it was that or put on the top I'd worn the day before.

I towel-dried my hair as best I could, dragged my fingers through it, then quickly grabbed my shoes from the bedroom before heading downstairs to the kitchen. Dex greeted me with coffee and a plate of pancakes, covered with maple syrup and blueberries.

"Breakfast of kings," he said with a smile, which I returned, took the plate and sank onto the nearest chair.

Dex sat opposite me. "Luca is going to be here in about thirty minutes." My fork clattered to the plate and my eyes jerked up to his. "You don't need to rush away. We can drop you off on our way to the record label."

"I ... ummm ... it might be best if I get out of here before he arrives."

"Why?" He sounded genuinely curious.

My cheeks flamed. "You *know* why."

A frown pulled his brows together. "You mean because he might ask why you're here?"

Sure, *that* was the reason. "Don't you think it looks weird?"

"He'll think we were fucking." Dex shrugged. "He won't care. We're both adults, Siobhan. If we want to get naked and have wild monkey sex, we can."

Chapter 9

WOLF IN SHEEP'S CLOTHING - SET IT OFF

Dex
PRESENT

Luca didn't react to Siobhan's presence in my house beyond a mumbled greeting, which ended on a yawn when he sauntered into my kitchen. It didn't surprise me. Luca had too many other things on his mind to worry about something that had happened months ago.

"Jet lag?" I asked and he grunted.

"Why the fuck are you so wide awake?"

"Didn't sleep. Secret of jet lag is to stay up and then hit the sack at your normal bedtime the next day."

"Do you *have* a normal bedtime?" He cracked another yawn. "Why did Karl call a meeting today? Couldn't he have held off a couple of days longer?"

"It's Karl. You haven't been home for two months. He's going to want to check in with you and check *up* on me. Plus you were supposed to travel *with* us, not hours later."

"He was in London the week before you turned up." He

crossed the room to help himself to coffee. "He dragged me to some seedy little bar to watch a band play."

"Oh yeah? Any good?" I took the fresh coffee he handed me.

"Not bad, actually. Reminded me of us when we were young, stupid and hungry."

"We're *still* young and hungry," I protested.

"And stupid," Siobhan muttered from her perch near the breakfast bar.

Luca swung to face her, one eyebrow arching. "And what *stupid* decision brought you here, little Spitfire?"

"Answering my cell at crazy o'clock," she replied, no sign of how she felt about facing Luca in her voice. "And letting your bass guitarist convince me he needed a partner to play pool with."

"Is that what you crazy kids are calling it these days?" A ghost of a smile crossed his lips when Siobhan's cheeks turned pink.

"Did Karl sign the band?" I ignored his comment.

"Not yet. He wants to take Marley over to see them first."

"And they're English?"

Luca shrugged. "Guess so. I didn't speak to them. They're pretty good, though. Covered a couple of our tracks. Not quite in Gabe's league, vocals-wise, but not bad." He drained his coffee. "You guys ready? Ryder's outside. I'm not awake enough to be trusted behind the wheel."

"*Ryder* is your new bodyguard?" I laughed. "Karl's pulling out the big guns. I don't recommend punching this one."

"So long as he doesn't annoy me, I won't."

"You know he has a black belt in Krav Maga?"

"You know I don't give a fuck?"

I knew he didn't. Luca had more black belts in various martial arts than any other person I knew. If he decided he was going to go head-to-head with Ryder for whatever reason, nothing would stop him.

"I'll remind you of that when you lose your temper with him," I said, grabbed my hoodie from the back of a chair and strode across the room. "We're dropping Siobhan off at her place on the way."

"Guessed as much," Luca's words ended on another yawn. "Let's go."

We stopped outside Siobhan's apartment building to let her out. I offered to walk her in and received a look of disgust in return. So, of course, I ignored it, pulled on a baseball cap, told Luca and Ryder I'd be right back and followed her out.

"I think I can make it to my apartment without help," she said.

"Wouldn't be very gentlemanly to not make sure you reached your home safely."

"Oh, so you're a *gentleman* now?" I saw her lips tilt up into a smile.

"When it matters." I held the door open and stepped back to let her through. "Have you found a new roommate now Harper has moved out?"

"Not yet."

"Are you looking for one?"

She arched a brow. "You looking to move out of your mansion and into a small two-bed apartment, Rock Star?"

I smiled at the use of her nickname for me. "Wasn't planning on it, but if you need help with the rent, you know all you have to do is ask."

We reached the front door of her apartment and I waited while she unlocked the door.

"I'm a big girl, Dex. I think I can manage."

I ignored her and walked inside. "Do you still have the same landlord?"

She didn't answer, and I swung around to face her. "What was his name? Donald? Drew?"

"David." She hung her jacket up and waited by the door. "Yes, he's still my landlord. Shouldn't you be leaving?"

"In a minute. There's no rush." I looked around. "It hasn't even changed. Same furniture, same decoration. Shit, Red, you even have the same television."

"Your point?" She folded her arms, and the movement reminded me she was wearing one of my shirts. I suddenly realized why Gabe always got a weird smile on his face every time Harper showed up wearing his clothes. There was something fucking hot knowing your clothes were resting against the bare skin of a woman you wanted naked in your bed.

I fought to keep a smile from my face at the thought. "There is no point. I'm just making conversation."

"There's no need. Luca is waiting for you. You have a meeting to go to."

I chuckled. "Fine, I'm going." Moving back toward the door, I stopped in front of her. "I'll call you later." I strode out without giving her the chance to respond and returned to the car where Luca waited.

"What's going on between you and the redhead?" he asked when I settled onto the seat beside him.

"Not a lot." The lie left my lips easily. And it *was* a lie. A carefully crafted one.

"Why was she at your place?"

I leaned forward to grab a bottle of water out of the small chiller. "I invited her over last night."

"But why? I thought whatever you had going on during the tour ended when she came home?"

"I never said that." I twisted the cap off and guzzled down half the bottle.

"Maybe not, but your actions certainly made it clear you weren't serious about her."

I shrugged, but didn't answer. Luca shot me a look—I didn't keep secrets from him. We didn't keep anything from each other. I could argue that something had broken between us since Lexi killed herself. He'd held things back from me, hidden what was going on between him and Seth's sister. But I was keeping things from him. In fact, I was keeping things from everyone, and had been for years.

I stretched out my legs, a wave of tiredness washing over me, and tipped my head against the seat.

"You remember when Gabe first tried to find Harper?" I said into the silence.

"After the first world tour when we supported Black Rosary, wasn't it?" Luca said after a second thought.

"Yeah. We'd just pocketed our first million." I nodded. "Gabe said it was time to reach out to Harper, but she'd moved out of the apartment she shared with her mom." I chuckled at the memory. "It would have been funny to see her face if she'd actually lived there when he turned up. Do you remember that? He dragged Seth to that seedy little apartment building and stood there for an hour hammering on the door and shouting."

"The couple who lived there called the cops, thinking he was a drug addict or a murderer."

"And it took a lot of fast-talking to keep it out of the press." I took another swallow of water. "We were all there in Karl's office the next morning when he chewed Gabe out."

"That's right, and Gabe lost his shit. Threw a temper tantrum if I remember right."

"Threw Karl's laptop against a wall." I smirked at the memory. "I wonder if Gabe ever told Harper about that. Anyway, all that could have been avoided because I knew where Harper lived. Had known for a while."

I felt the seat move as Luca twisted toward me. *"How?"*

"Because, unlike our idiot lead singer, I didn't cut her out of my life. Well, that's not strictly true," I amended quickly. "I didn't hang out with her, or talk to her. I kept tabs on where she was at. She was part of our life for too long for me to be able to just walk away. Gabe did it, and I get why he did. But he'd never have forgiven himself if something had happened to her while he was busy fucking other women to prove to himself she wasn't in his blood."

"So you appointed yourself her... what? Designated stalker?"

I snorted a laugh. "No, I appointed Siobhan."

There was a long moment of silence and then...

"What the actual *fuck?*"

CHAPTER 10

ALL TO MYSELF - MARIANAS TRENCH

Dex
AGE 22

"You don't have to come with me," Siobhan said for the hundredth time.

"And yet here I am," I replied patiently.

After our initial meeting on the train, I had managed to get her to agree to swap numbers and hang out with me. Lunch had turned into dinner and that turned into me joining her in a cab to take her home. It became a habit. Whenever I found myself at a loose end, I'd turn up at her apartment and take her out for food and drinks. She commented that I worked odd hours—but so did she—and I turned up at weird times, but she always let me inside her apartment and never refused to hang out with me.

It would have been the perfect opportunity to tell her I was a member of Forgotten Legacy, but I didn't. I liked that she treated me like a normal guy—she'd even argue with me over paying whenever we went out. We weren't well known enough yet for me to worry too much about being recognized, but I was aware that our popularity was growing and a time *would* come when I'd either have to come clean or risk being ambushed by fans or media while we were out. Until then, I enjoyed her company and the way she treated me like any other person.

I think she liked having me around as well. That was helped by the fact I'd been right about her landlord, because on the one occasion she returned home with me in tow and David had been hanging about, he backed off and stopped hassling her about finding alternative ways to pay the rent.

"You could just drop me off."

"Cherry Pie." I turned on the seat to look at her. "I meant what I said. I'm coming in with you. Besides, I'm curious about where you come from. You never talk about your family."

"Nor do you!" she retorted.

I shrugged. "There's nothing to say. My mom was a drug addict. My dad is a felon. He spends more time in prison than out of it."

The cab parked beside the entrance to the nursing home and I threw open the door. "Lead the way."

The look she sent in my direction told me she didn't really want me there but couldn't find a way to express it without sounding rude, and I found that fascinating. In the few times we'd spent together, she never struck me as the type to stay silent when she didn't approve of something and yet here she was going along with my crazy scheme ... almost as if she had her own brand of crazy going on.

I paid the cab fare, then followed her up the steps to the facility, and waited quietly while she spoke to the nurse at the desk. The smell brought back memories I'd long forgotten—a vague recollection of visiting an older person in a similar kind of place, but I didn't recall who it could have been or why I would have been there. I must have been very young.

"Ready?" Siobhan's voice refocused me on the now, and I nodded.

"She has her own room down the hall. I come and visit her most weekends, but I'm going to have to work more hours to make the rent and won't be able to get up here as often."

"She has friends here, though, right?" I waved a hand toward the communal room where I could see lots of old people. Some seated, noses in books, others watching television, and still others playing games or doing arts and crafts.

"Sure, but it's not the same as seeing family, is it?" She paused outside a door and tapped gently. "Grandma? It's Siobhan. Can I come in?"

"Of course you can!" a waspish voice called out. "I don't know why you need to ask every single time."

With an apologetic glance toward me, Siobhan pushed open the door.

"Wait!" I caught her arm. "What's her name?"

"Delores... Delores Walters."

"Okay. Got it."

She stepped into the room, with me close on her heels. The smell was the first thing to hit me—it wasn't bad, but it was *strong*.

Lavender and rose, I think. Wasn't that the typical smell of old people? Lavender and piss? I'd give the old woman that, there was no stink of urine in the room, not that I could tell, anyway. The second thing was the lack of photographs. The walls were bare, broken up by one oil painting of some kind of yellow flower. Daffodils, maybe.

And then there was the woman herself. I'd half-expected someone frail looking, but the woman seated in the chair near the window resembled a tank. She was brawny, with linebacker shoulders and a jaw to match and I couldn't help but compare her to Siobhan, who barely reached my shoulders and would probably be blown off her feet by a strong wind. She was curvy in all the right places, but she wasn't built like her grandmother.

"Gran, this is..." I heard the short hesitation before she settled on my name. "This is Dex."

I found myself looking into Siobhan's eyes, only set in an older face, and knew where the younger woman had inherited them from.

"Ms. Walters." I held out a hand and the older woman stared at it, her lips puckering. I thought she was going to ignore me, but then she grasped my hand and shook it firmly.

"And why are you here with my granddaughter?" she demanded.

"Grandma," Siobhan protested. "A little manners."

"Pfft." The older woman released my hand and waved it at Siobhan. "At my age you learn that manners only waste time." She returned her attention to me. "Are you sleeping with my granddaughter?"

I hid a smile and debated whether to lie, but Siobhan answered before me.

"No, he's not!"

"Then why bring him here? Getting my hopes up that you've finally found a man you can keep. You know you don't bring random men to see family, not unless there's something serious between you."

"We're just friends."

Her grandmother harrumphed. "Men and women can't be *just* friends, Siobhan. When will you learn that?" Her head turned and nailed me with a glare. "Isn't that right? I've heard about this *friendzone* rubbish—all that means is it's telling the man that he's wasting his time."

I grinned. "Sorry, Red, but she's got me there. We're not friends, Ms. Walters. I *definitely* have every intention of getting your granddaughter into my bed."

"Honest." She gave a sharp nod. "I like that. Sit down, young man. I have questions."

The incredulous look Siobhan threw in my direction told me this was out of character for her grandmother and I sent her a cocky smirk before lowering myself onto the edge of the bed, since there were no other chairs in the room.

"How did you meet my granddaughter?" she asked me.

"I proposed to her on a train."

"He eavesdropped on a conversation I was having," Siobhan

answered at the same time.

"Hush, Siobhan, I'm talking to Dex. Go and make drinks if you want to be useful, and leave us alone."

"But—"

"I want coffee. Dex, would you like something?" The old battleaxe angled a frown at Siobhan.

"Coffee would be great, thanks." I didn't look at Siobhan, but I could feel the outrage coming from her, and knew I'd be paying for siding with her grandmother as soon as we were alone.

I found I couldn't wait for *that* battle to commence.

She slammed the door when she left, and I swear I heard the old woman snicker.

"Siobhan never brings men with her. How did you convince her?"

I had to give the old lady her due; she didn't waste any time on niceties, and went straight for the throat.

"I didn't really give her much choice."

"You must be even more stubborn than she is. I should warn you, if you are serious about starting something with my granddaughter, she's the most stubborn girl I've ever met. She looks like butter wouldn't melt in her mouth, but that tongue of hers can draw blood."

"I'm pretty sure I know where she gets that from," I responded dryly.

"Yes, well. We don't have long before she comes back. Are you going to put a ring on her finger?"

Well, *shit*. This woman didn't waste any time. I liked that because I didn't believe in wasting time either.

"Considering it. You know what they say, right? If you like it, put a ring on it. And I *really* like it." I smirked.

Siobhan's grandmother gave a bark of laughter. "I like you. Call me Delores." She reached out and patted my hand, where it rested on my thigh. "Now tell me your intentions and *why* she insists you're only friends."

"It's a long story, Delores. Not one I can possibly tell you in the time it'll take Siobhan to bring coffee. So, let's say I've got her to agree to marry me, with stipulations, and she's a work in progress." *Telling me she'd only marry me if I was the last man on earth counted as a stipulation, right?* "But, believe me when I tell you that I have the best of intentions and I *am* going to make her happy." *Also true. When I finally convinced her to climb into bed with me, I'd make her very happy.*

The older woman gave me an unreadable look. "I actually believe you," she said after a moment's pause. "But you're not telling me everything. Like, for example, why Siobhan claims you're nothing more than friends."

I shrugged. "Like I said, she's a work in progress. We'll get on the same page eventually. Tell me about her parents?"

"Her mother is called Josephine, my daughter. Her father … Well, Derek is a lot of things, but father-material isn't one of them."

"You don't like him?" It was obvious from her tone.

"There's not a lot *to* like about him— Ahh, there you are …"

She broke off when Siobhan entered the room with a tray balanced between her hands.

The redhead's eyes met mine, and I gave her a smile, which I hoped would put her at ease, but I saw her shoulders tense slightly, and knew I'd failed.

"What were you talking about?" she asked, setting the tray down and handing her grandmother a mug.

"The ring your young man plans to put on your finger," Delores answered, and Siobhan froze in the process of lifting a second mug.

Her face paled, then turned a shade of pink. "Ignore everything he's told you."

"Really?" Delores replied. "You never could lie to me, child. Don't start trying now."

I snorted a laugh. "I told your grandmother I was on a mission to marry you."

"For the sake of repeating myself for the thousandth time today, that's *not* going to happen."

"Never say never, Cherry Pie." I reached forward to take the mug from her hand and lifted it to my lips with a wink.

The rest of the visit with her grandmother passed quickly and the sun was setting by the time we stood to leave. Siobhan was out of the room when Delores caught my arm.

"I don't know what's really going on between the two of you," she told me in a low voice, "but take care of my granddaughter, Dex. She's not the tough cookie she presents to the world."

I patted her gnarled fingers. "You can trust me, Delores. I have no intention of hurting her."

CHAPTER 11

LONELY DANCE - SET IT OFF

Siobhan

PRESENT

I needed to find someone to share my apartment with. I couldn't really afford to keep it since Harper moved out, but I wasn't going to let *her* know that—the rent had risen gradually over the years, but with two of us we'd managed to always keep on top of it. My landlord had a reputation for spending more time than necessary around the apartments when he knew single women lived in them. The problem was the apartment was one of the cheapest I could find in an area where I didn't have to look over my shoulder constantly in fear of someone breaking in. It happened, but not as often as other places where the rent was more affordable.

I hadn't yet informed David that Harper had moved out—which made dealing with him and his less than savory personality easier to deal with. I'd been dipping into my savings to make the rent payments, but that, as well as taking three months off work to go on the tour to keep Harper company, meant I was fast reaching a point where I'd either have to move or take an extra job to meet them. Unless I could find a new roommate before it reached that point.

Standing beneath the shower, I catalogued all the things I needed to do. Write up an ad, find somewhere to put it that wouldn't attract creeps, interview potential candidates … replace Harper with someone new. I lathered up my hair to wash it, my thoughts wandering back to Dex and his quip about helping with my rent.

I hadn't expected to hear from him after Paris; had actually planned to avoid any events Harper invited me to where there was a chance he would be attending. In the cold light of day, after Lexi's suicide, I realized that what had happened on the tour was a moment out of time, not real. Like everything that had gone on between us before.

Nothing about Nashville or South Carolina had been real life. The entire tour had been a surreal experience. A once-in-a-lifetime thing. I wasn't famous. I wasn't connected to anyone famous. Harper didn't count. *She* was the one dating a rock star, not me. I was just her friend. A friend who was keeping a secret from her. There was no way she would believe I hadn't known about her history with Gabe once she discovered I had known Dex all those years ago.

Rinsing off, I stepped out of the shower, grabbed a towel and dried off. Wrapping it around my body, I returned to my bedroom, dressed, and perched on the edge of my bed to dry my hair. My cell buzzed while I was twisting it into a braid. I reached out and hit the loud speaker.

"Hello?"

"What are you doing today?" Harper asked.

"Grocery shopping and then maybe eating a gallon of ice cream while I watch movies."

"A *gallon* of ice cream? Who upset you?"

I laughed. "No one. I have an ice cream craving, that's all. Ice cream and maybe Chris Hemsworth. Ice cream *on* Chris Hemsworth." I licked my lips. "Yeah, that sounds like a plan. Does Gabe know him?"

"You know he's married, right?" My friend's voice was dry.

"We can pretend he's rehearsing a scene for a movie." I tied off my hair, picked up my cell and moved to the living room, shrieking when an unexpected body rose from the couch.

"What? Oh my God! *Siobhan?* What's happening?" Harper demanded.

I scrambled to regain my balance and glared at the man smirking at me. "Nothing. Sorry. A spider ran across my foot." I pointed at the door. *Get out*, I mouthed. When he didn't move, I frowned. "Sorry, Harper, I need to go. That spider was huge and I don't know where it went."

I heard her laugh down the line. "Okay, fine. Go kill the eight-legged demon, then call me back."

I made sure the call was disconnected before I spoke. "How did you get in here?"

David Colton lifted a bunch of keys and shook them.

"Just because you have a key, doesn't mean you have the right to walk in," I told him.

His smile was a flash of white teeth. The man was good looking, but something about him raised the hairs on the back of my neck.

"I knocked, but you didn't answer. I worried that something had happened to you, so I let myself in."

"And then what? You made yourself at home?" I skirted around him, so the front door was at my back.

"I'm doing my duty as your landlord." He held out an envelope. "And also to make sure you got this."

I took it. "What is it?"

"An increase in the rent. This is your two-week notice of the change."

I felt the color drain from my face. I was barely making the rent as it was. An increase was going to ruin me.

"I keep telling you, Sioban." I bit my lip to stop myself from correcting his pronunciation of my name. He *never* got it right. "There's no reason why we can't come to an alternative arrangement." His smile spread wider. "Especially now Harper has moved out."

Shit, how did he find out?

"Get out." I stifled the urge to rub my temple and kept my voice even. I'd figure it out. I *always* figured it out.

"Come on, sweetheart." He took a step closer. "We could have a lot of fun, the two of us."

I lifted my cell. "If you don't get out, I'm calling the police."

David laughed. "For what? It's *my* property."

"That doesn't give you the right to walk in here for no reason."

He glanced around. "I'm sure I can find one."

"I have rights as a tenant, David." I refused to let him see how uncomfortable he was making me.

"Only as long as you pay the rent on time, sweetheart." His smile was oily and he started toward me. I stepped to one side and watched as he opened the door. "I'll be seeing you soon, gorgeous."

I dumped the bag of groceries on the countertop, returned to the front door, jammed my key in the lock and turned it. I'd bought a door chain, which I would need to fit, but for the moment my key would stop anyone if they tried to open the door from the other side.

Once I was certain the door was secure, I unpacked my meagre stash of groceries. The rent increase was going to take another two hundred dollars a month out of my earnings and David, bastard that he was, had timed the increase to coincide with when the rent was actually due at the end of the month, instead of it starting at the beginning of the next one.

Guess I'd be going on that crash diet I kept threatening myself with.

Even if I found a new roommate, they wouldn't be moved in with enough time to cover this month's rent, but if I didn't get an ad up soon I'd end up in the same position next month. I didn't know what was stopping me from taking that step. I *knew* Harper wasn't going to move back in, she was happy with Gabe and *I* was happy for *her*. I didn't think I was ready to share my space with someone new.

My cell lit up with an image of Harper and I connected the call.

"You didn't call me back," she said.

"I know. I'm sorry. I got distracted. Dav—" I cut off before I finished his name. I didn't want to tell Harper about David being in the apartment *or* that he'd raised the rent. This was something I had to deal with myself. "The spider escaped, so I evacuated and went grocery shopping."

"Are you back home now?"

"Yep, just putting everything away." I wedged the cell between my shoulder and ear and did exactly that, then grabbed an apple and flopped down onto the couch to chat with Harper. "I didn't think I'd hear from you for a couple of days, at least. Bored with Gabe being back home already?" I teased.

Harper laughed. "He had to go to a band meeting. We're going out to dinner later."

"Oh? Is he taking you anywhere nice?"

"Joyeuse, I think. We're meeting Seth and Riley there. You should come."

"And be the fifth wheel? I'll pass."

"Von, you know—"

"I have a date with Chris Hemsworth and ice cream," I

reminded her.

"I'm sure he wouldn't mind if you canceled."

"Maybe not, but *I* would be devastated."

"If you're sure ..."

"Harper, stop worrying about me and go have fun with your sexy rock star boyfriend."

"But—"

"Oh ... what was that? Chris is waiting for me, Harper. You know how he gets when I ignore him."

Harper laughed. "Fine! Enjoy your ice cream. I'll call you tomorrow."

"*Don't* call me tomorrow. Pretend I'm out of contact. Gabe has been out of the country for *two weeks*. You guys need some alone time. I'll call *you*. Now go!"

Eventually, I convinced Harper to hang up and reached for the television's remote control. I clicked through the channels for something to watch, smiling to myself when I discovered there actually was a Chris Hemsworth movie playing.

"Looks like we got a date after all," I said to the screen, collected my tub of ice cream from the freezer, grabbed a spoon and settled in for the evening.

CHAPTER 12

THINK I'M CRAZY - TWO FEET

Dex
PRESENT

I flushed the toilet, screwed on the cap for the little sample bottle, and strolled out of the cubicle. Handing the little piss-filled bottle to Diesel, who was propped against the wall waiting for me, I washed and dried my hands and then hiked an eyebrow.

Diesel didn't respond, merely pushed away from the wall and walked to the door to hold it open.

"Good chat," I muttered.

The rest of the band were in Karl's office when I returned. Gabe and Seth were both displaying complete disinterest in anything going on around them as they held a quiet conversation about something they were watching on Gabe's cell.

Luca sat in a chair with his feet resting on top of Karl's desk, twirling a drumstick between his fingers. His cell was in his other hand as he rapidly typed with his thumb.

Business as usual ... mostly.

I made my way across to where Luca was and flopped down beside him.

"Who are you texting?"

He glanced over at me and stuffed his cell into a pocket. "No one. Just a wrong number."

"Luca, get your feet off my desk," Karl barked before I could answer. "Gabe, Seth, put the cell away." He shut the door behind him and strode across the room.

"Sorry, *dad*," Gabe snarked and Karl threw him a look which immediately silenced our lead singer.

Guess our manager meant business this morning.

"This past year has been a rocky one for Forgotten Legacy," he began as he sank into his chair behind the desk. "While business-speaking, you're more popular than you've ever been, on a personal level you're walking fucking disasters. I'm sick of seeing news articles about you."

Gabe bristled and opened his mouth to speak.

"Don't even!" Karl stabbed a finger in his direction. "Let's list the drama, shall we? You—" Another glare at Gabe. "*You* decide to get back your childhood sweetheart, but instead of being an adult about it and ... *oh, I don't know ... calling* her! You play games. Fuck around with interviews and her. Your bodyguard—a man who's been with you for almost the entire time you've been famous—tried to *kill* you. Almost killed Harper. And why? Because *you* fucked his sister." His gaze nailed Seth. "And you ..."

Seth stared back impassively.

Karl sighed. "You've had your fair share of hardship this year," his voice softened slightly. "But that doesn't dismiss the fact you made some questionable decisions."

I braced myself when his attention turned to me. "One word for you, Dex. *Rehab*. You have meetings. Go to them."

"That's seven words."

"*Don't* fuck with me." Before I could respond to that, he focused on Luca. "And you ... Why the fuck didn't you come to me?"

Luca shrugged.

"Silent and moody doesn't do anything for me, I'm not a hormonal teenage girl. If you *ever* find yourself in a situation where it could affect any of your bandmates, you don't keep it a secret," he roared. "And then to top it off, you don't run away to a different country. YOU ... COME ... TO ... ME!"

"It wasn't that simple," Luca growled.

"Yes, it is!" Karl shouted, face reddening with anger. "I'm your manager. The clue is in the title, you fucking idiots. I *manage* you. That means *everything*. Every *fucking* detail of your lives."

Silence greeted his words as we all stared at him. Karl didn't lose his temper very often—he was the epitome of calm, *nothing* ever ruffled him. He'd been in band management for a long time; he'd seen *everything*. Hell, I'd heard stories about Black Rosary's early days that put our behavior to shame and I was sure, if I asked Marley, I'd hear Karl never lost his cool once with the band.

Karl's eyes swept over the room. "Nothing to say?"

Luca looked at me. I looked at Seth. Seth shrugged. Gabe

shifted in his seat, but didn't speak. Karl shook his head.

"Fine." He leaned back in his chair. "I've booked you for a photography session. We need to get moving on the cover for the album. Yes, Seth," he snapped when our guitarist opened his mouth. "Riley will be taking the photos, but we still needed to book a location. Keep Tuesday free and I'll have the details sent to you all." He studied Gabe for a second. "What are the chances of you talking Harper into agreeing to be photographed with you?"

Gabe's brows pulled together. "What do you mean?"

"Riley has this idea. She's listened to most of the songs you've recorded." He sliced a glance at Seth, who smirked. "And she thinks they tell a story. *Your* story. So, she wants to put you and Harper on the cover as well as the video for the first single."

"I don't know," he said slowly. "She doesn't like all the attention. You know that."

"Well, try. Otherwise we'll have to bring a model in. Will she prefer to see you draped all over some other woman and tongue-fucking them?"

Gabe rubbed a hand over his face. "Fuck no. I'll talk to her and see what I can do."

"I could get Riley to call her?" Seth offered and he nodded.

"Yeah, it might be a workable plan." He paused to grin. "If I ask her, she'll think I'm trying to get my freak on. If Riley tells her about it, she might take it more seriously."

"The fact you think she'll immediately wonder if you're trying to get freaky doesn't raise a red flag for you?" Seth quirked a brow.

Gabe laughed. "I'd be more worried if she *didn't* automatically think that. I've worked hard to drag her mind down to live with mine in the gutter."

"As long as you keep it *out* of the papers," Karl snapped. "I mean it, Gabe," he continued at Gabe's eye roll. "I don't want to deal with another sex tape, or grainy photographs of you and Harper having sex somewhere you shouldn't." He reached into a drawer, pulled out a piece of paper and tossed it across the desk. It landed on my lap. "That's your next therapist appointment. It's in an hour. Do *not* sleep with this one, Dex."

"Dr. Santos?" I asked, checking out the name and address. "Is she hot?"

"She is a *he*."

"Well, I'm hardly likely to sleep with *him*, am I?"

"Keep it that way." He rose to his feet. "Now get out. Luca, you stay. I'm not finished with you."

"Sorry, man. We'll wait for you outside." Gabe jumped out of his seat and strode toward the door, pausing to pat Luca's shoulder.

Seth and I followed at a slower pace.

"Close the door behind you," Karl called after us.

Seth whistled low beneath his breath. "Someone's in more trouble than he thought."

I snorted a laugh. "Luca's a big boy. I'm sure he can handle it."

"Are you and Riley still on for Joyeuse tonight?" Gabe asked when we caught up to him.

"Yeah," Seth replied. "You coming?" He glanced over at me.

I shook my head. "No interest in watching you lovebirds count the minutes till you can leave and get naked." I looked between them. "Unless you're having some kind of orgy? Then I might join in."

"Not happening," Gabe growled.

Seth was more hands-on, shoving my shoulder until I moved back a step.

"Ready to go?" Diesel asked from the doorway.

"Go where?"

"The therapist's office. It's a forty-minute drive from here."

I blew out a breath. Gabe's hand landed on my arm.

"You got this," he murmured. "Do the session. We'll hit the studio tomorrow and lay down some tracks. We've got a table booked at Joyeuse for eight. If you want to show up, there'll be a seat for you... and Luca, if he'll come."

I nodded. "I'm good, man. You guys have fun." With a wave, I walked across the reception area to the elevator, and leaned against the wall to wait for Diesel to catch up.

Guarded Addiction

CHAPTER 13

MIDDLE FINGER - BOHNES

Dex

SEVEN MONTHS AGO

My foot tapped a constant rhythm against the carpeted floor, while I flicked a guitar pick back and forth across my knuckles. I wanted to get up and leave, but knew if I did my position in Forgotten Legacy would be gone. I was a liability, a danger both to myself and to the band, or so Karl had told me when he drove me to the *prestigious*—my lip curled up into a sneer at the word—Red Wood Complex, well known as a private clinic with a reputation for the highest rehabilitation success rate of drug addicts, amongst other things.

I rolled my eyes. Couldn't wait to introduce myself to the other inmates.

Hi, my name is Dexter Cooper, and I'm not *a drug addict.*

I *wasn't* a drug addict, no matter how many times people claimed otherwise. I didn't touch heroin or meth. I liked to smoke a joint to relax, maybe do some 'shrooms, or occasionally drop some acid to help with creativity. Okay, so now and then I'd also freebase cocaine, but I didn't do that often enough to qualify as an addict. Everyone knew cocaine was a recreational drug. Other than that, the only vices I had were women and tequila.

All right, so I'd misjudged and fucked up at the kid's graduation. That could have happened to anyone. It didn't mean I had a problem. I simply needed a little pick me up to help me get through something as tedious as a school event. None of us went to our *own* graduation because we'd agreed it was a waste of time, so why Gabe had insisted we go to that one—fuck only knew.

I thought it went quite well, personally. I don't remember any of it—which was the aim of dropping acid before we got there. Waking up in the hospital with a furious Karl looming over me, on the other hand, was not something I wanted to repeat in a hurry.

I'd never seen him so angry, or such an interesting shade of purple. Not even when Gabe and Seth were caught sneaking out of some European princess's hotel room by the paparazzi had he lost his cool. Apparently, that special occasion was reserved for me.

I'm so lucky.

I genuinely thought he was going to end up in the hospital bed next to mine from popping a blood vessel, so I agreed to every demand he threw at me without really listening to them. And that's why I was here, cooling my heels, waiting for my new-age, tree-hugging therapist to try and head shrink me.

I yawned, not bothering to cover my mouth, and tipped my head against the back of the seat.

"Mr. Cooper?" The brisk voice of the woman behind the desk

reached me.

Oh yeah, I'd forgotten she was already in the room. I lifted my head and squinted at her. "How did you pay your way through college?" I asked. "Waitressing? Dancing? *Stripper?*"

I straightened from my slouch and scanned my eyes over the professional blouse and jacket she was wearing, and made a bet with myself that her skirt was figure-fitting and short beneath the desk. I'd have it off her before my hour-long session was over.

"We're not here to talk about me," she replied, and I let my lips form into a slow smile.

"But *I'm* paying for your time, so aren't we supposed to talk about whatever I want?"

"Your record label is paying and we're here to talk about your drug addiction."

"What drug addiction?" I yawned again and heard her sigh.

"When was your first experience of drug use?"

I shrugged. "My parents were high for most of my childhood. Does that count?"

"Did your mom take drugs when she was pregnant with you?"

"How would I know? I was in the womb, not outside watching."

There was a long beat of silence. "Mr. Cooper ... *Dex* ... this won't work if you don't try."

"I like how my name sounds on your lips." I smirked when those pink painted lips parted, and heat stained her cheeks. "Know what would be even better?"

"Mr. Cooper, your behavior is highly unprofessional."

"You want to know though, don't you?" I leaned forward and lowered my voice. "Admit it, doc."

"Mr. Cooper, this kind of deflection is absolutely normal for someone in your position. But you must focus."

"Oh, I *am* focused." My eyes dropped to the curve of her breast. "*Very* focused. You didn't answer my question."

"You haven't answered mine, either," she countered.

"Okay. Yes, my mom took drugs while she was pregnant with me. Now answer *my* question."

"I don't recall what you asked."

"Sure." I laughed. "I asked if you knew what would be better than my name on your lips."

"Mr. Cooper..."

"Do you?" I pressed. When she didn't answer, I told her anyway. "My dick. Your lips wrapped around my dick would be a thousand times better than my name."

"I'm going to have to ask you not to say things like that." Her voice was prim, but I saw the way her eyes dropped to my thighs and her tongue snaked out to wet her lips.

"What do you say, doc? Wanna sample it for yourself?" The offer hung between us.

Four orgasms—three for her, one for me—and an hour later, I sauntered out of her office with a smile on my face and a new appointment date scheduled for two days' time. I made another silent bet with myself that she'd seek me out before twenty-four hours had passed. Maybe spending the month in this place wouldn't be so bad, after all. Not with the lovely Doctor Shaw available to help pass the time.

I found my way back to the room I'd been assigned, went inside and flopped down onto the bed. When Karl had brought me here, I'd been given a pamphlet—like the place was a hotel with facilities instead of a regimented drug rehabilitation clinic—detailing all the different things they offered. I wasn't interested in any of them. My sole aim was to get Karl off my case, get out and get back to doing the things I loved—making music, fucking women, getting drunk and getting stoned. Until then, I'd play the good boy and check all the boxes I needed to check. Or, at least, I'd do whatever I wanted and try not to get caught until it was time to check out.

Three weeks later, Doctor Shaw had been reassigned or fired—I wasn't sure which—after a colleague walked in while I was fucking her on her desk. In her rush to get my clothes off and fuck her favorite rock star, she'd forgotten to lock the door.

I was sent to my room like a child with a slapped wrist, and that's where Karl found me a couple of hours later. I was lounging on my bed, feet propped up on a chair, playing the bass guitar they'd allowed me to bring inside with me when I arrived. He burst through the door, shoved my feet off the chair and pulled the guitar out of my hands.

"What is *wrong* with you?" he demanded.

I pursed my lips. "Other than being bored almost to death?"

"It's not funny. You were fucking your therapist."

I shrugged. "She could have said no."

"Did she smuggle drugs in for you as well?"

"What? No. I'm not a fucking addict, Karl. I haven't touched a thing since I got here." I would have killed for a drink or a joint, not because I was suffering from withdrawal, but because I was so fucking *bored*. The cold sweats and nightmares I had were nothing to do with withdrawal. I wasn't about to admit to any of that, though. I don't think Karl would have appreciated it.

"They want you to leave."

"Thank fuck for that."

"It's not a joke, Dex." He sat on the chair and handed me a manila envelope.

"What's this?" I asked, taking it from him.

"Your new contract." He watched while I tore it open.

New contract? What the fuck?

"If you won't take rehab seriously, then you're leaving me no other choice than to do it this way."

"I don't have a problem. I enjoy a smoke and a drink, but so does the rest of the band. Why am *I* the one with the problem?"

"Gabe barely touches any drugs, and he's not constantly drunk. Seth was borderline but he's got a handle on it. Luca... well, Luca's issues aren't drug or drink related." He folded his arms. "I haven't had to watch their stomachs getting pumped or had calls to collect them from the hospital after being found overdosing."

Okay, so I may have taken a few too many drug cocktails a couple of times. It could happen to anyone.

I pulled the new contract out of the envelope and glanced at it. "Give me the cliff notes."

He sighed. "Weekly sessions with a *male* therapist and drug tests. If you test positive, you're out."

"And the rest of the band agreed to this?"

"They don't get a say in it. It's the label's decision."

"I see." I scratched my jaw. "What if I have a headache and need to take something for it?"

"Don't be an ass." He stood. "Get your stuff packed. We're leaving within the hour."

"Just like that?"

"Yes, Dex. Just like that. The tour with Black Rosary starts soon. I was hoping you would have been able to make it through a month here and you'd come out with the tools you'll need to stay clean. But I see now that was a mistake."

"I'm *not* an addict."

The look he threw at me raised the hackles on the back of my neck.

"Spoken like a true addict. Dex, you have a problem. But until you're ready to admit to it, there's very little anyone can do. Get packed. I'll wait at the reception desk."

CHAPTER 14

NOVOCAINE - THE UNLIKELY CANDIDATES

Siobhan

PRESENT

A tub of ice cream, a Chris Hemsworth movie marathon, and a bottle of cheap wine—that was my evening. I crawled into bed shortly before midnight, and my eyes were drifting shut when I heard a quiet tap on my window.

I jolted upright, head twisting around. My window was closed, the curtains drawn so no one could see inside.

Had I dreamed the noise?

I lay back down, heart hammering loud in my ears, and strained to listen above it. And *there* it was! A soft rapping against the glass.

I crept from my bed, moving slowly and checking to make sure my shadow didn't fall across the window to alert whoever was out there. Part of me was terrified it was David, but I dismissed that. I couldn't see him climbing up onto the palisade simply to knock on my window. Carefully, I eased the curtain away from the wall and tried to see who was beyond the glass. I jumped back when a hand came into view, curled into a fist and knuckles hit the window—harder this time. Something glinted in the moonlight and I frowned, inching closer.

I recognized the ring on his little finger. My eyes narrowed and I threw open the window to lean out.

"What the hell are you doing?" I whisper-shouted.

Dex grinned at me from where he was precariously balanced on top of the small palisade fence which separated the apartment building from the street.

"Came to see you," he slurred.

"Are you *drunk*?" I hissed and grabbed his sleeve when his balance wavered and he almost fell backwards. "For christ sake, get down before you hurt yourself!"

"Don't think the fall will kill me, Red."

"No, but *I* might if you wake anyone up. Get *down!*" I leaned further out of the window to look up and down the street. "Where's your bodyguard?"

Wasn't the guy supposed to keep Dex sober and out of trouble?

Dex waved a hand. "Tol' him I was goin' to bed and he left." His voice lowered. "Didn't tell him *whose* bed I was going to be in." His leer would have been comical if I wasn't already annoyed with him.

"I'll call you a cab." I started to withdraw back into my room, and he lurched forward and caught my hand.

"Aww, come on, Cherry Pie. I came all this way to see you."

"I doubt that." I took another glance up the road. "How did

you get here, anyway?"

"Drove."

My jaw dropped. "You *drove?* Dex, you're out of your mind! What if you'd crashed or been pulled over by the cops? What if you'd *hit* someone?"

"Didn't do *any* of those things. What are you complaining about?" He swayed again.

"Oh, for god's sake!" I snapped. "Get down and come inside." I slammed down the window before he could speak, dragged on the bathrobe hanging on my door and hurried through my apartment, tying the belt as I went.

By the time I unlocked and threw open the door, Dex was there, swaying in the hallway. I sighed and grabbed his arm.

"Get in here before anyone sees you." I pulled him through the doorway. "You're unbelievable. What if someone spotted you? It's bad enough that Gabe put our address on the map, without *you* starting it all up again." I kicked the door shut behind him, released my grip on his arm and glared at him.

He blinked, then gave me a slow smile. "You're so pretty when you're mad."

I rolled my eyes. "How much have you had to drink?"

He lifted a hand and separated thumb and finger by about an inch. "Little bit."

"Little bit, my *ass!*"

His head tilted and he licked his lips. "It's a *really* nice ass."

"*Really*, Dexter?"

"Yeah, really. Wouldn't say it if it wasn't true."

"I'm calling Harper." I started to walk past him so I could grab my cell from the bedroom and his hand shot out to catch my arm and stop me.

"Sorry, can't let you do that." He tightened his grip and pulled me back into the center of the living room. "If you call Harper, she'll tell Gabe. Gabe will turn up here. Questions will be asked." He threw his arms wide, and shot me a sly grin. "And you *really* don't want them asking questions, do you, Cherry Pie?"

Guarded Addiction

CHAPTER 15

CRAZY - AEROSMITH

Dex
PRESENT

The question hung between us, and I waited to see how she reacted to it. Disappointingly, she *didn't*. So I tried again.

"Gonna offer me a drink, Cherry Pie?" I asked, and a pair of catlike green eyes nailed me with a glare I felt all the way down to my dick.

"I think you've had enough, don't you?"

This fucking woman.

"So prim and proper." I tutted. "I like the other version better."

"What other version?" She moved away from me to sink onto the couch, curling her legs beneath her.

"The one spread out across my hotel bed, screaming my name while I made her come."

The fire in her eyes matched the heat in her cheeks. "Get out, Dexter."

I smirked. "Make me."

Something passed across her face, a shadow gone before it

really registered. I cocked my head and reached out a hand to tug at one fiery lock of hair. "What?"

She frowned and swatted my hand away. "Go home and sleep it off. I'll call you a cab."

"Why would I go home? I only just got here." I spun and dropped onto the couch beside her. Well, *fell* onto it, really, since turning so quickly unbalanced me, but I managed to make it look like I'd meant to do it and grinned at the redheaded spitfire next to me. "Anyway, I thought you were planning on saving me."

"The only person who can save you is *you*." She rose to her feet. "I'll make coffee. You need to sober up."

"I'm not drunk."

She spun to face me. "You shouldn't even be *drinking!* What are you thinking?"

"I was thinking I wanted a drink, so I had one." I scowled up at her.

"You're supposed to be sober."

"I'm not an alcoholic, Red."

"You're an *addict!*" she yelled. "It doesn't matter *what* it is. Drink, drugs—you're not supposed to be touching any of it."

I lurched to my feet, the happy buzz from the tequila I'd been drinking fading at her words. "You're not my fucking keeper, Siobhan. I didn't come here to get a lecture from you."

"A keeper is *exactly* what you need. You can't be fucking trusted alone." Her hands slammed against my chest and shoved me. "Look at you. You're a mess. You're back in the country *one night* and you're calling me because you've already got drugs in your house and now ... *this!*" Her eyes raked over me in a look of disgust. "Look at the state of you."

"The state of me ..." I repeated flatly. "The *state* of me didn't bother you in Vegas, Nashville, or South Carolina. You *liked* the state of me *a lot*."

"You weren't drunk or *high* in Vegas." She turned away from me again.

I stepped toward her. "What about Nashville?" I asked silkily. "We were *all* drunk that night."

"Go home, Dex."

I was sobering up rapidly. This wasn't why I'd come here.

"*Go home, Dex*," I mimicked her voice. "That's all you ever fucking say to me. Fine, I'll go *home*." I made my way toward the door, threw it open and stepped out into the hallway. "Have a nice fucking life, Cherry Pie." I patted my pockets as I walked toward the exit, located my cell and fumbled with the lock screen. "Fuck." The curse left my lips when it slipped from my fingers and hit the floor.

A hand topped with cherry-red nails picked it up before I could reach it. I lifted my head to meet Siobhan's gaze.

"Come back inside," she said tiredly. "If anyone sees you out here ..."

"I get it," I snapped in return. "You don't want your quiet life disrupted by my fucking presence."

"It's a little late for that, don't you think?" she replied tartly, holding out my cell.

I snatched it from her hand. "I'll call a cab."

"You'll come inside and drink coffee."

"For fuck's sake, Siobhan," I blew up. "I'm feeling like a yo-yo here. Go home. Come back. Which is it?" Her lips pressed together and I knew she was fighting to stop herself from saying something. "Just fucking spit it out."

"You're being irrational," she said softly. "Why are you so angry? Don't you think *I* should be the angry one in this situation? You turn up in the middle of the night, *drunk*, and cause a scene."

"*I'm* being irrational?"

"Yes, you are. You say *you* feel like a yo-yo. How do you think I feel? Have you ever thought about that? You bounce in and out of my life without warning, expecting me to drop everything for you, and what do I get from that?"

"Good sex?"

My head snapped sideways from the force of her slap, and the sound echoed along the hallway. Slowly, I brought my face back to meet hers and smirked.

"That the best you got, Cherry Pie?"

Her hand lifted again, but this time I was ready and caught her wrist before she made contact. I propelled her backwards until her back slammed into the wall.

"First one was free, second one you pay for," I warned her.

She glared at me, but said nothing. A door creaked open behind us, and Siobhan's eyes jerked to look over my shoulder.

"Siobhan, dear, is that you? Is everything all right?"

"Everything's fine," I replied when Siobhan didn't answer.

"Siobhan?"

"Tell the woman everything is fine," I demanded in a low voice.

She wet her lips and I half-expected her to scream. "It's all right, Mrs. Montgomery," she said instead. "I'm okay."

"If you're sure ..." her neighbor didn't sound convinced.

"I'm sure." Green eyes locked on mine and I smiled.

"Good girl," I whispered and stepped closer. The scent of cherries enveloped me and it transported me back to the first time I spoke to her, when she was on the train arguing with her landlord. I dipped my head to the curve of her throat and inhaled. "So what am I doing, Cherry Pie? Am I leaving or staying?" My lips brushed against her skin as I spoke and I felt her shiver.

"I can't do this with you again," she protested. "I *can't*."

I ignored her, pressing butterfly kisses along her neck until I reached her ear. "Do you remember your safeword?" I breathed and a shudder rocked her.

"Dex, I can't," her voice was barely audible.

"Tell me what it is, Red."

There was a heartbeat of silence and then her lips moved.

"Pinea—" I kissed her, cutting off the rest of the word ... like I did *every* time she said it.

CHAPTER 16

BAD HABIT - THE KOOKS

Siobhan

PRESENT

I should have stopped him the second he kissed me, but I didn't. Instead, I tangled the fingers of my free hand into the front of his shirt and hauled him closer because if he insisted on kissing me, I'd damn well make sure I enjoyed it.

His thumb stroked over the inside of my wrist where he gripped it and then he moved, raising it above my head to pin against the wall. His other hand wrapped around my throat, thumb and forefinger exerting pressure on my jaw to tip my head back to a better angle.

My nipples tightened, heat pooling between my thighs, as my body responded to his touch—I remembered how *this* felt, the position he had me in, even though I'd blocked it out of my mind. My body reminded me how much I *liked* it when he shed the playful exterior and showed his true nature. The one he hid from most people, hid from *himself*, pretended didn't exist in favor of the easy-going, laid-back stoner rock guitarist. I knew better.

There was nothing easy-going or laid-back about Dex Cooper.

His tongue stroked over mine, the piercing adding an extra layer of sensation to the caress. The hand on my throat flexed when I nipped his bottom lip, stopping my intake of air for a brief second, but then he relaxed his grip and lifted his head. In a quick move, he released my wrist and dropped both hands to hook under my thighs and lift me, before striding back into the apartment.

He kicked the door shut behind him, crossed the room and lowered me onto the couch. I didn't get any opportunity to protest before his mouth was back on mine, and he was pushing a knee between my legs and a hand inside my robe. His fingers found the small hoop piercing my nipple and he gave it a gentle tug.

"Dex!" I hissed his name, my back arching up, and he chuckled against my mouth before lifting his head and kissing his way down my neck.

"I've missed the sounds you make for me," he murmured.

The reply died in my throat when his tongue traced around my nipple.

When had he opened my robe? When did I stop caring?

"Dex, stop," I whispered, and he raised his head.

"*Stop* stop, or pause?"

I licked my lips. I couldn't answer him because I didn't *know*. He cocked an eyebrow, blue eyes on my face. When I didn't reply, he smiled, rolled off the couch and dropped his hands to his belt buckle. "That's what I thought."

I watched as he slid the belt from around his waist and tossed it to one side. His jeans followed and, *the entire time*, I didn't move from where I lay—saying nothing as he peeled away layers of clothing until he was naked, revealing a toned body covered in tattoos and piercings. Naked and completely unconcerned by the fact—he came back to the couch and straddled my thighs.

"You're overdressed, Cherry Pie," he said with another slow smile, and pulled my robe open wider.

I was going to sleep with him, I acknowledged to myself. *I was going to let him win. I was going to give him what he wanted—me, my body, my time, and my attention.*

Tomorrow I'd deal with the aftermath, the self-hate, the anger at my inability to say no to him. I'd tell myself it was the last time and I wouldn't do it again. But right now? Right now, I'd be what he needed—a distraction, a moment out of time, a pretence that everything was right in the world. I'd do it because it was something he wanted that I *could* give him, something which wouldn't send him looking for another way to get high.

I lifted slightly so he could remove my robe and toss it on top of his clothes. He swept his gaze over me, and I knew he was processing any changes I'd made since the last time I was naked in front of him. His eyes dropped to the tattoo on my hip and his brows pleated, but he didn't comment on the change I'd made to it.

A finger traced along the edge of my panties before hooking beneath and peeling them downwards. One corner of his mouth tipped up when he saw I was bare, no trace of hair—

just how he liked me.

His hand reached down to grip his dick and stroke it. My heartbeat kicked up a notch when he bent and pressed his lips to my tattoo.

"I remember when you got this," he said. "Who distracted you from the pain when you added the extra detail?"

"No one."

One eyebrow rose. "No?"

I could feel my face heating up. "I don't do things like that any more." I didn't do things like that *ever* with anyone ... except him. Dex always managed to convince me to do things I would *never* consider doing with anyone else.

"Shame. Did you go to the same tattooist?"

"No!"

He gave another stroke of his dick. "I don't know whether to eat you or fuck you." His smile widened. "I bet you're already wet enough for me to slide right in." The finger holding my panties moved to my pussy and spread my lips apart.

I knew what he was looking for and satisfaction showed on his face when he found the barbell piercing still in place.

"Well, at least you didn't change *that*."

"Why would I? It's the gift that keeps on giving." I saw the flare of anger in his eyes before he lowered his lashes and masked it. "What's wrong, Rock Star?" I taunted him. "Don't like the thought that the gift you bought me got someone else off?"

He lifted himself up off my legs, fingers toying with the bar piercing the hood of my clit. "Take the panties off."

I tried to ignore the pleasure building like lightning bolts from his touch and held his gaze. "You need me naked, you do it." I was being purposely antagonistic, trying to keep some control over the situation.

"I don't *need* you naked, Cherry Pie." His smile was dark. "Leave them on then. I'll work around it. But don't say I didn't give you the chance to get rid of them."

I immediately kicked out of them. I knew Dex and when he said he'd work around it, I knew it would be in a way which would leave me feeling dirtier than I would think possible once he was done with me.

He laughed and reached down to pick up the condom wrapper he'd taken from his jeans pocket before removing them. Tearing it open with his teeth, he eased it over his dick, carefully stretching it over the piercings around the head. He caught me watching, my tongue licking over my lips, and cocked his head.

"You remember how this feels, don't you?" He shifted position until he was above me, one hand braced to the side of my head and one leg between mine. He ran his dick over my pussy and I couldn't stop the shudder which rocked through me. "Now should I dive straight in or do you want me to play for a while?"

It was a good question. I *did* know how it felt—the piercings he had made *everything* about sex more intense. Orgasms were guaranteed—at least for me, anyway. But I also knew what he could do with his mouth and that tongue piercing. Any woman who caught Dex's attention enough for him to want to fool around with them was in for the night of their life.

The downside of that was he *knew* how good he was and wasn't against using it to his advantage. He was also unpredictable and a little bit crazy, but that was another problem entirely.

I hooked my hand around the back of his neck and dragged his weight down on top of me.

"Just fuck me already!" I snapped.

Guarded Addiction

CHAPTER 17

BEAUTIFUL MISTAKE - MAROON 5

Dex
PRESENT

Wasn't really much I could say to that demand, so I wound a hand around the back of her knee so I could pull her leg up over my hip and lined my dick up. Her bottom lip was caught between her teeth and those huge green eyes darkened more with every inch I pushed inside her. I had to fight to go slow, to ignore the demand to drive myself into her so hard she couldn't deny who she belonged to. She was wet, ready, but so fucking tight and I wasn't exactly average-sized. Add that to the piercings I had and it meant rushing to sheath myself inside her body could be a fucking disaster in all kinds of ways, so I gritted my teeth against the agonising need to slam myself as deep as I could possibly go and took it slowly.

When one of her hands curved over my ass and dug her nails in, I knew I was green-lit to relax the hold on my control and surged the rest of the way into her. Her eyes closed as a part-moan/part-sigh of appreciation escaped her lips.

My head dropped to her shoulder and I kissed my way along her throat. She threw her head back, hips arching to meet every thrust I made, and the temptation was too great. I wanted to mark her, make it clear she'd been possessed, *owned*. Reaching up, I wrapped my hand around her throat, and used my thumb to turn her head to the side, then bit her. I sucked on her soft, fragrant skin like I was a starving vampire and she was my *mostly willing* victim. I marked a path down her throat and over her breast. Her nails dug into my ass and the sharp sting warned me she'd drawn blood.

But she didn't tell me to stop. Instead, she arched her back when I lifted my head and tried to drag me back down.

"Did you miss this, Cherry Pie?" I grunted, withdrawing almost completely from her body just to see her reaction.

"Shut up!" she hissed and wrapped her legs around my hips to anchor me back in place.

My laugh was ragged. "Who put you in control?" I tightened my grip on her throat, heard her breath hitch, saw her nipples harden. "Should I stop, love? Leave you on the edge?"

"Dex!" The whine in her voice made me smile.

Who needed drugs to get high when I could reach the same level of ecstasy every time I had a taste of this woman?

I lowered my head and nipped the lobe of her ear. "Say please."

Her fingers flexed against my ass, and she tried to force me into movement. I resisted, holding steady, my lips finding their way back down to the pulse beating at the base of her throat.

"Ask me nicely, Cherry Pie."

She dragged her fingernails up my spine and I relished the sting. Her fingers tangled into my hair and she tugged at me until I lifted my head.

"If you don't make me come *right now*, Dexter, I'll do it myself."

I arched a brow. "Will you now?" Reaching back, I caught her wrist and pulled it down between our bodies. Flattening her palm against her stomach, I linked my fingers with hers and sought out her clit. "Let's play together then."

With every thrust, I flicked her piercing, and stroked her clit using her own fingers. I stoked the flames until I could feel us both burning up, until she was babbling incoherent nonsense and I was slamming into her in an uncoordinated rhythm as we came.

Siobhan didn't stir when I levered myself up from the couch a few minutes later. I glanced at her. Her eyes were half-closed, her breathing still a fraction too fast, but she didn't speak or acknowledge me when I stooped to grab my clothes and headed into the bathroom to get rid of the condom.

It wasn't until I was returning to the living room that I realized in my haste to get her naked and beneath me, I hadn't closed the front door completely. It was slightly ajar. If anyone had walked past ... I stifled a laugh. Well, let's just say they'd have gotten an eyeful and possibly an education. I closed the door properly and turned to face the room.

Siobhan was where I'd left her, only now she was asleep, curled on her side with her ass on display. I could see the bruises forming where I'd bitten along her throat, my fingerprints on her thighs where I'd gripped her a little too hard—she'd always bruised easily, I'd forgotten that. I smiled to myself. She was going to be pissed when she realized what I'd done. I considered waking her so we could battle it out now, but decided against it. The fight would be far more entertaining if she was rested, plus I was kinda tired myself. Besides, fighting with Siobhan would turn into fucking and I wanted to give that the attention it would deserve.

If I could bottle whatever it was Siobhan did to me, I'd never touch another drug or drop of alcohol again. The high I got from her body, from her temper, from simply being *around* her, was like nothing else. It left me relaxed and calm, sleepy even, instead of agitated and strung out. In fact, I wanted nothing more than to crawl into bed and lose myself to sleep, but I knew I had to leave, get back to my house before Diesel did a check and realized I wasn't there.

My gaze fell on the sleeping redhead again. Could I risk putting her to bed or would she wake? Guess there was only one way to find out.

I crossed the room and carefully lifted her into my arms. She gave me a sleepy frown, but didn't open her eyes. I waited until she settled, and then carried her through to the bedroom and set her onto the mattress. Pulling the covers over her, I dropped a kiss onto her forehead and straightened.

"We'll go for round two tomorrow, Cherry Pie," I murmured, eased the door closed behind me and left her apartment.

Contrary to what I'd claimed earlier, I *hadn't* driven to Siobhan's apartment myself. Being caught over the legal limit by the police and then having to face Karl's wrath was something I planned to avoid at all costs. No, I'd called a cab. I only told *her* I'd driven myself there to see her reaction...

There was a company Marley Stone had introduced us to who he, and now *we*, used for ferrying us around when we didn't have a driver, or we wanted to take off alone. They had a reputation for being closed-mouthed and secretive about their clientele and, in all the years we'd used them, I had never heard of any of the drivers talking to the press.

I called them, ordered a car and was picked up less than ten minutes later. Climbing in, I rested my head against the backrest and closed my eyes. A yawn cracked my jaw and I fought not to fall asleep. Delayed jet lag, alcohol, and good sex—the perfect combination to combat my inability to rest. I would have liked a joint to round it off nicely, but *that* would show up on the next drug test so I wouldn't risk it.

I was drifting off when Luca's ringtone broke the silence of the car. I connected the call.

"S'up," I said on another yawn.

There was muffled shouting, and then Luca's voice reached me. "Are you home? Can you come and pick me up?"

"I'm in a cab, I can redirect it. Where—" I broke off, listening to the background noise coming through the speaker. "Are you *fucking* kidding me? You're at the cages? What the fuck are you doing there?"

"Needed to burn off some steam. How far away are you?"

Leaning forward, I tapped the driver's shoulder. "Can we take a detour?" At his nod, I gave him our new location and sat back. "Be there in about ten minutes. Did you win, at least?"

Luca laughed and I could hear a slight edge to the sound. "Of course I fucking won. Let me know when you get here." He ended the call.

People thought *I* was fucked up and unpredictable. They had no clue how deep the crazy ran with my best friend.

"Are you sure this is the place?" The driver spoke up ten minutes later as he carefully drove down the pitted and pothole ridden road toward a dark warehouse.

"Yeah. Pull up in front of the doors over there." I nodded toward the entrance while I texted Luca to tell him we were there, rolled down the window and let out a sharp whistle when I saw his familiar shape slip through the gap between the doors. He trotted toward us, and I threw open the car door for him to climb in.

"Where to now?" the driver asked.

"Back to my place. The original address I gave you," I replied and turned to Luca. "How many fights did you have?"

"Three."

"And you won all of them?"

He grunted in reply.

"I'll take that as a yes. How much?"

"Fifty thousand."

"Nice. What are you going to do with all that cash you don't actually fucking need?"

"Sure I'll think of something."

I rolled my eyes.

"Why are you out this late, anyway?" he asked me.

I felt a smile curl my lips up. "Decided to remind Siobhan of a few things."

CHAPTER 18

DRUGS AND CANDY – ALL TIME LOW

Dex

AGE 23

I put the joint to my lips and drew the smoke into my lungs. My eyes slid closed and I held my breath, waiting until I felt the drug start to work its magic, then exhaled. Gabe and Luca were bickering in one corner of the studio, while Seth played some riff on his guitar that was *almost* recognizable. The name of it hovered on the edge of my awareness. I didn't bother forcing myself to remember it; it wasn't *that* important.

"Fuck it," I heard Gabe snap. "I'm out of here. You coming, Seth?"

I heard Seth set his guitar down. "Where are we going?" he asked.

"Somewhere that *isn't* here," our singer grunted.

I took another hit from the joint and opened my eyes. "You should go to Trudy's."

They both swung around to face me.

"Why?" Gabe demanded. "We haven't been there in years."

I sat up, squinting at him through the smoke of my joint. "It's up for sale. I bet whoever buys it will tear it down."

Gabe's entire body stilled. I wasn't sure he was even breathing as he stared at me.

Seth's dark eyes swung from him to me. "And how do *you* know that?"

I shrugged. "Because unlike you two, I haven't cut off everyone from our days pre-fame."

Truth was, I'd seen the For Sale sign in front of the building during one of my weekly drive-bys to check out Harper's apartment building. I couldn't tell Gabe that, though. He'd lose his shit.

Any mention of the girl he'd grown up with caused him to fall into a self-destructive spiral that lasted weeks. It resulted in some great songs, but the unpredictable behavior that came with it wasn't worth the hassle.

At some point the idiot would figure out that Harper was his one and only. If you cut him in half, you'd find Harper's name painted all over his soul. He wasn't ready to admit to that, though, and until he was, we had to put up with the behavior caused by *not* having her in his life.

That was why I kept an eye on the girl. The last thing any of us needed was Gabe discovering she'd gone and got married, or had kids, or something equally as stupid. So far, I hadn't had to step in and make her aware of my presence or let Gabe know I was watching her.

A kick to my foot brought my attention back to the two men glaring at me. I cocked an eyebrow.

"What?"

"Who are you still in contact with?" Gabe was scowling and I could see his mind working as he tried to figure out who I could be talking to.

"Why? Aren't I allowed to have friends outside of the band?"

"Fuck you, Dex." Gabe spun away and I knew his mind had gone to Harper.

"You're not my type. Sorry, man."

Seth rolled his eyes at me and followed Gabe out of the room.

"How did you *really* find out about Trudy's?" Luca dropped onto the couch beside me, propping his feet up on the coffee table.

"Drove past and saw the For Sale sign."

He laughed. "You know it's going to eat at him whether you've been talking to Harper, don't you?"

I threw him a grin. "Of course I do. Maybe the fuckwit will go and see her."

"You know he won't."

My grin faded. "I know." Pinching the end of my joint, I stuffed it into a pocket. "Want to get out of here and find someone to play with?"

My head was pounding when I woke up, or regained consciousness—could have been either. I untangled myself from the body beside me and sat up on the bed to look around the unfamiliar room.

Where had we ended up? I checked to see if Luca was present and found him on the opposite side of the bed, two girls separating us. He was still asleep, face buried into the pillow, with one of the girls wrapped around him.

Yawning, I eased out of the bed, grabbed my pants and dressed quietly. With any luck, I could wake Luca and we'd both get out of here before either of the girls realized we'd gone. First though, I needed to find out where we were so I could call a cab.

Padding out of the bedroom, I discovered we were in an apartment and found my way to the front door. Opening it, I stuck my head outside. The hallway was empty and quiet, and very clean. A more upmarket building then. Retreating back inside, I went back into the bedroom and rounded the bed to shake Luca awake.

His eyes opened as soon as I touched his shoulder.

"Time to go," I whispered.

He grunted and reached back to unwrap the girl's arm from his waist. I handed him his clothes and he pulled them on, while I kept an eye on the sleeping girls. Neither of them stirred, not even when Luca tripped and hit the wall with his shoulder. We both froze in place and then, stifling our laughter, sprinted out of the apartment.

Out on the street, we headed down the sidewalk until we found a street name. Luca pulled out his cell and called a cab and, no more than half an hour later, we were back in my home on the other side of town.

Luca headed into the guest room where he kept clothes and used the shower there, while I did the same in my own room and we met in my kitchen a short while later.

"Do we have anything on today?" he asked, handing me coffee.

"Don't think so." I yawned and swallowed a mouthful of the scalding hot drink. "I might hit up Travis."

"Again? Didn't you see him a week ago?"

Travis was my supplier, my dealer. Not that I had an addiction. Sometimes I really needed a distraction from the crazy inside my head.

"Only for Mary Jane. I want something to help me sleep."

"You should come to the cages with me."

I snorted. "You're the fighter, not me. I'd be dead in five minutes."

"And you'll be dead just as fast if you keep putting all that shit into your body."

"I sometimes need a little boost now and then, that's all." He didn't reply, although I could see he wanted to. I fired off a text to Travis, asking him to arrange a drop, then glanced back up at Luca. "What are your plans?"

"Hit the gym. Work out the kinks."

Travis had come through for me and delivered a small package a couple of hours after Luca left. I stashed the baggie of pills in the medicine cabinet, where I would be able to find it when I needed them. My intention was to drop a couple of pills when I was ready to sleep. Until then, I had things to do.

First one being to check in with a certain redhead.

ME - Hey Cherry Pie. You busy tonight?

It was over an hour before she replied, and I spent the time playing bass guitar, smoking weed, and drinking coffee.

CHERRY PIE - Been working all day. Movie and an early night.

ME - Want some company? Your fiancé is back in town.

The last time I'd seen her had been when I went with her to meet her grandmother. A couple of days after that the band had headed out on a small US tour, supporting a couple of bigger bands. I'd texted her occasionally, but I wanted to see her and make sure she hadn't had any more issues with her landlord.

CHERRY PIE - Sure. You know where I live.

I was knocking on her door less than forty minutes later. She let me in, greeted me with a warm smile and a critical once-over, before leading me over to the couch in the center of the living room.

"Can I get you something to drink?"

"Beer, if you have it." I shrugged out of my jacket and dropped heavily onto the cushions. The couch creaked beneath my weight.

"Don't break my furniture, Dex," she warned.

"Already sounding like my wife and I've only been in the room for half a minute." I twisted to watch as she bent to grab a bottle of beer from the refrigerator. She caught me admiring her ass when she straightened and I smirked. "Had any trouble with Dickhead Dave?"

"No. I told him you work away which is why you're rarely here." She handed me the bottle.

"Thanks, love." I twisted off the cap and took a long swallow. "He lives in the building, doesn't he?"

"Yeah." She sat beside me, a respectable distance between us.

"I'll make sure he sees me then. You can say I'm home on leave or something."

"Or you came to have a serious talk about breaking things off."

I pointed my beer bottle at her. "Not gonna happen. I've decided we're getting married. No divorce, either. You're stuck with me for life."

"Then I guess we'll have a terrible court battle, since I want my freedom." She smiled at me and took a drink from her own beer. "I have grounds. You're never here and can't keep me satisfied."

I arched a brow. "I've never had any complaints."

She laughed. "Then I guess it's because you're cheating on me while you're out of town."

"Nah, I wouldn't do that. Not if we were really together." I reached to put my beer down and lifted her legs, placing them across my lap. She settled back against the arm of the couch, a pillow beneath her head. "You have sexy toes." I pinched one between my fingers and she wiggled them.

"There's no such thing. Feet are gross."

"Yours are cute." I ran my finger over the sole of her foot and she squirmed. "Ticklish, too."

"Cut it out," she told me.

"Are you ticklish all over?"

"If you try to find out, I'll stab you."

I chuckled. "That's a yes, then." My finger ran over her ankle.

"Grounds for divorce, Dex," she warned in a low growl. One that didn't so much threaten me as wake up my dick.

"I'd risk it." I muttered, and twisted in a quick move to lean over her, hands braced either side of her head. "Are you completely opposed to the idea of me kissing you?" I asked.

She lifted a finger to trace over my lips. "I'd be lying if I said I hadn't thought about it."

My tongue came out to lick her fingertip. "I think about it a lot. That, and your ass," I couldn't help but add, just to see her roll those big green eyes at me.

Guarded Addiction

CHAPTER 19

WOLF - HIGHLY SUSPECT

Siobhan

AGE 22

I hadn't given Dex Cooper much thought since the last time I'd seen him. He'd been fun to hang with. I definitely appreciated the fact he'd helped get my seedy landlord off my back, but then he disappeared back to wherever he came from. I didn't hear from him for months, other than a couple of texts telling me he had to go out of town and wasn't sure when he'd be back. So when his text message dropped, I had to take some time to consider whether I wanted to see him again.

He was cute, but there was an air about him that told me he was into some things I wanted no part of. He smelled of weed and his eyes were always slightly unfocused. I wasn't sure if he was using more than marijuana, but if he *was* taking something stronger than that—I didn't want to get any more involved with him than I already was.

So, if that was the case, why was I lying on my old couch, with him poised above me, having a discussion on whether or not I was going to let him kiss me?

His blue eyes were intent, his lips within reach, but he didn't make any move. All I had to do was lift my head slightly. He was waiting for me to make that first step. It was one thing pretending to be in a relationship with him as a means to fend off my landlord, but *kissing* him would turn our still-new, slightly oddball friendship into something more ... wouldn't it?

"What are you thinking, Cherry Pie?" he asked, and my eyes tracked the movement of his lips as he formed the words.

"A kiss," I said and lifted one finger between us. "*One* kiss ... just to see what it's like."

His lips quirked into a lopsided smile. "What if you want *more* than one?"

"What if I don't?"

"Oh, you will." He lowered his head until there was barely any space between our mouths. "Because I guarantee you will like it *a lot*."

I could feel his warm breath on my face, a faint hint of spearmint and the beer he'd been drinking. But he *still* didn't kiss me.

"What are you waiting for?" I asked, and the words came out as a breathless whisper. I'd never anticipated the touch of a man's mouth as much as I was waiting for his.

"You."

"Me?"

"If you want it, Red, take it. I'm not doing all the work for you."

Our eyes clashed, his daring me to make the first move.

"One kiss," I repeated.

"Just one," he whispered in reply.

I took a steadying breath, then closed the gap between us and placed my mouth over his in a perfectly chaste kiss, lips pressed firmly together.

He chuckled when I let my head drop down against the cushion and smiled up at him.

"Well played, Cherry Pie." He brushed his nose along mine. "Your safe word is pineapple."

I frowned. "Why do I need a safe word?"

"I'm not saying you *do*. But it's better to *have* one and not need it, than need it and not have it. Say it. *Pineapple*." He drew the word out in a long, low drawl and I laughed.

"Fine. Pinea—" His mouth swallowed the rest of the word, his tongue sliding between my lips and silencing me.

The kiss didn't last long, barely enough time for my eyes to close and my hands to lift and link around his neck, at which point he nipped my bottom lip and eased back.

"Come away with me for the weekend."

"Where?"

"Anywhere. Somewhere that isn't here."

I threaded my fingers through his hair, tugging it loose from the tie which held it back from his face. "Are you okay?"

His tongue licked over his lips. "Why wouldn't I be?"

"I don't know."

He dived back down for another kiss, and for a time I lost

myself in his taste, the feel of his lips against mine, but then he drew back and smiled.

"So this weekend? I'll pick you up in the morning. Pack an overnight bag, yeah?" His voice turned brisk, as he rolled to his feet, stood and stretched, before reaching down to pull me upright. Cupping my face between his palms, he pressed a kiss to the corner of my mouth, then backed toward the door.

"Wait. Are you *leaving*?"

"I need to make some plans. Be ready at nine."

"But—"

"Nine sharp, Cherry Pie. Don't keep me waiting."

I *was* ready, packed and waiting by eight thirty. Nine, nine-thirty, ten o'clock passed, but Dex never showed.

And I didn't see him again for almost a year.

Guarded Addiction

CHAPTER 20

IDFC - BLACKBEAR

Siobhan

PRESENT

I rolled onto my front, burying my face into the pillow and yawned. My body ached in all the right ways, the after-effects of good sex...

My eyes snapped open.

Dex! Oh fuck.

The bed was empty other than me, and I couldn't remember finding my way to it. My last real memory was lying in post-orgasmic bliss on the couch and Dex's warmth leaving me when he disappeared into the bathroom.

I sat up and looked around. *Had he stayed?* I couldn't *hear* anyone else in the apartment, or see any evidence of him being there. The sun shone between the gap in the curtains. *How long had I slept?*

Throwing back the covers, I rose to my feet, found my robe hanging on my door and dragged it on.

"Dex?" I called. Silence greeted me.

He hadn't stayed over then.

A shower, coffee, and then I'd head out to put up a 'roommate wanted' notice in the local community center. I entered the small kitchen and flicked on the coffeemaker, then made my way into the bathroom for a quick shower.

Stripping out of the robe, I stepped into the shower and turned on the water, making sure to step back out of reach for that first couple of seconds. The shower was temperamental and when you first turned it on, it would either send out a stream of water so hot it would scald you or so cold you'd freeze to the spot. Sadly, unless you stood *inside* the shower you also couldn't reach the controls to switch it on.

Today, the water was going for cold, but eventually it warmed up and I stood beneath the spray. I tried not to think about the night before, of what I'd done, my lack of willpower where Dex was concerned. I *knew* what I was doing. I wasn't even drunk. There was no point in regretting it now, and part of me *didn't* regret it. How could you regret being made to feel *that* good? Another part of me knew it had been a mistake, one I really *shouldn't* repeat—but I would. I always did.

I reached out for the body wash, poured some onto the sponge and lathered it over my body. My skin was sensitive, my nipples still tender from the attention Dex had given them, and the bath sponge felt rougher than usual. Rinsing off the soapy suds, I glanced down and stilled.

Was that a bruise?

As the soap washed away, more marks appeared. My breast was covered in them. I craned my neck, trying to see further up my body. There was a fucking trail of them.

He'd bitten me. *Marked me!* Oh fuck, where did they end?

I hit the button which controlled the water and stepped out onto the bath mat, grabbed a towel on my mad dash to the mirror that mounted the sink and leaned forward. Wiping away the steam, I studied my reflection.

That fucking rat bastard!

I peered closer, running my finger down my neck, following the trail of bites. How was I supposed to cover them up? They were *everywhere!* The left side of my throat, across my shoulder, and my left breast looked like it had been savaged by a hungry vampire. Makeup and a high-necked top was *not* going to hide all of them.

"I am going to *kill* him," I fumed. How the hell was I supposed to conceal all of them?

I considered calling him, but dismissed the idea. He'd find it funny, maybe even expect me to freak out at him. No, I had to play it differently this time, and not give him the reactions he was looking for.

After I dried, brushed my teeth and dressed, I found some paper so I could write up an ad for a new roommate, and then headed out. I was pulling the door open to exit the building when I heard my name ... well, *not* my name exactly, but the butchered version of it only one person used.

"Sioban!"

I briefly considered pretending I hadn't heard him and keep going, but knew that was only delaying the inevitable, so I stopped and turned. His eyes dropped to the bites visible above the collar of my jacket and a faint trace of pink colored his cheeks.

"Do you need something, David?" I asked.

He crossed the small hallway until he was less than a foot away. His eyes drifted to the bites again.

"Have you found someone to replace Harper yet?"

"No, I'm just on my way to put an advertisement up."

He nodded. "If you need more time … a payment holiday, perhaps?"

"It's fine."

"Did …" He paused to wet his lips. "Did you have someone over last night?"

I felt my cheeks heat up. I could hardly deny there'd been someone with me, not with the evidence clearly on display. "My husband came by." It felt weird saying that out loud. It had been so long since I'd thought about the story we'd told my landlord all those years ago.

"I thought you were separated."

"We are." I cleared my throat.

"Did you reconcile?"

My hand lifted to touch my throat. "No, I … umm." I gave a helpless shrug. "You know how it is."

His lips thinned. "No, actually, I *don't*."

"Oh ... well." I checked the time on the screen of my cell. "I have to go." I backed toward the door, not wanting to turn my back on him. I don't know what it was about David ... no, that wasn't true. I *did* know what it was—the man was a creep and he made me *very* uncomfortable.

Once I was outside the building, I turned and darted down the steps. I wouldn't put it past him to follow me, and I wanted to be out of sight before the thought occurred to him. I didn't slow my pace until I'd rounded the corner.

CHAPTER 21

HEAD LIKE A HOLE - NINE INCH NAILS

Dex
PRESENT

"Are you *fucking* stupid?"

That was Gabe's snarled greeting after I walked through the door of the studio with Luca. I knew it wasn't directed at me. *I* wasn't the one sporting a black eye and split lip. My scratches were hidden beneath my clothes where no one could see them.

"What the fuck are you thinking? We've got a photoshoot in *two* days and you turn up looking like this?" Gabe waved a hand at Luca's face, his own expression furious. "What the fuck is wrong with you?"

"What's wrong, Gabe? Harper not putting out? You need to find some side-piece, get laid and chill the fuck down." Luca's response was greeted by silence.

I traded glances with Seth and we both moved simultaneously—me to grab Luca, him to tackle Gabe. We were both seconds too late, and Gabe's fist connected with Luca's face. Blood exploded outwards as the resulting punch split Luca's lip again.

I managed to wrap my arms around Luca's waist and haul him backwards just as he buried his fist into Gabe's stomach. Seth hooked his arms around Gabe and we dragged the pair of them apart.

"Get the fuck off me," Gabe snarled, twisting to shove Seth away so he could stalk back toward Luca.

"Not happening." Seth stepped in front of him and slapped both palms against Gabe's chest. "When will you stop fucking rising to the bait?"

I saw the fury in Gabe's eyes and winced, knowing what was about to happen. The crack as Gabe's fist met Seth's jaw echoed around the studio.

Nobody moved for almost thirty seconds, and then Seth retaliated.

"Oh, for fuck's sake," Luca muttered and jerked out of my grip.

When Gabe and Luca fought it was usually a quick trading of punches, but when it was Gabe and Seth, things got damaged. And neither of us were willing to step in between that level of violence.

We both watched as Gabe and Seth traded blows, and then Gabe's foot caught on a wire draped across the floor and lost his footing. Seth's hand flashed out, catching his arm before he hit the ground and hauled him upright.

The two men stared at each other and Gabe's shoulders loosened, the tension leaving his body. He hooked an arm around Seth's neck and they both swung to face us.

"Is *that* likely to cause trouble?" Seth asked, flicking a finger at Luca's face.

Luca shook his head. "Nah, I was at the cages." He grinned, wiping away the blood dripping down his chin. "You should see the other guys."

Gabe scrubbed a hand down his face, looking tired. "Karl is going to lose his shit," he sighed.

"You're the face for the photoshoot, not me," Luca pointed out.

"He still wants band photographs, asshole."

Luca shrugged. "It'll be fine. The swelling will have gone down by then, and I'm sure the makeup girls can hide the bruising."

Gabe drew breath to speak, the fire kindling in his eyes again. Seth rested a hand on his shoulder. "We'll figure it out on Tuesday," he said before Gabe could say anything. "What about you? Anything you want to admit to?" he directed his attention at me.

"Nope. I'm just over here doing my thing," I said and wandered across the room to pick up one of my bass guitars.

Seth didn't believe me. I could see it in the look he gave me, but he didn't press. Luca disappeared into the bathroom, presumably to clean up, and there was a moment of tension when Gabe followed after him. When no sound of fighting reached us and the two men returned, chatting amiably, we relaxed and a few minutes later the whole thing was forgotten in our shared love and passion for making music together.

🍒

Diesel and Remy were outside when we left the studio a little over six hours later. Their voices reached us across the parking lot, too low to make out the words, but the conversation stopped when they saw us.

"Talking about me or you?" I asked Gabe.

"Could go either way," he replied. His lighter was in his hand, the flame flickering as he opened and closed it.

"Everything okay with you?" We all knew Gabe's habit of playing with his lighter when he was stressed.

"Define okay?" he muttered, then laughed—it seemed forced. "Yeah, man, everything's absolutely peachy."

He peeled away toward his car before I could question him further, but I saw Seth watch him walk across the parking lot, a frown pulling his brows together.

"Is there something going on with him that we need to know about?" I asked our guitarist in a low voice.

"Not sure," he grunted. "Something is bugging him, but he's not ready to air it yet. We'll just have to wait and see."

"Him and Harper okay?"

Seth gave a soft laugh. "Yeah, I think they're good. I'm pretty sure whatever has crawled up his ass doesn't have anything to do with that."

"How about you and Riley?"

He smiled. "We're working it out."

"Problems?"

"No, not really. We're feeling our way. She spends more time at my place than at her own. I'm thinking about asking her to move in permanently, but ..." he trailed off.

"Worried about the age thing and how it'll look?"

"Closer to her mom will lose her shit if we rush into it, and I don't need to cause any trouble with her dad. He's already pissed about her dating a rock star. So, we're taking small steps. We'll get there."

A car drove into the parking lot and rolled to a stop. Riley, in her typical cut-off jeans and one of our band t-shirts, climbed out of the back. Seth's smile widened and I snorted a laugh.

"Man, you got it bad."

Seth's head turned and a dark eyebrow rose. "And you don't?"

"What are you talking about?"

"You're not as subtle as you think you are. Take some advice. Come clean before it destroys friendships." He turned away before I could respond to greet Riley. "Hey, Shutterbug. Ready to eat?"

I didn't hear her reply as Seth wrapped an arm around her shoulders and walked back to the car. I looked around for Luca, and spotted him leaning against the wall by the door, his head bowed over his cell as he typed out a message.

"Want to grab a drink?" I asked, and he jerked, head lifting to search me out.

He pocketed his cell. "Nah, I'm gonna go home and sleep." He threw me a grin. "Was a busy night last night and I'm fucked."

"Which home?" I asked, and his smile faded.

"I only have *one* home, D. The other one is just for show." He pushed away from the wall and walked over to where his car was parked, Ryder already in the driver's seat.

"And then there was one," I muttered to myself, waved a hand at Diesel and headed for my own car. "Why do we all need separate drivers?" I questioned as he slid behind the wheel.

"Because all four of you sitting together in a small vehicle for longer than ten minutes is a recipe for disaster," my bodyguard replied.

I huffed a laugh. "Fair point."

"Where are we headed?"

I thought for a minute, then gave him Siobhan's address.

Guarded Addiction

CHAPTER 22

DRUGS - EDEN

Siobhan

PRESENT

"Get dressed," Dex said when I opened the door and found him standing there.

"Who died and made you the boss?" I sniped, stepping back so he could walk inside.

"Nobody died. I just took the role out of the goodness of my own heart." He stopped, turned toward me and smiled. He was looking at the bite marks he'd left on my throat and waiting for me to say something, to acknowledge what he'd done.

Well, he could die waiting.

"Go put some clothes on, Cherry Pie," he repeated when I didn't say anything *and* didn't move.

"I had no plans to go out."

"Well …" he sauntered past me and dropped onto the couch. "Now you do."

I folded my arms across my chest. "No, Dexter. I *don't*."

He raised an eyebrow at me. I glared at him.

"Come on, Red," he said eventually, when he realized I had no intention of complying with his demand. "I have a meeting and I don't want to go alone. We can grab some dinner after." He delivered the explanation softly, with no trace of his former arrogance.

I stood firm for a second longer, then nodded my head. "Fine. What time is the meeting?"

"In an hour. But it's a twenty-minute drive from here, *if* the traffic is good."

"Okay. Wait here."

I left him in the living room while I went into my bedroom, closing the door firmly behind me. If he really wanted to come in, a door wouldn't keep him out but I hoped it would send him the message that I *didn't* want him in here with me.

I pulled on jeans and a t-shirt, tried to conceal the bites he'd covered me in with makeup, left my hair loose and darted back out to where he waited. I don't think it took more than ten minutes, but he was on his feet and pacing when I returned.

"Is everything okay?" I asked.

"Yeah. You ready?" He swept his gaze over me, lingering on my throat.

"Let me grab a jacket and my keys."

He waited, impatience dripping from him, while I tugged on a jacket, grabbed my purse and stuffed my keys into it, then slipped my feet into a pair of flats. "Okay, I'm ready."

He had the door open and was in the hallway before I finished speaking.

"Diesel's out front with the car," he said, holding the door to the apartment building open and waving me through. "The SUV across the road. See it?" He pointed and I nodded.

"Hard to miss."

His laugh seemed brittle. "You're not wrong. Wouldn't be my first choice, but since Miles nearly killed Gabe and Harper in the Mustang, Karl has decided we need to travel everywhere by tank."

"Didn't Gabe get the Mustang repaired?"

"Yeah. It's sitting in a storage locker somewhere." His voice held a hint of ... *something* I didn't recognize. "That car was his pride and joy. His prized possession. The one thing he loved, other than Harper, from his childhood."

"Was?"

"He nearly lost Harper when they were in it. He's had it restored, but I don't think he's ready to get back behind the wheel yet." He sighed. "I don't think he's ready to deal with a lot of things right now."

"Him and Harper are okay, though, right?"

He waved a hand. "Sure, they're tight." Diesel materialized from around the car and opened the back door. Dex stepped back to let me climb in first. "But he's not settled. There's something bothering him," he continued once we were inside.

"Do you know what it is?"

"Not a clue. The first person to find out will be Harper or Seth. My money's on Seth. It's *always* Seth. Harper being back in his life won't change that."

We sat at the back of the NA meeting. Dex had a ball cap pulled low over his face and the collar of his jacket turned up. The person in charge seemed to know him and gave us a nod when we slipped through the door and sat down. He never spoke to Dex or tried to draw attention to him during the meeting. As people began to leave, a little over an hour later, he came over to where we sat. Dex rose to his feet and shook his hand.

"You know everything said in here is confidential. No one is going to say they've seen you. One day I'd like for you to tell your story," he told Dex.

"Siobhan, this is Max." Dex ignored his words.

Max gave me a smile. "This is the first time you've brought someone with you."

"She'll stop me from taking a detour on the way home and buying something to get through the night."

"You feel like that's a possibility tonight?" Max asked, and I couldn't hear any sign of condemnation or accusation in his tone. Nothing more than simple curiosity.

"I think it would be more than a possibility," Dex admitted roughly.

"Is that why you asked me to come?" I blurted and both men looked at me.

And then Dex's lips tilted into a slow smile, eyes losing the dark look and glinting with sudden humor. I realized what I'd said and pointed a finger at him. "Do *not* say a word."

His smile widened. "I never ask, love, I demand."

I rolled my eyes. "I told you not to speak."

"But you didn't say please."

Max cleared his throat. "As entertaining as this is, Dex, if you *do* need help ..."

"I'll be fine."

"I'll get him home and make sure he doesn't do anything stupid," I said and Max nodded.

"If you need me, you have my number." He took Dex's hand and shook it again. "Any time, *day or night*," he stressed.

"Got it." Dex's hand found the small of my back and exerted enough pressure to make me step forward. "We have a dinner reservation. Catch you later, Father."

"He was a *priest?*" I asked when we stepped outside.

The SUV glided forward and we were inside the car seconds later.

"I can't believe you lied to a priest," I continued once the car was in motion. "You didn't make dinner reservations."

"I might have." Dex tossed the ball cap to the floor.

"No, you didn't. Neither of us are dressed to go to a place that requires reservations."

"Can't fool you, huh?" He pulled out his cell. "What do you want to eat? I'll get us a table."

"It's that easy?"

"Perks of fame." He lifted a hand to rub the back of his neck. "C'mon, Cherry Pie, humor me. I'm starving. What do you feel like eating?"

I thought for a moment. "Italian food. I *really* want Italian."

He eyed me, then scrolled through his contacts. "Good thing Luca isn't here. I know the perfect place." He tapped one of the numbers and waited for the call to connect. "Hey, Lola? It's Dex. Don't suppose you could fit in a table for two?" He paused, listening to the reply. "In about ... ten minutes?" Another pause. "You're a star. Thanks, sweetheart. See you soon."

"Who's Lola?" I asked.

"Jealous, Cherry Pie?"

Yes, I was.

There had been an easy familiarity in the way he spoke to her. "No, I've just never heard anyone mention her before."

"She works at Tallorico's." He named an Italian restaurant in East Hollywood. I'd heard of it but never been there.

"There isn't a dress code?"

He snorted. "At *Tallorico's?* No, it's a dress as you want kind of place."

"You go there often?" There was something in his tone that I couldn't place.

"Not that often, no. But I know the family who owns it."

"How? Ex-girlfriend?" I couldn't help but ask.

"Fuck no." He glanced over at me. "You're not going to leave it at I know the family, are you?"

"No. Did you go to school with one of them?"

One shoulder lifted in a half-shrug. "You could say that."

"Stop being so secretive." I punched his arm.

He laughed. "The restaurant belongs to Luca's parents."

"Luca's *parents?*" My mouth dropped open in surprise.

"You know he wasn't hatched from an egg, right? He might act like a grumpy-assed dragon but he is human." Dex's voice was dry.

CHAPTER 23

IT WON'T LAST - BLACKTOP MOJO

Dex
PRESENT

I was taking a huge risk going to Tallorico's. If Luca discovered I'd been there, then there was a high chance he'd kill me—*really* kill me. But Siobhan wanted Italian, and *no one* prepared authentic Italian food like Luca's parents—a skill Luca had inherited but rarely used. I doubted she would tell him, the pair of them barely talked, and I *knew* Lola wouldn't say a word, she wouldn't get the opportunity, because Luca had cut his family out of his life a long time ago.

Lola was waiting at the front of the restaurant when I guided Siobhan inside fifteen minutes later. She greeted me with a huge smile, the female equivalent of Luca—all dark eyes, dark hair and temperamental mood. When she threw her arms wide, I dropped my hand from Siobhan's back and stepped into the other woman's embrace.

"Hey, Lo-Lo, it's been a long time." I pressed a kiss to her cheek. "How's the folks?"

"Mama is ready to corner you and demand information. Papa is preparing your favorite ravioli."

"And Leo?"

If I hadn't been watching for it, I would have missed the way her eyes dimmed. "He still behaves as though you and Luc no longer exist."

"Don't let it bother you, Lo. I doubt Luca gives it any thought at all."

She squared her shoulders, drawing herself up to her full height and sighed. "I wish he would. I miss my baby brother." A small head shake followed her words and she turned away. "Come, come. Let me show you to your table."

I held out the chair for Siobhan, who gave me a curious look before sitting. Once she was settled, I rounded the table and sat opposite her. "What was that look for?" I asked.

"You playing the gentleman."

"That hurts, Cherry Pie."

"The truth generally does," was her smartass reply.

I canted my head. "That mouth of yours is going to get you into trouble one of these days."

"What are you going to do, Dex? *Spank* me in the middle of the restaurant?"

"Think I wouldn't?"

"Think I'd let you?"

I hid a smile. *This* was why I kept coming back to her. She distracted me from the craving that constantly itched under my skin.

"I'll remind you of that confidence when you're sucking my dick later and begging for me to let you come."

"You mean when you're dropping me off at my apartment and I'm blowing you a kiss goodbye?"

"It won't be a kiss you're blowing." I smiled at her. She was coming home with me, and then I'd make her *eat* those words ... *and* my dick.

"What are you grinning about?"

I rested my elbows on the table and propped my head on one hand. "I was thinking about last night."

Red filled her cheeks. "Don't get any ideas. *That* shouldn't have happened and won't happen again."

"Are you telling me it was a mistake?" I asked.

She was saved from replying by Lola reappearing, another older woman behind her. I rose to my feet and was engulfed in the other woman's arms.

"Dexter!" She peppered my face with kisses.

I gently untangled myself. "Ledia. You look as gorgeous as ever."

"Oh, stop!" She grabbed my cheeks and pinched them. "Look at you!" Her eyes were shining with unshed tears, and I waited for the question I knew would inevitably follow. "Is he coming to meet you?"

"No, I'm sorry." She deflated before my eyes. "He doesn't know we're here." I knew Siobhan was watching curiously from the other side of the table, and slowly turned Ledia to face her. "This is Siobhan, my ..." I hesitated, her eyes narrowed in warning, and

I chuckled. "My friend."

Ledia reached out a hand and tipped Siobhan's chin up. "Your friend or your chew toy?" Siobhan's cheeks darkened. "Shame on you. Where's the respect I taught you?" She nailed me with a glare, reminding me where Luca's temper came from.

I shrugged. "Heat of the moment, mama. I got carried away and..." I gave the older woman a knowing smile. "She tastes *so* good."

Ledia threw her arms up in disgust. "Men!"

"You would be lost without us," a quiet male voice said, and I twisted around to find an older, shorter version of Luca standing beside the table.

"Allesandro," I greeted him cautiously.

"It's been a long time, boy." His eyes tracked over me, noting the expensive jeans and band t-shirt I wore. "Although you're no longer a boy, are you?"

"Was I ever?" I quipped and he sighed.

"No. I sometimes think you, Luciano, and ... well, you were born older than your years." He carefully set the plates he held onto the table. "Who is this?" He angled his gaze at Siobhan. "You mark her like property. Is that what she is, son? A possession?"

"No, sir."

"Then why do it? Are you trying to scare off competition, perhaps?" His brow arched. "Maybe you think you're not good enough to hold onto her and need an outward sign of ownership."

Fuck. I'd forgotten where Luca got his snark from. His father had years more experience in cutting us down to size. I glanced over at Siobhan, who was watching the exchange with undisguised amusement.

"A *strong* man doesn't need to have visible signs of ownership on their women," Allesandro continued. "They have other ways to ensure their females do not wish to stray."

Ledia slapped her husband's arm. "You're embarrassing the girl, Sandro. Stop now." She turned back to me. "Tell me about my son. Is he happy? I see him on the television. He has grown so tall, so *handsome*."

"He's enjoying our life, mama," I replied carefully. I wasn't about to tell her Luca was going through some kind of identity crisis. He might have cut his family out of his life, but that didn't mean his family had stopped loving him. I *liked* Ledia and didn't want to upset her any more than our presence must have been doing already.

"Will you ..." she hesitated. "Tell him I love him and miss him."

"I will." The lie came easily. Chances are I *wouldn't*. Luca wasn't interested in hearing it.

"Come." Allesandro caught his wife's arm. "Let them eat before the food grows cold." He waved a hand at the plates on the table. "They came for food, not tears and regret."

He tugged her away from the table, but I could see her casting backward glances at me and knew she'd be back before we left if she could. Siobhan didn't speak as I slid one plate over to her, took the other and tucked into the food. The flavor exploded on my tongue and I swallowed a moan of delight.

I'd forgotten how good Allesandro's cooking was, where Luca had got his culinary skills from, and made a mental note to demand he start cooking more often.

Siobhan never commented on the fact we didn't look at the menu once, yet Lola appeared with a second course, and then a rich, decadent dessert without being summoned. A server also appeared early on with a bottle of red wine, which he poured into two glasses before leaving the bottle on the table and disappearing as silently as he arrived.

We barely spoke through the entire meal, small smatterings of comments about the food, the wine, the restaurant itself. The craving I'd been feeling all day finally relinquished its grip and was replaced by a relaxation and calmness I often found around Siobhan … when she wasn't driving me to the brink of crazy or lust, anyway.

After the final mouthful of food was scraped from my plate, I pushed it away with a satisfied groan and eyed Siobhan over the top of my wine glass.

"Coffee?" I asked. "Or do you want to get out of here?"

"Coffee would be nice," she replied.

I lifted my hand, knowing Lola would be watching and, sure enough, she appeared a few seconds later. "Tell papa everything was fantastic. We'll grab coffee, if you don't mind, and the check."

"Dex … will you …" Lola licked her lips and shoved a small piece of paper at me. "Ask Luca to call me. I miss him."

I looked down at the paper she held and slowly took it from

her. A cell number was scrawled across it. "I'll give it to him. I can't make any promises though, you know that."

"I know, but I'd *really* like to talk to him."

I pocketed it and nodded. "I'll see what I can do."

"Luca never talks about his family," Siobhan said once Lola was a safe distance away. "Even the press doesn't touch it."

"It's complicated." My voice was clipped. It was Luca's story to tell, not mine, and I wasn't about to start gossiping about my friend—not even with a woman who shared her body with me.

"You don't have to get defensive. I'm not looking for a story to sell, Dex," she snapped. "I'm just making conversation."

Chapter 24

NEVER ENOUGH - TWO FEET

Siobhan

PRESENT

Unlike the earlier silence while we were eating, which had been comfortable, the silence which came after I snapped at him was charged and awkward. The server—Lola—set down our coffee, glancing from him to me and back again, picking up on the tension. She placed a little tray beside Dex's elbow and he dropped his credit card onto it without looking.

"Are you coming home with me?"

I choked on the mouthful of coffee I'd just taken. "I already told you I wasn't going home with you," I said once I caught my breath again.

"Didn't think you meant it."

"Dex," I said quietly. "This … this *thing* … it's not good for us. It never has been."

"Bullshit. If that was true, we wouldn't be sitting here right now."

I shook my head. "It's physical attraction, that's all. A habit that won't die."

His eyes darkened at my words.

"A *habit?*" Dex gave me an incredulous look. "You're comparing me to a fucking *habit?*" He broke off when Lola reappeared with his card, pocketed it, rose to his feet and strode around the table. Hooking his hand around my arm, he pulled me off the chair. "Let's go."

"Go where?"

"Somewhere I can prove to you this isn't a fucking habit, a physical attraction, or not good for us."

I dug my heels into the carpet, stopping his forward motion. "Dex, stop."

He did, but only long enough to turn, cup my face between his palms and kiss me. I didn't even get enough time to draw in a breath, his mouth covering mine, tongue pushing past my lips to invade and possess. He tasted of coffee, a hint of chocolate from dessert and something else—something that tantalized my senses, a decadent flavor that was unique to him. Before I realized what I was doing, I was kissing him back, my arms reaching up to wind around his neck.

A cleared throat and a muttered *'we're in a family restaurant'* brought me back to my senses and I jerked back, pulling my mouth from his.

"Tell me again how it's only physical attraction, Cherry Pie," he murmured, grabbed my hand and, ignoring the man who had complained, pulled me out of the restaurant.

The car pulled up almost as soon as we exited and Dex threw

open the door to hustle me inside; I assumed before anyone spotted him. Wrong assumption it turned out, since the minute the door shut and the car pulled away, he was pushing me down onto the seat and lowering himself on top of me.

"You can protest and deny it all you like, Red, but I *know* this isn't as shallow as you're trying to keep it. That's not who you are, it's not who *we* are. It never has been." His lips found the pulse beating at the base of my throat, and I shivered at the light touch. "I've seen the real you, Siobhan. I *know* you. You're never going to find what we have with someone else."

"You don't know that." My protest was a soft whisper, my body already aligning itself to his. My head fell back against the soft leather of the seat as he bit and sucked his way down to the neckline of my top.

"I *do* know that." His fingers, warm and roughened from years of playing guitar, crept beneath my shirt and found the way to my breast, peeled away the lace of my bra and stroked over my nipple. "I know that like I know my own name. I know it because when you look at me, you see the real *me*, too. You know me, Red. You know me and you want me anyway."

His words were like honey, and part of me questioned whether he was using them to get what he wanted, chosen purposely to make me succumb to the temptation he posed. Another part, the part I tried to ignore, whispered he was being honest. And if he was right? That thought scared me.

The man kissing his way across my body was broken in the

worst possible way. A time bomb waiting to explode. An addict who had torn out my heart more than once. And yet here I was, in his arms again, letting him touch me, taste me—a willing victim to the fire he set alight inside me. And I did that, fully aware that there was a chance he would break me again, because when he touched me ... He was right ... I knew exactly who he was and I *did* want him anyway.

"Come home with me, Cherry Pie."

We tumbled out of the car, clothes askew, and he walked backwards into his house, his mouth still on mine.

I made the decision somewhere between the restaurant and his house that I was going to have one more night. One more taste of him, and then I'd cut him loose. I'd end this self-destructive pattern I'd returned to since discovering the Dex I'd fooled around with all those years ago was the same troubled rock star who was often emblazoned across the news. The same one who'd looked right through me one night and denied he knew who I was.

I didn't argue when he linked his fingers through mine and led me upstairs to his bedroom. Once inside, he turned to face me, his blue eyes dark with desire, released my hand and cupped my face.

"Cherry Pie," he whispered, and kissed me.

He kissed me until I was breathless, clutching at his shoulders to stay upright, held me captive with only his mouth, and made me hungry for more. I wanted him to feel the same way I did—out of my element, unable to breathe, *needy*.

I lifted my hands to his chest and pushed at him until he took a step back, then another … and another until his legs hit the bed and he dropped onto the mattress. Without giving him a chance to speak, I climbed onto him, straddled his legs, and kissed him again. His hands were on my waist, beneath my clothes, sliding up my spine and I groaned into his mouth, then drew back to snatch in a breath.

My hands dropped to the button on his jeans. "What's the safe word, Rock Star?"

"Am I going to need one?" Rich amusement combined with desire made his voice deeper than usual.

I crawled off him, wedged my leg between his and dropped to my knees. "I think you might," I told him while I worked on his zipper.

He made no move to help, watching me with a slight smile on his lips, when I finally freed his dick and licked my lips. Raising my head, I met his eyes, smiled and then gave his dick a long lick from base to tip.

My tongue swirled around the piercings surrounding the head, and he groaned, his hands landing in my hair, fingers curling against my scalp. Maintaining eye contact with him, I lapped my way around his shaft, and up to the tip, then slowly slid my lips over him and took him as deep as I could into my mouth.

It took a minute to adjust to his piercings but after a second or two, I found a rhythm. My tongue swirled, licked, making him wet enough for my lips to slide up and down with ease. I ran one hand up his inner thigh and between his legs to cup his balls, stroking and teasing them while I sucked.

His fingers tightened their grip on my hair when I changed my pace, wrapped a hand around the base of his dick and sucked harder, squeezing his shaft with my fingers as I stroked up and down, took him to the back of my throat, *fucked* him with my mouth.

And then something happened … a slight loosening of his fingers, a soft exhale of breath … I couldn't pinpoint exactly what it was, but I knew I'd lost him. His attention had wandered.

What the hell?

I thought he was into what I was doing.

He'd appeared to be enjoying it.

I stopped moving, and lifted my eyes to look at him.

"I'm fine," he grunted. "I just lost myself for a minute."

I narrowed my eyes. *Lost himself?* That wasn't something you wanted to hear from a guy when you were giving him a blowjob. Pulling my mouth off his dick, I rocked back on my heels and scowled up at him.

"I'm swallowing your dick and you *wander off?* Fuck you, Dex!" The fact I hadn't been able to keep his attention from wandering stung. Embarrassed, I rose to my feet. *Had it been that bad?*

"Come on, love. It was a momentary lapse."

"Do you even remember my *name?*" I knew that wasn't fair, but I was dying from embarrassment at my failure to keep him in the moment the way he always did for me.

His features darkened. "That's a fucking stupid question. Of course I remember your name." He stood and dragged his pants back up. "Why the fuck wouldn't I remember your name?"

"I don't know, Dex. Why would you be having *daydreams* while I'm sucking your dick?" I was mortified and lashing out, but I couldn't seem to stop. Spinning away, I fixed my clothes and headed for the door.

"Where are you going?"

"Home!" I snapped.

"Red." The nickname was a soft sigh and he moved to intercept me.

"Get out of my way."

"No. You're overreacting."

"What were you thinking about?" I demanded.

His hesitation hurt more than I expected it to. *Had he been thinking about someone else?*

"Goodbye, Dex." It was time to end it. I *had* to end it. I reached for the handle and the next words from his mouth froze me to the spot.

"I'll tell Harper we're married."

I spun to face him, the knowing smirk on his face making my temper rise.

CHAPTER 25

SNOW WHITE - DENNIS LLOYD

Dex
AGE 24

I flicked my cigarette to the ground and stood on it, watching as the door to the apartment building opened. The light inside shone on the bright red hair of the woman darting down the steps and into the waiting arms of the man by the car.

I heard her laugh from where I stood, low and throaty, and ground my teeth together when she raised up on her toes to press a kiss to her companion's lips. His hand landed on her ass, squeezed, and I started forward before I could stop myself.

"Cherry Pie," I said quietly from behind her and saw her stiffen.

The guy she was with gave me a disinterested look, and curled his arm around her waist. "C'mon, babe. We're gonna be late."

She didn't even look in my direction, allowing him to draw her toward his car without any argument.

"I'll be here when you get back, Red," I called and sat on the step.

That stopped her in her tracks. Slowly she turned to face me.

"Babe ..." Her boyfriend asked

She pulled free from him and moved toward me. I tipped my head back to watch her approach, admiring the sway of her hips in the short dress she wore.

"What are you doing here?" she demanded in a low voice.

I lifted a shoulder in a shrug. "Came to see you."

"Well, you can turn around and go back to wherever you disappeared to."

"You don't want to hear what happened?" I leaned forward, my elbows on my knees and cocked my head.

"No. It's been a *year*. You're clearly not dead, so there's no reason why you had to wait this long."

"Babe? Siobhan?" Her boyfriend, I guessed, came toward us.

I rose to my feet and reached out to wrap a lock of her hair around one finger. "It was complicated. Give me five minutes."

"You *ghosted* me, Dex. For a *year*." Her head tilted back, eyes tracking over my face. We both ignored the guy hovering behind her. "Give me one good reason why I should even bother giving you one *second* of my time right now."

I gave a tug on the lock of hair I held, and she stepped forward. Bending my head, I watched her lips part, and smiled.

"This right here ... this is why," I whispered. "Can't deny it, Cherry Pie."

"What the fuck do you think you're doing? Get away from her."

I glanced at the idiot still lurking. "You're wasting your time," I told him.

But his words had broken the spell, and Siobhan wrenched

herself away from me.

"Let's go," she told the dickhead she was with, caught his hand and walked away without a second look at me.

The asshole threw me a smirk over his shoulder and I scowled. I was certain she'd stop and come back and yet she slipped into the passenger seat of his car and they drove off. I was left staring after them.

I couldn't fucking believe it. She'd walked away. I had arrogantly believed she'd want to hear my explanation.

Fuck it.

Standing there on the steps to her apartment, I fished out a pack of cigarettes from my jacket pocket and popped one between my lips. I was lighting it when I saw a figure coming toward me.

"You're a fucking asshole." The words reached me moments before Siobhan did, and she slapped the cigarette away from my mouth. "You ask me to go away with you and then you disappear. I thought you were *dead*. I had no way of contacting you. Your cell number was disconnected." She shoved at my chest. "I thought you were dead, Dex."

She shoved at me again, and I caught her wrists. "I know. I'm sorry."

"It's been a year!" She was shouting now, struggling to free her hands from my grip. "A fucking year!"

"I know," I repeated calmly. Releasing one hand, I wrapped an arm around her waist. "I can explain, I swear. But not here. Come with me?"

"Where?"

"A drive. We'll take a drive."

I waited for her nod, then led her to my car and unlocked it. She didn't wait for me to open the door, throwing it open herself and climbing in. I rounded it and settled into the driver's seat, turned the key and pulled away. Silence reigned. I'm not sure why that surprised me. I think I half-expected her to demand answers the moment I joined her in the car.

I leaned forward and flicked on the stereo to mask the silence, and caught her sidelong glance. 'Midnight's Playground' by Black Rosary filled the car for all of three seconds before one pink-tipped finger switched it off.

I gave a quiet sigh, but let her have her way, and concentrated on the road. It took her almost forty minutes to question where I was taking her. We were cruising along Foothill Freeway when she finally spoke.

"Where are we going?"

"Vegas."

"*What?* No. Dex, turn the car around. That's at least a *five-hour* drive from here."

"I can do it in four."

"You said we'd take a drive. I didn't agree to you kidnapping me."

"In my defense, I never said how long the drive would be. Also, you got in my car willingly, so it's hardly kidnapping."

"We won't even get there until midnight. Can't we pull over somewhere and talk?"

"Nope. I need to get out of the city for a while."

"Dex, I *can't* go to Vegas. I have work tomorrow."

"Call in sick." I didn't take my eyes off the road. "This isn't a whim, Cherry Pie. But I need you to trust me, okay?" I knew it was a big ask—especially since I'd walked out of her apartment a year ago and not returned. "I have a place in Vegas. We'll go there, talk, and I'll bring you back tomorrow... if that's what you want."

"You have a place in Vegas?"

"Yeah. An apartment for when I want to get out of LA for a while."

"Is that where you've been for the past year?"

I slid a quick glance in her direction. "No."

"Dex—"

I uncurled the fingers of one hand from the steering wheel and reached out to take her hand and squeezed her fingers. "I swear, I'll tell you what happened. Just drive with me, okay?"

She gnawed at her bottom lip while she digested my words. "You *swear* we'll come back tomorrow?"

"Scout's honor."

I pulled into the underground parking lot of the building where I had an apartment at a little past midnight. Siobhan had fallen asleep a couple of hours earlier, the movement of the car and the rumble of the engine lulling her, I guessed. I'd reduced my speed and took my time, turning on the stereo and keeping it low so it didn't wake her. She stirred when I cut off the engine, her eyes fluttering open.

"Are we there?" she mumbled around a yawn.

"Yeah. Come on, Cherry Pie." I climbed out of the car, stretched, then strode around to open the door for her.

My eyes were on her legs as she twisted and stepped out.

"My face is up here," she said primly and I laughed.

"I know where your face is, Red, but I wanted to admire your legs. It's been a while since I saw them. Follow me. The elevator is over here." I rested my hand on the small of her back and guided her across the parking lot. The elevator doors slid open as soon as I pushed the button and we stepped inside.

Siobhan moved to the far left corner and watched while I tapped the button for the sixteenth floor. I prayed the doors wouldn't open on any other floor; I didn't want her to see that I kept a place in one of the most expensive apartment buildings in Vegas. So long as we made it to my floor, once we were inside she wouldn't be able to tell.

I let out a sigh of relief when we reached the sixteenth floor without stopping and the doors slid open.

"Down here," I told her and directed her to the left when we exited into the hallway.

"Are you sure this is the right place?" she asked, her eyes darting around.

"Pretty sure. At least, they haven't had me arrested for breaking and entering yet." I stopped outside a door and fished out the key from my jacket. Unlocking it, I stepped back and waved her through. "Come on in."

CHAPTER 26

I REMEMBER WAY TOO MUCH - MOD SUN

Siobhan

AGE 23

When I was walking out of my apartment building to meet Jason—a guy I'd been dating for two months—and heard a voice that sent shivers down my spine, my mind had gone blank. I hadn't known how to react, how to respond. I wanted to ignore him, walk away without acknowledging his presence but, like every other time, I couldn't do it.

The arrogant belief that I'd drop everything because he'd decided to grace me with his presence was all over his face, and that gave me the strength to walk away and climb into Jason's car. I even let him pull away, but I could see Dex through the rear-view mirror and, in my mind, I thought about how tired he'd looked.

"Stop the car," I instructed Jason before I even realized I was unbuckling my seatbelt.

"What?"

"I'm sorry. I need to go back and talk to him."

"Siobhan? What the fuck? Who is that guy?"

"I'm sorry." It wasn't fair on him, I knew that. But I'd never be able to stop questioning and wondering if Dex just hadn't been *that* into me if I didn't get answers.

I climbed out as soon as the car stopped moving, heard Jason curse me, accusing me of being a tease, of using him, but none of it mattered because I could see *him* standing there… waiting for me.

When he suggested we go for a drive, I *knew* it wouldn't be as straightforward as it seemed, and I was right. And yet, again, I let him talk me into going along with him and woke up in Vegas hours later.

His apartment wasn't what I was expecting. I couldn't say what that would have been exactly, but this large airy space with dark wooden floors, a brushed leather sofa and a wall-mounted television complete with surround sound speakers wasn't it.

"Can I get you something to drink?" Dex asked and I turned to find him standing near a door. "Kitchen's through here."

"I … sure." I followed him through the doorway and entered another large room. At one end there was a dining table big enough to fit six. At the other, stainless steel worktops and dark wood kitchen cabinets. A large range cooker took up the space along one wall.

"Alcohol or something warm?"

"Umm…"

Fingers touched my chin and he tipped my head up to meet his eyes. "Concentrate, Cherry Pie. What would you like to drink?"

"Wine?" I said the first thing that came into my head.

"Red or white?"

"Either." I moved further into the room, looking around. "This is your place?"

"Yep."

My fingers trailed over the countertop. "Did it come already furnished?"

He snorted. "Not what you expected, huh?"

"Well... no." I hadn't really given much thought to what Dex did when he wasn't with me. When we were together, it felt like snatched moments out of time—and our *normal* lives were set aside. "How can you afford it?"

"I have a job that pays *very* well."

"You're not a drug dealer, are you?" I knew Dex dabbled, occasionally at the very least. I wasn't sure with what, but I knew he smoked marijuana often and he'd been stoned at least once when he'd been around me.

He placed a glass of wine in front of me. "No, I'm not a dealer."

"But—"

"I don't want to talk about work," he interrupted. "If you want to know all that, then we'll talk about it some other time. Not now, not today."

"I shouldn't even be here now. I called *hospitals* trying to find out if you'd been hurt."

His lashes dropped, shielding his eyes, and he turned away to open the refrigerator and take out a beer.

"I'm sorry about that."

"What happened?"

"When I left your apartment that night, I had every intention of going home and making arrangements to come out here for the weekend. I'd just bought this place and thought it'd be fun to have you help me furnish it." He paused to take a drink from the bottle. "I got a call when I was driving home from ... a friend."

"A friend?" I asked sharply. *Had he gone to see another woman?*

"A guy called Phillip. He's someone who can keep me supplied in ..." He shrugged. "Well, whatever I want, really."

"You mean drugs?" My voice was flat.

He rubbed his jaw with one hand, but didn't answer me. "Instead of going home, I went to meet him. Whatever he sold me was ... well, I woke up four days later in the hospital."

"You overdosed," I whispered. "You overdosed and nearly died."

He gave me an easy smile. "Nothing that drastic, Cherry Pie. I'm not an addict. Whatever was mixed in with the batch he sold me caused a reaction and made me ill."

Sickness churned in my stomach. His words were those of an addict in denial, blaming anything but the truth.

"I think I should go home." I set my glass down.

"No. I promise, Red, that was it. I haven't touched that stuff since. My cell was smashed. I think I had a fit and dropped it. My ... boss ... insisted I change my number so Phillip couldn't reach me ... and wiped all my saved numbers other than the ones he recognized."

"You knew where I lived."

He inclined his head. "And the state I was in? If I'd turned up like that, you wouldn't have given me the time of day. I fucked up, Red. I *know* that. I thought it was better if I stayed away until I got a handle on things. Then I had to go out of town with work. I didn't get back into LA until a month ago." He reached out to tug my hair. "I thought about you a lot. I wondered if you'd met someone else, moved on."

"I *did*."

"That douche you were with tonight?" His lip curled up into a sneer. "He was never going to keep hold of you, love."

"And you know that *how*?" I demanded.

He gave an exaggerated glance around. "Well, he's not here, is he?"

"Only because I…" I trailed off. *Fuck.* I'd chosen Dex over Jason.

Dex placed his bottle down onto the countertop and stepped closer to me. "Know what we should do?" He looped his arms around my waist to pull me against him so he could dip his head and nuzzle my cheek. "We should get married."

"*What?*" I flattened my palms against his chest and attempted to push away from him. His arms tightened around me.

"Hear me out. We're in Vegas. We can go buy a ring and just *do* it."

"Get married?" *How crazy was he?*

"Why not? It makes sense."

"In what reality does it make sense, Dex?"

"*Every* reality, Red."

I eyed the hand hovering in front of me.

What are you doing? I asked myself. This entire thing had escalated more and more and I had rapidly found myself losing control of a situation I hadn't ever expected to be in.

After announcing we should get married, Dex had sent me off to a bedroom and told me to sleep on it. I didn't do a lot of sleeping, tossing and turning most of the night—which was why I was about to choose a ring and marry a man I barely knew. Or, at least, that's what I kept telling myself.

Okay, one who I'd flirted with *a lot*. One I was definitely attracted to ... and one that had a very, very obvious drug problem, even if he wouldn't admit to it.

Dex Cooper was trouble wrapped up in a layer of temptation and sin. From his messy dark hair that looked like he'd dragged a hand through it one too many times, to blue eyes which danced with a wicked charm ... as well as that lazy drawl which always held a hint of amusement to it—as though he was laughing at a joke only he knew the punchline to.

"Enjoying the view?" The dry tone snapped me out of my internal musing and I took his hand to climb out of the car, feeling myself blush.

"You're not exactly ugly, are you?" I said to hide my embarrassment at being caught looking at him.

"Man, you can't even say it, can you? Repeat after me ... 'Dex, you're a fine-looking man and I want to make babies with you.'"

I couldn't help but laugh. "I'm not saying that."

"Which part was the deal breaker?" He caught my hand in his and set off down the sidewalk. "It was the babies, wasn't it? That's another reason to divorce you." He referenced the conversation we'd had when we first met, all that time ago.

"I think it's more how crazy you sound."

"I do not sound crazy, I sound... *practical*."

"Sure."

He huffed a laugh. "Down here," he said, and turned down a side road.

I followed him and we stopped outside a door to a building that *did not* look like a jewelers.

"Are you sure this is the place?" I asked him.

"Positive." He rapped on the door. "Don't worry, there's nothing illegal going on in here." The door creaked open and a grey-haired head popped through the gap.

"Dexter?" The old man squinted up at the man beside me. "What are you doing here?"

"Hey, Murphy. I need a ring."

The old man's pale blue eyes turned to me. "What did you do now? Is she pregnant? She doesn't *look* pregnant."

"I'm not pregnant," I responded firmly when Dex said nothing.

"Hmph," the man grunted. "I thought I warned you to always put something on the end of it? Getting a girl pregnant is not what you need."

"She's not pregnant, I swear," Dex replied and stepped inside. "Come on, old man. I just need a ring."

"What do you need a ring for?"

"To give to my new fiancée." He nodded toward me.

"You're getting engaged and she's *not* pregnant?" The man scowled. "Have you lost your mind?"

"Yes. I've been reliably informed that I'm crazy. Now are you going to give me the ring to use or not?"

The man pouted. No joke, his lips moved into a pout and then he spun and disappeared down the hallway. "Come along then. I don't have all day."

Dex threw me a smile. "You heard the old grump. Let's go get engaged."

The room at the end of the hallway was large and bright—a far cry from the dark and seedy entrance. There were long display cases covering one wall, full of gorgeous rings and necklaces. The other wall was made up of a work area—presumably where the old man did his work.

"What did you have in mind?" He directed us toward the display cases.

"Something with rubies. Red to match her hair … and her temper."

"Gold band?"

"Platinum. I think the color would look better against her skin."

"So you don't want *a* ring, you want *the* ring?" Murphy said

I looked from Dex to Murphy. "You know I'm standing right here?"

"We know, love, now shut up while we talk." He smirked at me, and I was almost tempted to punch him in his arrogant, sexy face.

"Don't I get a say in the ring?"

"No. This is my idea, so I'm choosing the ring."

"But what if I don't like rubies?"

"Of course you like rubies. They're red, like blood. You fucking love red. It's your favorite color."

I scowled at him. He was right. I *did* love red—but how did *he* know that? Instead of arguing, I wandered away to look at the necklaces displayed on one of the stands. One in particular caught my eye and I cast a quick glance over at Dex to see whether he was looking at me, but he was in deep conversation with Murphy.

I stroked a finger along the fine silver chain, then hooked a nail beneath the intricate cross. Each point had a tiny red stone set in it, and at the center was a diamond star.

"Try it on." Dex's voice, behind me, made me jump and I dropped the chain back onto its stand and spun.

"No."

"Siobhan," he sighed. "Try it on." Reaching past me, he lifted the necklace and held it out. "I never took you for a cross wearer. Are you religious?"

"Not me, no. My grandmother. She firmly believes that wearing a cross keeps her close to God and is always telling me I should get one. She'd like this one." I couldn't resist reaching out again to stroke a finger over the cross. "And it's subtle."

"Crosses aren't subtle, Cherry Pie." He handed it to Murphy, who appeared beside him. "We'll take that too."

"I'm not buying the necklace, Dex."

He smiled at me but didn't respond.

"Don't ignore me."

"I'm not. I'm just not acknowledging your protest."

I heaved an irritated sigh. "I'm not sure we'll survive being engaged very long before I murder you."

One eyebrow shot up. "Wow, that escalated fast. Marriage, divorce, and now murder? Whatever next?" He tutted. "No, don't answer that. Let it be a surprise. It'll be fun."

"Fun," I repeated, and he threw me another one of his grins.

"Come on, Red, live a little. This is fun, right? Didn't you ever play make believe when you were a kid?"

"Not like this. Please, Dex, slow down for a second. Are you *sure* about this? You don't think it's crazy? You're joking, right? Seeing how far you can take it before I tell you to stop?"

"No, and no." He stepped around me and headed across the room.

I darted after him, caught his arm and hauled him back around to face me. "At least admit this is all a little crazy."

His eyes tracked over my face, and then a slow smile curled his lips. "Of course it's fucking crazy, Cherry Pie. That's what makes it so much fun. And we're not hurting anyone. It's not like we're ruining someone's life. We're adults. We're attracted to each other." He lowered his voice. "And I can't wait to fuck you while you're wearing nothing but my ring on your finger."

A cleared throat brought both our heads around to find Murphy standing nearby.

"This should suffice," he said and held out a small box.

Dex took it from him and looked at me. "Ready?" he asked.

"For what?" For some reason my heart was pounding, my mouth was dry and my breath was coming in short bursts.

This felt real, felt more than it was. I was marrying a man in Vegas—it wouldn't last; I *knew* that. It was a moment of madness, yet it felt like something was happening here that would change us in ways we hadn't yet considered.

Dex flipped open the box and closed his fingers around the contents. "Give me your hand, Cherry Pie," he instructed, and held out his palm.

I laid my hand on top of his, and licked my lips. He grinned.

"Gonna make an honest man out of me?"

"Not sure that's possible," I croaked.

"Well, it's a nice fantasy, yeah?" As he spoke, I felt him slip something over my finger and looked down.

The platinum band almost glowed against my skin, the small clusters of diamonds interspersed with deep red rubies. It looked obscenely expensive and oh so beautiful.

"I can't take this," I whispered.

"It's only make believe, Red," he coaxed. "Play the game with me."

"But—"

"Didn't you ever want to be the princess? In her diamonds and ball gown?" He lifted my fingers to his lips and pressed a kiss to each one. "It's perfect, Murphy. All sharp edges and bloody intentions."

"Don't lose it," the old man admonished.

"I won't," I said.

Murphy snorted. "I wasn't talking about the ring, girl. I mean it, Dexter. Don't mess this up."

"Then what—"

"It's not important," Dex cut in. "Let's go. We need to go get the dress next."

"A dress? What for?"

"I'm not marrying you in jeans, love."

He shook hands with Murphy and set off for the exit. "Thanks, Murph. I'll call you and let you know how it goes."

I found my hand engulfed by his again and he half-escorted, half-dragged me out of the building. I glanced down at the ring on my finger, the sun catching on the diamonds, making them gleam and shine.

"I chose well, huh?" His gruff voice cut through the silence and I glanced at where he moved along beside me at a steady lope.

"I still can't believe I'm letting you talk me into this. Where are we going now?"

"Dress shopping," he smirked. "Good job Vegas never closes, isn't it?"

I vented a wry laugh. "You seem to have this all worked out. Anyone would think you've been planning your wedding for a long time."

That smile flashed on again. "I'm just quick on my feet." He let loose a shrill whistle and a cab glided to a halt beside us.

Guarded Addiction

CHAPTER 27

NINE IN THE AFTERNOON – PANIC! AT THE DISCO

Siobhan

AGE 23

I'd done it. I'd married a man I had spent less than ten days with over the past two years, and yet … I felt like we'd known each other for a lifetime. We left the small chapel arm in arm, laughing, and I'd never felt so … *free*.

My parents were going to kill me.

"What should we do now?" Dex asked, then stopped. "I know. Tattoos."

"Tattoos?" I repeated blankly.

He nodded. "I've been meaning to get one. Now seems like the perfect time. Let's go." He caught my hand and headed down the sidewalk. "I know a place that'll fit us in."

"But I don't think I want a tattoo."

"Cherries … that's what you need to get. Dex's Cherry Pie." He ran his finger over my hip. "Right there."

I laughed at him. "I don't think so. What about you?"

He smiled. "You'll see."

The tattoo parlor he took me to was a fifteen-minute walk from the chapel, but he finally stopped outside a building with dark tinted windows and an imposing black door. He pushed it open and led me inside.

"Well, if it isn't Dex Cooper." A large man rounded the desk and engulfed Dex in a hug. "Where've you been hiding, boy?"

Dex laughed. "Around. You know how it is. Can you fit us in?"

"Us?" The bearded behemoth glanced at me. "Your little lady friend here wants some ink?"

"Do you still have those designs we worked out last year?"

He nodded. "Sure do."

"Got time?" Dex asked.

"It's your lucky night." He waved a hand around the empty interior. "Come on through."

I found myself escorted through to the back of the shop. Dex peeled off the shirt he'd worn and handed it to me. The tattooist reclined the chair and Dex lay on it, face down.

"Where do you want it?"

"Side, that way I can add to it," Dex replied.

The tattooist nodded and set to work preparing everything he needed. I watched as he wiped over Dex's skin, presumably cleaning the area, then placed what looked like a temporary tattoo sheet onto him. He wiped over it, smoothed it out and then carefully peeled it off, leaving the outline of what looked like a tree... to me, anyway.

"What do you think?" he asked, holding a mirror up so Dex

could see.

Dex nodded. "Perfect."

"Let's do it then." The tattooist smoothed some oil over the design and then picked up the tattoo machine and turned it on.

The slight buzz filled the room, and he swept it over Dex's skin, leaving behind a smooth black line. Dex didn't even flinch, and as time passed his eyes drifted shut.

"Doesn't it hurt?" I asked a little while later.

Dex opened his eyes and looked at me. "I find it quite relaxing, actually."

"You're crazy."

He chuckled. "Your turn next, Red. Don't chicken out on me."

"I never agreed to get one."

His smile was lazy. "Gotta commemorate the day."

Another hour passed before the tattooist lifted his head. "Done. See what you think." He gave the new tattoo one final wipe over and rubbed something into Dex's skin—I guessed some kind of lotion—then lifted the mirror again.

"Excellent." Dex grinned at me and rolled off the chair. "Your turn, Cherry Pie."

He caught my hand and pulled me to my feet. "I don't even know what I'd get," I protested.

"I've already had it designed," Dex told me and I gaped at him. "*When?*"

His eyes shifted away from mine. "Last year … when I asked you to come away with me."

"You designed a tattoo? Are you serious?"

"One hundred percent." He tugged my hand again. "Come on, Red."

"Show me. I'm not getting a tattoo I haven't seen." I couldn't believe I was even entertaining the idea of getting a tattoo *at all*.

He heaved a sigh and turned to the tattooist. "Frank, can you show it to her?"

"I need to wrap yours up and take a photograph," Frank said, pulling another stencil out of the folder he'd taken Dex's from. He handed it to me.

"Cherries?" I said, looking down at it.

"Cherries for my Cherry Pie." He gave me a smile. "I thought we'd start small for your first ink."

"First?"

"You might find you enjoy it. Stop stalling. Hop up on the chair."

"I can't believe I'm letting you talk me into this," I muttered. "Wait ... how is he going to do it? I'm wearing a dress."

"You'll have to pull it up."

"It's okay, honey. I have a sheet you can throw over yourself." Frank nodded to where a folded sheet lay to the left of the chair. "I need your hip and stomach area clear. You get yourself comfortable while I finish up with Dex."

The dress I was wearing—yes, it was red like Dex said it would be all that time ago—was form-fitting and easy to roll up. I dragged the sheet over my legs, covering my panties and settled back. My stomach churned with nerves. After listening to the buzzing while Dex got his tattoo and seeing the blood being wiped away after each stroke, I wasn't sure I'd be able to go through with it.

But, I *had* always wanted to get a tattoo, and the cherry design Frank showed me *was* pretty... and *small*.

"Ready?" Frank turned back while Dex pulled on his shirt, covering the now-wrapped tattoo.

"As I'll ever be," I said, my voice wobbly with nerves.

Dex dragged the stool I'd been sitting on closer. "Don't worry, Red. I'll hold your hand."

I jumped at the coolness of the alcohol wipe when Frank spread it over my hip and stomach. "Please try to stay as still as you can," he explained. "We'll put the stencil on first so you can get an idea of how it looks."

I gave a jerky nod and Frank got to work.

When he peeled away the stencil to show me how the design would look, I was surprised. The double-cherry design with a bow tying them together was girly and cute and *not* something I thought Dex would have chosen, but I liked it.

"Happy with it?" Frank asked and I gave another nod. "Settle back then and we'll get it done."

The first stroke of the needles across my skin was like fire and I yelped. "No! Stop!"

Dex laughed. "He barely touched you."

"It *hurt*! Leave it, I don't want it. I've changed my mind."

"Baby, you have a black line tattooed on your skin. You can't leave it like that." He squeezed my fingers. "Look at me." I turned my head toward him. "The first stroke is always the worst because you don't know what to expect. It gets easier, I promise."

I shook my head. "I can't do it."

"Sure you can. You like the design, yeah?"

I *did* like it, but... Dex must have seen something in my face because he hopped off the stool and dragged it closer.

"I can distract you, if you like? Take your mind off it while Frank works."

"How?"

He smiled and rested one hand on my stomach. "Just remember, you have to stay still, okay?"

I narrowed my eyes at him uneasily. "What are you going to do?"

"Kiss you." The hand on my stomach smoothed over my skin... down toward the sheet covering my hips. "Amongst other things."

I caught his wrist, stopping his downward motion. He bent his head until his face was close to mine.

"Come on, Red. Live on the edge with me," he whispered, and kissed me.

His tongue parted my lips and delved inside and it hit me that I'd married a man I'd barely kissed, *never* had sex with and barely knew—and now I was getting a tattoo, marking his presence permanently onto my body.

On the edge of my awareness I heard buzzing, knew Frank was about to press those white-hot needles against my skin again, but Dex's tongue, teeth, and lips distracted me, held my attention as he devoured my mouth, demanding a response. And then another sensation intruded, one that had me gasping into his mouth.

The hand resting on my stomach moved, found its way beneath the sheet, into my panties and between my legs.

I tore my mouth from his, intending to protest, only for his other hand to wrap around my jaw and bring my mouth back to his.

"Focus on me. Nothing else," he said against my lips. "Just me, Cherry Pie, and what I'm doing to you."

His fingers were on my clit, the touch featherlight as he stroked in a small circle.

"Hold still now." Frank's gruff voice reminded me we weren't alone, and I tried to pull my mouth from Dex's again.

"Ignore him." His hand slid from my jaw to my throat and squeezed slightly, making my breath hitch and heat pool between my thighs. "You need to relax, Red. He's busy. He's not interested in what we're doing."

Two fingers pushed inside me at the same time his tongue wrapped around mine and I moaned, the sound swallowed by his mouth. Everything but the sensations he was building in me was forgotten as his thumb brushed over my clit and his fingers pumped in and out in a slow rhythm.

I could feel an orgasm building, being stoked by the touch of his fingers inside my body, his thumb teasing my clit, his tongue against mine.

"You can't come until the tatt is finished, Red," Dex warned softly. "Stay still. Almost there."

"I can't…" The pressure was building, I could feel it in the way my nerves tingled, and my legs trembled.

I no longer cared that there was another man there, one who was tattooing an image onto my body. The only thing I could focus on was chasing the high Dex was building. He pushed a third finger inside me and I whimpered, the added pressure driving my orgasm closer.

"Dex ..." I panted his name, clutched at his wrist, trying to slow his movements down and he gave a soft laugh.

"Almost there," he crooned, his voice filled with rich amusement. He kissed along my jaw, nipped at my ear, and then the buzzing which had filled the room stopped. "Come for me now, Cherry Pie," he whispered and, almost as if his words were the trigger, I did.

My hips arched up, his fingers still filling me, and I cried out, letting the waves of bliss crash down. The only sound in the room was my breathing, harsh and fast, as I sucked in air—and then mortification took over when Frank spoke.

"Well, now. I feel like I should be paying *you*," he drawled.

Guarded Addiction

CHAPTER 28

MADNESS - MUSE

Dex
AGE 24

"You shouldn't have done that," Siobhan said the second we exited the tattoo parlor.

"You could have stopped me at any time," I told her, throwing an arm over her shoulders and steering her down the sidewalk. "I gave you a safe word. Have you forgotten it?"

"That's not the point."

"No, the point is you got a tattoo *and* an orgasm. You should be happier." I ducked the punch she swung at me and laughed. "Don't argue with me. It's our wedding day. We're supposed to be ecstatically happy. You know, wedded bliss and all that?"

"I can't believe we did that either!" she exclaimed. "You're a bad influence on me."

"I'm a *great* influence on you. Tattoos and orgasms today. We'll get piercings next."

"Definitely *not* getting anything pierced."

"Maybe not today, but you will. I can feel it in my boner."

"You mean your bones."

"Nope, I mean my boner ... which we need to go and do something about."

She rolled her eyes at me. "You're such a child."

I laughed and hailed a cab. "Let's go back to the apartment and I'll show you just how much of a man I am. Watching you come has me hungry for the main course."

I saw the cab driver's eyes jerk to the rear-view mirror, overhearing me as we climbed into the back of the car, and the blush that hadn't left her cheeks since leaving the tattoo parlor deepened further.

I gave the driver the address and settled beside Siobhan, my arm resting over her shoulders. I toyed with the strands of hair close to my hand. I honestly didn't know what it was about her—she fascinated me, had done since first setting eyes on her. I wanted to push her boundaries, test every limit she had, just to see her eyes flash fire at me. Every time she fell in line with my crazy suggestions, I loved her a little more. But I knew it was the kind of love that had the potential to burn us both up if I didn't control it. It wasn't safe and tidy, it was dark, messy and I was under no illusion that it would destroy us both eventually—or, more accurately, *I* would destroy it.

I leaned close to her so I could press my lips against her ear. "Take off your panties."

She sliced a look at me and shook her head.

"Sure?" I licked the shell of her ear, felt her shiver, and smiled.

"Last chance to change your mind before I work around it." My hand dropped to her thigh, slid up beneath her dress and found the edge of her panties. "How about I do this…" I eased my fingers into her and sank my teeth into the lobe of her ear.

"The driver …" she gasped.

"Needs to keep his eyes on the road or we'll fucking crash." I couldn't get enough of her, needed to see her come at least once more.

"Dex—"

"He can't see a thing, not unless I push your dress up." I lifted my head from where I was biting along her throat. "I could do that. Do you want him to watch? Did you like knowing Frank was watching what I did to you?"

"We're here." The cab driver's voice was a rough bark in the darkness of the cab, and I felt Siobhan jerk away from me.

I chuckled. "Saved by the bell," I quipped. I paid for the ride and threw open the door. "Let's go." I helped her out of the car and we walked into my apartment building.

She stopped, staring around with wide eyes.

Fuck.

We'd driven to Murphy's, taken a cab to the chapel and I'd been that wound up after having my hands on her at the tattoo parlor, I'd forgotten all about my car.

"*This* is your apartment building?" she demanded.

"Appearances are deceptive," I replied. "It's not as expensive as it looks."

"*Really?*" Her tone said she didn't believe me. No surprise there, considering it *was* one of the most exclusive places to live in Vegas.

"I ... know someone who cut me a great deal on the place," I said with a smile. Not strictly a lie, I *did* know someone and I did get a good deal but it still cost me a cool half million to buy. I wasn't about to admit that, though.

I caught her hand and pulled her into movement, and we crossed the foyer and entered the first available elevator. She moved to stand in the far corner, and I faced her, propping my back against the wall and folding my arms.

"You okay?" I asked.

"Yeah ... I think so. It's just all ..." her teeth sunk into her bottom lip. "What have we done? Got married? Tattoos?"

I could hear the slightest hint of hysteria in her voice as the events of the past few hours finally caught up with her. She'd gone along with my crazy antics, swept up in the fun and excitement and now ... now we had stopped and stood in relative calm, so her mind started working overtime.

"Hey ..." I crossed the small space and cupped her face between my palms. "We're not crazy."

"Dex, we got *married!*"

"I know. Do you know why?"

"Because you're crazy and I bought into your insanity."

I smiled. "I won't deny the possibility, but that's not why." I kissed the tip of her nose. "Ask me why I talked you into marrying me, Cherry Pie."

"Why?" Her lips formed the word, but I could barely hear her whisper.

"Because," I said, pressing a kiss to the corner of her mouth, "there's this crazy," another kiss to the opposite side, "attraction between us." I let one hand slide down to circle her throat gently, my thumb brushing along her jaw. "One that, no matter how much time we spend apart, fires back into life the minute you're close to me again." I angled her head up so I could taste her lips. "I felt it when we met, and every time since. We *belong* together, Red."

CHAPTER 29

I DON'T LIKE THE DRUGS - MARILYN MANSON

Dex
PRESENT

"If you *ever* tell Harper about that, I swear I'll kill you." She advanced on me, fire in her eyes and, sick fucker that I am, my dick sprang to attention. She had gone from horny to furious in less than three seconds, and that turned me on more than anything else could.

The memory of my hands being covered in blood while I fought to keep someone alive was receding in favor of the angry redhead stalking toward me, and I embraced the distraction.

"Maybe I'm tired of being your dirty little secret," I threw at her, just to see her reaction, but the second the words left my mouth I knew it was the truth.

There was a beat of silence and then her palm hit my cheek. "*My* secret? *Mine?*" she shouted. "Unlike *you*, my memory is sound. *You* denied any connection to me. You told the hospital you had no idea who I was."

I let a smirk pull my lips up, ignoring the urge to rub my face.

"Heh, yeah I did say that, didn't I?" The amusement in my voice was a far cry from how I actually felt about it.

"You're unbelievable," she seethed. "I don't know why I keep letting you convince me you've changed. You're *never* going to change. I'm done. *We're* done. Goodbye, Dex."

She twisted, threw open the door so hard it banged off the wall and walked out. Searching around, I found my cell on the floor beside the bed and reached down for it. Unlocking it, I tapped out a text for Diesel asking him to pick her up from outside the house and take her home.

I wouldn't go after her ... not yet. Let her think we were done. I knew better.

Diesel replied, confirming Siobhan was in the car, and I tossed my cell onto the bed. My eyes fell on the small tin sitting on top of my nightstand, and I frowned. I recognized it as the container I always kept my weed in. I'd handed it over to Karl, along with almost everything else I used, after I collapsed at Riley's graduation. So what was it doing in my bedroom? I skirted the bed, eyeing it as though it was going to bite.

Maybe it was only the tin and there was nothing in it? Maybe I should open it and check.

My hand was shaking when I reached out, and I snatched it back before I touched the metal.

What if it wasn't empty?

My mouth was dry, and my heart rate was speeding up. I wanted to open it *so much* it scared me. All thoughts of Siobhan, sex, and my past fled, leaving me with nothing but the memory of how it felt to get high, get stoned, and leave this world alone for a few hours.

Fuck, I wanted to experience that high again *so much*. One joint wouldn't kill me ... right? Hell, it was used for medicinal purposes these days. I reached out again, my fingers tracing over the embossed design—the Forgotten Legacy wings and my name beneath it.

Had it been sent back to me by accident? Maybe someone had seen it in Karl's office and thought I'd left it there? I dismissed that as soon as I thought about it. *Everyone* knew what I used it for—it wasn't a secret. And I doubted Karl would have left it lying around somewhere on show.

I eased off the lid, the familiar smell reaching my nostrils, and my eyes closed. I could almost *taste* it, *feel* the effects of it, and I wanted that *badly*. Forcing my eyes open, I checked the contents. Three joints had been made up and there was a little baggie filled with what looked like around an eighth of marijuana.

I took out one of the joints, my hand shaking, and lifted it to my nose. I inhaled the smell, almost groaning with the need to light it, to lose myself.

A voice was whispering inside my head, reminding me how good it felt, how easy it would be to light it and go back to a state of numbness, of not caring, of not *feeling*.

It was between my lips, and my lighter was hovering at the tip when I came to my senses.

Fuck.

I threw the tin across the room and spat out the joint.

What the fuck are you doing?

I had to get out of the room, maybe out of the house. Grabbing my cell, I fired off a text to Luca.

ME - Are you at the cages?

LUCA - No, Damnation.

ME - On my way.

Damnation was heaving, as usual. Diesel kept the fans back when they spotted me, and we forced our way through to the entrance and up to the VIP room. Luca was sitting on one of the curved couches, feet propped up on a table in front of him, cigarette hanging from his lip as he chatted with Ryder, who leaned against one wall.

The conversation stopped when I walked in, Luca's eyes narrowing when he saw me.

"You coming down with something?" he asked, and I shook my head, silently heading directly for the bar to pour a large shot of Tequila. "You look like shit."

"Thanks, you're looking as fuckable as ever." I raised my glass in a toast, downed it, poured another, then went to join him.

"Want to talk about it?"

"Do I look like a girl?"

One side of his lip curled up. "Sometimes." He patted his lap. "Come on, D. Climb on daddy's lap and tell me all about it."

I snorted an unwilling laugh. "I appreciate the offer, but daddy kink doesn't do it for me."

"I could spank you?" he offered.

"Thanks, but I'll pass."

"Speaking of daddy kinks, where's your redheaded brat?"

"Siobhan doesn't have a daddy kink, either."

"Not denying she's a brat, though, I see," Luca pointed out.

"Oh, she's definitely a brat. But I think that's her default setting." Bantering with my friend was easing the agonising hunger I felt after running from my house.

"What's the story there? You said you've known her for years, yet I never heard anything about her until Harper came back."

"Long story."

"I'm not going anywhere."

I sighed. "I don't think there's enough tequila in the club to untangle that mess right now."

Silence fell, broken only by the muffled beat from the music through the thick glass of the window.

"Do you want to find a hookup?" Luca said finally.

"No." I didn't even have to think about it.

"Got it bad, huh?" Amusement dripped from his tone, and I slanted a glance at him.

"Apparently, I *really* like cherries. Who knew?"

He lifted his beer bottle and tapped it against my glass. "I wish you luck locking that down. I feel like you're going to need it."

CHAPTER 30

SECRETS - ONEREPUBLIC

Siobhan

PRESENT

Tuesday morning started out quietly. After leaving Dex on Saturday, I hadn't heard from him at all. I'd blocked his number from my cell, and spent the rest of the weekend expecting him to turn up at my apartment.

But he didn't. Tuesday morning came around, and he *still* hadn't tried any form of contact.

And that made me nervous.

Harper called me while I was getting ready for work.

"What shift are you on today?" she asked.

"Days. Start in an hour."

"Oh."

I frowned at the note in her voice. "What's wrong?"

"I was hoping you had the day off today."

"Did you need me for something?" I sat on the edge of the bed.

"The band has a thing today. A photo shoot ... and a video for the song they're planning to release before they announce the new album."

"Okay..."

"Gabe has to make out with a woman in it."

I could hear the uncertainty in my friend's voice. "Harp, it's just acting. You know he loves you."

"No, that's not the problem," she hurried to say. "They... umm ... they want me to be the woman he makes out with. Riley thinks it would be perfect and everyone else seems to agree with her."

I stifled a laugh at the thought of Harper in the limelight. I knew she was uncomfortable with the attention, and hated that aspect of Gabe's life.

"But that's great. The chemistry between the two of you is off the charts and will come across. Sex sells, Harp."

"I know, but ... would you come along? For moral support?"

I chewed on my lip. I couldn't really afford to take the time off. I wouldn't get paid if I didn't go in, but Harper rarely asked for anything and I didn't want to let her down.

"Okay," I said finally. "Send me the details and I'll meet you there."

I'd figure something out. Hopefully, someone would reply to my roommate ad before the end of the month.

"Oh thank you!" The relief in Harper's voice was worth it. "I love you, Von!"

I forced a laugh. "Yeah, yeah."

The studio where they were shooting the photographs and video was in downtown LA. I got there a little after ten and found a place to park.

Two burly men stood at the entrance, blocking the way in. I eyed them over my coffee.

"I'm expected. Siobhan Rawlings ... Harper's friend?"

They gave me a blank look and didn't move. Sighing, I juggled my coffee and pulled out my cell to call Harper.

"There are two gorillas outside refusing to let me in. I have hot coffee and I'm not afraid to use it," I told her when she answered.

Harper laughed. "I'll send someone down to let you in."

Gabe's assistant, Candice, arrived at the door a few minutes later. She pushed it open and waved me through. I threw the two security men a wink and a smirk and walked past them.

"Harper is a bundle of nerves," Candice told me as we walked through the building.

"She doesn't like all the attention."

"She's going to need to overcome that. Once this album is released, it's only going to get worse," the other woman cautioned.

"She'll work it out."

Candice didn't reply, pushing open the door and leading me inside. The room beyond was a hive of activity. I could hear voices shouting directions, people arguing as they moved scenery and cameras around.

I spotted Harper seated in a director's chair on the opposite side of the room, a makeup artist leaning over her, and I walked over.

"The cavalry's arrived," I quipped. "No, don't get up," I added when she started to hop off the chair. "Let the woman do her work."

I shared a smile with the makeup artist. "Is she being awful?"

The woman laughed. "No, not at all. I'm done now, anyway. Do *not* drink or eat anything until after the shoot, or I'll have to do it all again," she warned Harper.

"Frosty?" Gabe's voice reached us. "You ready?"

Harper turned pale beneath the makeup. "I think I'm going to be sick," she whispered.

"It's not like some stranger is about to stick his tongue down your throat. It's *Gabe*. You'll be fine," I said. "Just pretend the cameras aren't there." The look she threw at me told me I wasn't helping. "You better get over there before they come looking for you," I prompted when she didn't move. "Come on, I'll walk over with you."

She stood and hooked my arm through hers and walked over to where Gabe waited. The frown on his face melted away when he saw her, and he smiled.

"Ready?" he asked.

"No?" Harper replied, a slight tremor to her voice.

"Relax, Frosty." He wrapped an arm around her waist and pulled her into his side. "We can send everyone out. It'll just be us... Riley... and the camera crew."

"So ten people and us, then?" she shot back at him and he laughed.

"There she is." He dropped a kiss onto the top of her head, careful not to displace the styling. "You got this."

He drew her away, and onto the set where a microphone stood in front of a bar which looked like it had been fashioned to mimic the interior of Damnation.

I looked around for somewhere to sit and settled down to watch. I'd never seen a movie or music video filmed, so I was interested to see how it all worked.

Six hours later, I discovered it involved a lot of stopping and starting, yelling, repeating the same actions over and over. It was also *very* hot inside the studio, which caused fraying tempers all round. I took another bottle of water from the selection available and drained half of it, fanning my face.

"Do you want me to take your jacket?" one of the assistants asked me, and I shook my head. The last thing I wanted to do was take it off, because the bites Dex had left all over my throat hadn't faded.

A commotion near the door stopped filming again and I glanced back to see Luca, Dex, and Seth walking across the floor. Gabe moved to meet them, draping an arm across Seth's shoulders and dragging him into a hug.

Harper came over to me.

"Aren't you hot in that?" She touched the sleeve of my jacket.

"I'm fine."

"She doesn't want you to see the hickeys she's hiding all over her neck."

I physically felt the color drain from my face at Dex's words. Harper's eyes widened.

"You've been seeing someone? You never told me! Who is it?"

"Of course she didn't tell you. It's a dirty little secret, isn't it, Cherry Pie?"

If there was ever a moment where I wanted the ground to open up and swallow me, that was it. I shook my head mutely, not trusting myself to speak.

Harper threw a confused frown at Dex. "Why would it be a secret?"

"Good question." His head swung toward me. "Why *is* it a secret, Red? Why haven't you told your best friend who you've been fucking?"

Guarded Addiction

CHAPTER 31

CRY BABY - MISSIO

Dex
PRESENT

I hadn't planned on saying anything, but when I saw Siobhan wrapped up in that fucking jacket like it was mid-winter in Alaska; it annoyed the shit out of me. She'd run out on me in South Carolina because I'd confronted her with a truth she didn't want to acknowledge, *refused* to admit to me or herself. Okay, so maybe I'd also behaved a little badly after the whole Nashville thing, but that was natural.

But *this*? This was killing me. We were never going to get beyond the bullshit if she insisted on pretending there was *nothing* going on between us.

"Please don't do this," she said.

"Do what?" Harper's gaze bounced from Siobhan to me and back again. "What's going on here?"

"Cherry Pie here has spent a lot of time in my bed." I held Siobhan's eyes while I spoke.

Harper laughed. "That's hardly news, Dex. The two of you

weren't subtle. You were all over each other in Nashville *and* South Carolina. I thought it was nothing more than a fling, though, while you were on the road."

My smile was a baring of teeth and Siobhan's eyes pleaded with me to stay silent.

"Oh, we were together *long* before that, Harper." I knew exactly what would happen when I dropped this bombshell, but fuck it. I was tired of hiding shit. Between pretending my body wasn't killing itself with its need to get high and hiding that Siobhan and I had any kind of relationship before the tour—the stress was eating me alive. There were already too many secrets and lies tearing this band apart, I wasn't going to be responsible for this one.

"Dex—" Siobhan began and I cocked an eyebrow at her.

"Want to take over the storytelling, Red?" She fell silent and glared at me. "Didn't think so." I turned my attention back to Harper. "Have you never wondered how Gabe knew where you lived?"

"Gabe? What?" Harper frowned. "I thought he used a private investigator or something." She looked at Gabe, who was scowling at me. "Didn't you?"

"No, Frosty. *Dex* told me where you lived."

"Dex? But... how?"

"Because without me, you wouldn't have lived in that apartment with Siobhan in the first place," I told her.

"I don't understand." She turned to Siobhan. "You put an ad up in the apartment building I was living in." I could hear the bewilderment in her voice, but I was committed to this, and plowed on.

"No, she didn't. She put it in the community center. *I* took it and pinned it to the door of your apartment."

"*You?*"

I shrugged. "Gabe was going to come for you eventually. We needed to make sure you weren't fucking around with anyone while he was working through his shit. Siobhan needed a roommate. It was an all-round win."

"What the fuck?" I heard Gabe growl.

At the same time, Harper turned to Siobhan and demanded, "You knew Dex all along?"

"It's not what you think," Siobhan began.

"Not what I think?" Harper repeated. She spun to look at Gabe, whose face had paled. "Did *you* know?"

"No. Harp—"

"Have you been laughing at me all this time?" she asked, her voice rising. "Stupid, naïve, *friendless* Harper? Did you ask her to pretend to be my friend?"

"No!" Gabe's denial was immediate.

"Did you know Dex before I moved in with you?" Harper asked Siobhan. When she hesitated, Harper spoke again, her voice hardening. "It's a simple question. Yes or no."

"Yes," Siobhan whispered. "But, I swear Harper, I didn't—"

"Please stop. No more lies!" Her eyes swept over us all, landed on Gabe briefly before jerking away to look at me. "How long,

Dex? How long did you know her before I moved in?"

"Three years, give or take a few months. We spent a lot of time together while you were looking after your mom."

She gave a jerky nod. "I need some air."

"Harper, wait." Gabe reached out to catch her arm and she shook him off.

"Don't."

The only sound was the click of her heels as she walked out of the studio, arms wrapped around her torso and her head bowed.

Gabe spun toward me. "What the fuck have you done?" He started toward me and then appeared to change his mind and turned back to look in the direction Harper had gone. "You know what? I don't fucking care. Sort your shit out." He took off after Harper.

Nobody moved for a long moment, and then Siobhan speared me with her eyes. "What is *wrong* with you?"

"Me? I'm the one owning my shit."

"By causing trouble for everyone else? Did you really think Harper would be okay with that? How do you think she feels now? She thinks our entire friendship was a lie!"

"Wasn't it?"

"No! You didn't tell her the part where I had *no idea* you'd moved the ad or that I didn't know you knew each other. Or the fact I hadn't seen you in *over a year* and didn't know you were even a part of this stupid band!"

I cocked my head. "Nothing stopping *you* from telling her."

Her palm hit my cheek. "I *hate* you. Stay away from me."

She twisted away and I grabbed her wrist, dragging her back around to face me.

"Didn't I tell you only the first one was free, Cherry Pie?"

The narrowing of her eyes was the only warning I got before her knee connected sharply with my groin. I doubled over, the pain making my eyes water.

"Stay *away* from me," she repeated, while I was cupping my balls and groaning, and fled.

"Well, that was interesting," Luca said into the ensuing silence.

I threw him an angry glare and straightened, fully intending on going after Siobhan. Seth's hand on my arm stopped me.

"Let her go," he said quietly. "I think you've caused more than enough drama for one day." He nodded to the window where we could see Gabe and Harper arguing in the parking lot.

We watched as Harper jabbed at his chest with one finger, her lips moving furiously. Gabe shook his head and replied. Harper responded by turning her back on him and walking away. He lunged for her, caught her arm and spun her back to face him.

Whatever she said caused everyone in the room to suck in a collective breath because Gabe's features blanked, and his hand fell away from her arm. They stared at each other, and then Gabe gave a slow nod and Harper walked away, leaving him standing alone in the parking lot.

No one moved as Gabe spun and hurled his cell phone against the wall, shattering it into pieces, before stalking toward the main entrance of the studio.

CHAPTER 32

GIRLFRIEND - BADFLOWER

Siobhan

PRESENT

I didn't stop until I was out of the studio and inside my car. Once there, I locked the doors, gripped the steering wheel and closed my eyes, sucking in a calming breath.

Had he really orchestrated Harper moving in with me?

He couldn't have ... could he?

How?

I hit the steering wheel with one hand.

Think!

Harper had turned up holding the ad I'd posted. She never mentioned where she saw it and I didn't ask—I remembered that. She would never believe me though, not with the way Dex had thrown the information out there. He made it sound like I knew exactly how it had happened.

I punched the steering wheel again, wishing it was his head.

Damn it, what was he thinking? Was this just another one of his stupid games—a way to amuse himself?

Surely he hadn't wanted to really hurt Harper or Gabe? But that's what he had achieved. Harper now thought everyone had a part in her coming to live with me. I *knew* my friend. I knew how her mind worked. She would be torturing herself with the thought of everyone laughing at how she didn't know, congratulating Gabe on how clever he had been to keep her somewhere he would be able to pick her up when he was ready.

I also knew reaching out to her right now wouldn't achieve anything. She wouldn't be ready to listen. I needed to give her a day to calm down, a chance to think about things rationally, and come to the realization it hadn't been how she was imagining.

Jamming the key in the ignition, I drove back to my apartment, found a place to park and walked into the building.

Oh great.

My landlord was standing in the hallway talking to one of my neighbors. They both fell silent when they saw me, and I could feel their eyes watching as I unlocked my door and went inside.

Throwing my jacket onto the couch, I went into the small kitchen and took the bottle of wine I'd opened the night before from the refrigerator. It wasn't quite six PM, but I didn't care. I needed a drink and that was the strongest thing I had in the apartment.

Pouring a large glass, I took it with me into the bedroom, pulled open the top drawer of my dresser and took out a small box. Sitting on the bed, I opened it and took out the rings inside.

One was a platinum band, set with rubies and diamonds. The other was plain and smooth—a wedding band. I held them in my palm, then slowly closed my fingers around them. I should have gotten rid of them years ago, but I hadn't been able to bring myself to do it.

Maybe now was the time? If I sold them, I could get enough money to make rent for at least six months. And why was I keeping them, anyway? They held nothing but memories—some of them good, sure, but one bad one outweighed them all. And, after today and the stunt Dex had pulled, I wasn't sure I wanted the reminder of him around any longer.

I stroked a finger over the wedding band, feeling the smoothness of the metal. I hadn't questioned at the time where he got the ring from, but looking at it and the engagement ring he'd given me together, I knew now he'd picked them both up as a set on the same day.

Even now, years later, I still found it hard to believe I'd done it—married him, *loved* him without question. And yes, I *had* loved him—hopelessly, dangerously, crazily. Over the course of a single week, we'd lived a lifetime—marriage, tattoos, piercings, sex … lots of sex. Who did that? Me, as it turns out.

And then, just as quickly, it was over. Done. Finished.

I shied away from *that* memory, dropped the rings back into the box and placed it on top of the dresser. Sipping my wine, I returned to the living room, found the television remote control and curled up on a corner of the couch to channel surf for a few hours before heading to bed.

A warm body pressing against my back woke me. A hand sliding beneath my thin tank top to cup my breast. Half-asleep, I swatted at him, and shrugged him off.

"Go home, Dex," I mumbled, rolling away. "I'm not talking to you right now."

He ignored me, his fingers finding my nipple and pinching, the action painful instead of pleasurable.

"Fuck, stop it! That *hurt*." I twisted to shove him away and froze, blinking.

Foolishly believing I was seeing things, I didn't react straight away. When the image in front of me didn't change, all remnants of sleepy confusion fell away to be replaced by icy fear. I scrambled toward the edge of the bed.

"David? What ... how? Get out!"

His hand grabbed my wrist before I managed to escape the bed and dragged me back toward him. "I saw you the other night. I saw what you like. *How* you like it."

"What? I don't know what you're talking about." I twisted in his grip, and his fingers tightened.

"The other night with your *husband*. I saw *everything*."

My mind flashed back to the last time Dex had been in my apartment, and I went cold.

How had he seen what we'd been doing?

"Let go of me, David." I tried to keep my voice calm. "You need to leave. Whatever you saw, whatever you think that means, you shouldn't be here." I tried again to free my wrist.

"You think you can put on a display like that and not get a reaction from me? You *knew* I'd be watching. That's why you left the door open. I know your type. You tease and flirt."

"No."

He was pulling me toward him. I clutched at the edge of the mattress, trying to stop him, but he was bigger, stronger, and I couldn't stop the forward momentum.

Maybe he was trying to scare me ... to get me to agree to taking his help with the rent so he could have some kind of hold over me?

Right, and maybe there's a box full of hundred-dollar bills beneath your bed, a voice whispered through my mind.

"David, listen. Let's go into the other room. I have an ad up for a roommate. I'm sure someone will move in soon," I tried to reason with him.

"We're right where we should be," he replied and gave one final jerk.

I slid across the bed, the fingers of my free hand trying to find purchase on the sheets.

"Fight this all you want. I saw how you like it, Sioban. You like to be controlled, held in place ... *dominated*."

"N-no ..." I shook my head. "That's not what you saw."

"Stop lying."

The pressure on my wrist increased, sending shockwaves of pain through me. I didn't *think* he'd broken it, but if he twisted it any more ...

"David, you have to leave." I tried again, and I couldn't keep the tremor of fear from my voice.

I'd heard somewhere that if you used someone's name, it could appeal to their humanity. If I could reason with him, maybe he would listen?

"Leave? Why would I leave? This is what *you* want. You've been teasing me for years, shaking your ass, flashing your tits, flirting with me. I tried to resist, tried to stay away, but that show you put on the other night for me ... that was a message. You *want* this."

I tried to kick out with my legs, but he anticipated the move and the air was driven from my lungs when his weight dropped down on top of me

"You're just a fucking prick tease," he said. "And it's time to pay the price." He kissed me, sinking his teeth into my lip.

I bucked, tried to dislodge his weight, and white-hot pain shot through my arm when he twisted it up at an angle beneath my back. His other hand found my throat and he squeezed, stopping my scream before it escaped my mouth.

"I know your type," he whispered against my ear before biting it, making me cry out. "All mouthy and tough until you're put in your place."

I could feel his erection pressing against my stomach and I fought against the need to panic. Tears filled my eyes, part fear, part pain, but I refused to let them spill. I had to stay calm. If I did that, I would find a way out of this. I *had* to find a way out of this.

Slowly, I inched my free hand toward the nightstand where

my cell lay. If I could reach it, and hit the emergency dial, *someone* would come. I couldn't let the fact I couldn't breathe, couldn't draw air into my lungs distract me. I had to ignore how tight his grip on my throat was.

I felt a laugh bubble up—hysteria, a detached part of my mind noted. His hand gripped me the same way Dex did, and yet it was different ... so, so different. Every time I moved, his fingers dug deeper, his nails biting into the skin below my jaw.

His mouth was still attacking mine, biting my lips, and the coppery taste of blood filled my mouth when he broke the skin. I tried to throw him off again, but I couldn't breathe, and the movement was weak.

Was this it? Was someone going to find my body in a couple of days when I didn't show for work?

NO!

I needed to reach my cell. But there was a roaring in my ears. I couldn't focus ... my vision was beginning to blur.

And then I heard a shout. My head snapped sideways. Something hit me with a blow that knocked me into a welcome darkness.

CHAPTER 33

HAPPY PILLS - WEATHERS

Dex
PRESENT

Gabe's fist connected with my face before I even realized he was back in the room.

"What the actual fuck are you playing at?" he shouted.

Yells and screams sounded around us, from those not used to our band's violent outbursts, as he threw punch after punch. I staggered back under the onslaught, regained my balance and then pressed forward, trading blow for blow, until someone grabbed me and hauled me out of his reach.

Wiping the blood from my face, I saw Seth had Gabe, arms pinned behind his back as he tried to surge forward again. I knew without looking that Luca had hold of me.

"I don't know what fucking game you're playing right now, D, but you need to stop," he told me in a low voice. "It's not funny anymore."

"There's no fucking game. I'm sick of all the secrets everyone is keeping." I snapped in return. "What's your secret, Gabe? What are you keeping from us?"

"Fuck you," Gabe snarled in return.

"Get him out of here," Seth threw at Luca, nodding at me. "Go home. Cool down."

"Harper's staying in a hotel," Gabe called after me, as I turned to follow Luca. "I hope you're fucking satisfied."

I stopped and looked back at him. "Did you tell her you didn't know anything about me and Siobhan?"

"Of course I fucking did."

"But she didn't believe you?"

"What do you think?" he snapped.

"You know what, Gabe? You should really take some time to think about *why* Harper automatically assumes you're lying whenever something comes up." Luca and Seth jumped in front of us again when Gabe surged forward.

I didn't wait around to hear if he had anything to say in response. I walked out and let the door slam behind me. My cell was ringing before I exited the building.

"Get your ass to my office right now," Karl barked down the line.

I rolled my eyes. "Did Gabe call you?"

"No. Candice did. I want the entire band here within the next thirty minutes." He cut the call.

"Karl?" Luca asked from behind me.

I nodded. "We've been summoned." I looked around. "I told Diesel he could have the afternoon off. I was going to hassle Siobhan until she agreed to talk to me. Do you have your car?"

"Yeah." Luca waved a hand to the left, where Ryder leaned against the side of a black Lincoln Navigator.

"New car?" I asked.

"Not mine. Ryder likes to pretend he's driving a tank or something."

The man in question straightened as we approached. "Where to?"

"NFG Records," Luca told him. "It seems we have a band meeting to go to."

We all sat in Karl's office—Luca and Seth separating me from Gabe—listening while our manager gave us a lecture on keeping internal problems private instead of putting them on display for the world to see.

It was obvious Gabe wasn't listening. His lighter was in his hand, and he was staring into the flame, his brow furrowed while he chewed on his bottom lip.

Karl's eyes were on our lead singer as he spoke, and we could see his concern. "All right," he said finally. "All of you get out. Gabe, stay put."

Gabe didn't even give any sign he'd heard Karl speak. The rest of us stood and moved toward the door. He surged to his feet before we made it and pushed past us all, ignoring Karl's shout for him to wait.

"Look, I don't know what's going on between all of you and, honestly, I don't think I *want* to know. But you need to fix it, and *soon*," he said.

"Families fight," Seth said quietly. "We'll be fine."

"Do *you* know what's going on with Gabe?" Karl questioned the guitarist, and Seth shook his head.

"He's not talking about it with anyone. That's part of the reason things blew up between him and Harper today. It's not completely Dex's fault." His dark eyes slid to me. "Although you *didn't* help the situation."

"Where's Harper now? Do we need to put someone with her?" We all looked at Karl.

"Riley is with her. I sent Carter along with them," Seth replied.

"Okay, all right. Riley is a good choice. She has no real history with either of them. What about you?"

"I'll catch a ride with Gabe." Seth threw a troubled look after Gabe, who was disappearing into the elevator. "I don't know what's going on with him, but I don't think he should be alone right now. I'll call you if I find out anything." Raising his voice, he shouted for Gabe to hold the elevator and took off after his friend.

"Do you have an appointment with Dr. Santos today?" Karl asked me and I groaned. I'd forgotten all about that.

"I can drop you off," Luca offered.

I glanced over at Luca. "You doing anything tonight?"

"Gym, food, sleep," he replied. "I could maybe wedge you in somewhere if you need entertaining."

"I think I do. Drop me at my appointment, then meet me

afterwards. We'll go grab food from somewhere."

"Stay out of trouble, the pair of you," Karl warned as we followed the same path Gabe and Seth had taken.

The session with Dr. Santos went well. He asked me about my childhood, I ignored him and played Candy Crush on my cell. He asked about my mother's drug addiction, I ignored him and … yep, there's a pattern here … played Candy Crush. He asked about my father's arrest history, I ignored him and, well … I don't need to keep repeating myself.

After an hour, he put down his pad. "This won't work unless you cooperate."

"My drug use has nothing to do with my childhood or my parents. I'm not suffering from some childhood trauma." I ignored the brief flash of memory of blood on my hands, of leaning over and vomiting until there was nothing left to bring up.

"Dex, until you acknowledge what set you on the path, you'll never get off it," he said gently.

I resisted the urge to roll my eyes at him. I *knew* why I took drugs. I didn't need to share that information with him.

"As long as I stay away from them and don't get high, that's all that matters, right?" Checking the time, I rose to my feet. "Same time next week, doc?"

He nodded. "I'll get my secretary to send you a reminder." Standing, he held out his hand. I took it in mine. "You understand that these appointments will continue until I feel you're in a place where I can sign you off?"

I grinned. "Maybe I just like your company." Dropping his hand, I sauntered out of his office and threw a cocky grin at the pretty receptionist. I wasn't interested in her, but she blushed and I smirked.

Ryder was waiting outside and we headed back to the car. Settling into the back, I fired off a text to Luca telling him I was on my way, then called Siobhan.

I was pretty sure she'd blocked my number and wasn't all that surprised when the call didn't connect. Maybe I'd surprise her and turn up at her apartment after dinner.

Guarded Addiction

CHAPTER 34

IN CHAINS - SHAMAN'S HARVEST

Dex

PRESENT

"You know what would round that meal off perfectly?" I asked Luca, pushing the plate away and leaning back on my seat.

"A good fuck?"

"Well, I was going to say a nice fat joint, but I like the way you think."

"Neither are on the cards. We could go to Damnation?"

I thought about it, then shook my head. "Gabe and Seth will probably be there. If we turn up, we might stop Seth from finding out what's going on with Gabe."

"What do you think it is?" Luca asked, waiving a hand to get the check.

"No idea. Whatever it is, he doesn't want to tell Harper." I smiled at the server who placed a tray at my elbow, pulled out my credit card and dropped it on top. "Take your usual tip, sweetheart."

She returned my smile and disappeared.

"So what's up with your current need to cause shit with

everyone? That's usually my role."

"I'm really tired of all the bullshit. It didn't bother me when I was stoned all the time, but ... *fuck me* ... the drama is almost constant right now. Gabe and whatever the fuck is going on in his head—he's losing his temper over everything. I thought once Harper agreed to marry him, he'd chill down a bit, but he's worse now than he was before he got her back. Seth and Riley ... although that seems to have sorted itself." I hesitated. "You and Lexi." I saw him lower his lids, veiling his expression. "Come on, Luc. You know what she did wasn't your fault. That girl was all kinds of fucked up."

"I know," he acknowledged quietly.

"I hear the words, but not the conviction."

"It's not that simple."

"Were you fucking her?"

Luca's headshake was immediate. "But I loved her, D. I fucking *loved* her, and I thought it'd be enough."

"Did she love you?" The server returned before he could answer and handed me my card. "Thanks, sweetheart." I drained the last of my beer and stood. "Ready to go?"

Luca nodded and we headed out of the restaurant. A flash of lights showed us where the Lincoln was parked, and we moved toward it. Ryder hopped out and opened the back door. We both climbed in.

"Thanks, man," Luca murmured and Ryder nodded.

"Where are we going?" he asked.

Luca looked at me. I bounced my head off the back of the seat and sighed. "Siobhan's." I gave Ryder the address and the car pulled out into the traffic.

"Is that wise?"

I chuckled. "No. But she's blocked my number and..." I threw my friend a smirk. "Well, I can't have that now, can I?"

"You're quite the asshole when you're sober, aren't you?" Luca laughed.

"It's her, man." I sighed again. "She brings out this urge to push her buttons ... *all* the fucking time."

"Make sure you don't push the one that makes her kill you," Luca's reply was dry.

"Can't make any promises. She's fun when she's feisty."

"Have you developed a death wish with your new found sobriety?"

"No, but I rediscovered my taste for cherry pie."

Luca snorted and shook his head. "What happened to *she's just a hookup. We're just fooling around while we're on tour ... it doesn't mean anything?*" He did a fair impression of my voice.

My smile faded. "Nashville happened."

"You know that was a one-time thing, right?" His voice grew serious. "And if I'd had any idea..."

"*I* didn't even know, how would you? I think it needed to happen to finally take the blinders from my eyes."

I felt the car come to a stop and reached to open the door.

"You know, I think I might come with you to watch the groveling," Luca said and followed me out of the car.

The road outside her apartment building was empty and silent when we walked back to where the main entrance was. Loping up the steps, I pushed open the door and we went inside.

Siobhan's apartment was the last one down the hallway and I led the way, Luca behind me. One of the hall lights was flickering, the bulb on its way out, and it cast odd shadows along the wall, reminding me of the hallucinations I'd had at times when I was high.

"Is she expecting you?" Luca asked.

"No, why?"

"The door is open." He nodded ahead and, sure enough, the door to Siobhan's apartment was slightly ajar.

"Huh, weird." I reached out, then stopped, canting my head. "Did you hear that?" We both stood, listening, then I shook my head. "Never mind. I must be hearing things."

There was a thud, then a low groan and I exchanged looks with Luca.

"If you're hearing things, then so am I," he said. "Is she seeing someone else?"

"No way." My denial was immediate. I knew Siobhan, and if there was any other man in her life she would *not* have let me fuck her. At least, I *hoped* that ... but what if I was wrong? A frown drew my brows together.

No fucking way.

I pushed the door open and walked in, my eyes immediately tracking the room, looking for evidence of another man. There was one glass on the coffee table, a single plate on the kitchen counter. Siobhan's jacket was thrown across the back of the couch.

My frown deepened, the hairs on the back of my neck standing up. Something wasn't right, but I couldn't pinpoint what it was.

"D, I don't think—" Luca cut off at the sound of a hand hitting flesh.

"Luc," I began, but my friend already had his cell out and I knew he was sending a text to Ryder.

I started for the bedroom door, Luca close on my heels. It took me half a second to process the scene I walked in on, my mind trying to tell me my eyes were seeing things wrong. It was only Luca's harsh curse which snapped me out of the denial train I was riding.

We moved as one, both reaching for the man on top of Siobhan. He was so focused on the woman beneath him, he didn't immediately react to our presence. Luca's hands curled around his ankles, while I went for his throat. I grabbed him by the back of his neck and lifted him as Luca dragged him backwards. He swung an arm, his fist catching the side of my head. It was a wild and uncoordinated punch, nothing more than a love tap, which did nothing for my mood. Gabe had hit me harder.

Between us, we hauled him to his feet. He struggled, attempting to free himself from my grip so Luca hooked an arm around his neck to hold him in place, whispering something which made the guy freeze, his eyes darting to me.

I ignored him and walked slowly to the bed. Siobhan's hair spilled across the pillows and, for a moment, I was back inside a memory where my hands were slippery with blood.

"Dex!" Luca's sharp bark shook me free and I moved forward, gently touching her face.

"Red?" I murmured.

She didn't respond and, with a shaking hand, I pressed my fingers to her throat, searching out her pulse. I let out the breath I'd been holding when I felt it fluttering strongly against my fingertips. Brushing her hair gently from her face, my jaw clenched at the blood on her lips, and the handprint around her throat.

I cupped her cheek, my thumb wiping away the drop of blood at the corner of her mouth. "Give me a minute, love," I whispered and pressed a kiss to her temple. She wasn't in any danger, I didn't think. Not right now, anyway.

Schooling my expression, I straightened, turned and stepped back to the center of the room where Luca still held the man in his grip. I stepped up to him and wrapped a hand around his jaw, forcing him to look at me.

"What the fuck were you doing?" I *knew* what I had seen, but I *had* to be sure.

His lip curled up into a sneer. "What she wanted."

"She invited you?"

He didn't answer. I looked at Luca, who tightened his grip. "Answer the man."

"What's happening here?" Ryder appeared in the doorway. The man in Luca's grip tried again to get free, maybe realizing there was no way he was going to bluff his way out of this.

"Ryder, come and hold this fucker still," Luca said.

Ryder took in the situation with one look around the room. His face hardened and he came to stand beside me in front of the guy.

"I asked you a question," I reminded him, and anyone would have been forgiven for thinking we were having a pleasant conversation. None of the anger I was feeling showed on my face or in my voice. On the outside I appeared calm, relaxed. On the inside, I was burning with anger, one step away from ripping his throat out... with my *teeth*. "*Did* she invite you?"

"I have a key."

"You have a key," I repeated flatly. I turned to Luca's bodyguard. "Ryder, I'm going to need you to call 911 soon. We're going to need an ambulance."

Ryder's head swung around to where Siobhan lay. "Why didn't you say something? Fuck..." He pulled his cell out.

"Oh, it's not for her," I said softly, and buried my fist into the guy's stomach. "And we don't need to call them yet." Another punch, this one to his nose. "You're her fucking landlord." My third punch loosened his teeth. "That key is not permission to assault women in their homes."

CHAPTER 35

MONSTERS - SHINEDOWN

Dex
PRESENT

The three of us studied the man on his knees, nose dripping blood, left arm hanging at an odd angle, whimpering and begging for us not to hurt him any more.

"What do you want to do with him?" Ryder asked, wiping blood, almost fastidiously, from his hands with a wet wipe.

"We could take him to the cages," Luca suggested. "They ask no questions there."

I shook my head. "Too easy." I tangled my fingers into David's hair and wrenched his head back. "Look at me," I demanded. "How many times have you done this?"

"N-none!"

"Why don't I believe you?" Ryder said before I could reply. He crouched in front of David, hooked his fingers into the man's bloody nostrils and yanked upwards.

David howled, trying to scramble to his feet. Luca's hands pressed down onto his shoulders, stopping him from rising.

"Here's the thing, asswipe," I said, leaning over him. "You're right *here*, in Siobhan's bedroom, so that raises the count to *one* immediately. So let's try this again. How many times have you done this?" I repeated my earlier question.

Ryder tightened his grip on David's nose when he didn't answer straight away.

"Okay, okay!" he snuffled.

Ryder released him and plucked another wet wipe out of the packet he'd found from *somewhere* and cleaned his hands again.

"The others all agreed to my ... *interest payments* so they could have a reduction on their rent."

"Interest payments," Luca muttered. "Is that what we're calling it?"

"How *many* others?" Ryder asked.

A soft moan from the bed distracted me and I swung away to check on Siobhan. Her eyes were fluttering open when I leaned over her. The look of fear that crossed her features was enough to make me want to return to the man on his knees and end his miserable life. I resisted the urge, and reached out to stroke a finger over her cheek.

"Hey, Red." I kept my voice calm and casual.

"D-Dex?" She winced and my eyes dipped to her throat, where I could see bruises forming in between the ones I'd left there, from where the bastard had squeezed.

I wasn't sure how much she remembered and I didn't want to stir anything up too quickly, so I sat on the edge of the mattress, blocking her view of the room, and palmed her cheek. "How are you feeling?"

"I..." she trailed off, her eyes widening. "David was... David was here!" She struggled to sit up and I moved quickly, stopping her.

"No, stay there. Tell me what happened. Do you remember?" The question I wanted to ask, I couldn't voice because I knew I wouldn't be able to hide the fury boiling inside of me.

"I... I was asleep. Something woke me and I thought you were here but... but it wasn't you. Dex," she clutched at the front of my shirt. "Dex, he was in my bed. He wanted to... tried to..."

I could hear the mounting hysteria in her voice. Covering her hand with mine, I squeezed. "It's okay. Breathe, Cherry Pie." I risked a glance back at where Ryder and Luca stood.

Ryder had one hand covering David's mouth, stopping him from making any noise.

"Get him out of here," I mouthed, and turned back to Siobhan.

"Did he—?" I cleared my throat. "Do you know if...?" I couldn't bring myself to say it, couldn't speak the words.

"I don't think so." Her reply was little more than a whisper. "I'd know... right?"

The uncertainty in her voice was killing me. I had no way of reassuring her, no way of telling her everything was going to be fine and the urge to kill the man Luca and Ryder were dragging out of the room grew stronger.

"Dex?" My name brought my attention back to the woman clinging to me.

"I think," I began slowly, "that we should get you to the hospital so you can get checked over. You were out cold when I got here. I want to make sure you haven't got some kind of head injury."

I should have done that before laying into David, but the anger at what I'd walked in on had been far stronger than thinking logically. I'd wanted his blood for what he'd done. Unpeeling her fingers from my shirt, I rose to my feet.

"Take her to the car." Diesel's voice startled me and I swung around. "Ryder called me," he explained in response to my surprised look. "I got here a couple of minutes ago. You and Luca take her to the hospital. We'll deal with the mess here."

"What are you going to do?" I asked.

Diesel's smile was sharklike. "The less you know the better. Get out of here. Luca's got the keys for the car. I've parked directly outside the building."

I turned back to Siobhan, who had pushed herself up into a seated position. "Can you walk?" I asked her.

"I think so." She swung her legs round and stood.

My eyes fell on her top. It had been torn partway through, but the shorts she'd been sleeping in were still right where they should be. "Let's get you something to wear and get out of here." My voice came out gruffer than I wanted and I pressed my lips together to stop myself from saying anything further.

She shot a look at me, but said nothing as she walked, a little unsteadily, to her dresser and pulled out a pair of loose sweatpants and a plain t-shirt. Once she was dressed, I led her out of the room.

There was no sign of Diesel, Ryder, *or* David. Luca was leaning against the wall near to the door, twirling the car keys around one finger. He straightened when he saw us. Catching my eye, he jerked his chin toward the bathroom, telling me where the rest of them were, and I nodded.

"Ready to go?" he asked.

"Just about." I grabbed Siobhan's jacket from the back of the couch and threw it around her shoulders, then took her hand. "Let's go."

She paused to slip her feet into a pair of sneakers, and the three of us walked out and through the silent building to the exit. Sure enough, like Diesel had promised, the car was parked right in front of the steps. I helped Siobhan in the back, then slipped in beside her.

I called Gabe on the way to the hospital—even though he'd ruined his cell at the studio, I knew he would have had a replacement delivered within hours. He ignored me the first three times, but finally picked up.

"What?" he growled down the line when he finally answered.

"I need a contact for the hospital. Is it Riley's mom who works there?"

"You don't *sound* high. Why do you need to go to the hospital?"

"I'm *not* high. Siobhan has … she … fuck, just give me the fucking number."

"What's happened, D?" Gabe's tone immediately changed from aggressive to concerned.

"Not now," I said. "I'll text you the details." I didn't want to get into what I'd seen and done while Siobhan could hear me from where she was sitting, tense and silent, on the back seat beside me. "Can you *please* get me into that hospital without a media circus?"

"You got it."

"Is Harper with you?" I asked.

"No." I heard the tension return to Gabe's voice. "She's staying at a hotel."

"Is there any way you could get her to come to the hospital?" I lowered my voice. "I think Siobhan might do better with a female presence nearby right now."

"I don't know, man. She's pissed. I mean, *really* pissed." He sighed and I could see him rubbing a hand down his face in my head. "I'll see what I can do and let you know." He ended the call.

I received a text a few minutes later, with instructions on which entrance to use and who would be waiting to escort us inside. I replied with a brief run down of what had happened, then pocketed my cell.

"We're here," Luca said quietly from the front. "Do you know where we need to go?"

"Yeah." I gave him the directions and he drove around to the parking lot Gabe had told us to use.

I helped Siobhan out, keeping one arm wrapped around her shoulders, as we walked toward the entrance.

When the door slid open with a soft hiss, Riley's mom stepped out to greet us and I was reminded of the last time I saw Siobhan before Gabe reconnected with Harper.

CHAPTER 36

EASY TO LIE - FOREST BLAKK

Dex
AGE 24

I rolled out of bed, careful not to wake Siobhan, pulled on my jeans and padded through to the living room. I'd been ignoring calls from the band for a week, other than a quick text here and there telling them I was alive and taking some time out from the crazy train. We spent two days in Vegas, and then came back to hole up in her apartment.

I needed to figure out how to tell her who she'd married and what that meant, but every time I tried, I stumbled over the words and ended up dragging her back to bed. Not that she complained. She seemed as hungry for me as I was for her. A build up of attraction over the years as we'd drifted in and out of each other's lives. Okay, *me* drifting in and out of *her* life. I wouldn't be surprised if she thought I was some kind of homeless vagrant—or would if I didn't have top label designer clothes and an apartment worth half a million in Vegas.

Yesterday, I'd taken her to get her nipple and clit pierced

and now I was regretting it because we couldn't have sex for two weeks. I hadn't considered that when I talked her into it, but I knew it'd be worth it … for both of us. But it made me restless. If I couldn't wear myself out with sex, I needed to get stoned to be able to sleep without nightmares.

I found the tin holding my weed, opened it to roll a joint with what was left and lit it. Wandering across the room, I opened a window and leaned out. It was almost three in the morning and the street outside was empty—no fear of being spotted smoking illegal substances.

Before I could take a hit, my cell buzzed in my pocket and I took it out, unlocked it and opened the message.

T - I have your order. Need it collected tonight. Usual place.

Fuck.

Glancing in the direction of the bedroom, I rapidly calculated the time it would take to drive to Belvedere. Ten minutes, I estimated, give or take. Add on five minutes for the usual social niceties, then ten minutes to get back here. Could I make it there and back without Siobhan waking to find me gone?

T - D? you coming?

"No brother, not if I have to take a drive out to Belvedere," I said to myself, laughing softly. While we couldn't have sex, it hadn't stopped Siobhan swallowing my dick like it was her favorite cherry-flavored sucker.

ME - I'll be there in fifteen.

I pinched the top of my joint and shoved it back in the tin to smoke later, then crept back into the bedroom. Locating my shirt, I dragged it over my head, grabbed my jacket and slipped out of the apartment.

I was halfway to Belvedere before I realized when I returned to the apartment I would have no way of getting back inside without waking Siobhan to open the door for me. I spent the rest of the journey thinking up reasons I could give her for why and how I'd locked myself out.

Travis was sitting on one of the ramps in Belvedere Skatepark when I pulled into the parking lot. I flashed my lights and watched as he hopped down and came over to me. He waited for me to unlock the door and climbed into the passenger seat, dropping an envelope onto the center console. I handed him a roll of bills, which he didn't bother counting before he shoved it into a pocket.

"Can I drop you anywhere?" I asked.

"Nah, man. Got another drop to make here." Travis sniffed and wiped his nose with the back of his hand. "Drop me a text when you want a top up, or something else." He threw open the car door and disappeared back the way he came.

I reversed out of the parking lot and made my way back to Siobhan's apartment. Parking outside, I opened the envelope, took out the baggie of weed and rolled a fresh joint. Cracking open the window slightly, I lit it and placed it between my lips.

My eyes snapped open and I jerked upright, only to be stopped by hands on my shoulders.

"Lay still." A male voice—one I didn't recognize.

I could feel my heart racing like I'd run a marathon and I felt disoriented and nauseous.

"What did you take?" The same voice, urgent and controlled.

"Wh-what?" I craned my head around, searching out the person talking to me.

"You overdosed. What did you take?"

"Can't have." I lifted a hand to rub at my head, trying to shake away the fuzzy feeling. "It was just a joint." I tried to sit up again, and the hands on my shoulders pushed me back down.

"We're not the police. We're not going to arrest you, but we need to know what you took."

"A fucking joint. That's it!"

"Look, son, you need to be honest with us, so we can help you."

I shook my head—a mistake when the world spun. I managed to roll over before I vomited all over myself and only got a little on the guy's boots. I congratulated myself on my aim, then flopped onto my back.

"Is there anyone we should call?" The EMT asked as they lifted me onto a stretcher and carried me into the back of the ambulance.

"My manager," I mumbled. "He's listed as the Emergency Contact in my cell."

"The girl who called us. Is she family?"

I lifted my head slightly and saw her, pale-faced, being held back by the EMT's partner. I met her eyes, then looked away.

Siobhan knew I smoked weed, and I knew she didn't like it. I couldn't drag her into this side of things. I couldn't introduce her to my life like this. Her first experience of the band, the record label and my manager could not be while he chewed me out for taking drugs. I didn't want him looking at her like she was part of the problem.

"No... No, I don't know who she is," I said tiredly, let my head drop back onto the board and closed my eyes so I couldn't see the hurt I'd caused.

I went into convulsions again two hours after being admitted into the hospital, leaving me drained and exhausted. I couldn't figure out what caused them and it was only when Karl demanded I hand over my stash and told the hospital to test it, waving money around to rush the results, that we discovered it had been laced with Fentanyl.

That explained why I felt like I'd been fucked up. I dabbled in a lot of shit, but *that* wasn't one of them.

A counselor came in to talk to me about my *habits* and I ignored him while he droned on and on. Gabe saved me from dying of boredom when he popped his head around the door.

"The nurses say a girl keeps ringing and asking for information about you," he said.

"Information? A reporter?" I asked.

Gabe shook his head. "No, she says she's your *wife*." His lip curled, telling me exactly what he thought of that. "Wants to know if you got admitted here and when she can come and see you. Got something you want to share?"

Fuck. It had to be Siobhan.

I forced a laugh. "I have a wife? When did that happen? It's more likely to be a crazy fan or a reporter who saw me being brought in and wants to get an exclusive."

Gabe nodded, accepting the lie at face value. "I'll inform security to keep an eye out, in case she tries to take it a step further than phone calls. I'll also emphasize to the staff not to give anyone other than Karl or the band any information."

Guarded Addiction

CHAPTER 37

YOU - TWO FEET

Siobhan

PRESENT

I sat on the bed while the doctor poked and prodded at me. After my third yelp, and Dex threatening to break the doctor's hand, I had to ask him to leave the room before he was thrown out.

"He seems very angry," the doctor commented, his voice gentle. "Is there something you'd like to tell me while he's not in here?"

"He's angry because he couldn't stop this from happening." I waved a hand at my face. "He didn't do it."

"Do you want to tell me who *did* do it?"

"Doesn't matter."

"Has he done it before?"

I gave him a humorless smile. "I'm not in a violent relationship. It was a home invasion."

"We can perform a …" He paused, then finished carefully, "a rape kit."

I shook my head. "He didn't get that far." I frowned at the

detachment in my own voice.

He gave me a thoughtful look, catching my expression. "It's natural to feel a certain amount of disconnection after going through something like this, as a means of distancing yourself from what happened. Trauma and shock has a way of coming back on you later, when you least expect it." He straightened. "Well, the good news is nothing is broken. I can give you something for the pain, but other than that ... time will heal the bruising. I'll leave you to get dressed and I'll fill out the paperwork so you can go home."

"Thanks, doc."

He left me alone in the small room and it wasn't until the soft click of the door intruded into the silence that I realized I hadn't moved. I turned my head to find Dex leaning against the door, arms folded across his chest as he stared at me.

"Just say it," I said.

One pierced eyebrow hiked. "Say what?"

"You told me so. You warned me about David years ago. That I should have moved out, found somewhere else to live when Harper moved in with Gabe."

"Seems like I don't need to say any of it. You're doing a real good job telling yourself all that without any input from me." He pushed away from the wall and walked over to me. "Get dressed, Red, so we can get out of here."

I slipped off the bed and let the hospital gown fall to the floor. Being naked in front of Dex didn't bother me. He'd seen everything up close and personal more times than I could remember, but I didn't count on the explosive tirade of curses that spilled from his mouth when he saw the bruises on my ribs.

"Did *he* do that?" he demanded.

I pulled on my clothes without answering him. I didn't need to, he *knew* without me having to tell him.

"Can you take me back to the apartment?" I asked him once I was dressed, and he scowled at me.

"Why the fuck would I take you back there?"

"Because I need to get my bank card, money and a change of clothes, then find a hotel for the night." My voice wobbled slightly before I regained control of it. "I can't stay there tonight, Dex." I hated the pleading note in my voice.

"Tonight, tomorrow, the *rest* of your fucking life. You are *not* going back there." He pulled his cell out and punched in a number. "Diesel? Are you still at the apartment?" His eyes were on me while he listened to the reply. "Okay, well can you go back there and grab whatever shit you think Siobhan might need?" He paused, frowning. "Fuck it. Pack everything you can." He listened for a moment longer, then cut the call.

"I can't take everything with me."

"You really think I'm going to let you stay in a hotel?" At my nod, he rolled his eyes. "You need your fucking head examined."

"Bit late for that, isn't it?" I retorted. "I married *you*, after all."

A shocked gasp sounded at my words and we both spun to the door and found Harper standing there, one hand over her lips, Gabe behind her.

"Dex?" Gabe queried.

"You're *married*?" Harper said at the same time.

"About six months before you moved in," I told her. "We separated almost straight away."

Dex snorted. "We weren't separated. We just weren't talking."

"That's not how I remember it." I crouched to find my shoes and slipped them on.

"Are you okay?" Harper's legs came into view and I lifted my head to look at her.

"I've had better days." I tried to smile, felt my lips tremble and looked away, straightening.

"Von?"

"I'm fine, I promise," I told her and found myself wrapped in her arms.

"I'm sorry," she whispered. "Do you want to come and stay with me?"

"She's coming home with *me*," Dex said before I could reply. "And *you* are going home with Gabe."

I felt Harper bristle.

"Don't fucking argue with me," Dex continued. "Gabe had no part in you living with Siobhan. *I* did that. Siobhan and Gabe had no idea. You needed somewhere to live after your mom died, and I didn't want Siobhan alone in that apartment for any longer than necessary."

"Is that true?" Harper swung to face Gabe. "Why didn't you tell me?"

Gabe's face was unreadable. "You didn't give me much of a

chance," he said finally.

Harper bit her lip, and I could see how much his words hurt her. I kissed her cheek. "Go home, Harp. We'll talk tomorrow."

"But—"

"No, you need to go home," I cut in. "I'll go with Dex tonight and stay at his place. Tomorrow we'll talk, okay?" I gave her a gentle push toward Gabe, who stepped back out of the room.

I watched them walk away and frowned. "They're not holding hands," I murmured. "Gabe always holds her hand. He didn't even reach for her."

"They'll be fine," Dex said. "Can we focus on *you* instead of everyone else for five minutes?"

CHAPTER 38

FIGHTING IN THE CAR - JOE P

Dex
PRESENT

I hated hospitals. I'd spent way too much time in them over the years. And the one thing I'd taken from those experiences was *nothing* good ever came of being there.

I've woken up in a hospital bed with faces looming over me, fearful and angry. I've seen people die there. *I've* almost died there... more than once.

The doctor returned to give Siobhan her prescription and paperwork so she could leave, all the while casting me furtive glances because he was sure I was the one responsible for her condition, regardless of her claims to the contrary. Granted, the blood splattering my shirt didn't help the situation, but I didn't care.

"Ready to get out of here?" I asked once the doctor left, with one final dark look in my direction.

She nodded, clutching the little slip of paper. "I have to go and get this prescription filled." She caught her lip between her teeth.

"I'm not going to steal your painkillers, Red," I told her dryly, correctly interpreting the look. "I haven't quite reached that level of desperation."

"I'm sorry." Her cheeks reddened.

"Don't be. It's nice to know you worry about it." And, in a warped way, it was. It meant I hadn't completely fucked up to the point of her no longer caring about me.

She didn't respond to my comment with anything other than a sidelong glance. I pushed away from where I was leaning against the wall and met her in the center of the room.

"Luca gave me the car keys before he took off, so let's get moving. I want to get you home before you collapse."

"I'm not going to collapse," she protested.

"You've looked on the verge of it for the past hour, I'm taking no chances." I placed my hand on the small of her back and urged her toward the door. "I'm supposed to be meeting the band at the studio tomorrow …" I paused and checked the time on the wall clock as we walked out in the main area. "Today, actually, but I think they'll understand if we rain check it."

"You don't have to do that."

As far as I was concerned, that didn't even deserve an answer, so I ignored it and we walked the rest of the way to the entrance of the hospital in silence, pausing to pick up her painkillers. It was only as we stepped outside and a camera flashed to my left that I realized my mistake.

Fuck. I was supposed to use a different exit. But it was too late and we were swarmed by reporters.

"Dex? There's a rumor that you beat up your girlfriend. Is that true?"

"Is that her? Can we get a look at your face, sweetheart?"

"Dex? Can we get a comment?"

"No comment," I ground out, wrapping an arm around Siobhan's shoulders and using my other hand to bring her head against my chest, so I could hide her face.

"Who is she?"

"Isn't that the girl Gabe's girlfriend lived with?"

For fuck's sake. I wasn't going to be able to walk away without giving them something.

"Keep your head down," I murmured to Siobhan, and stopped. "No, I didn't beat up my girlfriend and, no, you can't see her face. Show some fucking respect."

"Then why are you here?" One of the vultures stepped forward, thrusting a camera into my face and taking a close-up shot.

"I suggest you take a fucking step back," I snapped. I could feel Siobhan's fingers gripping my shirt, heard her panicked breathing as the crowd of reporters surged forward.

And then Diesel was there, shoving them back, and relief flooded through me.

"Where did you come from?" I asked as he forced a path through the reporters, and led us to the car.

He held out a hand for the keys, and I passed them to him once I'd unlocked the car and helped Siobhan inside.

"Luca told Ryder he'd left you at the hospital, so I got him to drop me off," he explained. "Figured someone would have dropped a tip to the press that you were here."

"Thanks, man. I appreciate it."

He nodded. "Part of the job. Get in, and we'll get out of here." He strode to the driver's side and climbed in. I did the same, sliding in next to Siobhan on the back seat.

She didn't speak the entire journey back to my place, and I didn't try to break the silence. She looked exhausted and I knew she was fighting against her body's need to fall asleep and heal. Her lids kept dipping and then snapping open again, while she blinked rapidly. I half-hoped she'd succumb and let sleep take her, but I should have known better. That wasn't who she was. Siobhan was a fighter, and she wasn't about to change now, even when giving in would be the best thing for her.

I shifted on the seat, draped my arm across her shoulders and drew her closer to me. She threw me a look, but didn't argue, and that told me everything I needed to know about her state of mind. I kept my head carefully turned toward the window, looking out at the scenery as it passed and, after a few minutes, my patience was rewarded when her head dropped to rest against my shoulder.

Guarded Addiction

CHAPTER 39

FOOLISH - BOY EPIC

Siobhan

PRESENT

The motion of the car and the heat radiating from Dex conspired against me and I fell asleep. I hadn't wanted to, had fought against it, tried to keep my eyes open. The thought of going to sleep, of waking up to find I wasn't really safe, that I was still in my bed with David pinning me down haunted my dreams. What if Dex turning up in time was just a fevered hallucination due to oxygen deprivation? What if I was already unconscious? What if I was *dying*?

I woke, a scream tearing from my throat, and fought to free myself from the arms trapping me in place.

"Hey… hey… breathe…" The hold on me loosened and hands cupped my cheeks. "It's okay. It's me. Hear me, Cherry Pie?"

Cherry Pie … only *one* person called me that, and the relief when I realized I hadn't dreamed him up was overwhelming. He grunted in surprise when I threw myself at him, wrapped my arms around his waist and buried my face against his chest, breathing him in.

One hand smoothed down my back, and I felt him press a kiss to the top of my head. "You fell asleep in the car," he said quietly. "I put you to bed in one of the spare rooms. You woke up long enough to ask me to stay. Do you remember that?"

I shook my head, not quite ready to trust my voice.

"Harper called a little while ago," he continued, his voice slow and soothing. "She wants you to call her back later today. Someone called Lou called your cell as well, asking about work. I told her you'd had an accident and wouldn't be back for a while. She said she'd arrange cover and to take your time."

My heart rate was slowing while he spoke, my arms loosening their death grip on him. I could hear the beat of his heart beneath where my ear was pressed against his chest, strong and reassuring, the rumble of his voice as he spoke vibrating against my cheek.

"Thank you," I whispered.

"Do you need anything? Painkillers? A drink? Something to eat?"

"No."

His hand continued to stroke up and down my spine, calming my initial panic further, and I let loose a shuddering sigh, relaxing against him.

"If you hadn't ... hadn't turned up when you did," I began.

"Don't go down that path," he said over the top of me. "I *did* show up. That's all that matters."

"But if you hadn't—"

"Stop it, Red." His voice was firm. "We're not going to play the 'what if' game. That way lies madness."

I took a deep breath, leaned away from him and looked around. We were lying in the center of the bed I'd slept in a few nights ago. Dex was sprawled on his back, one palm resting above the curve of my ass, his thumb stroking in a small circle. His other hand lifted to brush a lock of hair away from my face and tuck it behind my ear.

"I need to report David to the police," I said.

"If that's what you want to do, we can go down there today," he replied, and there was a note to his voice that made me pause.

"You don't think I should?"

"I think I've heard enough about how women are treated in assault cases that I don't like the idea," he replied slowly.

"But that means he'll get away with it."

"Trust me, Cherry Pie, he's not going to get away with anything." He stroked a finger over my cheek and then touched my bruised bottom lip carefully. "I don't want you to worry about him."

There was something in his voice, a certainty that made me believe him ... and worry.

"What are—" The finger on my bottom lip moved upwards until it covered my mouth.

"Don't ask. The less you know, the better. All you need to know is it's being taken care of."

"What have you done?" I persisted and saw him smile.

"Me? What could I have done, Cherry Pie? I've been with you the entire time." His finger traced the outline of my lips. "You should get some more rest."

He was right, I knew that, but I didn't want to sleep. I was tired but I didn't think I *could* go back to sleep, not yet.

"Didn't you say you're supposed to be at the studio today?" I asked instead.

"This afternoon, yeah. I can reschedule. It's not a problem."

"No." I rolled away and sat up.

His hand curled around my arm. "Where are you going?"

"I can't lie in bed all day, Dex." I threw him a smile, hiding a wince when the movement pulled at the small bites on my lip.

"Sure you can. We could order in and watch movies."

"Or I can get up, get dressed and arrange to meet Harper at the studio, instead. That way you don't feel like you have to stay here and babysit me."

"Siobhan." I stilled at my name, the seriousness of his tone. Dex *rarely* used my name, preferring to call me by the various nicknames he'd picked out—Red and Cherry Pie being his favorites.

The mattress gave as he moved until he sat beside me. "No one is going to blame you for taking a day. What happened isn't something anyone expects you to just ignore."

I gave a jerky headshake. I didn't *want* to take a day and think about what had happened—that was the problem. Losing myself inside my head over it, over what might have happened if Dex hadn't had such a stubborn nature and came to see me when I told him to stay away … that wasn't something I wanted to dissect. And I knew that's what would happen if I sat around with nothing else to do.

I needed to wipe the memory from my mind, wash away how his hands had felt pinning me down, tearing at my clothes.

"Red?" Dex's concerned question drew my attention to the fact my breathing had quickened, my fingers curled and nails digging into my palms.

I twisted to face him.

"Will you do something for me?"

"Anything. You know that. What do you need?" His response was immediate.

"You."

"You already have me. I'm here."

"No." I reached for him and dragged his shirt up so I could slide my hands beneath it. "I *need* you."

CHAPTER 40

LEAVE ME ALONE - I DON'T KNOW HOW BUT THEY FOUND ME

Dex
PRESENT

It took a minute for her meaning to sink in.

When it did, I knew what she was trying to do and I wish I could say I was going to be the better man, and find another way for her to deal with what had happened. But where she was concerned, I'd *never* be the better man. If she offered herself to me, I was *always* going to accept because that was the temptation she posed for me.

I leaned forward to brush my lips carefully over hers, but before I made contact, the sound of someone pushing the gate's intercom rang through the room. I jerked my head back, frowning.

"Diesel will get it," I grunted, knowing my bodyguard would be in the house somewhere, and threaded a hand through her hair to draw her closer to me.

I was losing myself in her scent, the taste of her skin on my tongue as I kissed my way down her throat when the door to the bedroom was thrown open. Siobhan jumped as it banged off the wall and I lifted my head to find two armed police officers framed in the doorway.

"Dex Cooper?" one of them asked, and I nodded. I could see Diesel behind them, being held back by a third officer.

"You're under arrest on suspicion of the murder of David Colton."

"What the fuck?" I rose to my feet, turning to face Siobhan, who sat on the bed with one hand pressed to her lips, her face white. The words of the officer faded as he read me the Miranda Rights because my focus was on her.

"Call Gabe," I told her, ignoring the officer who was pulling my arms behind my back to cuff me. There was no point in fighting him, it wouldn't help my case and could even escalate the situation. "He'll know who to contact."

"I'm afraid that won't be possible," the other officer said. "She needs to come with us too."

"I want my lawyer," I said. "So does she. Red, ask for your lawyer." I wrenched myself free of the officer's grip when I saw the other haul Siobhan to her feet roughly. "Get your fucking hands off her."

"Dex, don't. Just go with them," she told me. "Can I get dressed first, Officer?"

The officer beside her scanned the room, eyes landing on her discarded sweats near the end of the bed. "Are they yours?"

Siobhan nodded. The officer picked them, patted them to make sure there was nothing hidden in the pockets, then handed them to her.

"Thank you." Siobhan pulled them on. "Do you need to cuff me?" I could see her willingness to cooperate was easing the officer's mood.

"No, ma'am," he replied. "That won't be necessary."

We were taken to the police station in separate cars. I refused to speak. This wasn't the first time I'd been arrested and I knew the process. Lawyer up—even if you were innocent. I caught a glimpse of Siobhan as I was led into one of the interrogation rooms, but wasn't given any opportunity to speak to her, to reassure her. I had to hope that she'd listened to me when I told her to demand a lawyer.

"Do you want to tell us where you were between the hours of one and five AM this morning?"

I raised my head to look at the officer sitting opposite me.

"Lawyer," I grunted, and then returned to the position I'd been in—head resting on my arms on the table.

"You know lawyering up makes you look like you have something to hide," he continued.

I smiled and said nothing.

"You think your fame and money will protect you?"

I yawned and closed my eyes, ignoring their words. I knew they were trying to draw me into conversation, get me to talk before my lawyer arrived, possibly incriminate me. But I had a rock solid alibi for being nowhere near David Colton when he was killed. I was at the hospital—there would be security footage available to prove that. The reporters had seen me leave, they had time-stamped photographs. My own security cameras attached to my house would show us arriving and not leaving again until the police showed up.

They had *nothing*.

I could tell them all of that, of course, but where would the fun in that be? No, they could wait for my lawyer to arrive and then the game could really begin.

It took them an hour but they eventually realized I wasn't talking and left me alone in the room. I didn't move. I was aware it was a ploy, a means to make me relax and lower my guard. They'd be back soon enough—offering a drink and something to eat. Hopefully, with my lawyer in tow.

I napped—a skill I'd learned over the years of touring with the band when we had to snatch short periods of sleep in between driving around the country promoting our music—and eventually heard the click of the door seconds before it swung open. I didn't move, didn't open my eyes. Outwardly, I looked the picture of relaxation. Inwardly, I listened intently, picking up the sound of a shoe scraping across the floor, breathing, the smell of stale sweat, and the familiar scent of expensive cologne, and the clipped upper-class voice of Matthew Carmichael, NFG Records' top lawyer.

I waited until he was seated beside me before lifting my head and affecting a yawn.

"Hey, man," I greeted him.

He looked down his hawkish nose at me, and I fought against a smile.

"I'd like to speak to my client alone," he said to the officers and waited while they grumbled, then walked out. "Did you do it?" He went straight to the point.

"No. Have you seen Siobhan?"

"Not yet. Jared is on his way to her now." He named one of his colleagues. "Tell me what happened."

I told him everything—from dinner with Luca, arriving at Siobhan's apartment and what we walked in on. I held nothing back, shared the details of how much damage we'd done to Colton before we left to take Siobhan to the hospital.

"He was alive when you left?"

"One hundred percent," I confirmed.

"And nothing you did to him could have been life-threatening?"

I shook my head. "I broke his wrist, his nose, maybe a couple of his ribs. Nothing he didn't deserve."

"Ms. Rawlings didn't report the assault?"

"We went straight to the hospital. I wanted to make sure she was okay. We didn't get back to my place til almost five. She was exhausted, so I put her to bed. We were talking about reporting it to the police not long before they burst through the door."

"And the relationship between you and Ms. Rawlings?"

I laughed. "You're not that clueless, Matt. Don't pretend you have no idea that I married her years ago. The minute you heard I was arrested and her name was raised, I *know* you'll have investigated. That's why it took you so long to get here."

"I knew you married her long before this morning. I looked into her when she kept calling the hospital after your overdose a few years back. You didn't seem to want to mention it, so nor did I. What I want to know right now is the *current* status of your relationship with her."

I sighed. "It's a work in progress."

"Not looking for a divorce?"

"Fuck, no. I'm looking for the two point four kids and white picket fence." I thought about that for a second. "Actually, scrap the kids. We'll get a dog or three, instead. We can just practice baby making."

Guarded Addiction

CHAPTER 41

TROUBLE - CAGE THE ELEPHANT

Siobhan

PRESENT

The female police officer had seemed sympathetic when she first led me into the small interview room. She offered me coffee and asked if I'd ever been interviewed by the police before.

I declined the coffee and told her I hadn't.

"Should I ask for a lawyer?" I asked and she smiled.

"You haven't been arrested. This is just us wanting to ask about what happened. We're trying to build a picture of David's actions prior to his death."

"Okay." I was a little dubious. I mean, I'd *seen* the television shows on how these things worked. But, I also wondered if demanding a lawyer and refusing to talk would make me look guilty of something. I *wasn't*. I hadn't done anything wrong, but…

"Why don't you tell me what happened last night? How did you know David Colton?"

"He was my landlord. He owns… owned the apartment building."

"And why was he in your apartment?"

"He …" I paused, wetting my lips nervously. "He had a key."

"So he came to see you regularly, then?"

"No! That wasn't what I meant."

"Then what *did* you mean?"

"He recently increased the rent and used his key to come into my apartment to hand deliver the letter."

"And that was normal behavior for him?"

"No. I asked him to leave. Th-then last night I woke up and he was in my bed."

"He thought you'd agreed to have sex with him to help with your rent payments?"

"No! No, I never gave that impression to him." I tried to explain to the officer what had happened, but no matter what I said, she seemed to twist it into me giving David some kind of sign that I was interested in him and open to his sexual advances. I was fighting back tears of frustration when the door opened and another stranger walked in.

"That's enough," he said crisply, striding across the room, one hand held out. "Ms. Rawlings, my name is Jared Kilroy. I'm your lawyer. Did the officers inform you that since this is merely an interview and you haven't been arrested, you can actually leave at any time?"

I shook my head and he swung to face the officer.

"This interview is over. Unless you plan on charging my client with a crime, I'm taking her out of here."

His hand curled under my elbow and drew me to my feet. Still a little dazed, I stumbled after him out of the room.

"Where's Dex? Is he okay?" I asked.

"He'll join us shortly. Through here." He nodded toward a door and led me through into a room where Forgotten Legacy's manager, Karl Daniels, was waiting.

I hadn't had much interaction with him, other than the odd word here and there during the short tour I'd joined them on, but he strode across to me, his concern etched on his features.

"Diesel told me what happened," he said. "Are you all right?"

"I th-think so." I stumbled over the words, not really believing them myself. "Have you heard anything about Dex?"

"I'm here." Arms wrapped around me from behind and turned me around until I faced the pierced and tattooed bass guitarist. He pulled me into his body and buried his face into my hair. I heard him take in a deep breath. "Are you okay?"

My own arms crept around his waist and I breathed in his scent, nodding against his chest.

"Let's get the two of you out of here," Karl said. "There are reporters outside. Do *not* respond to any questions. Let Jared and Matthew deal with them."

"Everything they have on Dex is circumstantial. With all the evidence proving he was nowhere near David Colton when he died, they have no case," Dex's lawyer said. "They're looking for a quick win and thought he would be an easy target to blame."

"But how did they know he was in my apartment?" I pulled free from Dex's arms so I could look at the lawyer.

"Someone reported a fight and saw you leaving with Dex and Luca," Jared replied. "Colton was found four hours later in his *own* apartment. His recorded time of death coincides with when you were both in the hospital."

"Why didn't they pull Luca in for questioning?" Dex asked.

"They did. I was with him before I came in for you," Matthew responded. "Same thing. He has witnesses who saw him in the hospital, and then there's traffic cams showing him being driven back to his apartment, as well as apartment security footage of him going inside and not coming back out. There's nothing to link either of you to his death other than the beating you gave him, which, incidentally, wasn't what killed him."

"What *did* kill him?"

"His throat had been ripped out."

Dex grunted over my gasp. "That'll do it."

"What happens now?" I asked.

"Nothing," Jared said. "Dex and Luca were both released without charge. They know they have nothing that will hold up and *you* weren't arrested."

"Diesel is waiting with the car. I need you to come to the offices, and then I expect you to go home and get some rest," Karl instructed. "Let's get out of here. And Dex? Stay *out* of trouble."

The amount of reporters outside the police station was more than triple the ones who had been outside the hospital the night before. Questions were shouted, cell phones thrust into our faces for comments and photographs. It was loud and terrifying, and gave me a taste of why Harper felt the way she did. Diesel, along with two other men, forced a path through to the car waiting for us at the bottom of the steps. Dex kept one arm wrapped around my waist and steered me in front of him, his other arm outstretched to stop people from getting too close, *if* they even made it past Diesel, Karl, and the two lawyers flanking us.

"Almost there." Dex's voice was low and close to my ear. "When we reach the car, don't look around, just climb straight in."

"Hey, Dex, who's your girlfriend?" one of the reporters shouted. "Is she the redhead who was on tour with you?"

Dex didn't respond, pressing forward grimly.

"I guess if you don't want to confirm or deny it, then you won't care if I put out the footage we captured of you, her, and Luca getting up *real close* and personal back in Nashville then?"

Dex stopped dead, and I felt what little color I had left drain from my face. I clutched at his arm. "Dex, don't." But it was too late.

Dex wheeled and punched the reporter, sending him crashing back into the others.

CHAPTER 42

BAD THINGS - JACE EVERETT

Dex

FOUR MONTHS AGO—NASHVILLE

Nashville—*Music City*—home to some of the most famous current music stars around. I don't know what it was that drew them to the city. Maybe it was the musical history, but so many people in our industry moved here. Me, though? I liked LA—the decadence, the shallowness, the *entertainment* to be had.

I sipped my beer and looked down at the dance floor where Riley and Siobhan were having fun. Seth stood beside me, and I could feel the tension radiating outwards from his body. The sooner he admitted he wanted Riley and fucked her out of his system or locked her down for good, the sooner he'd relax, but telling him that only made him angry. And an angry Seth was not something anyone wanted to deal with.

We both watched as Riley said something to Siobhan and left her on the dance floor alone. I knew Seth tracked the brunette, but my eyes remained fixed on the redhead … watching her, the way I'd been doing pretty much since the tour began.

Like a creeper.

She behaved like we had no history, like I hadn't made her scream my name, like I didn't know what she tasted like, like she didn't have my name tattooed on her fucking skin. And, I admitted to myself; it annoyed the ever-loving shit out of me.

She breezed along on the tour, that fucking cherry sucker in her mouth, hanging out with Harper, flirting with Jazz and Deryn. I'd even caught Marley smiling in her direction a time or two.

I watched as she gyrated against one guy's groin while another danced in front of her, his hands roaming over curves he had no business touching. Without turning my head, I waved Jason, my current babysitter, over to me.

"Go and retrieve Siobhan from the dance floor. Those two are getting a little ... *handsy*," I told him.

He gave me a quick nod and padded away silently.

"Looks like Harper's spitfire friend is looking for a good time," Luca remarked from beside me.

I swung to face him. "Maybe she is."

"Then maybe you should stop standing up here glaring at her and show her one?" I saw him smile out of the corner of my eye.

"Maybe we should." If Cherry Pie down there was looking to be double-dicked, the only dicks she was going to see would be Luca's and mine.

"We?" His eyebrow rose in query and I shrugged.

"At least we know she'll have a good time *and* be safe."

My friend gazed down at Siobhan, who was arguing with Jason about leaving the dance floor.

"You sure that's what you want to do?" he asked. "The way you watch her, I thought maybe you were a little more serious."

"Whatever gave you that impression?" I scratched my jaw. "She looks like she'd be up for a bit of three-way fun. You in?"

He didn't answer straight away, taking a swallow from his drink, but then nodded. "Sure, why not? I don't have anything else planned," he said finally, as Jason ignored Siobhan's struggles and firmly led her from the dance floor.

We both turned as one to watch when the door swung open and Jason pulled Siobhan through. Before it shut, Seth pushed his way out with Carter in hot pursuit.

Green eyes, blazing with irritation, met mine. "You're not my boss, Dexter. Why are you throwing your weight around?"

"Me? Sweetheart, all I'm doing is standing up here drinking and relaxing after a hard night working." I smirked at her. "What's your excuse?"

"I *was* having fun until you sent your pet dog down to break it up."

I saw Jason's lips quirk up into a half-smile and I was sure he murmured the word '*wolf*' in response to her insult, but my attention was on her and not him. If he preferred to be compared to a wolf, then it was no business of mine.

"You'll have more fun up here, Red," I told her.

Her lip curled up into a sneer as she swept her eyes over me.

"With you, Rock Star? I don't think so."

"How about me, then, Spitfire? Want to have some fun with me?" Luca asked from beside me.

Siobhan's eyes shifted to him. "I've heard things about you, Luca," she said. "Have to admit I'm curious what's true and what isn't."

He laughed. "You're more than welcome to find out."

Her lips pursed, eyes darting back to me, and I knew she was gauging my reaction. I smiled at her. Anyone watching, Luca included, wouldn't even guess at the history between us. I wondered briefly what he'd say if he knew, then discarded it as irrelevant. She wanted to act like I meant nothing to her, then I'd treat her like the hookup she was pretending to be ... and that meant playing the game everyone expected me to play.

"What are you drinking, Red?" I asked.

"Tequila," she replied.

I nodded and left her with Luca to go to the bar. Tequila for Siobhan and me, bourbon for Luca. Returning to them, I handed out the drinks. One drink became two, became three ... became more until Siobhan was laughing, dancing between the two of us in time with the music coming from the dance floor below.

At some point the music changed, became slower, heavier, and I found myself standing behind her while she swayed against me. One arm was hooked back around my neck while her other was looped over Luca's shoulder, her glass held between her fingertips.

He was smiling down at her, winding a lock of her hair around one finger, and I had a sudden visual of her between us, naked and writhing, and felt my dick harden.

"One for the road," I said, and downed my tequila in one swallow.

Siobhan's head tipped back against my shoulder, her eyes narrowing at the challenge in my voice, and she threw her head back to down her shot.

"Well, all right then," Luca chuckled and followed suit.

"Let's get out of here and go somewhere more private," I said, hooked my hand around Siobhan's arm and led her to the door. Jason materialized in front of us. "Find the nearest motel," I instructed him.

He glanced between the three of us, but didn't do anything other than nod his head and lead us out of the club.

Siobhan sat between us on the back seat of the SUV, while Jason drove through the quiet streets. Luca was sprawled on the opposite side, completely at ease flicking through his cell, unaware or uncaring of the tension I could feel building.

I reached out and dropped my arm across Siobhan's shoulders. She tensed beneath my touch but didn't pull away. I wondered how long it would be before she put the brakes on what was happening. Rolling my head sideways, I placed my lips against her ear.

"Do you remember the night we talked about our fantasy bucket lists?" I whispered. "You said you'd always wanted a threesome. You told me that you thought the idea of two men focused completely on you was hot ... do you remember that?" She ignored me, but I felt a shiver run through her and her nipples beaded beneath the thin dress she wore. "We'll be at the motel in a few minutes. If you want to back out, I can tell Jason to take us all back to the bus. No harm, no foul. But the minute we enter the motel room, Red... you better remember your safe word, because you're going to need it."

My hand gripped her chin to turn her face to mine, and I kissed her, my tongue pushing between lips that parted immediately. The flavor of cherries and tequila exploded on my tongue, from the alcohol and the cherry suckers she loved so much, reminding me how addictive the taste of her was. When I lifted my head, her eyes were closed. I glanced at Luca, who was watching us. Exerting gentle pressure on her jaw, I turned her head to him.

"Taste how sweet she is," I told him, and lowered my mouth to her throat, fingers pushing down the straps of her dress until I could free her breast and stroke over the hardened tip with one finger.

She moaned, the sound swallowed by Luca as he moved closer, capturing her lips with his.

Guarded Addiction

CHAPTER 43

BAD GIRL - AVRIL LAVIGNE (FT MARILYN MANSON)

Siobhan

FOUR MONTHS AGO—NASHVILLE

I was swimming in sensation and tequila. I knew I was on the verge of drunk, not enough for it to be obvious, but I could feel that slight buzz, a numbness at the tip of my nose. Clear signs that I was at the limit of my alcohol intake before I tipped over into a place where I could not be held responsible for my own actions.

But right now I *knew* what I was doing, what I was agreeing to, when Dex whispered in my ear. I knew if I said *anything*, gave any hint that I wasn't comfortable, he would take me back to the bus without argument. I knew I was *safe*, even with the issues between us, and could call a halt to what was happening at any moment.

Tomorrow, I'd acknowledge that maybe it was the drink that was driving me, but tonight... *tonight* I was going to live the fantasy. One thing I'd learned in the crazy short-lived relationship I'd had with Dex was that living in the moment was not always a bad thing. I might regret it tomorrow, but I would have experienced something *new*. Something that, before him, I would have been too scared to admit to, let alone *do*. I *loved* that he had opened my eyes to the understanding that taking a leap, making a crazy decision, giving in to temptation sometimes was not going to kill me.

Luca's kisses were more forceful than Dex's, more demanding. He controlled everything about it, exploring my mouth, my lips, his tongue stroking against mine. I could feel Dex's lips on my breast, his teeth teasing my nipple, tugging slightly on the hoop piercing it.

Hands pulled down the rest of my dress until I was completely uncovered from the waist up, but I didn't care. I couldn't think beyond what their touch was doing to me. Luca's mouth pulled from mine, and he bent his head to my breast.

Two men, two mouths, two very different sensations as they both sucked, licked, and bit at my nipples. My head fell back against the seat, an orgasm ripping through my body and shocking a curse out of me.

Dex lifted his head, and ran his tongue up my throat to my mouth. "Did you just come, Red? From nipple play alone? You're going to need to pace yourself, love, or you won't survive the night. We're not even at the motel yet."

In reply, I slid my hands into his hair and pulled his mouth down onto mine. He chuckled, resisted my attempts to kiss him, and cupped a hand around my jaw.

"What's your safe word? Do you remember?" he whispered,

too low for Luca to hear.

"Pineap—" His mouth swallowed the rest of the word.

"We're here. I've booked you a room. Here's the key." Jason's voice intruded and I jerked my mouth from Dex's and attempted to cover my breasts.

Luca's hands caught my wrists and held them still, never stopping his teasing of my nipple with his tongue.

"I'm parked right outside the door you need to aim for." Dex's bodyguard continued, no indication of what he thought about the scene playing out in the back of his car evident in his voice. "I'll wait out here."

Luca lifted his head, flicked my nipple with one finger, then dragged my dress back up. Dex climbed out of the car first, held out his hand to me and helped me out, Luca followed. Both men wrapped their arms around my waist and guided me toward the door Jason had indicated.

Dex unlocked it and ushered me inside. Luca flicked on the light, Dex locked the door, and then both men turned to face me.

"Take the dress off," Luca said.

Before I could react, Dex moved around until he was behind me, and his fingers hooked into the hem of my dress and slowly pulled it upwards.

"Lift your arms," he whispered against my ear.

Luca watched, his eyes following the movement of the dress as it was peeled away from my skin, up over my hips, my stomach, my breasts, and then off over my head.

"And the panties," he directed.

"Keep your arms up, baby, and arch your back. Show him how gorgeous your tits are." Dex kissed his way down my spine as he crouched and dragged my panties down my legs, until I could step out of them.

I fought against the need to cover myself, saw Luca smile as if he knew what I was thinking, and stiffened my arms, linking my fingers together and arching my back to push my breasts forward.

"Turn around," he instructed.

I did, turning slowly until I faced Dex. Warmth at my back told me Luca had moved closer. His hands closed over my hips and pulled me back against him, his erection pressing against my ass. Dex stepped forward and I was sandwiched between them.

"Are you sure you want this?" Luca asked, his head bending so he could kiss my shoulder. "We can still stop."

I caught Dex's eyes. He was silent, his blue eyes dark and unreadable, but his dick was hard against my thigh. I shivered, the idea of having both of them, feeling them both pressed up against me, sent a frisson of excitement through me.

"I want this," I forced the words out. Not because I *didn't* want it, but because my teeth were chattering and I was shaking from nervous anticipation.

"Safe word?" Luca spoke again.

"Pineapple," Dex said before I could. "Sweet yet acidic." He leaned close and pressed two fingers against my cheek. "But if your mouth is too full to speak, you can use two fingers to tap one of us on the arm or leg. Two taps for stop, three for slow down." He tapped my face gently. "Got it?"

I nodded.

Luca's hand slid from my hip around my stomach and up to cup one breast and lift it, almost in offering. I saw a smile flicker across Dex's face before he dipped his head and ran his tongue around my nipple. A hand wrapped around my wrist and lowered my arm, directed my hand between my legs until my fingers were sliding into my own wetness.

"There's something about watching a woman make herself come," Luca breathed against my ear. "Seeing how they touch themselves, fuck their own fingers, taste their own juices. It can tell a man a lot about what the woman they're with needs. Show us what you need, little Spitfire."

His arm around my waist tightened and I was drawn backwards. Dex matched us step for step, and then I was guided down onto the bed, hands on my thighs pulling my legs apart, another on my wrist keeping my hand between my legs. Those hands joined mine, fingers slippery with my arousal, circling my clit, pinching, stroking, until I was panting with the effort not to come.

Dex leaned over me, his mouth finding mine in a searing kiss and I felt two fingers push inside me, then another... and a fourth.

Christ, it was both of them.

I whimpered into Dex's mouth, my back arching up to meet the thrusts of their fingers.

"If you come," Luca's voice was low in my ear, "we'll have to start all over again." His teeth nipped at the sensitive skin beneath my jaw.

"But if you don't," Dex whispered against my mouth, "we'll have to try even harder to make you lose control."

They both laughed softly when I opened my eyes and attempted to glare at them, but succeeded only in crying out when Luca's teeth closed over my nipple, and Dex's hand wrapped around my throat to trap the breath I tried to suck in.

Guarded Addiction

CHAPTER 11

DO IT FOR ME - ROSENFELD

Dex

FOUR MONTHS AGO - NASHVILLE

She looked like a goddess of sin, splayed out on the bed, pussy glistening with her arousal, fingers digging into the sheets while Luca teased her nipples into stiff peaks. Her cheeks were flushed, and her bottom lip caught between her teeth as she fought to stifle her whimpers. Whether that was from Luca's attention on her breasts, or the fact we both had two fingers buried deep inside her was anyone's guess.

I pulled my fingers free and pressed them to her lips.

"Open," I demanded. Her eyelids fluttered open, lips parting. "Good girl. Lick." I pushed my fingers into her mouth and her tongue lapped at them, tasting herself.

She shifted restlessly, her other hand reaching up to clutch at my shirt. "I need you naked," she pulled her mouth away from my fingers to say. "Please?"

For a moment, I wondered if she'd forgotten we weren't alone, but then her head turned and she plucked at Luca's shoulder. He rose up, without speaking, and dragged his shirt off, tossed it to the floor and then settled beside her on the mattress.

"Think it's time you paid for those orgasms, little Spitfire," he said, his hands going to the buttons of his jeans and popping them open.

Siobhan watched him, her green eyes focused on his fingers as they opened each button to reveal his hard dick. He caught my eye, winked, and I shook my head, laughing, as I pulled off my own clothes. I knew what those lips could do. Luca was amused now, but he'd be experiencing a very different emotion as soon as his dick was free and she could wrap her mouth around it.

I stilled as a surge of … *something* … went through me. Jealousy? No way. Luca and I shared all the time.

But this is Siobhan, a voice whispered.

I shrugged it off. "Roll over, Red." I tapped her thigh. "Up on your hands and knees."

She moved languidly, rolling onto her stomach and then slowly rose up on her knees, putting her ass at the perfect height for my dick. I smoothed my palm over her silky skin, and down her leg, tugging it further apart from the other, and dipped my fingers back into her pussy. A shiver rocked her, and she pushed against my hand.

Luca rose from the bed to strip out of his jeans, and then settled back onto the mattress, fisting his dick.

"Bring your mouth over here," he told her, reached out a hand to wrap in her hair and used it to pull her down onto her elbows.

I watched as her mouth slid over the end of his dick, her eyes closing as she angled her head to take him as deep as she could. I ignored the sharp pang of ... *whatever it was* ... and reached for the condom in my jeans pocket. Taking it out, I tore it open and rolled it over my dick, stepped back up behind Siobhan and eased myself into her. She groaned around Luca's erection, one hand reaching back to clutch at my thigh.

My eyes closed as I sank into her body. Fuck, she felt good... *too* good. Had she always felt this good and I hadn't realized because I'd always been high more often than not when we fucked?

Her nails dug into my leg, and I realized I'd stopped moving. Shaking my head, I drove myself deeper into her, searching out her clit with my fingers so I could play with her. My fingers found the piercing decorating it and my mind flashed back to when she'd got it. I'd spread her open on the chair in the tattoo parlor and eaten her out, got her pretty little clit good and excited, making it easier for the piercing to happen.

"D?" Luca's voice dragged me out of the memory and I lifted my eyes to meet his.

He was frowning at me, one hand in Siobhan's hair, holding her still. I didn't speak but whatever he saw on my face made him tug Siobhan's mouth off his dick. Swinging his legs off the bed, he stood and reached for his jeans.

"You know," he said, a smile teasing one corner of his mouth. "I think I'm done for the night. Too much bourbon. I'm fucked. I'm going back to the bus. I'll send Jason back to get you."

He patted my shoulder as he walked past, pulling on his clothes as he went. When the click of the door told me he'd left the room, I reached forward, wound my hand around Siobhan's hair and yanked her head back because I realized, once Luca left, that I was *fucking* furious. Anger was the feeling that had been slicing through me while I watched her sucking Luca's dick. Fury that she'd willingly agreed to being shared.

"What the *actual* fuck?" I snarled and shoved her away from me. Her eyes snapped open at my angry tone.

I stepped away from the bed, stooped, found her dress and threw it at her.

"Put your fucking clothes back on."

She twisted on the bed, dress clutched to her chest. "*You* wanted this."

"Did I?" My voice was flat as I disposed of the condom and dressed. Carefully tucking my still-hard dick into my pants. That was what she did to me. Even when I was angry with her, angry with *myself* for pushing the situation we were in, I still fucking wanted her.

She'd been driving me crazy for the entire month we'd been on tour, watching me with that fucking cherry sucker stuck in her mouth. Tormenting me with brief touches as she moved around the bus we were all living on, fluttering her eyelashes, pursing her lips, making me *want* her.

Well, *congratu-fucking-lations*, it worked. I spun back to the bed where she was still sitting, her eyes huge as she reached up to pull the dress over her head, her breasts rising, and I felt myself harden more.

Oh, what the fuck ...

I almost sighed out loud in defeat when I kicked back out of my jeans and moved back to the bed, my hands finding the material of her dress and throwing it across the room.

I shoved her back onto the mattress, followed her down and pinned her there, my body heavy on hers. My hand wrapped around her throat, and I forced her head up to look at me.

"You will forget how he tasted, how he felt, and how he touched you," I told her through gritted teeth. "You will forget *everything* except how it feels when *I'm* fucking you. Do you understand me?" Her eyes widened at the aggression in my voice. "You don't need to speak. I don't want to fucking talk to you right now. Just nod."

Anger sparked in her green eyes and she glared up at me.

"Fucking ... nod," I ground out.

She gave me a jerky nod, as much as she could with my hand still gripping her throat.

"If you need to fuck, you find *me*. Got it?" Another nod and her tongue snaked across her lips. "Hands above your head." I released her throat and stood. Searching out my belt, I bent and picked it up.

Turning back to the bed, I found Siobhan had done as I'd demanded, arms stretched above her head. I leaned forward, looped my belt around her wrists, then snapped it tight and buckled it around the headboard, leaving enough slack for her to turn onto her stomach if I needed her to. She didn't say a word, watching me out of those green eyes. I rounded the bed, curled my fingers around her ankles and pulled her legs apart so I could crawl between them.

"I want you to describe what I'm doing," I told her. "Every single thing." I ran my tongue over the outer lips of her pussy. "Start talking, Red."

"No." Her voice was defiant.

I nudged her legs wider, until every part of her was on display to me. "Then you don't get to come. I'll fucking edge you all night long until you do as I say. Until you learn that this," I dipped my head and swept one long lick over her clit. "This is *mine*."

"Fuck you, Dex."

My smile was cruel. "Yes, yes, you will. But not until you beg me for it."

She tried to hold out, to stay silent, but I knew *exactly* how to make her scream, how to make her beg and I used that knowledge ruthlessly to take her right to the edge of orgasm again and again, until she was sobbing breathlessly.

"Tell me what I'm doing to you," I demanded again, and she shook her head, biting her lip.

I added a third finger to the two I was already pumping inside her and used my teeth to tug on the barbel piercing the hood of her clit. She cried out, hips jerking upwards, but she still refused to speak.

"If we were back at my place, I'd have you on your hands and knees." I circled her clit with my tongue, then leaned back. Easing my fingers out of her body, I rolled her onto her stomach and lifted her up, so her ass was in the air and her face was buried into the cushions with her arms still bound above her. "I'd use your own arousal as lube so I could slip a finger into your ass." As I spoke, I stroked backwards to that tight little hole.

She tensed.

"I'd use one finger to prepare you," I pressed my fingertip against her ass, pushing it in slowly. When she whimpered and tried to pull away, I reached around and pinched her nipple sharply in warning. "I'd fuck your ass with that finger until I thought you were ready to take another one. And then I'd add a second." Another finger joined the first, and I heard her breathing hitch. "I'd fuck your ass with my fingers until I thought you were stretched wide enough to take my dick." I leaned over her, using my free hand to grip my dick and rub it against her pussy. "And then I'd fuck you until you screamed." I pulled my fingers free and reached for a condom. "But you're not being a good girl for me, Red."

I rolled the condom on and stroked my dick against her again. "You're soaking wet. Anyone would think you're enjoying what I'm doing to you. But you won't tell me, so we'll never know." I pinched her clit, and she bucked against my hand. "Want to reconsider your decision? What am I doing to you, Red?" I whispered and reached around to drag a nail over her nipple.

There was a beat of silence, broken only by her panting

breaths, then whispered words spilled from her lips, stilted at first. Her confidence grew when I groaned at how she told me pinching her nipples made her wet. How being helpless with her hands tied above her head excited her. How full she felt when I pushed my dick inside her. How *fucking* turned on she was by what I was doing to her.

I played with her body like it was my bass guitar, made her scream for me until her words became incoherent sobs, pleas for me to let her come. She pulled against my belt restraining her wrists. The more I tormented her, the dirtier her words became, until I forgot I was angry with her, angry with *myself*, and I lost myself to the ecstasy that was her body.

Guarded Addiction

CHAPTER 45

WHERE IS MY MIND - MILKY CHANCE

Siobhan

PRESENT

A muscle ticked in Dex's jaw as we were driven to NFG Records with Karl and the two lawyers in the back of the car. His replies to Karl were monosyllabic, refusing to be drawn into a discussion of why he'd punched the reporter. He stared moodily out of the window, the fingers of one hand drumming against his thigh.

I sat beside him, fingers curled into my lap, praying the questions wouldn't be directed at me. I didn't want to talk about that night in Nashville. I didn't even want to *think* about it, or what had happened afterward. Nerves had my stomach twisted up in knots, and I chewed on my lip waiting for Karl's attention to swing to me. When the car pulled up in the underground parking lot for NFG Records without that happening, my short-lived relief turned to tension when Forgotten Legacy's manager looked at us.

"Both of you upstairs to my office *now*," he barked and climbed out of the car.

Dex didn't acknowledge his words. The two lawyers glanced over at him and followed Karl, Jared slamming the door shut behind him and sealing us both inside. When Dex moved, twisting to look at me, I couldn't withhold a flinch. His brows pulled together.

"You've reopened the cuts in your lip." He touched my bottom lip with his thumb. "What did the cops say to you?"

"They wanted to know why David was in my apartment."

"Did you tell them what happened?"

"They didn't believe me."

"Accused you of giving him mixed signals, did they?"

I nodded. He sighed.

"I'm sorry, Cherry Pie."

"Dexter!" Karl bellowed, making me jump. "Don't try my patience!"

"Who killed him, Dex?" I asked.

He quirked an eyebrow. "Karl? No one yet, but the day is young."

"You know who I mean."

"Colton? Red, I was with you. How would I know who killed him?" He sounded convincing, but I didn't believe him. He *knew* what had happened to David, but he wasn't going to tell me. "Karl's going to have a coronary if we don't get moving." He threw open the car door and stepped out.

I followed him more slowly, wincing a little. My body was starting to feel the effects of what had happened the night before; bruises throbbing and my ribs aching. I must have made some kind of noise because Dex stopped and twisted to face me. His blue eyes tracked over my face and he leaned past me to rap on the driver's side window of the car. The window lowered slightly.

"Hey, Diesel, can you go back to the house and pick up Siobhan's prescription? It's in the bathroom."

"Sure thing," his bodyguard replied. "Don't leave the building until I get back."

"If we do, I'll let you know where to find us."

"You didn't have to do that," I said as the sound of the car's engine echoed around the parking lot.

"You're hurting. Don't be a martyr, Red." He draped an arm over my shoulders and turned me toward the elevator bay. "Let's go before a search party is sent out to track us down."

It felt like walking into the principal's office when we finally reached the floor where Karl Daniels was waiting for us. He stood in the doorway, his expression stern and I felt nerves fluttering in my stomach as we crossed the thick, expensive carpet and came to a stop in front of him.

"Inside," he barked at Dex, who gave a faint sigh, urged me forward and into the office. "Sit."

With a nervous glance at Dex, I sank into one of the seats. Dex sprawled into the one beside me, legs outstretched, oozing with a completely relaxed rock star vibe. Karl strode around to the opposite side of the desk and sat. He regarded us impassively for what felt like a lifetime and then sighed.

"In all the years I've been involved with band management,

I have *never* had to deal with one of my stars being arrested on suspicion of murder. Drug busts, trashing hotel rooms, fighting, even orgies, but *murder*? No, that's definitely a first for me."

"I didn't murder anyone," Dex said.

"And yet the police felt they had enough to pull you in and question you. So, tell me, Dex, what *did* you do?"

"Stopped an attempted rape." Dex cast an apologetic look in my direction when I flinched. "I'm sorry, Cherry Pie, but that's what was happening."

"I don't think he would—" Dex's derisive snort cut me off.

"You were out cold, how the fuck would you know what he would do? What I walked in on was him pulling his dick out, Siobhan." He jumped up from where he sat and spun to rest his hands on the arm of my seat, looking over me. "What the fuck do you think he was going to do with it? Take a photo and send someone a fucking dick pic?"

I blinked up at him, the echo from his shout bouncing off the walls of the small office.

We stared at each other, and then he jerked upright, rubbing the back of his neck with one hand.

"Fuck sake," he muttered. "I need a drink."

"There's bottled water in the refrigerator," Karl told him and Dex's lips twisted.

"Not the kind of drink I was hoping for."

"Well, why don't you go and see if there's anything in Marley's office? I can talk to Siobhan while you're gone," Karl suggested.

I stiffened. *Talk to me?* But Dex didn't seem to see anything unusual about Karl's words and was already moving toward the door before I could protest. I rose to my feet, meaning to go after him.

"Sit down, Siobhan," Karl said, his voice quiet and firm.

I froze, casting a look at Dex's retreating form.

"I'm not going to bite, but I need to talk to you while he's distracted. Please, sit down."

I lowered myself slowly back onto the seat, fingers clutching at the arms, ready to bolt at the first opportunity. I couldn't even say why I was so nervous about being alone with the man who managed Forgotten Legacy and its members' lives. That wasn't me. It wasn't who I was, I didn't get shy or nervous around people.

"Luca told me what happened last night." He wasted no time in getting straight to the point. "He also said he thought that maybe there was more to things between you and Dex than anyone realized or understood. So, Ms. Rawlings, would you like to tell me what I'm missing?"

I swallowed. "I don't... I mean..."

"Please don't lie to me. Not only have I managed Forgotten Legacy for almost ten years, I also manage Black Rosary and, let me assure you, the boys in Forgotten Legacy don't even come close to what Marley and his boys got up to in their youth. There's *nothing* you can tell me that will shock or surprise me. But I need to know whether what you two are hiding is going to affect the rest of the band."

"No, it's nothing like that."

"I'm giving you the opportunity to be honest with me here, *before* the media gets hold of all your secrets and emblazons them across their pages for all the world to see. I heard what Jamieson said." He referenced the reporter Dex had punched. "I'm not an idiot, and I was also young once, believe it or not."

I laughed softly at his wry tone.

"My point is, Siobhan, that all boys go through a phase when they're full of spunk and bullshit. They do things which can sometimes have a nasty habit of coming back to ruin them later. Don't be that mistake." He leaned forward, steepling his fingers and looking at me over the top. "So, consider this an opportunity to make sure that doesn't happen."

I bit my lip, winced when it stung, and took a breath. "We got married," I blurted.

Karl snorted. "I *know* that. It was you who called the hospital a few years ago when Dex was picked up off the street. Did you really think I wouldn't have your claims investigated?"

"But ... *how*? I didn't leave my name."

"No, but Dex said it enough times for me to make a connection between his *Cherry Pie* and the girl frantically begging the nurses for information every ten minutes."

My cheeks flamed at hearing the nickname Dex called me come out of Karl's mouth.

"What I want to know is what Jamieson has on you all from Nashville."

I didn't think my cheeks could heat up any more than they

already were, but I could feel myself reddening further.

"Look, I get it. Being on tour with a bunch of rock stars who, more often than not, do everything to excess, can be exciting. If they talked you into something, and I'm fairly sure I know what that something was, and one of them videoed it—"

"*Nothing* happened ... not completely, anyway."

"But *enough* of something happened?"

"Luca left before we did more than fool around," Dex said from behind me, a distinct bite to his voice. "The only thing that fucker will have footage of is us in the club or walking into the motel together. Beyond that, he has nothing."

"Then why did you punch him?"

Dex shrugged, and lifted a beer bottle to his mouth.

"Dex," Karl warned.

"I didn't like the way he was talking about Siobhan."

"We were outside a *police* station."

"Should be glad I didn't murder him, then." He set the now-empty beer bottle on the desk. "Where's Luca?"

"The police released him before you and, *unlike* you, he behaved himself and went straight home."

"Sure he did."

I shifted in my seat, trying to ease the ache in my ribs and Dex swung to face me.

"Ready to go?" he asked.

"Go? I thought we were supposed to wait for Diesel?"

"You need to get home, take some painkillers and relax. He's taking too long." Apprehension at the thought of going back to my apartment must have shown on my face. "*My* home, Cherry Pie. If you think I'm letting you go back to that place, you're crazy. I had Diesel pack up as much of your stuff as he could and take it to the house last night. We'll go back and you can check and see if he missed anything important."

"I can't stay with you, Dex." People would talk, dig. My parents would find out what had happened. The thought made me nauseous.

"It's already done. Anyway, your apartment will be classed as part of the crime scene and taped up so no one can disturb anything."

I stared at him.

Crime scene?

And then everything crashed down onto me—David breaking into my apartment, finding him in my bed, trying to force himself on me, finding out he'd been killed ... and my mind blanked.

Guarded Addiction

CHAPTER 16

I DON'T LOVE YOU - MY CHEMICAL ROMANCE

Dex
PRESENT

"*Fuck!*" I caught Siobhan as her body swayed forward out of her seat and swung her up into my arms.

Casting a look around, I strode over to the small couch in the corner of Karl's office and carefully placed her onto it. "Do you have smelling salts or anything?" I demanded.

"Why, for the love of God, would I have something like that in my office?" he retorted, rising to his feet and following me. "Stop yelling and give her a minute. She's already coming around, see?"

"What the fuck happened?" She'd lost all color, even in her lips. The bruising on her face stood out against the stark paleness of her skin. My mouth dried up, my own vision swimming as my heart-rate increased—the sound loud in my ears—as I pressed two fingers to the pulse in her neck, needing to make sure she was still with me. Panic threatened, a state I recognised from when I walked into her apartment and found David there.

Her soft moan brought me back to her, and I dropped to my

haunches beside the couch, reaching out to brush her hair from her face.

"Hey, Red," I said gently, no sign of my internal worry showing in my voice or expression. "Look at me, love."

Her head turned toward the sound of my voice, and relief coursed through me when her eyes fluttered open.

"Hey, Rock Star." Her voice was soft, warm, and it twisted my insides because ... how long had it been since she looked at me like that—all the barriers down and her feelings for me shining bright in her eyes? And then realization and memory kicked in, and I saw the warmth in her eyes leach away, to be replaced by wariness as she frowned in confusion.

"Steady," I warned her when she struggled to sit up. "Slow down. You fainted."

"Give the girl some space, Dex," Karl said from behind me. He leaned past me to hand Siobhan a glass of water. "When did you last eat or drink?"

Her eyes jerked to me and I frowned, thinking. "It has to have been before I came to the apartment last night. We didn't have a chance to eat anything this morning because the police turned up before we got out of bed."

Karl's sigh spoke volumes and I bit my tongue so I didn't say anything to make the situation worse. Now wasn't the time to get into an argument with my manager. I heard him moving around the office, and then a click as he picked up the telephone on his desk.

"Merry, can you send someone out to the nearest café

and bring back some sandwiches?" He put his hand over the mouthpiece. "Any dietary needs?"

I shook my head.

"No. Order something of everything. Then can you call…"

I zoned out and returned my attention to Siobhan.

"Are you okay?" She gave me a silent nod. "He's right. You haven't had anything to eat or drink. That, delayed shock, and stress over this morning are all going to be factors in you fainting."

"Speaking from experience?"

I fought a smile. *There she was—my sarcastic, fiery Cherry Pie.* I must have failed to keep the amusement from my face because she scowled at me.

"What are you doing, Dex?"

I didn't even pretend to misunderstand her question. "Do you really want to have that conversation here right now?"

"I want to know what game you're playing. Your unpredictability was exciting five years ago, right up to the moment you decided to leave me. But we're older now and I don't want to play games anymore. I'm *tired* of the games, Dex."

"There's no game."

"With you, there's always a game."

"Not this time."

The look she gave me made it clear she didn't believe a word I was saying. Not that I could blame her. Our entire relationship had been built around games, pushing boundaries, stepping outside our comfort zones and into the unknown. Taking chances, taking *risks*.

"Do you remember when you took me to meet your grandmother?" I asked.

"The way I remember it is *you* invited yourself along."

I ignored that. She wasn't wrong. "How is she? Have you been to see her lately?"

"Last weekend."

"Does she know about me?"

"Know *what* about you?" She pushed up into a seated position and I moved to sit beside her.

"That I'm back in your life. That we're together again."

"No. Because you're not and *we're* not."

I shot her an amused look. "Hate to break it to you, Cherry Pie, but we totally are." She opened her mouth to argue and I pressed a finger to her lips. "Okay, so if we're done ... completely over and finished ... why have you never filed for divorce?"

"I didn't know where you were. I had no address for you. I had no intention of ever getting married again. We got married in Vegas, it doesn't count." She reeled off her reasons. "Pick one."

I snorted. "Vegas weddings are still real. If you divorced me, you'd have been entitled to half my assets."

It was her turn to laugh. "You can *keep* your assets. When I married you, I thought you were a broke, crazy stoner with very little to his name."

"And you married me anyway," I pointed out. "Because you loved me."

"I was swept up in your craziness," she argued.

"And you loved me," I told her.

"I didn't. You were good in bed."

"I still am. But that wasn't the reason. You married me because you loved me." I reached for her hand and lifted it to my lips, kissing each finger with each sentence I uttered. "Not many people accept me just the way I am, Red. You knew I took drugs. You knew I drank too much. But you let me into your life anyway. Into your bed. You let me mark your skin, push your limits." I smiled at her. "But, no, I agree, of course you don't love me, but that's all right because it's obvious to everyone that I don't love you either. I didn't corner you on that train because you fascinated me. I didn't come back because you were constantly on my mind. I didn't marry you because I needed to know you were mine." My eyes dropped to the tattoo on her hip, the one she'd changed. "And you didn't let me put my name on your skin to keep me close when we were apart."

The clearing of a throat broke the spell I was weaving and Siobhan snatched her hand back and looked away, but not before I saw the memories taking hold in her eyes. I smiled and looked up at Karl.

"There's food and drinks in the main waiting room. Go and eat something. I've checked in with Diesel. He'll be here soon to take you both home." He gave no indication that he'd overheard anything I said. "Matthew wants you to stay close to home in case the police have any further questions."

"Do you think they will?" I asked.

"I don't know."

"I didn't kill him, Karl. I *wanted* to, but I didn't."

Karl gave an abrupt nod. "I believe you. Get out of here." He waved a hand toward the door. "I have work to do. I swear, between you and Gabe I'm going to be bald before the year is over."

"You live for the drama. It's why you chose to work in the music business ," I told him. Standing, I held out a hand to Siobhan. "Hungry?" When she didn't answer, I reached down and curled my fingers around her wrist. "The correct answer is '*Yes, Dex, I am.*'"

Harper called while we were in the car on our way back to my house and Siobhan spent the majority of the journey fielding questions and reassuring her friend that she was okay.

I don't know if Harper believed her, but *I* wasn't convinced. Not even twenty-four hours had passed since the assault and other than the few short hours of sleep we got before the police arrived, she hadn't had time to stop and process what had happened. There was a reaction coming. I just couldn't predict when it would arrive or what form it would take. But it *would* happen, and I was watching for it.

She was still talking to Harper when Diesel parked outside the house and she followed me inside. I directed her into the kitchen, waited until she was seated at the table, still engrossed in her conversation, then walked upstairs to the bathroom.

Diesel had unpacked her toiletries onto one of the countertops and I sifted through them until I found what I was looking for. Turning to the tub which took the central position in the room, I turned on the faucet and poured a healthy amount of the cherry-scented bubble bath into the water. While that filled, I found towels and placed them close by.

My eyes strayed to the medicine cabinet. I hadn't had a craving to take anything for a couple of days. Not surprising with everything that had been distracting me. Still, knowing there were pills that could give me a high so close to me made my skin itch with a need so strong, it took me by surprise.

"I'm clean," I muttered to myself and turned my back on the cabinet.

I'd come this far, succumbing to the temptation they posed was a backwards step I no longer wanted to take. It didn't stop my body from trying to convince me to do it. It certainly didn't ease the cravings I felt, and I knew it would be *so easy* to slip back into being the happy little space cadet. All it would take was a little push, a whisper stronger than my willpower, and I'd be back inside the cycle of getting high, crashing down, overdosing and, eventually, dying.

A year ago, I wouldn't have cared. I'd have jumped straight back onto the roller coaster and freebased my way to hell. A year ago, a certain redhead hadn't yet crashed back into my orbit and knocked me off the path of self-destruction I was on.

I could admit that losing myself to getting high or stoned made me an easier person to deal with. Without drugs in my system, I was a lot more irritable, prone to mood swings, erratic behavior—but I wasn't about to collapse, froth at the mouth and die. I had to find a way to manage the memories that had driven me to turn to drugs in the first place.

One step at a time, I told myself and turned to check the temperature of the water in the tub, cut off the flow of water, and straightened to leave the bathroom so I could go in search of Siobhan.

She was exactly where I left her—sitting at the kitchen table—but her call with Harper had ended. She looked up when I walked in.

"Follow me," I instructed her, waited for her to stand and led the way out of the kitchen.

When I opened the bathroom door and ushered her inside, she stopped and turned to look at me.

"Strip," I told her. "And get in the tub."

"Is this some kind of new kink I don't know about?" she asked slowly, her eyes darting from the bubble-topped water to me and back again.

I laughed. "If I could think of a way to turn it into something kinky, trust me, I would. But no, I would have done this last night but you were out cold by the time we got back here." I reached out to tweak a lock of her hair. "Get naked, and get wet." I smirked and stepped closer, lowering my head until our lips were almost touching. "And then if you want kinky *and* you're a good girl, I'll make you wetter," I whispered.

Guarded Addiction

CHAPTER 47

KEEPING ME ALIVE - JONATHAN ROY

Siobhan

PRESENT

My eyes shifted from Dex, ignoring his innuendo, and went back to the tub filled with fragranced water and bubbles. I could see the steam rising and any thought of arguing went out of the window. I peeled off my top, stepped out of the sweats I was wearing and moved toward the bath. My bra and panties were next, thrown to one side seconds before I stepped into the water, sank down into the heat and closed my eyes with a moan of delight.

"Scoot forward." Dex's hand on my shoulder snapped my eyes back open, in time to see one long tattooed leg lift and step behind me.

"What are you doing?" The water sloshed as he lowered himself into it and settled behind me, legs appearing either side of mine.

"Relax, Cherry Pie." An arm snaked around my waist and slid me backwards until I half-reclined against his chest.

"How can I relax when I can feel your dick against my back?"

"I could put it somewhere else," he offered and squeezed my waist when I tensed. "I'm teasing, Red. Relax. I'm not going to try anything."

His fingers brushed my hair away from one shoulder and I felt his lips press a kiss to my bare skin.

"I thought you said you weren't going to do anything?" I said, and hated the breathlessness in my voice.

"I'm not. Lie back and close your eyes." He slid down into the water and the palm on my stomach exerted gentle pressure until I was lying on top of him. "There's something soothing about a hot bath, don't you think?"

Sure, I thought. *When you're alone!* There was absolutely *nothing* soothing about being wrapped up in Dex's arms, naked in a tub full of water.

"Cherry Pie?" Dex broke the silence a few minutes later, his voice a husky whisper close to my ear. I jumped at the sound, and he chuckled. "You're not relaxing."

"And that surprises you because …" I was amazed my voice came out steady because my heart was racing.

"Because I'm not doing anything."

"Dex, we're naked in a bath together."

He was silent for a moment and then gave a soft laugh. "Couldn't exactly climb in with my clothes on. That'd be weird." He shifted position, drawing his legs back so he could raise up onto his knees. Warm water cascaded over me as he picked up a bath sponge and ran it over my shoulders and back. "Do you remember the night we got married?"

"Of course I do."

"When we got back to my apartment in Vegas, we took a bath together. Just lay there in the water, you remember that?"

I hadn't until he mentioned it. I tried not to think about those times too often. It hurt too much.

"I've never felt so ... *at peace*. I could have stayed there for hours." His voice was a soft caress, matching the gentle strokes of the sponge as he washed my body. "I didn't feel the need to get high, stoned, or drunk." His lips touched the back of my neck. "I thought doing this might help you relax a little."

I twisted in the water to face him. "You never told me that." The words came out like an accusation.

A smile tugged at his lips. "We were having fun, remember? No pressure, no strings." Leaning forward, he kissed the tip of my nose before rising to his feet so he could climb out of the tub. He reached for a towel to wrap around his hips. "This isn't going the way I planned it in my head," he laughed.

"What were we thinking?" I blurted. "We got *married* without really knowing each other." I'd asked myself that so many times.

Why had I married him? Why had I let him talk me into doing something so dramatically life-altering? Piercings, tattoos—all things that wouldn't affect me long-term, but *marriage*? I'd married a man I barely knew, let his charm and the attraction I felt stop me from thinking logically. The result? A broken heart and years of questioning whether the overdose I'd witnessed had been my fault.

It had taken me over a year to reach a point where I was willing to let a guy close to me, but even then I wouldn't entertain anything serious. Party, have fun, no attachments—that was my outlook and I repeatedly told myself it worked for me. Until the day I walked into Damnation's VIP room and set eyes on the tattooed and pierced bass guitarist again.

"Why did you do it?" I asked.

He crouched beside the tub and stroked a hand down my cheek, his blue eyes tracking over my face. He didn't need to ask what I meant. It was written all over his face. Catching his lip piercing between his teeth, he toyed with it and, for a long moment, I thought he wasn't going to answer me, but then he sighed.

"Look, Siobhan, I *know* I'm an addict, okay? I say I'm not because admitting it means ..." He broke off to shake his head. "I don't know ... that I'm *weak*? That it controls *me* and not the other way around. I didn't want you to be a part of that. Meeting the band, finding out what I do for a living, who I am? Those things alone can be intimidating for anyone who isn't part of our world. Add that to my drug abuse and it was a recipe for disaster. I didn't want your first introduction to the band, the life I lived, to be me overdosing and puking all over the place. That would cement you as someone who enabled my addiction, and I didn't want that for you." He looked away, blowing out a breath. "So I cut you loose."

"I called the hospital. No one would tell me anything. I thought you'd died." The memory of the panic I felt, the sickness twisting my insides when the ambulance drove away with him inside, came roaring back.

"I'm *so* sorry, Red. You have to believe that. But it was the right thing to do at that moment in time. I needed to hit rock bottom to get a clear view of what I was doing to myself." He picked up a towel, unfolded it and held it spread wide between his hands. "Ready to get out?"

I stood and stepped out. Dex wound the towel around my body. He didn't move straight away, his arms holding me close. His chest moved and he drew in a breath, as though he was about to speak, then his arms dropped and he stood back.

"Your clothes are in the guest room. I'll let you get dry and dressed. Meet me downstairs when you're done?"

CHAPTER 48

COTTON CANDY - YUNGBLUD

Dex
PRESENT

I backed out of the bathroom, attempting not to look like I was running away—but I couldn't deny to myself that was exactly what I was doing.

What had I been thinking by climbing into the tub with her?

I should have left her alone to relax instead of wrapping myself around her like some kind of weird creeper. When she stripped out of her clothes and I saw the marks David had left on her ... I needed to hold her, to reassure myself she was here, *with me*, and safe.

"Hey, Rock Star?" her voice said from behind me and I wheeled to face her as she exited the bathroom, surprised she was already done.

She came toward me, and it took my brain a minute to catch up with my body when her arms snaked around my neck and pulled my head down so she could kiss me.

"Red?" I broke away from her lips long enough to say her

name, meaning to caution her to be careful because of the damage David had done to her lips, but her fingers speared into my hair and dragged my mouth back onto hers.

She moved forward, pressed against me and kept going, forcing me to move backwards along the hallway until I hit the wall and then she pulled her mouth from mine.

"You know this is a terrible idea?" she whispered, but there was a gleam of humor in her eyes.

I wrapped a lock of her hair around one finger. "The best ones usually are." I twisted; changed our position and found her mouth again. When I finally came up for air a few minutes later, I ran my nose along hers. "Want to relocate to my bedroom?"

I didn't give her the chance to reply, wrapping an arm around her waist so I could lift her off her feet, and strode into my room.

She didn't argue, looping her arms around my neck and pressing kisses along my jaw instead as I walked inside, and kicked the door shut behind me. Reaching back, I unhooked her hold on my neck, and holding her hands in mine, led her toward the bed.

My hands were shaking when I peeled away the towel from around her body and cast it to one side. I couldn't say why, but this felt different, like it was the first time I'd had her in my arms, in my bed. I think she felt it too, because her palm trembled when she rested it on my side, atop the tattoo I'd got the day I stole her away to Vegas and married her.

"I didn't recognize what this was when you got it," she whispered, letting her fingers trail along the trunk and branches of the tree wrapping around my left side and covering my chest and back. "But I do now."

"What is it?" I dipped my head to press a trail of kisses along her shoulder.

"A cherry blossom tree. But it wasn't this big or detailed when you got it."

"It's grown over the years, and spread its branches all over my body." I sat on the mattress and pulled her down with me, until we lay side by side. While she stroked over my tattoos, my fingers found the one on her hip. "Why did you change it?"

"I was angry with you. After Nashville and then the night in South Carolina."

"You kept it all those years and *that* was the trigger to have it changed?" My fingertips spelled out what it used to say—*Dex's Cherry Pie*. She'd had it redesigned to read *Sex & Cherry Pie*.

"When I saw you with Luca," I admitted roughly. "I didn't like it. I'm sure you've heard the rumors, the talk about the things we liked to do together ... the sharing. And I'll be honest, Red, I thought watching you with Luca would be hot." I cleared my throat. "The reality was, I *hated* it. I hated seeing his hands on you, his mouth, but I didn't recognize it for what it was. I thought I was in control, I thought I was cool with us all hooking up and having fun. But when I saw you take his dick in your mouth, I knew I was actually punishing myself for the way I'd behaved."

My hands stroked over her thigh, her stomach. I flicked the silver charm piercing her navel, and smiled when I realized it was a cherry.

Her favorite fruit, favorite scent, favorite color.

And mine.

I shifted closer, my hand reaching her breast, curving over the soft swell, my thumb seeking out her nipple and sweeping over it in a gentle caress. It hardened beneath my touch, and she arched slightly, pushing herself more firmly against my palm. I ignored her. She liked me to be rough, loved when I manhandled her, pinned her down and possessed her. She protested, but she liked it when I pushed her limits and took her outside of her comfort zone. Her protests were simply part of the game we played and why I'd given her a safeword. If she really wasn't into something, she knew she could say it.

But today I needed something else from her, something *different*.

Rolling, I leaned over her and lowered my head until our mouths were almost touching. "There aren't many things I regret doing," I said quietly. "But that night in Nashville is high on the very short list. I shouldn't have pushed you into it."

"You didn't." Her reply was soft. "I made the choice to go with you both that night."

"You wouldn't have done it, if I hadn't pushed your buttons." I kissed the corner of her mouth. "I'm thankful that Luca realized something wasn't right because, I gotta tell you, love, if we'd gone through with that … I'm not sure I could have dealt with it afterwards." Another kiss to the opposite corner. "Apparently, I'm not the sharer I thought I was."

Her green eyes were locked on mine, and I wanted to fall into them and forget the entire world around us. I dropped my forehead to rest against her shoulder, breathing in her scent of cherries.

"I've fucked up so many times, Red, and in so many ways. But chasing you and marrying you? *That* wasn't a mistake. That was the best decision I ever made."

My lips found the imprint of David's fingertips on her throat and I placed a kiss to each mark he'd left there.

"I hate seeing what he did to you."

I searched out each bruise he'd left, kissed every one as I made my way down her body, until I was kneeling between her thighs and my mouth was where I wanted to be the most.

I didn't taste her straight away. I wanted to prolong the anticipation—for me *and* her ... or maybe I wanted to torture us both. Instead I nibbled along her inner thigh, kissed my way back up to her navel, and down the other side.

"You know what amazes me?" I asked suddenly, resting my head against her thigh and looking up along her body.

"No," her voice was a breathless whisper, thick with desire and need.

"The fact that we're right here. You've let me *this* close to you." I ran my tongue along the outer edges of her pussy. "After everything I've done, everything I put you through, you still give yourself to me." I licked her again, felt her piercing against my tongue and flicked it. "Do you remember what I said to you in the bathroom?"

"N-no?"

"If you were a good girl …" I pushed two fingers inside her. "And you *are* a good girl, aren't you, Cherry Pie?" I circled her clit with my tongue. "If you're a good girl, I'll make you wetter."

She whispered my name, and her fingers found their way into my hair while I used my tongue and my fingers to fuck her to orgasm.

When she was quivering, hovering on the edge, I rose up until I could kiss her, thrusting my tongue inside her mouth and used my hand to stroke my dick over the slick wetness of her pussy.

"I want to fuck you bare, Red. I want to feel you around me without anything separating us." I kissed her again. "I'm clean. I've been tested. I haven't been with anyone but you in almost a year."

I was tormenting myself, sliding my dick along her clit, and then withdrawing. Her nails dug into my ass and I stilled, unsure whether she was saying no or yes. I held myself above her, one arm braced to the side of her head, my other hand around my dick, waiting for her to tell me what she wanted to do.

Her green eyes gazed up at me, and I felt like she was staring straight into my soul. She smiled, her fingers covered mine where they gripped my dick and I felt my stomach flip.

"I trust you," she whispered and guided me into her body.

I jerked awake from the dream, eyes snapping open, my heartbeat rapid and loud in my own ears. It took me a minute to get my bearings, to remember that I was in my own home, my own bed and not a thirteen-year-old boy trying to stop blood from gushing out of a knife wound.

"Dex?" A sleepy voice beside me spoke my name, and the sound of it was what I needed to pull me that final step out of the memory.

I rolled onto my side, wrapped an arm around her waist and drew her against me.

"Bad dream," I murmured into her hair. "Go back to sleep."

She nuzzled into my shoulder, her hand reaching up to wind around my neck. "What was it? Your heart is racing."

"Nothing. I don't remember." I didn't want to lie to her, but I didn't want to talk about it either, not right now. I eased out of her arms and sat up. "I'm going to get a drink," I said, twisting to drop a kiss to her cheek. "Go back to sleep, I'll be back soon."

I waited until she'd burrowed back under the covers before I stood. I watched her for a minute, unable to tear my eyes away, part of me wanting to crawl back under the covers, wake her up and make love to her again.

Make love.

I almost laughed aloud. That wasn't what I did—sex was always about getting off, not making a connection. It was fooling around, having fun, *fucking*. But last night? That had been something else, something new, something *deeper*.

I gave myself a shake, grabbed a pair of sweats from on top of the dresser, and crept silently out of the bedroom, before I let temptation rule me.

In the kitchen, I opened the refrigerator and grabbed a bottle of beer, then hesitated, Siobhan's words from a few days ago coming back to me.

"You're an addict! It doesn't matter what it is. Drink, drugs—you're not supposed to be touching any of it."

Deep down, I knew she was right. It wasn't only drugs I had an unhealthy interest in, alcohol was a close second. I looked at the amount of beer bottles in the refrigerator, mentally catalogued how many bottles of tequila I had. Chewing on my lip ring, I walked across to the sink, twisted the cap off the bottle and poured it away.

Drugs and alcohol had been my crutch for years, a way to mute the nightmares caused from watching one of my best friends die in my arms. Maybe it was time to find a new way to deal with the memories, a way that wouldn't send me to join him in death.

Guarded Addiction

CHAPTER 49

MY NAME IS HUMAN – HIGHLY SUSPECT

Dex
AGE 13

"Hey, Dex, wait up." I slammed my locker shut and turned to watch as Luciano and Lazaro Tallorico loped toward me.

Classed as identical twins, most people couldn't tell them apart, but I could. They weren't quite as identical as people thought. Not when you *knew* them. There were little things that you picked up if you spent enough time with them. Laz's eyes were a deep dark brown, while Luca's eyes were a slightly lighter shade with gold flecks. Luca was an inch taller than his twin, but Laz was broader across the shoulders. Laz was louder, more aggressive, more ... *everything*.

One thing they did have in common, though, was their talent for getting into trouble. If something was going on in school, you could almost guarantee that Laz would be involved, with Luca backing him up.

Laz hooked an arm around my neck and rubbed the top of my head with his knuckles. I elbowed him in the stomach.

"Fuck off, Laz."

"Someone's grumpy today," Luca commented.

"The parents were up half the night fighting. I didn't get much sleep."

"Should have cut loose and come to our place," Laz said.

"It didn't kick off until after midnight. There was no way I was going to get past them, so I just plugged in my earphones and listened to music." I slung my bag over one shoulder. "We better get to class."

"It's only math. We could ditch it instead?" Laz suggested.

"I've got a better idea." Luca nudged me and nodded toward the lone figure walking down the corridor toward us.

Christian Baker—the football team captain's brother—alone, without his friends. It was almost too good to be true. I glanced around, saw Luca smirking on one side, while Laz was cracking his knuckles on my right.

None of us were bullies, but Christian made everyone's life miserable and hid behind the popularity of his brother to make sure he got away with it. He and his friends had caught me unawares a week ago, smashed up my cell phone and destroyed the one good jacket I had. Luca and Laz had been out for his blood since, but he was *always* surrounded by the football team which made him untouchable … until now.

We waited for him to notice us, but he was engrossed in whatever he was doing on his cell, and didn't spot us standing there until he was almost on top of us … and by then it was too late.

Luca and Laz moved as one, stepping forward on each side of him and hooked their arms beneath his and lifted him off his feet.

"Got time for a chat, Baker?" Laz asked.

"Because we *really* want to talk to you," Luca added.

I stepped forward and plucked his cell from his hand. "You're not going to be needing that."

"Shout for help, I *dare* you," Laz said when Christian opened his mouth.

Whatever he heard in Laz's voice stopped him. His teeth snapped back together and he remained silent.

"Why don't we find somewhere quiet to have a chat?" The twins, both a good few inches taller than Christian, manhandled him backwards until we reached one of the bathrooms. I opened the door, and they dragged him in. The door swung shut behind me, and I leaned back against it. Luca and Laz loosened their grip on Christian and stepped back.

"If you touch me, my brother will kill you," he said.

"Oh, we're going to do more than touch you," Laz laughed. He moved forward and prowled around Christian, coming to a stop beside him. Grinning, he draped an arm across the other boy's shoulder. "See, you broke my boy over there's cell, so I think it's time you apologized."

"Fuck you."

"Are you offering? Because sure, I could go for a blowjob right now." He tightened his grip of Christian's shoulders. "It's what the mouth can do and not what it's attached to, right? So if you want to *try* and suck your way out of this, be my guest. Can't make any promises though. Depends how good you are."

"Laz, cut it out," Luca told his brother.

Christian tried to pull out of Laz's grip, and Luca's brother shook his head.

"Not so brave now you don't have your friends here, are you? Are you going to apologize?"

"No."

Without any change in his expression, Laz buried his fist into Christian's stomach and the other boy doubled over.

"Want to change your answer?"

"Fuck you, Tallorico," he wheezed.

Laz tutted. "You're not very quick, are you? Let's try again." He fisted Christian's hair and yanked his head back. "Apologize to my friend," he demanded.

I traded glances with Luca. Neither of us could ever be called the kind of kids who went out of our way to make trouble, we kinda fell into it by following Laz. Out of the three of us, I was the quietest and the smallest, which is why I got targeted a lot. It wasn't that I couldn't take care of myself—one on one, I was a match for any of them. But they never came at any of us when we were together, and never when they were alone.

Christian ignored Laz, staring sullenly at me.

"He can keep his apology," I said.

"No." Laz stepped backwards, dragging Christian along with him. "If he won't apologize, then we'll have to make it clear that he isn't going to get away with the shit he's pulling anymore."

"Let him go, Laz, it's not worth it." I knew as soon as I said it that Laz would ignore me. Once he decided on something, he wouldn't let it go until it was finished. And whatever he was planning to do with Christian, I knew it wasn't going to be pretty. He'd been waiting for an opportunity like this for way too long.

"Not so brave now your brother isn't here to save you, are you?" Laz said.

Christian sneered at him. "Like you're going to do anything to me," he mocked. "You're too much of a pussy."

Laz's face darkened and he tightened his grip on Christian's hair. "Say that again."

"You're a fucking pussy," Christian repeated.

I saw the moment Laz lost his temper. He shoved Christian forwards, grabbed his shoulder and spun him around, then nailed him in the mouth with a right hook. The other boy staggered backwards, hands lifting to his face and eyes widening in surprise.

"You fucking hit me!" he yelped.

"No shit," Laz snapped and did it again.

Christian dropped to the ground, and Laz followed him, raining blow after blow to his head. When the other boy lifted his arms to protect his face, Laz kicked him in the stomach, winding him.

"If you ever come for any of us again," Laz said, punctuating each word with another kick, "I'll fucking put you down for good."

He spun around and stalked out of the bathroom, leaving Christian wheezing and bleeding on the tiled floor. With one final glance at the boy on the ground, we followed him out.

I went back to Luca and Laz's place after school. I'd been friends with them both for years, and by that point, his family were *my* family and I spent more time there than I did in my own home.

His parents were a far cry from my own. They were happily married, for a start. They had their own business—a restaurant where all four of their children helped after school and on weekends. At some point over the years, I'd become their unofficial fifth child and was expected to do my part. They fed me, taught me how to cook, and even paid me in return for helping in the restaurant alongside Luca and Laz.

When we all bundled through the door of the apartment they kept above the restaurant, laughing and jostling each other, it was to find Allesandro Tallorico standing in the hallway, his expression unusually stern, and his arms folded across his chest.

"Come straight in here please, boys." He waved a hand to the living room. "We need to talk."

Trading glances, we all trooped in and sank onto the couch.

"Which one of you is going to tell me why I had a phone call from the principal today?"

We exchanged glances, but stayed silent.

"None of you want to explain?" Allesandro sank into the armchair opposite us. "Not one of you wants to tell me why Christian Baker has two broken ribs and a broken nose after being seen getting dragged into the boys' bathroom by the three of you?"

"Nothing he didn't deserve," Laz broke the silence.

"If you were having trouble with this boy, you should have come to *me*."

Laz's lips twisted. "That's not how it works. Having our parents fight our battles would make things worse. We *had* to deal with it ourselves."

"And now you're in trouble for taking it *too far*!" his father roared. "His parents want to press charges for assault. They're willing to keep the police out of it *if* you make a public apology."

"No fucking way," Luca growled from beside me.

"Language, Luciano!" Allesandro barked.

"He's *done worse* to other kids," Laz argued.

"But *he* didn't get caught on camera doing it, you fool!" His eyes swept over the three of us. "Tomorrow you will go to the principal's office when you arrive at school. Christian and his parents will be there. You will apologize and you will accept whatever punishment the school deems fit.

"*What?*" Laz jumped to his feet. "Christian is the fucking problem, not us."

"You will *sit* down!"

"Fuck this." He stormed out of the room, leaving Luca and me staring at each other.

Allesandro sighed. "Boys, listen to me. I know it may seem wrong, or harsh, but you *must* do this otherwise his parents will involve the police and things could get much worse for you."

"It doesn't *seem* wrong, it *is* wrong," Luca said. "We shouldn't be apologizing to *him*."

"You will do as you're told."

Guarded Addiction

CHAPTER 50

I WANT MY LIFE BACK NOW - THE WRECKS

Dex
AGE 13

I stayed at Luca's for dinner, and we were both conscious of the empty seat where Laz should be sitting. I caught his mom casting troubled glances toward his dad, but neither of them said anything.

By the time we'd eaten and it was time for me to head home, Laz *still* hadn't returned. I sat on Luca's bed, lacing up my boots, while he texted his twin.

"Something is wrong," he said, his voice agitated while he gnawed on a thumbnail.

"Where do you think he's gone?" I asked. "He wouldn't have faced Christian without us... would he?" The moment I said it, I wondered. Laz had a temper and didn't always think his actions through.

"No ... maybe? I don't know." He rose to his feet and grabbed his hoodie from the back of the door. "Something is wrong," he repeated, his voice was urgent. Throwing open the bedroom door, he stuck his head out and shouted for his father.

Allesandro appeared a few seconds later.

"We need to find Laz," Luca told him. "He's in trouble."

"He's fine, Luca. He's doing what he always does. Hiding away until his temper cools."

"No! There's *something* wrong," Luca insisted. He pulled his hoodie over his head. "I'm going to find him."

"Luca!" Allesandro moved to stop his son. "It's past nine. You shouldn't be wandering the streets."

"Nor should Laz!"

"It's okay, I'll go with him," I said. "I have to go home, anyway. We'll hit Laz's usual haunts. He's bound to be at one of them."

"You could come with us. We could take the car," Luca said.

Allesandro sighed. "You know I can't. I have to get back down to the restaurant. Your brother will be home. He rarely stays out for too long."

Luca shook his head. "This time it's *different*." He pushed past. "I'm going to look for him."

"Luca!" Allesandro called after him, but Luca ignored him.

"I'll stay with him," I told the older man quietly. "We'll find Laz and bring him home."

Laz wasn't at any of the places he usually went. It was close to midnight and Luca's father had been blowing up his cell for the past forty minutes demanding he come home.

"There's one place we haven't looked," I offered into the silence after he cut off his dad again.

Luca's eyes lifted to meet mine. "The cages."

As a rule, anyone under eighteen couldn't get in, but we'd figured out a way to slip past their security a while ago. Luca and Laz liked to watch the fights—both of them claiming that one day they'd join the ranks of the underground fighting scene.

In silent agreement, we set off. It was a half-hour walk from where we were to the cages. My parents wouldn't care I wasn't home—they were usually drunk or high, so I was sure they wouldn't even notice—but Luca's parents weren't like that and we both knew when we *did* finally catch up with Laz, the pair of them would be in trouble when they got home.

The abandoned warehouse used for underground fighting, commonly known as *The Cages,* was dark and silent when we got there. No signs of life or security, which meant there had been no fights otherwise the place would have been a heaving mass of bodies and noise. Luca switched on the flash light app on his cell and we made our way inside.

"Laz?" Luca called his brother's name, unconcerned about being heard. His voice echoed back at us, but his brother didn't reply.

"Maybe he didn't come here," I said after a few minutes.

Luca shook his head. "No, I think he's here."

I didn't argue. Luca and Laz often had this weird twin thing going on. If Luca thought Laz was here, there was a high chance he was.

"Maybe we should split up and look around? You go search around the actual cages, I'll check where the fighters get ready," I suggested. "I'll shout if I find anything."

We set off, Luca walking off into the darkness. I stood for a second longer, then turned and headed down the narrow corridor which led to the area which had been sectioned off for where the fighters could prepare for upcoming matches.

Without a cell, I had no way of lighting my way and it was fucking *dark*. I knew there was a light switch somewhere, so I inched forward, one hand pressed against the wall searching it out as I moved.

I finally found it on the wall beside the doorway to the changing rooms and flicked it on. Light flared and I blinked, waiting for my eyes to adjust to the change in brightness.

"Laz?" I called out.

Nothing. Where the fuck was he?

We'd searched *everywhere*. He had to be here. And then I heard a noise … a groan … and my head swung around, scanning the area.

"Laz?" I hissed. "Luca?"

Neither answered. Was I hearing things? I stepped further into the room, the smell of stale sweat hitting my nose and then I heard another groan.

Someone was definitely in here.

I crept forward, staying close to the wall, listening for further sounds and then I rounded the corner and stopped dead, my skin going cold.

"Luca!" I screamed my friend's name, hoping he'd hear me,

and flew across the uneven floor to crash to my knees beside the figure lying there.

Laz was lying on his side, knees bent to his chest, eyes closed, skin pale. I touched his face, and his eyelids fluttered, lips parting on a silent gasp.

"Laz? What's happened?" I asked.

His hand reached out to grip mine weakly. It was wet in my grip and I looked down, eyes widening in horror at the red coating his fingers.

"Luca!" I shouted for him again and heard footsteps growing louder as they ran toward me. "Call 911!"

Laz shook his head. I saw his lips move, but the words were too faint for me to hear, so I bent closer. He licked his lips. "Too late, D."

"What happened?" I demanded again, and hated the way my voice shook.

His fingers waved feebly toward his stomach and bile rose up in my throat when I spotted the wet red stain covering the front of his shirt.

"Knife," he whispered. "Did..." He sucked in a shuddering breath. "Didn't see them."

"Laz?" Luca dropped to his knees beside me. "What the fuck?"

I silenced him with a look, and reached out to peel my friend's t-shirt up slowly. The wound beneath made me swallow. It was bad... *really* bad.

"Call your dad," I whispered.

"I need to call for an ambulance." He hit 911 on his cell.

I took a deep breath and pressed my palm against the wound, trying to stem the flow of blood, but it seeped beneath my fingers. I held Laz's eyes. He knew what was coming, what was happening. His hand covered mine and I saw his eyes flick toward Luca.

"Luc," I breathed. "You need to call your dad."

But Luca wasn't listening. He was talking to emergency services, demanding an ambulance, his voice frantic.

My eyes returned to Laz, who gave me a half-smile. "Always said I w-wouldn't make it to tw-twenty."

"How can you even joke?" I hissed, my voice choked.

"L-look after my b-brother." He didn't answer my question.

"Please ... hold on," I begged. "The ambulance will be here soon."

"S-sorry, D. Can't."

"Fuck. Hold on!" I pressed down harder on the knife wound in his stomach and he hissed. "Luc!"

Luca turned back, his face draining of color when he saw the blood covering my hands. "Laz?" his voice broke. "You can't do this."

"Sorry," his twin breathed. "I ... held on for as long as I could ..."

He was unconscious by the time the EMTs found us and they tried to get us to move to one side so they could help him. Not that we would accept their help. We fought to stay with him, tried to wake Laz, slipping in the pool of blood in our determination not to leave his side, until more than our hands were covered in it. Eventually the two male EMTs managed to drag us away. They must have called for backup because another ambulance was waiting outside and we were manhandled inside and kept there while they went back for Luca's brother.

The rest of the night passed in a daze. I remember arriving at the hospital, of being asked questions I couldn't answer. All I could see was the blood on my hands, on my clothes. All I could hear was the last rattling breaths as Laz slipped away from us; the shouts as the doctors and nurses ran around trying to bring him back; the broken sobs of his mother when he was pronounced dead.

And all I could think was that if we hadn't stood up to Christian Baker, it wouldn't have happened.

CHAPTER 51

COULD YOU BE MINE - BILLY RAFFOUL

Siobhan

PRESENT

I woke up alone. It was dark outside, I could see that through the gap in the curtains. The other side of the bed was cold, which told me Dex hadn't returned after he'd gone to find something to drink. Climbing out of the bed, I grabbed the first shirt I saw, pulled it over my head and went in search of my missing rock star.

I found him in the kitchen standing in front of the sink, hands gripping the edge and his head bowed.

The room *stank* of alcohol.

Had he been drinking? Looking around, I found a stack of beer bottles on the drainer and … *was that two bottles of tequila?*

"Dex?"

He spun at my voice, and my eyes dropped to the bottle in his hand.

"Is everything okay?" I asked cautiously.

His brows pulled together, then he glanced down at the bottle he held and his expression cleared.

"Oh …" His grin seemed forced. "I haven't been drinking." He waved a hand toward the sink. "I was pouring it away."

"Pouring it away?" I repeated slowly. I could hear the confusion in my voice and knew Dex heard it too.

He set the bottle down with the rest and came toward me. "I had an epiphany," he told me, and dropped a kiss to my lips.

"You're not making any sense." I pulled my mouth away from his. "Why don't you start with why you're pouring all the alcohol down the drain?"

"Because you were right." His arm slipped around my waist and we walked over to the kitchen table. Dex pulled out a chair and I sat down. He sat opposite me. "You told me I shouldn't be touching drugs *or* alcohol. I had it in my head that only drugs were the problem, but I was wrong. I'm never going to stay clean if I don't work at it, and to do that I have to get rid of *anything* else I've been using as a crutch. Alcohol is another way of ignoring the actual issue." He paused and threw me a smile. "Well, *almost* everything. There's one thing I refuse to give up."

I rolled my eyes. "Sex?"

"Close, but no cigar." He tapped the end of my nose with one long finger. "*You*, Cherry Pie. I refuse to give *you* up."

I glanced over at the drainer where there had to be at least twenty empty beer bottles. "You got rid of *all* of it? That's what you've been doing while I was sleeping?"

He nodded. I swallowed. I don't know why I felt on the verge of tears, but I wanted to cry. Blinking rapidly, I stood, stepped forward between his legs and wrapped my arms around him.

"Red?"

I shook my head, burying my face into his throat. "I can't believe you did that. I'm so proud of you."

His arms crept around my waist and he pulled me tighter against his body. "I had a moment of clarity. I could keep the addiction or I could keep you." His lips found my throat. "This time I'm making the *right* choice. I'm picking you, Siobhan. I should have *always* picked you." He pressed a kiss to the pulse beating at the base of my throat, then carefully stood and set me back. "Want to help me get rid of all this?"

I helped him box up all the empty bottles and place them in the recycling bin outside the kitchen.

"I think there might be more in the game room," he said once we were done.

"It doesn't all have to be done at once," I said.

"It does," he said over the top of me. "If it's here, I'll drink it. I may not be an alcoholic, but I've definitely been drinking more since cutting out drugs. I think, at least for a while, I need to avoid anything that could be addictive."

I nodded. "Okay, let's do it."

It took us an hour to search out all the alcohol in the house. It wasn't that he'd been hiding it, there was just *a lot* more than I expected there to be. Even Dex seemed surprised at the quantity once we had it all stacked in the recycling.

"I'm not an alcoholic," he said softly, eyeing the bottles. He wasn't trying to convince me, but himself.

"I know." I slipped my hand around his arm. "Most of those bottles had never even been opened. I bet a lot of them were brought by guests or given to you as gifts." I don't know why, but I thought he needed the reassurance of hearing that I believed him.

He placed his hand over mine and squeezed my fingers. Frowning, he angled his head down and lifted my hand from his arm. His eyes were intent as he looked at my fingers.

"Is everything okay?" I asked and his eyes jerked up to mine.

"Do you still have your rings?"

I bit my lip. *Did I want to admit to him that I'd kept them? What would that say about me?* But then I thought about his words earlier, about how he should have picked me, and nodded.

"If I asked you to ..." He hesitated, and his piercing caught the light as his tongue stroked over his lips. "Would you wear them?"

"You want me to wear my wedding ring?" I looked pointedly at his ring finger—the only one with no ring on it. "You don't wear yours."

"I ... uhh ..." he cleared his throat, and I was struck by how uncomfortable he suddenly looked. "I do wear it. I always have."

"No ... you have tons of rings, but I think someone would have commented if you'd worn a wedding ring."

His smile was sheepish. "I had it melted down and turned into my lip and nose piercings."

"*What?*" I gaped at him.

"I knew, after I refused to tell anyone who you were, that if I wore the ring questions would be asked. But I ... uhh ... I wanted to keep it close, so I went to see Murphy. He turned the ring into these." He flicked the ring piercing his lip and then the one through his nose.

"Dex ..." I didn't know what to say. For most people, maybe it would have seemed weird, but to me? It was possibly one of the most romantic things he could have done.

"I'll get another one. I'll call Murphy. We'll drive up there today," he rushed to say, misunderstanding my tone of voice. "You can even pick it out this time."

"Are you telling me you want to go public?" I breathed.

"I want everyone to know you're off the market." He reached out to loop a lock of my hair around his finger. "I'm a better person with you," he muttered and I smiled.

I stepped forward to wind my arms around his neck. "Why, Dex Cooper, there *is* a sweet side to you after all. Who knew?"

CHAPTER 52

HEAR ME NOW - BAD WOLVES

Dex
PRESENT

I let Siobhan have her moment of teasing, then swept her off to bed to remind her I wasn't as sweet as she was making out. Seeing the marks Colton had left on her body made anger course through me every single time my eyes fell on them, but none of that showed in my expression or my touch. Like I had the night before, I sought out each mark and kissed it. I made love to her body with my mouth, my fingers and, eventually, my dick. But not until I made her beg and plead.

I teased her, took her to the edge over and over again, so that when I finally sheathed myself into her body, she came almost immediately. Her nails clawed at my back, drawing blood. Her teeth bit into my throat, my shoulders, and the more it stung, the more I liked it.

Afterwards, we lay in a tangled mess of sweaty limbs and I slept peacefully for the first time since Laz had died, without the need of drugs or drink to keep away the dreams.

She woke me the next morning with my dick in her mouth and I was thrown back to the days following our marriage in Vegas, where we spent two days in bed doing nothing but learning each other's bodies.

I'd spent years having one-night stands, scratching an itch with a stranger I'd never see again, never wanting to get close to anyone, or let them see *me* instead of the rock star they all wanted a part of. I told myself it was because I wasn't interested in anything more. Quick, no-string fucks were easy. There was no expectation of more, no demands on my attention, no *connection.*

But here, with Siobhan, I realized it had all been a lie. I'd spent the years since leaving her bouncing from one bed to another because, deep down, I *knew* nothing would ever come close to what I had with her. That connection, that added *intensity* of being with someone who knew you, who could predict what you wanted from a single moan or touch, held an added dimension that I couldn't have handled with anyone *but* her.

I threaded my hands through her hair, her tongue swirling over the end of my dick, licking from base to tip before swallowing me back into her mouth, and my eyes rolled back at the sheer bliss of it. I could feel my orgasm building and tightened my grip on her hair so I could pull her mouth off me.

"Come up here." I directed her and she crawled up my body, until she could straddle my hips and lower herself onto me. "Fuck," I groaned. The feel of her, the *scent* of her, invaded my senses, and it was a battle not to come the second I was as deep as I could get inside her.

I watched her breasts bounce as she rocked above me, and my mouth watered for a taste. I wrapped an arm around her waist and dragged her down so I could take a nipple into my mouth. Her moans were like music, those soft gasping sounds she made which told me her orgasm was close. I rolled, pinning her beneath me and took control, driving myself into her, feeling her body spasm around mine as she fell over the precipice. Her orgasm triggered mine, and I followed her down.

We took a first-class flight to Vegas—it was quicker than driving and, after telling Karl what I'd planned, I agreed it was better to go there and back in one day, in case the police decided they wanted to speak to me again. I left Diesel with the task of arranging a car to pick us up from the airport, and hunted Siobhan down in the shower for another round of sex, which nearly made us miss the flight.

We made it with minutes to spare, and annoyance painted the faces of the passengers as we made our way through the first-class section of the plane. We were unbuckling our seats after takeoff when the hostess appeared beside us.

"Can I get you anything, Mr. Cooper?" she asked.

"Diet Coke would be great, thanks," I replied. "What about you, love?" I asked Siobhan.

"Coke is fine," she replied.

"Don't want champagne?" I said and she shook her head. "You know you can drink around me, right?"

"I know, but I don't want to." She rested her hand on my thigh and smiled up at the hostess. "Coke, please."

I was about to argue with her but was distracted by a sparkle as the sun through the window hit the ring on her finger. A smile pulled my lips wide, and something relaxed inside me. She was wearing the rings I bought her—the ruby and diamond engagement ring shone brilliantly, and her wedding band fit snugly against it. Unable to resist, I lifted her fingers to my mouth and kissed them.

The hostess's eyes widened when they fell onto the rings, but she didn't speak and I *knew* the minute she returned to her colleagues, the news would spread like wildfire.

I turned to Siobhan once the hostess left and grinned. "Do you think she's going to tell her friends that I'm having an affair with a married woman or that I secretly got married?"

"Affair," Siobhan's response was immediate. I fucking loved how she was completely on my wavelength and didn't even need to ask what I meant. "You're not wearing a wedding ring."

"I totally am," I argued and she rolled her eyes at me.

"Not in a way any *sane* person would."

"Are you saying I'm not normal?"

"There's not a single member of Forgotten Legacy that could be described as normal, Rock Star." She laughed. "You're all crazy in your own unique ways."

And that set the tone for the entire flight. We laughed and teased each other, shared kisses, and held hands. I knew the other passengers as well as the flight staff were whispering and talking.

I guessed they were also taking sneaky photographs while trying to figure out who she was and why she had a wedding ring on, but with Diesel sitting close by and ensuring no one disturbed us, theories were all they had.

No one bothered us as we made our way through the airport and into the car Diesel had arranged, after we landed. He took the driver's seat while we climbed into the back, and I gave him directions to Murphy's.

"Know what we should do?" I said as we followed Murphy inside a short while later.

"I'm scared to even try to guess," she replied.

"Get a tattoo."

She laughed. "We've been down that path once already."

"But we need to fix your tattoo, now you're no longer mad at me."

Murphy, a few steps in front of us, barked a laugh. "Boy, that girl is going to spend half her life mad at you. You might as well get used to it. I warned you when you brought her here the last time not to lose her, and what did you do?"

"Yeah yeah," I muttered.

He opened a door and led us into his workroom, then left us to go over to a bench on the far side.

"Get your backside over here, girl," he snapped when he realized we hadn't followed him.

Chapter 53

YOU'RE MINE - DISTURBED

Siobhan

PRESENT

I glanced at Dex, who smiled and waved me away.

"He got to pick your ring, it's only fair you choose his ring this time around," Murphy said when I reached him. He pulled open a drawer beneath the desk and placed a tray of rings in front of me. "As you can see…" He pointed to a row. "These ones are similar to the wedding ring you're wearing."

I stroked a finger over them. "They're nice."

Murphy nodded. "They are, but …" He looked to see where Dex was and lowered his voice. "Your rings are part of a set. There's a matching man's wedding band, if you want that."

"Wasn't that the one he turned into his piercings?"

"Oh, no. I wouldn't have allowed him to do that."

"Oh?"

He frowned at the interest in my tone. "He hasn't told you, has he?" he said slowly.

"Told me what?" I glanced over at Dex nervously. He was

leaning against the wall, his eyes on his cell as he either texted someone or played a game. Either way, he wasn't taking any notice of us.

"Those rings on your finger belonged to his grandmother."

"What?" My voice came out as a whisper.

"I don't know how much you know about Dex's childhood, but his grandmother distanced herself from his parents long before he was born. She lived here in Vegas and when Dex started finding fame with his band, he tracked her down. His grandfather had died a few years before and when she died, she left Dex everything—including the jewelry. He asked me to look after them." He crouched and pulled out a little black velvet box from the drawer. "Imagine my surprise when he turned up here with you less than a month after her funeral."

"A ... month?"

Murphy sighed. "He didn't tell you that either?"

"No."

"Didn't tell you what?" Dex said from behind me and I jumped guiltily.

Murphy tapped the little box between us and Dex's eyes jerked down. "You need to stop keeping secrets, my boy," the old man told him. "Starting here."

"Is that the ring you're picking?" Dex asked me, his voice hoarse.

"I think so." I picked up the box, then paused to look at Murphy. "Will it fit?"

Murphy nodded.

"Give me your hand, Rock Star."

His hand was shaking when he lifted it and I opened the box to reveal a wedding band similar to mine, but a little thicker. I took it out carefully and slid it onto his finger. It fit perfectly.

"I guess it's official then," I said, and couldn't help a nervous laugh.

Dex didn't speak. Instead, he lifted his hands to cup my cheeks and kissed me. A cleared throat broke us apart a few minutes later, and Dex turned his head to grin at Murphy.

"This means it's serious now, huh?" he said to the older man.

Murphy grunted. "Try not to lose her this time." Even though he sounded irritable, I could see the smile he was trying to hide.

"No, sir." Dex wrapped his arm around my shoulders and turned me toward the door. "Thanks, Murph," he threw over his shoulder as we made our way back to the exit where Diesel waited.

Dex got his way and we ended up in the tattoo parlor where I'd got my original tattoo all those years ago. I don't *think* Frank recognized me or, if he did, he acted like he didn't. Dex held my hand while Frank turned the S back into a D, resulting in my tattoo now saying "Dex & Cherry Pie" which, according to Dex, was even better than the original. Being such a small change, it was over quickly and we were in and out within forty minutes and Diesel drove us to the apartment Dex owned.

Stepping inside his apartment was like taking a step back into the past. Kicking my shoes off, I let my feet sink into the thick carpet and looked around. *Nothing* had changed.

"What time is the flight back to LA?" I asked as he moved across the room toward the kitchen.

"We have a couple of hours to kill. Want to order some food, Mrs. Cooper?"

The name startled me and I stared at him. I'd never used his name, hadn't even considered it because our marriage had been over almost as quickly as it began and I didn't feel right using the name of a man who wasn't in my life. But now?

"Siobhan Cooper," I said slowly, testing how it sounded, and he smiled.

"Has a nice ring to it, don't you think?"

Reporters were camped outside the airport when we landed back in LA later that evening. *Someone*—my money was firmly on it being one of the flight attendants—had raised questions with them about Dex's traveling companion ... *me* ... and my marital status. They mobbed us as we walked out of the exit, shouting over each other in their desperation to get a story. Camera flashes went off, blinding me, causing me to misstep and stumble, and I felt Dex's arm wrap around my waist to guide me toward the car.

Before we reached it, he stopped and bent his head to whisper in my ear. "If we don't give them something, they'll make up their own stories."

"What do you want to do?"

He smiled. "Want to go public with me?"

"*Now*? Before you even talk to the band?"

"It's not like they don't already know. You really think Gabe wouldn't have told them?" he pointed out.

He wasn't wrong. If Gabe didn't say anything, I was certain Harper would because, with everything else that had happened, she would have wanted to know if they already knew about it. I gave him a slow nod.

"Okay... what do you have in mind?"

He straightened and turned to face the pack of reporters, tracking over them until he found a familiar face.

"Jefferson." He pointed a finger at a man near the back.

The reporter smiled and pushed his way through. "Thank you. I have a couple of questions, if you don't mind."

Dex shrugged.

"You were arrested yesterday, but released without charge. Can you tell us anything about that?"

"Not a lot, really. I walked in on a guy trying to assault my..." He hesitated, squeezed my waist, then continued. "... my wife. We fought, and then I left and took Siobhan to the hospital. Next we knew the police were dragging me to the station and accusing me of his murder. I was in the hospital when it happened and neither myself nor Luca had any involvement in the man's death." His brows pulled together. "Can't say I was sad to hear about it, though."

"Your wife?" Jefferson leaped on his description of me.

Dex's frown turned into a smile. "Best kept secret in LA. None of you sniffed that one out, did you? We were on a break for a while."

I huffed. "We were *not* on a break. We were separated."

"We were never separated. We were on a small hiatus!" he argued good-naturedly.

I shook my head, while the reporters watched on with rapt fascination.

"And how long have you been married?" Jefferson asked.

"A few years. We ... reconciled a few months ago, but wanted to keep it quiet until we were sure it was what we both wanted," Dex replied. "Now, if you don't mind, it's been a long day and we'd like to go home."

He opened the car door and waited while I climbed in, then followed, ignoring the follow-up questions being shouted by the rest of the reporters.

Jefferson simply smiled and waved as Diesel pulled the car into the traffic.

Guarded Addiction

CHAPTER 54

20 DOLLAR NOSEBLEED - FALL OUT BOY

Dex
PRESENT

Siobhan had gone to bed a couple of hours ago. More accurately, I'd *put* her to bed because she'd been falling asleep on the couch under some misguided attempt to stay awake with me. When her eyes had closed and stayed closed, I'd scooped her up and taken her to bed without her waking up, then slipped back out and returned downstairs. I wasn't quite ready to try to sleep yet.

A noise behind me had me turning around. Diesel stood in the doorway.

"I've set all the alarms," he told me. "So no sneaking out and making me look for you."

I laughed. "Come and play pool with me ... unless you're heading to bed?" Diesel walked into the room and I moved past him to close the door. "Grab a cue."

Diesel won the first game, I won the second.

"Best of three?" I suggested and he nodded.

I waited for him to take his shot, lined up my own and glanced over at him. "So what went down with David Colton?"

"No idea," Diesel didn't miss a beat. "We took him back to his apartment, dumped him inside with a warning that worse would happen if he didn't turn himself in and left."

"Did you see a dog in his apartment?"

"No, why?"

I took my shot. "Apparently, he had his throat ripped out. I find it hard to believe a person did it. So it had to have been a dog."

"Huh … that's weird."

I'm sure I saw him smile out of the corner of my eye, but when I turned to look at him fully, his eyes were on the pool table, gaze completely focused on where the ball was going.

"You don't own a dog, do you?"

He shook his head. "Nope, no pets."

"What about Ryder?"

Diesel laughed. "Ryder has no pets, either. Seriously, Dex, he was alive when we left. Neither of us killed him. I think someone saw what happened and took the opening we provided. I doubt Siobhan was the only girl he's tried that with."

I wasn't convinced he had no part in what happened, but I also wasn't worried. If Diesel was as confident as he appeared, then I was pretty sure that there would be no way the landlord's death could be connected to any of us.

We finished up the game with Diesel beating me *again*. He placed his cue on the table.

"Time to grab some sleep," he said. "You should as well. Don't forget you need to be at NFG at eight."

"Fuck. Yeah." I scrubbed a hand down my face. I *had* forgotten about that. Karl wanted a band meeting—probably to shout at me and Luca again with Seth and Gabe as witnesses.

My bodyguard patted my shoulder and walked out. I spent a few minutes resetting the pool table, then headed up to my own bedroom. Creeping inside, I smiled at the way Siobhan was sprawled out in the center of the bed, taking up as much space as she could … which, considering how big my bed was and how small *she* was, wasn't a lot.

I grabbed clean underwear as quietly as I could and disappeared into the ensuite bathroom to take a quick shower before slipping beneath the sheets beside her and letting sleep claim me.

I woke up to the scent of cherries in my nose and my alarm screeching on the nightstand. Opening my eyes, I groped for my cell and turned off the noise. Siobhan was burrowed against my side, an arm flung over my waist and a leg tucked between mine. She mumbled something I didn't quite catch, but I was fairly confident it was a complaint about how early it was.

I pressed a kiss to the top of her head and untangled myself from her, so I could stand.

"Sorry, Red, work calls. Stay in bed, I'll call you once the band meeting is done." She was asleep again by the time I finished dressing.

Diesel was in the kitchen when I finally found my way downstairs.

"I wondered if I was going to have to wake you," he commented, handing me a coffee.

"I was tempted to stay put," I admitted on a yawn. "But it'd just make Karl yell for longer and no one needs that."

I dropped a text to the band's group chat while I drank my coffee. Luca replied immediately, telling me he was already at NFG. Seth took a few minutes longer. Gabe didn't respond at all. Opening a separate message, I texted Seth.

ME - Is everything okay with Gabe?

SETH - Not sure. Harper went back to the apartment and I know they had a long conversation. The bombshell you dropped didn't land well.

I knew it wouldn't, but I hadn't really thought Harper would jump to the conclusion that *Gabe* had been the one behind her moving in with Siobhan. I found Gabe's number.

ME - Are you coming to the band meeting?

He didn't reply until we were in the car and halfway to the NFG Office, and when he did, it was short and to the point.

GABE - Yeah.

ME - About Harper. I'm sorry. I didn't mean to cause shit between you.

GABE - Like fuck you didn't. But it's sorted now.

ME - I'll tell her you had nothing to do with it.

GABE - No need. Just leave it alone.

There wasn't much I could say to that, so I didn't respond. A few minutes later another text came in.

GABE - How is Siobhan? Is she with you? Harper wants to see her.

ME - She's at my place. Still in bed when I left. Get Harper to call her or go over. I know she'd be pleased to see her.

GABE - When did you get fucking married?

ME - Years ago. Long story.

GABE - Make time to tell me. I'll see you at NFG.

Okay, so Gabe was in some kind of mood—that was clear from his messages. This meeting was going to be all kinds of fun.

I stepped out of the elevator and into the reception area outside Karl's office as my cell rang. Without looking at the caller ID, I connected the call.

"Hey, D. Been a while."

I stopped in my tracks. *What the fuck?*

"*Travis?*" I spun away and walked along the corridor toward the bathrooms. "How did you get this number?"

"Got a text last night, man, from someone telling me you'd changed your number. Gave me this one and said I should call you to arrange a drop."

"I ... *what*? Who told you that?"

"I didn't ask their name."

"Can you send me the number?"

"Sure. So, about that drop? I can do tomorrow night. Want your usual?"

And just like that, the craving hit from out of nowhere. A desire to get high so strong it made my entire body shake.

I swallowed, cleared my throat, swallowed again.

"D? You there?"

"Yeah ... yeah, I'm here." I sucked in a steadying breath. "I'm good. I don't want anything. I got clean a few months back."

"You did?" Travis's voice brightened. "That's great, man. Congratulations."

"D?" Luca's voice sounded from behind me, and I lifted a hand to silence him.

"Don't take this the wrong way, but could you do me a favor and lose my number?"

Travis laughed. "Sure thing. *After* I send you the number you want, right?"

"Please."

"You got it." He paused. "And, D? Seriously, man, congratulations. Don't call me, yeah? You stay clean, you hear me?"

What fucking planet was I on where my dealer was pleased I'd got clean?

"Thanks, Trav." I ended the call and turned to face Luca.

"Why the fuck are you talking to Travis?" he demanded.

"Strangest fucking thing," I replied and told him about the conversation.

"Who do you think it was?" Luca asked when I was done.

"I have no idea, but add that to someone slipping me some freebase at the airport and then my weed tin appearing in my bedroom... someone is trying to fuck with me."

"Someone gave you *cocaine*?" Luca demanded. "Why the fuck didn't you say something?"

"That's why Siobhan was at my place," I admitted. "I called her and asked her to come over."

"Have you told Karl?"

The question hung between us, and I looked away.

"Fuck sake, D. You need to tell him about this. What if someone slips you something and you fail the next drug test?"

"I know. I just..." How could I explain I'd been way too deep in denial to want to admit to anyone that I had a problem? "I'll tell him after the meeting today."

"If you don't, I will," Luca warned.

CHAPTER 55

WHOLE LOTTA LOVE - HOLLYWOOD VAMPIRES

Siobhan

PRESENT

Remy dropped Harper off at midday, with a warning not to leave until he was sent to pick her up. I caught her eye roll as she walked away from the car and hid a smile.

"Gabe still not letting you out alone?" I asked as we walked through to Dex's kitchen.

She sighed. "You have no idea. I thought he'd get better over time, but I swear he's getting worse." She pulled out a chair and sat. "So spill. I want all the details. Starting with how you're feeling and what happened the other night."

"Coffee?" I offered and she nodded.

"Yes, but talk while you're making it. I want to know *everything*."

And that's what I did. I told her everything. From how I met Dex, to marrying him, his overdose and why we separated and right up to present day. The only thing I didn't mention was the almost-threesome with Luca. There were some things you didn't share—even with your best friend.

"So, I didn't *mean* to keep it a secret," I said eventually. "But I couldn't see a way to explain it to you without it sounding so …"

"Crazy?" she supplied.

I laughed. "Yeah, that. But really, Gabe had nothing to do with it *at all*."

Harper's face grew serious. "I know. I think I was so shocked by the way Dex told me. I just … I didn't know what to think."

"I can understand that."

"What about you and Dex now? Are you together again?"

I lifted my hand silently to show her the rings and she gasped. "Oh my god, they're gorgeous."

"I think we're trying to give it another go. He took me to Vegas yesterday to replace his wedding ring."

"You *think*? Have you seen the papers this morning? There are photos of you and Dex all over the place. Did he really give an interview?"

"Reporters caught us coming out of the airport last night. He stopped to talk to them for a few minutes."

"Then it's more than just *think*, Von."

"I don't know. I'm not sure we're good for each other. When we're together, it's like …" I paused, trying to explain how he made me feel.

"Like nothing else in the world matters but the two of you? Like without him, you feel incomplete? Like you're on a ride that's spinning out of control, but you can't stop getting back on for one more go?" Harper sounded almost sad and I frowned at her.

"Yes, just like that. Is everything okay with you?"

She smiled, but her eyes were distant. "Yeah, I'm fine. We're talking about you. You don't get much more committed than being married to Dex. And if he's telling the world…"

"I know."

"You don't sound convinced."

I couldn't help but laugh. "When he's here and he talks, it's like everything he says makes sense. But once he leaves and I have time to think…" I shrugged.

"They've always been like that, you know," she said softly, a wealth of memories in her eyes. "Their enthusiasm for things can be overwhelming sometimes and you find yourself swept along in the excitement before you realize it."

"Exactly." I paused, biting my lip. "But then, when everything slows down, I remember what he said to me when we were in South Carolina, and I question *everything*."

Harper's head tilted to the side. "What happened in South Carolina?"

Chapter 56

HABITS (STAY HIGH) - TOVE LO

Siobhan

FOUR MONTHS AGO - SOUTH CAROLINA

The atmosphere in the private function room, where the band gathered for a meal in the hotel, flowed from tense to relaxed and back to tense again depending on who you were talking to.

Gabe seemed lost in thought, although whenever Harper spoke to him he responded and smiled at her. Riley's eyes seemed permanently attached to the door. I don't know who she thought she was fooling, but it was clear the girl was head over heels for Seth, and *him*? Well, he was doing a terrible job of pretending he wasn't attracted to her. Not that he was here. I don't know what was going on, but he hadn't turned up for the meal for whatever reason.

Dex sat on the opposite side of the long table, Luca beside him. I tried to avoid looking in his direction and, whenever I did make the mistake of looking up, it was to find his blue eyes on me—still as dark and angry as they'd been in Nashville. Luca, on the other hand, seemed completely unconcerned by any of the potential drama building in the room. He was chatting with Lexi, who appeared to be almost as unhappy as Gabe.

I counted the minutes until I could escape without raising any questions, told Riley I would be sleeping elsewhere and got the hell out of Dodge before anyone could stop me. My plan was to grab a single room and hide out until it was time to take the flight to Paris.

But like every best laid plan—that imploded almost before I could set it into action.

I was at the front desk when I was grabbed by the arm and spun around.

"Where are you going?" Dex's voice was a low growl.

"Take your hands off me," I told him, my own voice flat.

"I *said* where are you going?" He ignored my demand, his fingers biting into my arm.

"I don't answer to you, Dex." I wrenched my arm free and turned back to the person on the desk. "I'm sorry about that," I told her, while she gazed at Dex with wide eyes. "Do you have a room ready for me?"

"Why the fuck do you need a room? You *have* a room."

I fought against snapping at him and turned slowly, once more, to face him. "I don't want to share a room tonight. I want to have some time to myself. Is that a problem for you?"

His jaw clenched. "Who are you meeting?"

"No one."

"Don't fucking lie to me."

"And you are basing that assumption on *what* exactly?"

"On the basis of Nashville when you were happy to spread your legs for me and—" I slapped him before he finished the sentence. His head snapped sideways.

The woman at the desk gasped, but didn't turn to look. My eyes were glued to Dex, who was slowly bringing his head back to face me. The smile that twisted his lips made my blood run cold.

"I think you need a reminder on who's in control here," he told me, his voice low. "But I'll give you a hint. It's *not* you." His hand curved around my arm again. "You can struggle and scream, if you like," he said when I tried to pull away. "But you won't like the outcome."

"What the hell is wrong with you?" I demanded. "Are you *high*?"

"No, I'm *not* fucking high," he ground out from between clenched teeth. "Move your fucking ass into the elevator." He gave me a push and I found myself inside the small compartment with the doors sliding shut before I could argue.

He wasted no time in herding me into the far corner, and braced his arms either side of my body to bracket me in.

"Who are you going to meet?" He was close enough for me to smell the alcohol fumes on his breath.

"I *told* you already. I'm not meeting anyone."

"Stop fucking lying to me!" he shouted.

Part of me acknowledged that maybe I should be scared of his anger, of what he could potentially do, but he wouldn't hurt me, no matter how angry he was. Another part of me was just as furious as he seemed to be. He had *no right* to be demanding anything from me.

"Look, Dexter, I don't know what you think is happening here, but you don't *own* me. You don't even *like* me. You've made that perfectly clear."

"Don't like you?" he repeated, his lips twisting. "Does this feel like me not *fucking* liking you?" He grabbed my hand and pressed it against the erection tenting his pants. "I like you well enough, Cherry Pie."

"Enough to fuck me, you mean." I pulled my hand free, as the doors slid open.

"Isn't that all that matters?" He grabbed my arm again, pulled me out of the elevator, and along the corridor until we reached a door.

Voices reached us as he unlocked the door and his head swung around as he listened. I drew in a breath, ready to shout for help, and he stepped up to me, pressed a finger to my mouth and lowered his head to my ear.

"Scream ... I dare you," he whispered.

I bit his finger. He laughed, a brittle edge to the sound. "Want to play biting games, do you?" he said, and nipped my ear lobe.

I couldn't stop a shudder at his action. He knew every single spot on my body which would cause a reaction and how to get it. On the edges of my awareness, I could hear the voices coming closer and I recognized one of them as Harper, but Dex's mouth had captured mine and I was drowning in the taste of him.

I heard a surprised "*Oh!*" from whoever was walking past, I was sure it was Harper, and then he was backing me through the door and into his suite. I didn't even bother pretending to put up a fight. *That* ship had sailed back in Nashville. I'd managed to resist the temptation before then, but once I got a taste of him, a reminder of how it felt to be *with* him ... my body would accept nothing less when it was offered another opportunity.

We tore at each other's clothes, throwing t-shirts to one side, kicking off shoes and jeans, and then the back of my legs hit the bed, and we fell onto it. Dex came down to rest between my thighs, his mouth still on mine, while his hands found their way beneath my bra. His fingertips, rough from playing the guitar for so many years, skated over my skin, sending sparks of desire through my veins and I arched into his touch. He pulled his mouth from mine and his blue eyes stared down at me.

"What's your safe word?" he asked, and the angry edge had gone from his voice, leaving it thick and husky with arousal.

"Pineap—" He cut me off with another kiss, tongue sliding between my lips to stroke along mine.

His fingers found my nipple piercing and he gave it a slight twist, hard enough to dance along the edge of pain and send bolts of pleasure through me. Moisture pooled between my legs and shifted restlessly, needing something—*anything*—to ease the ache building. Almost as if he could sense it, one hand dropped and pushed beneath the waistband of my panties and found my clit.

"This what you want?" he asked against my lips, and pushed a finger inside me.

I grabbed his wrist, stalling his movement, and he lifted his head to look down at me. I met his gaze, searched his eyes for ... I don't know what ... *something* that told me this was more than just an anger-induced hookup, but his features were unreadable. Oh, there was passion and desire there—it was clear in the way his blue eyes had darkened—but beyond that it was impossible to figure out what he was thinking.

His thumb swept across my clit piercing, and my breath stuttered.

"Changed your mind?" he asked, and I decided I didn't care if it was a hookup going nowhere. I released his wrist and dragged him down on top of me.

"No."

Guarded Addiction

CHAPTER 57

POWER - ISAK DANIELSON

Dex

FOUR MONTHS AGO - SOUTH CAROLINA

The urge to get high had been strong all day, so when we met for dinner I drank too much, trying to ease the hunger. Any other time I'd have dragged Luca out, picked up a girl and lost myself in fucking and fooling around. But he was deep in conversation with Lexi and I couldn't even stand the thought of picking up some other woman—not since I'd buried my dick into Siobhan's willing body back in Nashville.

When I saw her stand up to leave, I followed her out and watched as she spoke to the reception desk. I overheard her ask for a new room and an image formed in my head of her with some unknown guy and … I lost it.

Hadn't she understood me when I told her in Nashville that *no one* was going to touch her except me? If she had a itch that needed scratching, it was *me* she needed to search out, not some fucking stranger.

Was my anger irrational? Sure. Did I give a fuck? Absolutely not.

There was a moment in my suite when I thought she was going to call a halt to what was happening. A flicker in her eyes that had me holding my breath, wondering if I'd pushed her too far this time. But then she wound an arm around my neck and hooked her legs around my waist until my dick was rubbing against her clit.

I pulled my finger out of her body and groped on the nightstand for a condom. Fuck foreplay, I needed to be inside her. She was ready, wet, and rubbing against me like a cat in heat. I leaned back to roll the condom on, ripped off her panties, then lined myself up and thrust home.

She let out a small yelp, her body tensing at my intrusion and I paused to give her a second to adjust to my presence inside her. When I felt her start to relax, I grabbed her hands, pinned them above her head and started to move. She fought to free her hands, but I was stronger, my grip firm on her wrists, holding her in place as I drove myself into her.

We didn't speak. There was nothing to say. She was angry with me. I was angry with her. Neither of us were reasonable where the other was concerned—we never had been. She made me burn just by being in the same room as me, and I wanted her up in flames beside me.

The only sounds in the room were our panting breaths, groans, and moans. The slap of flesh against flesh, soft gasps and guttural curses as we both came. I'd barely finished coming when she wrenched her arms free, shoved me off her and scrambled off the bed. I rolled onto my back and watched as she grabbed her clothes and dragged them on without looking at me.

"Running away, Red?"

She jerked at the sound of my voice, but didn't respond.

I rose to my feet and went into the bathroom to dispose of the condom. When I came out, she was standing by the door, about to leave.

"Next time you have an itch that needs scratching, you know where to find me," I told her.

I knew I was being an asshole. I had no right to demand anything from Siobhan, but that didn't stop me. I loved seeing the fire in her eyes—it made me feel alive.

"If I get an *itch*, I'll know who to blame," she retorted and yanked the door open.

Before she could storm out, I caught her arm and spun her back to face me. "Blame me for whatever you want, Red, but keep in mind I gave you every opportunity to say no. You can admit you have an unhealthy addiction to my dick. I don't mind. No judgement here. Hell, I'll even feed that addiction."

Her hand lifted to slap me, but not quickly enough. I caught her wrist, twisted it up behind her back and pulled her against my body. "Need some more, Red? Not satisfied enough yet?" I leaned forward and kissed her, biting her bottom lip before I pulled away. "Just say the word, love, and I'll take it to the next level."

She shoved at me with her free hand, forcing space between us. I dropped her wrist and stepped away, bending to pick up my jeans from where I'd thrown them and pulled them on. A joint fell out of the pocket and I heard her sharp intake of breath.

"Are you using again?" she demanded.

"No." My reply was curt.

"Then why do you have *that*?" She reached down and snatched up the joint before I could.

Good question. One I couldn't answer without admitting to things I didn't want to talk about.

"It's just weed." I shrugged, feigning a disinterest I didn't feel.

I'd bought an eighth of marijuana after that night in Nashville because I couldn't get her out of my head and it was either get stoned, drunk, or search her out. I'd opted to get drunk instead, because I knew the weed would show up in the drug tests Karl forced me to take... but it didn't stop the craving.

She stared at me. "That's the real reason you fucked me, isn't it? To stop yourself from getting stoned."

I forced a smirk. "An orgasm gives a similar high." It wasn't a denial and she knew it.

She looked hurt for a second, then blanked her expression, green eyes hardening.

"You used me to distract yourself." Her voice was flat. "That says a lot about you."

"You let me," I countered. "I'd say it says more about *you*."

I could have told her that the high I got from her was so much more than anything drugs or alcohol would give me. I could have told her that I didn't *need* to get high when I was with her. I could have told her that she made me want to be better.

But I didn't.

I stayed silent and let her leave, the joint crushed in her fist, believing that I'd used her as nothing other than a distraction from my addiction.

CHAPTER 58

BANG - AJR

Dex
PRESENT

"That video is going to drive the fans crazy," Seth said.

Karl had brought the finished footage with him into the meeting and played it on the wall-mounted tv. The electric attraction between Harper and Gabe had been captured perfectly. Seth was right. The fans were going to love it. I had doubts about whether Harper would. This was going to propel her directly into being the center of attention and, judging by the look on Gabe's face, he didn't think she was going to be happy about it.

"Do you have a copy I can show to Harper?" he asked, and Karl handed him a USB flash drive. He blew out a breath. "She's gonna lose her shit over this, you know that, right?"

"Why?" Karl asked. "She looks great. The chemistry between the pair of you is off the charts. What's the problem with it?"

He scratched the stubble on his chin. "There is no problem, not really. It's just Harper. She'll be weird about it." He huffed a sigh. "I'll figure it out." Pocketing the usb drive, he stood. "Is there anything else?"

Everyone looked at him. He was usually the last to leave, the one pushing for discussions and ideas of what was next for the band.

"What the fuck is going on with you?" Seth was the one to voice what we were all thinking. "And don't fucking say nothing. You've been acting odd for weeks."

"It's nothing." He walked to the door of the office.

"Like fuck it's nothing."

Gabe spun around. "You need to leave it alone, okay?" His grey eyes scanned the room. "I've got somewhere to be. I'll see you all at the studio tomorrow."

I was the first one to look away and caught the look of concern which crossed Karl's face. It had cleared before the rest turned back.

"Is there anything else?" Karl asked.

Luca looked at me. "Someone gave me cocaine in the airport when we came home from London, and then left my weed tin in my bedroom a couple of days later," I said and waited for the explosion.

It never came. Instead, Karl studied me from across his desk.

"Your drug tests came back negative for any drugs in your system."

"I didn't touch any of it." I slid a glance at the others. "I *wanted* to ... but I didn't."

"What did you do with it?" Karl asked.

"Siobhan got rid of the cocaine. The tin ..." I patted my pockets. "I have it here. I wanted to ask if you'd sent it back to me."

Karl shook his head. "If I was going to do that, I would have had it cleaned out first. The last time I saw it, it was on the shelf." He waved a hand toward the bookcase along one wall.

"Could Merry have seen it and thought I'd left it here?"

Karl pursed his lips. "Possibly. I'll check with her. Other than that, are you okay?"

"Yeah. I …" I rubbed the back of my neck with one hand, glancing around at my bandmates. "I … uhh … I quit drinking. I think if I'm going to stay clean, I need to do it the whole way—no drugs, no alcohol, no smoking. I don't think I can do it otherwise," I finished in a rush.

Silence greeted my admission, and then Seth stood up. "I'm proud of you, Dex," he said and hauled me out of the chair and into a hug.

I froze. Seth wasn't a hugger … not with anyone other than Gabe, anyway. His laugh was quiet in my ear and he patted my shoulder before releasing me.

Luca took his place. "You've got this, D," he said.

"You're such a fucking asshole." An unexpected voice said from behind us and we all twisted to see Gabe in the doorway.

He strode forward and wrapped an arm around my shoulders to haul me against him. "I love you, man. We got your back."

"I thought you had somewhere to be."

He shrugged. "This was more important." He shoved me back down onto my seat and reclaimed his own. "What do you need us to do to make it easier?"

"I don't know. Don't do drugs?" I laughed. None of them joined in. "Too soon? Fine. Try and keep the drinking to a minimum around me for a time, while I get a handle on it." I pulled my cell from my pocket and checked the messages. As promised, Travis had sent me the number I'd requested. "One other thing, someone sent Travis a text telling him I was in the market for a new supply." I handed my cell to Luca. "Does anyone recognize the number?"

Luca looked at the text, and checked it against the numbers saved in his own cell, Seth and Gabe followed suit and all of them shook their heads.

Karl frowned. "It seems someone might be trying to sabotage you. I'll see if we can get the number traced and go from there. In the meantime, if anything else happens you *tell* me immediately, got it?"

"Yes, boss," I said and received a scowl in response.

"The police got in touch this morning. They've removed you and Luca as suspects, but that doesn't mean you shouldn't be vigilant. If they can't pin it on someone new, they might circle back to you."

"It wasn't us," Luca said. "There's no way they can make that stick."

"It doesn't mean they won't try. So, please, try and stay under the radar for a while. Don't do *anything* that might bring their attention to you again." He rose to his feet. "If that's everything?"

Everyone stood up.

"Gabe, can we have a quick chat?" he asked when Gabe started for the door.

For a moment, I thought our singer was going to refuse, but then he took in a deep breath, turned and sat back down.

"Sure."

"Mr. Cooper?" I looked up at my name. "Dr. Santos will see you now."

"Thanks, sweetheart." I stood and walked across the reception area to the open door the woman stood beside.

She gave me a smile as I passed. Once upon a time, a lifetime ago, I would have stopped to get her number, maybe talked her into joining me in the nearest bathroom for a quick round of fun, but this time I walked past without stopping. The door closed softly behind me.

"Dex!" Dr. Santos rose to his feet, hand outstretched. "I have to say, I was surprised to hear you arrived for your appointment today. After the last session, I was half-expecting you to cancel completely."

"Yeah, about that." I shook his hand and then dropped onto the couch, swung my legs up and lay back so I could rest my head against the arm.

Dr. Santos quirked an eyebrow but slowly rounded his desk to sit on the chair to the side of the couch.

"This is ... new for you."

"I had an epiphany, doc." I rolled my head sideways to look at him.

"What kind of epiphany?"

I ignored his question. "I got married. Did you know that?"

"Recently? Congratulations. Is she aware of your ... history?"

"Not recently." I lifted my hand to show him the ring on my finger. "But we reconciled and are giving it another go." I sighed. "I gave her my grandmother's rings when we got married."

"Were you and your grandmother close?"

I laughed softly. "Not really. She wasn't around when I was a kid. I found her once I had the resources and was able to pay someone to do the legwork. I knew her for a couple of years before she died." I smiled. "She'd have loved Siobhan."

"Siobhan? Is that your wife?"

"Yeah." I sat up and reached into my back pocket for my wallet. Flipping it open, I pulled out a photograph. "She'd never let me forget it if she saw this," I said and handed it to the doctor. "I took it when we were on tour."

She'd been standing beside the stage watching Badinage's set, cherry sucker in her mouth as she talked animatedly to Harper, hair falling in bright red waves down her back. It was before Nashville, before anger and guilt had come between us... *again*.

"She's pretty. A redhead, as well. Does she have their temper?"

I chuckled. "Oh yeah." I took the photograph back and tucked it back in my wallet. There was another photograph of her in there. One from our wedding day. I handed that one to Dr. Santos.

"You look very happy together."

"We were. Looking back, it amazes me how she let me talk her into it. We barely knew each other, but when you know... you know."

"Love at first sight?"

"I'm not sure it was for her, but me? Knocked me six ways to hell and back the first time I laid eyes on her." The second photograph rejoined the first, and I shoved my wallet back in my pocket. "I drive her crazy most days. Pretty sure she wants to kill me more often than she wants to fuck me. But she makes me want to try harder, you know?"

"Was that the epiphany?"

"I guess. I've messed up so many times, and she keeps catching me, keeps putting me back on track. I need to make it work this time, I need to show her I'm in this for the long haul." I let myself drop back until I was reclining again. "So what do I do now?"

The silence stretched between us, and then Dr. Santos reached for his notebook.

"Why don't you tell me about the first time you took drugs?"

CHAPTER 59

Dex

AGE 13

I woke up in a cold sweat, scrubbing my hands down my sheets, wiping away blood that wasn't there. My heartbeat was loud in my ears, tears wet my cheeks and my breath was coming in short panting gasps. Another nightmare. Another night of reliving Laz's death. Another night of feeling helpless.

As my heart rate slowed, and my brain caught up to the fact I was in my bed and not back at the cages, the sounds of the television, of voices talking in the other room reached me. I rolled out of bed, dragged on a t-shirt and opened the door.

My mom sat at the small square card table we used to eat at, a cigarette between her lips as she watched some tv show on the small television balanced on the unit at the other end of the trailer. Her eyes flicked to me when I appeared and her head cocked sideways, taking in my damp cheeks and hair sticking up in sweaty spikes.

"Everything all right, son?" she asked—voice raspy from the twenty-a-day she smoked.

"Can't sleep," I said.

Her lips thinned as she swept her blue eyes—the same blue as mine—over me. "Another nightmare?"

"I keep seeing Laz," I admitted. "If we'd gotten there sooner, maybe we—" My voice broke and I bit my lip.

"Dex, what happened *isn't* your fault." She stood and walked over to me so she could wrap one thin arm around my shoulders. I realized, with some surprise, that I was almost taller than her.

"I can't get it out of my head, Mom," I whispered, dropping my forehead against her shoulder. "Every time I close my eyes, I see him. I feel his blood on my hands, hear him talking."

"It's going to take time, honey, but it will get better, I swear." She guided me back to the table. "When did you last sleep?"

"I don't know." I sank onto the chair next to her and glanced around. "Where's Dad?"

She shrugged. "Who knows." She exhaled the smoke from the cigarette in her mouth and eyed me. "There is something you could try."

She reached down and picked up a small box. Opening it, she took out a joint and held it out to me. "I wouldn't normally suggest it, but it might help. It's safer than sleeping pills or anything else a doctor might prescribe to you."

My gaze bounced from her to the joint and back again.

Was my mother really offering me drugs?

"It's one joint, Dex. It won't hurt you. It will just make you feel more relaxed." She stubbed out her cigarette and put the joint to her lips. Lighting it, she took a long pull, held her breath for a couple of seconds and then let it out. Smiling, she held it out to me.

I licked my lips and slowly reached out to take it from her.

That first joint hit me hard. I remember my dad coming home to find the pair of us giggling like little kids on the couch over some stupid program on television. He took one look at the pair of us and started yelling.

I grinned up at him, not understanding half of what he was saying and not caring. Nothing mattered. I felt numb, at peace. Nothing bothered me.

It was a perfect existence.

CHAPTER 60

UNDER THE BRIDGE - RED HOT CHILI PEPPERS

Dex
PRESENT

"I slept like a baby after that. Every night before I went to bed, I'd go to my mom, who'd hand me a joint, give me a smile, and we'd smoke it together. I'd crawl into my bed and wouldn't surface until my alarm went off the next morning."

"Your *mother* introduced you to drugs?" Dr. Santos couldn't hide his outrage.

I cracked open an eye and peered at him. "You have to understand that my mother was a drug addict *long* before she had me. She wasn't a bad person, but the drugs made her make decisions that were a little … *out there*."

"You're making excuses for her."

"She did the best she could." My mom and I had a weird relationship. She wasn't what anyone could term a great role model, and we hadn't spoken to each other in years, but I wasn't about to sit and let someone else criticize her.

"Dex, she gave you marijuana when you were *thirteen*."

"I could have said no." I swung my legs off the couch and sat up. "Look, I know what she did, but she wasn't to blame. She was trying to help. I chose to take it, like I chose to experiment with other things."

"Okay." I think he realized it wasn't a topic I was prepared to discuss, and changed the subject. "What about your father? You say he was angry when he came home?"

"Yeah, but not for the reason you think. He wasn't annoyed that I was getting stoned. He was angry that it was *his* weed I was smoking." I stood up and began to pace around the room. "The problem was that after a while the weed stopped helping, so I started looking for other things to help me sleep. Alcohol, sleeping pills, whatever I could find. My mom had a stash which she thought I didn't know about and I started stealing a couple of pills here and there. After my dad was arrested and jailed for another botched robbery, she hooked up with one of her dealers." I threw him a wry smile. "That made it a *lot* easier for me to access what I needed. Unlike my mom, he didn't give a fuck so long as I could pay for what I wanted."

I glanced at the wall clock. It had been over an hour since I'd arrived, yet the doctor hadn't said a word about running over the appointment time. I turned to face him.

"Think my time is up, doc," I said. "Same time next week?"

"Dex, wait," he said. "Sit down for a minute."

I frowned, but did as he asked, dropping back onto the couch and stretching my legs out in front of me.

"This girl you married ... Siobhan?" He waited for my nod. "Why did you marry her?"

"Are you married, doc? Dating? Have a significant other?"

He hesitated. "Married."

"How long did you date before that happened?"

"Four years."

I nodded. "I wasn't dating Siobhan at all. We'd kissed once, barely spent any time together. But I *knew*. Whenever I saw her, everything made sense. Everything felt *right*." A smile curled my lips. "I married her because ... how could I not? Do you believe in soulmates? I do. She's mine. I knew it almost the second I saw her. I wanted to wrap myself around her and never let go." I snickered, an image of myself hanging onto her leg popping into my mind. "If I did that, she'd stab me. So I did the next best thing. I put my grandmother's ring on her finger and tattooed my name on her body." I stood and stretched. "And now I really *do* need to leave."

Diesel was waiting for me outside and I followed him back to the car.

"Where to, now?" he asked once I was inside.

"Home," I told him, and pulled out my cell with the intention of texting Siobhan to see if she wanted to go out to eat.

I was distracted by the folded piece of paper which fell out of my pocket and onto the seat. Picking it up, I unfolded it.

Lola's cell number ...

I'd forgotten I had it. Well, not *forgotten* exactly, just set the memory aside. Unlocking my phone, I opened my text conversation with Luca.

ME - I took Siobhan to Tallorico's the other night.

Luca's name flashed on the screen almost immediately, showing an incoming call. I connected it and braced myself.

"What the fuck, D?"

"She wanted Italian, and you know—"

"I don't give a flying fuck."

"Come on, man. It's been fifteen years."

"And? You think there's a magic number and Laz will come back?"

"Of course not, but Lola misses you. So does your mom."

"They can reach me through NFG."

"It's your fucking *mother*, Luc. She shouldn't have to go through a third party to get hold of you."

Luca hung up. All things considered, I felt it went better than expected.

"Did you order anything?" Diesel said as we approached the gates to my house.

"No, why?"

"There's a parcel by the gate."

I lowered the window and poked my head out. The box was small, with no identifying marks on it.

"Stay in the car," Diesel told me, parked the car and climbed out.

"Pretty sure it won't be a bomb," I called after him and he ignored me.

I watched while he examined the parcel, then pulled a knife from his back pocket.

Who the fuck carried switchblades around? Apparently, my bodyguard did.

He sliced along the parcel tape and carefully pulled back the flap. Whatever he found inside caused him to scowl.

"What is it?"

"Stay there," he said, rose to his feet, and turned in a slow circle, his head slightly tilted and eyes narrowed.

"What the fuck are you doing now?"

"Get in the driver's seat and go up to the house," he told me, and the note in his voice made the hairs on the back of my neck rise.

"What's going on?" I demanded.

"Don't argue, Dex. Go up to the house, go inside and *stay* there."

I quickly climbed out of the back and into the driver's seat, pushed the button to open the gates and drove through. I chanced a quick glance at the box at Diesel's feet, but he'd closed it and I couldn't see inside. My mind was whirling with possibilities though.

I'd joked about it being a bomb, but what if it was? I'd heard of celebrities being targeted, but didn't really consider myself someone who would generate the kind of emotion to cause someone to want to blow me up. Maybe it was a crazy fan—we all had them. It could even be something that wasn't meant for me. But I felt that wouldn't have made Diesel react the way he had... which took me back to the bomb idea.

I parked the car at a haphazard angle outside the house, and went inside.

"Siobhan?" I shouted. "You here?"

"Kitchen," she called back. "You're just in time. I made cookies."

I found her in front of the stove, taking a tray out, and the smell of freshly baked cookies teased my nostrils.

"Fuck, they smell good. I didn't know you baked," I said while simultaneously kissing her cheek and swiping a cookie. "Ouch, fuck those are hot!" I dropped it onto the table and blew on my fingertips.

She rolled her eyes at me. "No, really? Who'd have thought it."

"Brat," I muttered and she laughed. "Did anyone buzz the gate to drop a package off while I was out?"

"No. I've been in here the whole time. Remy came to pick up Harper about an hour ago. He's the only person who's dropped by since you left this morning." She paused, then asked, "Are you expecting someone?"

I shook my head. "No, but a package was left by the gates. Diesel is checking it out."

"What was in it?"

"I have no fucking idea." I bit into the cookie and moaned in delight. "I think you need to make more of these. A dozen is not gonna cut it." She stacked them onto a plate. I took the tray from her, set it down and looped my arms around her waist. "I missed you today. I thought we could go out tonight. Go for a meal somewhere disgustingly expensive." I ran my nose along hers. "I want to show you off."

"Because I look so attractive with my black eye and cut lip."

"All that says is that you're a badass and it makes you even fucking sexier to me."

Her arms lifted and curled around my neck. "Why are you being so nice?"

"That's brutal, Cherry Pie. I'm *always* nice." I brushed my lips over hers. "And—"

The sound of a cleared throat brought my head up to find Diesel standing in the doorway, face serious.

"I've called Karl. He's on his way over."

My brows pulled together. "And why did you do that?"

Diesel moved deeper into the room and tossed the box I'd last seen outside my gates onto the table.

"Don't touch that," he barked when I dropped my arms from Siobhan's waist and reached for it.

My fingers froze mid-air.

"We need to call the security company in charge of the alarm system here and get the gate footage for the past twelve hours."

"And we need to do that because …" I quirked a brow. "What the fuck is in that box, Diesel?"

"Cocaine."

I backed across the room rapidly, putting distance between myself and the table.

"Powder?" I asked.

Diesel shook his head. "Freebase."

"What the fuck?" I whispered. My eyes sought out Siobhan. "I didn't ask for that. It's not mine, I swear."

CHAPTER 61

ANGELS AND DEMONS
Siobhan
PRESENT

I'd never heard him sound so desperate before. There was a pleading note in his voice and a look in his eyes which sent me flying across the room to stand between him and the box on the table.

"I know you didn't," I told him firmly. "Look at me, Rock Star. Someone is messing with your head. Think about it. Who would want to drive you back into addiction?"

"No one. What would it achieve? There's no one lining up to take my place in the band." He twisted to look at Diesel. "You said Karl was on his way over?"

"Yeah. And no, *not* because he thinks you're high," Diesel said before Dex could say another word.

"Why else would he come rushing here?"

I touched his cheek, and turned his face toward me. "Why don't we go outside? I've been here a few times now and you haven't even shown me what's out back. Do you have a pool?"

Diesel nodded in approval when I linked my arm through Dex's and drew him toward the door set against the far wall. Dex let me pull him across the kitchen, but stopped as we reached the door. He turned back to look at Diesel.

"Call me when Karl gets here."

"Stay on the grounds," Diesel warned us both. "If someone *is* trying to stir up trouble, they might still be watching to see how you react to the package."

Dex opened his mouth, frowned, shook his head and then rubbed the back of his neck. I could see the uncertainty in his eyes.

"I don't get it," he muttered finally.

We walked outside and I looked around curiously. The few times I'd come to Dex's house, I'd rarely ventured further than five rooms: bedroom, bathroom, guest bedroom, kitchen, and game room. While Harper had been visiting, we'd stayed in the kitchen, and then afterwards I'd spent time baking, so this was the first time I'd actually stepped outside into the private grounds at the back of the house.

There was a kidney-shaped pool with a second higher section connected by a low waterfall, rocks and various greenery near the house. A gravel path led around it to an archway which was covered in climbing plants, and we followed the path through it. As we stepped beneath the archway, I stopped, my eyes wide.

"Dex?" I said slowly, my eyes sweeping over the little grove of trees.

"Yeah, they're cherry blossoms." He regarded the trees ahead of us. "I was surprised to discover the flowers on them are pink, not red. I have a gardener who comes in and takes care of them because I was scared I'd kill them." He gave a small laugh. "I'm not plant-friendly." He fell silent and I could see him toying with the ring in his lip with his tongue.

"Is there something in there?" I asked. I thought I could see a building beyond the trees.

He glanced at me. "There's an arbor inside and a small koi pond. I go there when I need to ... escape, I guess. It's peaceful. Because it's surrounded by the trees, it's like stepping outside of the world for a few hours ... Do you want to go and see it?"

I nodded. My mind was racing. Those trees weren't new, they hadn't been planted recently. In fact, they looked like they'd been there quite a while ... *established*. How long ago had he planted them?

I followed him along the path and between the trees. A small arbor sat on one side of the grove, corner-shaped, with enough seating for maybe four people. I wondered if it was a custom build, because it seemed to have been designed to blend into the trees, with various plants and flowers I didn't recognize growing around and through it. A wind chime, shaped like music notes, hung on one corner and there was a small table in front of the seating. An open book lay, face down, on top of it—Mr. Nice by Howard Marks, I saw with a smile. Trust Dex to be reading the autobiography of a former drug dealer.

On the far side of the grove was a pond, like he'd said, carefully designed to look like it was a natural part of the landscape, and I could see flashes of color from the fish within its waters. Pink, white, and yellow water lilies floated across the top.

He was right, there was an air of peace inside the grove, a feeling of being able to escape, and I could see why it held such appeal. I turned in a slow circle.

"It's beautiful," I told him, my voice hushed.

We stayed in the grove for an hour, curled up on one of the seats, talking about nonsense and avoiding anything to do with drugs or the box of freebase cocaine in his kitchen, and gradually I felt him relax ... at least until Diesel appeared between the trees.

"Karl's here," he informed us, and Dex immediately tensed beside me.

I reached for his hand and intertwined my fingers with his. "We'll get this figured out."

Karl wasn't the only person waiting for us when we returned to the house. The record label's lawyer, Matthew Carmichael, was also seated there, along with Marley Stone. The latter rose to his feet to pull Dex into a rough hug, then turned to me.

"Hello, trouble," he greeted me in that low, slow drawl which affected women the world over.

I smiled at him. "Marley."

We'd connected during the tour, not in any kind of sexual way, but I'd hung out with him and the rest of Black Rosary a lot while I was trying to avoid Dex. During that time I discovered that, below that "still waters" exterior, Marley possessed a wicked sense of humor, a need for everything to be exactly how he wanted it and very little patience when things didn't go his way.

He touched the bruise on my face and then the cut on my lip. "That should never have happened. If the fucker wasn't already dead, I know a few people who would have taken care of him."

I caught his hand and squeezed his fingers. "I appreciate that."

"Are you okay?" he asked and I nodded.

"It could have been much worse. If Dex and Luca hadn't turned up ..." I broke off, hearing my voice waver. I was trying very hard not to think about what had happened, trying to keep away from falling into the darkness of 'what if' scenarios.

Almost as if he sensed the direction of my thoughts, an arm wrapped around my waist and I found myself pulled into Dex's side. He dropped a kiss to the top of my head. "She'll be fine," he said, his voice firm. "One day at a time, right, Cherry Pie?"

There was a short silence, then Karl cleared his throat. "The security company has emailed over the footage for the past twelve hours. Matthew has hired someone to go through it and see what they can find. Hopefully, we can work out who dropped your ... *gift* ... off. I've also had a conversation with a detective I know. He'll be here shortly to take the evidence. I want you to give him your tin as well—he'll see if there are any prints that can be connected on both items."

Dex nodded. "Whatever you need." His gaze shifted to Marley. "Why are you here?"

"I was with Karl when Diesel called and," Marley's dark brows pulled together, "I gotta tell you, man, it brought back memories."

"Memories?"

"When Black Rosary first hit the scene, we all went through the whole sex, drugs, and rock 'n' roll thing." He threw an apologetic glance toward me, and I waved a hand telling him to continue. "We all did our fair share of drink and drugs. When we became established, found our places so to speak…"

Karl snorted. "Grew up, you mean."

Marley's lips curled into the half-smile he was famous for. "There was a reporter who didn't like the fact that there were no front-page stories to be made from us anymore, except for our music. No hotel room trashing, no public fights, no crazy break-ups with women and no incriminating photographs of us drunk or high. Jazz had a similar experience to you, he was sent *gifts*—usually high-end drugs. We could never prove it, but we *think* it was a particular reporter who was desperate both to make a name for himself *and* be the one to break that killer story."

Dex sank onto one of the chairs. "You think that's what is happening here?"

"When I tell you who the reporter was, I think you'll agree with me," Marley replied.

Dex quirked a brow. "Who?"

"The one you punched at the police station. Sam Jamieson."

"You think he's setting me up just to get a story?" Dex leaned forward and I placed a hand on his arm to keep him from jumping to his feet.

"I think it's not the first time he's done it," Marley said. "But this time we might have the evidence we need to put an end to it."

CHAPTER 62

I KISSED A GIRL - TWENTY ONE TWO

Dex
PRESENT

The detective friend of Karl's arrived shortly after Marley shared his theory. He took my weed tin, as well as the box with the freebase cocaine, and handed them over to his partner to take back to the station.

"We'll check for prints and also look through the video footage Karl forwarded to me. Is there anything else you can think of that might help?" he asked me.

"No. Wait… Actually, yeah." I pulled my cell out of my pocket. "I got a call from the guy who … well, my dealer. *Ex*-dealer," I amended. "Someone had contacted him to say I wanted to place an order. He forwarded the number to me." I hesitated before handing my cell over. "I want your word you won't go after him."

"If it makes you more comfortable, just give me the number of the person who contacted him. Your dealer isn't our main priority right now."

I nodded. "That works. Red, can you grab a pad and pen out

of the drawer over there?" I pointed to the one she needed to look through, and she did as I asked.

"Do you think he had anything to do with the death of David Colton?" I asked while I wrote down the cell number.

"It's a possibility that we'll look into, but I'll be honest with you, we've found nothing to link that to anyone so far."

"Except me," I pointed out and slid the number over to him.

The detective scratched his chin. "I hate to speak ill of my colleagues, but that was a rookie move. There were too many witnesses to prove you were elsewhere, and no offence, but you'd have to be a fucking idiot to commit *that* crime the same night your girlfriend was attacked by him."

"I've been called worse."

"I'm sure you have." He rose to his feet and shook my hand. "Okay, I'm going to take all this back to the station and see what I can find out. In the meantime, be careful. If this guy has tried this before, he might have a few more tricks up his sleeve yet."

"Thanks, man," I said.

"I'll walk him out," Karl said and disappeared out of the kitchen with the detective.

"I'd put money on it being Jamieson," Marley said. "If we can take this fucker down once and for all, it'll be a day of celebration." He stood. "Right, I'm out of here." He waved a hand as I moved to walk out with him. "I'll see myself out, and drag Karl along with me." He winked at Siobhan. "Keep him out of trouble, honey."

I turned my head to look at Siobhan. "So … dinner? Where do

you want to go?"

She gaped at me. "After everything that's happened, you *still* want to go out?"

"I'm not letting all this bullshit stop me from living my life. I told you we'd go out for dinner, so that's what we're doing. Anyway, Diesel will be with us, so it'll be safe enough." I checked the time. "Do you want to change or go as you are?"

"Is there something wrong with what I'm wearing?" She bristled and I hid a smile, sweeping my eyes over her.

"You're a little overdressed for my tastes..."

"*Over* dressed?"

I let my grin fly free. "I prefer you naked."

She rolled her eyes at me. "I don't think there are any nudist restaurants in LA."

"I bet I could find one."

"That wasn't a challenge, Dex. I'm not sitting naked in a restaurant so you can get your kicks."

"What about one of those where you eat food *off* someone's body? I could cover you in food."

"We don't need to go out to do that."

My dick stirred. "Maybe we should stay home, then."

She gave me another eye roll. "I thought Gabe was the one with the food fetish?"

I shrugged one shoulder. "I'm wondering if he's onto something. Can't deny there's a certain amount of appeal in the thought of licking things off your body." I tugged her up out of her chair. "Go on, get freshened up. You smell like cookies ... which I have no problem with, but I'm sure you want to smell of something less *edible*. I'll book a table somewhere."

At Diesel's suggestion, I booked a table at a small local restaurant not far from my house instead of going somewhere that risked having reporters lurking around. We arrived a few minutes before our booking time, ate and didn't linger afterwards. That wasn't to say we didn't have an enjoyable meal or took our time, but we were both *so* conscious of everything that had gone on over the past few days that we didn't want to stay out in public for too long.

I didn't admit it to Siobhan, but I was also fucking *tired*. Not so much physically, but mentally exhausted—drained, even. I wanted nothing more than to crawl under the sheets, wrap myself around her and sleep like the dead. I felt a certain degree of relief when we got back to the house and she told me she wanted to go straight to bed. I couldn't even summon up the energy to make a lewd comment, simply followed her upstairs, stripped off and fell into bed.

I think I was asleep before she joined me because when I next opened my eyes, the sun was shining through a gap in the curtains and the scent of cherries was teasing my senses. I stretched out an arm and found my cell on the nightstand. Checking the time, I contemplated staying in bed, but a text came through from Karl and I eased out from Siobhan's arms and headed downstairs to make coffee.

KARL - Call me when you're awake. I have

`news that I'd prefer not to share via a text.`

A grin pulled my lips up. Karl *hated* using text messages, preferring phone calls and leaving voicemails. I would have been willing to take a bet that he'd made Merry send the text instead of doing it himself.

I tapped the call button and he picked up on the first ring.

"You're awake early," Karl said.

"Went to bed early, too. Apparently, that's my thing now." I moved around the kitchen, filled the coffee machine and turned it on.

Karl chuckled. "So, they arrested Jamieson last night. The cell number you gave Detective Conway was also registered to him. There are too many things which link the reporter to being behind this whole thing. His fingerprints were all over the box delivered to your place and your tin."

"How did that end up back in the house?"

"Merry," Karl sighed. "He paid her to take it out of my office and give it to him. And then he dropped it at your house. The lady who keeps your kitchen stocked picked it up and put it in your room."

"He hasn't really broken the law, though, has he?"

"No, but there are technicalities. *Technically*, he bought drugs with intent to supply."

"That's grasping at straws."

"Maybe so, but the fear of it resulting in a prison sentence may stop him."

"I guess."

"What are your plans today?"

"Not sure. I'll see what Siobhan wants to do." And wasn't that a weird thing for me to say? Usually, if there wasn't anything band-related to do, my answer was simple—either stay at home and get stoned, or meet up with Luca and get drunk. Here I was a day or two into trying the whole relationship thing without getting high or drunk, and I wasn't hating it.

I chatted with Karl for a little while longer—ever since he introduced himself to the band and became our manager, he'd always acted somewhat like a father figure to us all. We were lucky to have found a manager like him. He cared beyond how rich we could make him and always had our best interests at heart. He treated us like the kids he'd never had. Yelled at us, lectured us, and was there for every new low we reached, ready to pick us up. I knew, without him, I'd have overdosed and died years ago.

I heard footsteps just as Karl was saying goodbye and turned as Siobhan entered the room. Her red hair was a tangled mess falling around her shoulders, and she was attempting to finger-comb it as she walked. I tossed my cell onto one of the countertops and moved to meet her.

Guarded Addiction

CHAPTER 63

BEAUTIFUL WAY - YOU ME AT SIX

Siobhan

PRESENT

We met in the middle of the kitchen, and it seemed perfectly natural to loop my arms around his neck and pull his head down for a morning kiss. When he lifted his head a few minutes later, his blue eyes were dark and hungry.

"I could get used to that," he murmured, his voice husky. "Coffee?"

"Yes, please." He prepared two mugs and set them down on the table.

"Do you want to do anything today?" he asked.

"I was supposed to go and see my grandmother today, but—" I stopped when a smile lit up his face. "What?"

"Delores?" When I nodded, his smile broadened. "She's still in the same place, right? We'll head up there today. What time were you thinking?"

"I usually get there for eleven and stay for lunch." I gave him a dubious look. "Are you sure you want to come?"

"Absolutely. I like her. I'll let Diesel know." He walked across to where he'd left his cell and tapped the screen—I assumed he was sending Diesel a text. He threw me a smile when he caught me looking at him. "All sorted. We should stop somewhere on the way and grab something for her."

"Like what?"

"A decent lunch. In fact, I have an idea." He messed around with his cell for a minute, then lifted it to his ear. "Hey, Lola ... I know, I know ... two conversations in a week ... Yeah, I did. He's not ready, sweetheart, I'm sorry."

Was he talking to Luca's sister again?

He paused, listening, face serious. "I'll keep trying. Listen, do you still do lunches to go? You *do*, excellent. Could you prepare three for me? A bit of everything. I'll send someone over to collect it in an hour. Thanks, babe." He cut the call and grinned at me. "Sorted. Hope Delores likes Italian."

"You're putting way too much thought into this," I told him and he laughed. "Are you really sure you want to come with me?" I asked him again.

I wasn't certain how my grandmother would respond to his presence. After the last time I'd taken him, she'd asked after him a few times and she'd been shrewd enough to notice how it affected me. Eventually she'd stopped mentioning him, much to my relief.

"Are you ashamed to be seen with me, Cherry Pie?"

"What? No!"

"Are you going to hide the fact we're married from her?"

My eyes dropped to the rings on my fingers. I had to admit

I'd considered it and I knew my silence told him that because he sighed and dropped onto the chair next to me.

"Siobhan, listen to me." One hand appeared in my line of sight and he tucked a finger beneath my chin to turn my head toward him. "I want this with you, you know that, right? This isn't a five-minute distraction for me. I'm not fooling around, it's not a hookup. We got married without really thinking about what we were doing, but I *want* it to be a real marriage." The seriousness of his voice matched the expression on his face. "I know I've been unpredictable. I haven't taken things seriously, but this is different. *Everything* is different now."

He slid off the chair and onto his knees in front of me, reaching for my hands. "If you need me to propose properly, with witnesses, then I'll do it. If you want to get married again, I'm there for that too." His head canted. "We should arrange to do something anyway so our friends can be there. I *want* this, Siobhan, and I hope you do too."

He lifted my hands to his lips and kissed my fingertips. "I knew back then that you were the one. That's why I gave you my grandmother's rings." He smiled at me. "She'd have loved you like *I* love you."

My bottom lip dropped in shock at his words. "You ... love me?" I whispered.

His laugh was low and rough. "I guess I haven't been as obvious about it as I thought, huh? It took me a while to figure out why seeing you flirting with the guys in Black Rosary was driving me crazy. But it was that night in Nashville which really drove it home. I love Luca, but man ... seeing his hands on you ... you touching him ... I was ready to kill you both. I couldn't do it, Red. I couldn't handle it ... and it was then I realized I was in deeper than I thought."

"You love me," I repeated, and smiled. I didn't care about how he'd come to the realization, only that he *had*. I pulled my hands free from his and curved them over his jaw. "You drive me crazy. I'm not completely convinced you're sane. You make me take leaps into the unknown." I leaned forward until my mouth was close to his. "I didn't believe in love until I met you."

The drive to Glendale, where my grandmother lived, was torture. Diesel had picked up the food Dex ordered from Tallorico's and the smell permeated the car, making my mouth water and my stomach rumble.

"I told you to eat breakfast," Dex told me for the fifth time, laughing at the sounds my stomach was making.

"I didn't have time. *Someone* decided joining me in the shower would be a good idea."

He grinned at me. "It was a *great* idea." He draped an arm over my shoulders and bent to press his lips to my ear. "I didn't hear *you* complaining. You seemed to call out for God a lot, though."

I elbowed him in the ribs, and he nipped my earlobe.

"You better behave while we're there," I warned him. "She's become even more outspoken over the years."

Dex snorted.

"I'm serious, Dex. She might not even remember you."

"She'll remember me." He sounded supremely confident.

Diesel parked and walked with us to the nursing home.

"I'll wait out here," he said. "Call if you need me sooner."

Dex held the door open and we walked inside. It was almost like a repeat of the first time I brought him here—the same nurse on duty, almost the same conversation, and then we were on our way down the hallway to her room. As I lifted my hand to knock on her door, Dex's fingers curled around my wrist.

"Hey, Red, before we go in. There's something I should—"

"Dex?" My grandmother's voice called out over him. "Get your fine, tattooed self in here! You didn't come to see me last weekend."

I gaped.

"Oh fuck," Dex muttered.

CHAPTER 64

SNAP OUT OF IT - ARCTIC MONKEYS

Dex
PRESENT

"What does she mean?" Siobhan demanded. "Why does she think you were supposed to come and see her?"

"Yeah, about that. I—"

"Dex Cooper!" Delores yelled again, and I heard the creak of her chair as she stood.

"Dexter, if you don't explain right now what's going on here, I swear to God, I'm walking out."

"Red—"

"Don't *Red* me," she snapped and swatted my hand away when I reached out to tweak a lock of her hair.

"It's not that big a deal, Cherry Pie."

"Why did my grandmother expect to see you last weekend?" Her voice was tight.

"I ... uhh ..." I was enveloped in the scent of lavender before I could explain, and two arms wrapped around me in a hug that almost broke my ribs. I managed to get my hand holding the bag full of food cartons away from my body before the older woman crushed them.

"What is happening right now?" I heard Siobhan mutter.

"Mary and Claire missed you last week," Delores said when she finally released me. Grabbing my hand, she dragged me into her room. I threw an apologetic look at Siobhan and followed her inside.

"I brought a peace offering and an apology," I told Delores, waving the food at her. "Hope you're hungry."

"Will you both stop and tell me what's going on?" Siobhan shouted and we both turned to face her.

"Siobhan," Delores greeted her granddaughter, her eyes flicked to Siobhan's face, and I knew she was looking at the damage Colton had done. "Come and sit down."

Siobhan folded her arms across her chest and glared at me. "Dex…"

"Okay, fine," I said. "Do you remember when I came to see you? You were heading out on a date, but ditched the asshat so you could come to Vegas with me?"

Her eyes narrowed. "You mean the weekend you married me. *That* time?"

I ignored her sarcasm. "Before I came to see you, I visited Delores."

"You did *what?*"

"Oh hush, Siobhan," Delores said. "He wanted to tell me he was finally going to marry you and get my blessing." She reached out to pat my hand. "Dex is a good boy."

I busied myself unpacking the cartons of food from Tallorico's and waited for the explosion.

"You *planned* on marrying me in Vegas?"

"Told you when I met you that I was going to marry you, Cherry Pie," I said.

"You didn't *mean* it!"

I paused and turned my head to look at her. "Of course I meant it. I even sat here and told your grandmother I was going to marry you."

"It wasn't serious, Dex! It was a ploy to stop David from … from …"

I straightened, strode across the room and wrapped an arm around her shoulders. "Baby, don't."

"I think it's my turn to ask what's going on," Delores said.

"Siobhan's landlord attacked her," I said, unable to hide the anger the memory woke from my voice.

"When did this happen?" Delores asked.

"A couple of nights ago." I tightened my arm around Siobhan, drawing her closer to me. "The guy got murdered the same night."

"I see," Delores said slowly. "Are you okay?" she asked her granddaughter.

Siobhan gave a jerky nod. "Dex got there before he could do anything. Now can you please tell me why you expected him to come and see you last weekend?"

"Don't get angry," I said and she glared up at me. "I've been coming to see your grandmother almost every month since you introduced us."

"But you said you came to see her before we went to Vegas."

"I did say that, but that was to get her permission to marry you. I'd been coming most months before that. When I could anyway. There were some months when I was out of town with the band."

Siobhan twisted out of my grip and faced her grandmother. "You *knew* who he was? You've been seeing him all this *time* and never told me?"

"I knew how you'd react," she replied.

"How come you were never here when I came to visit?" she demanded.

I flicked my tongue piercing against my teeth. "There were a few times when you were here and I kinda just... hid until you left."

"You *hid*?" Her outrage struck me as funny and I laughed. "There's nothing remotely funny about this, Dex!"

"I'm sorry, Red. I know... but it *is* kinda funny. I lurked like a creeper so many times waiting for you to leave because I knew neither of us were in the right place to be together. But I wanted to be in your life so bad, so I'd come and hang out with Delores and she'd keep me up to date with what was going on in your life."

"He's a good boy, Siobhan. He's made some mistakes, but he loves you."

Siobhan's jaw dropped. "He *told* you that?"

"For the last time, Cherry Pie, I wouldn't have married you if I didn't love you." I caught her hand and stroked a finger over the rings I'd given her. "I certainly wouldn't have given you my grandmother's rings if I wasn't certain."

"How did you know I wouldn't pawn them?" she demanded.

I shrugged. "I didn't. It was a risk I was willing to take."

"If you loved me so much, why did you walk away from me?"

"I walked away *because* I loved you. I'm an addict, Siobhan. I'm *always* going to be an addict, even if I never touch another drug for the rest of my life. That risk is still there. One slip up is all it takes. Leaving you was the least selfish decision I've ever made in my life."

Her eyes swung to Delores. "And *you* knew all this?"

Her grandmother gave a slow nod. "He came to visit me when he got out of hospital, after he overdosed. I told him then that unless he was positive he could choose *you* over drugs, that he should stay away and leave you to live your life."

I couldn't read the expression on Siobhan's face as she looked between us. She hadn't pulled her hand free of mine, though. That was a good sign … right?

"Tell me you haven't met my mom and dad without me," she said eventually.

"Oh hell, no. I'm not *that* crazy."

Her hand lifted to stroke along my jaw. "I don't even know why I'm surprised. Nothing you do is normal." She looked at her grandmother. "And *you*. I have no words. You're a devious old woman."

Delores laughed. "It's boring in here, Siobhan. We have to find ways to entertain ourselves. Now, can we eat before Mary and Claire come and steal the food?"

We spent most of the day at the nursing home, and Siobhan got front row seats to how many relationships I'd formed with the people who lived there. They dropped in and out of Delores' room to see me, dishing out hugs, kisses, and dating advice—most of which was suspect at best. I could feel Siobhan's eyes on me as I asked about sons, daughters, and grandchildren, but she didn't comment.

When it was finally time to leave, Delores swept me into another rib-crushing hug and then grabbed Siobhan, taking her by surprise.

"Marriages have been started with less than what you two have," she told her granddaughter. "Anything worth keeping is a battle. Don't give up. Fighting is part of the fun, making up afterwards is the prize."

"Gran!" Siobhan's cheeks turned fiery.

Delores tutted. "I was young once too, you know. *You* wouldn't even be here if it wasn't for me and your grandpa getting frisky."

"Oh my god! I don't want to hear this!" Siobhan pressed her hands over her ears and backed away.

Laughing, I threw my arm over her shoulders, blew Delores a kiss and led Siobhan out of the room. It took another fifteen minutes to get out of the building because residents kept stopping to chat, but eventually we made it outside and back into the car.

"I can't believe you've been visiting her all these years," she said once we were in motion.

I sliced a sidelong glance at her. "You're not angry about it?"

"I was ... a little. But, not now. Mom and Dad rarely come to visit, and I try to get there as often as I can, but it's not always possible. So I'm glad someone else has been able to see her."

"I didn't know my own grandmother for long before she died, but Delores reminds me of her. No-nonsense, doesn't pull those punches. I like her."

"Why didn't you tell me you were visiting her?"

"I didn't even think about it until we got here. And then it was too late." A thought occurred to me. "Did you ever tell your mom and dad we got married?"

"Christ no! They would never have understood."

"That you married someone you barely knew? How did *they* meet?" I asked.

"Childhood sweethearts. Dated in school, Mom got pregnant soon after she graduated. They got married. And now they live in marital hatred. Dad has affairs, Mom drowns her sorrows in a string of meaningless hookups. Neither willing to be the one to make that first step toward divorce."

"Sounds cozy."

She laughed. "Very. I try not to spend too much time with them. I call them every couple of months to remind them I'm still alive."

"You know you're going to have to tell them we're together, or they'll see it in the news. You can own the narrative if you tell them first."

"What do you mean?"

"Well, the news will report it however they feel like. But we can give your parents our own version. Our eyes met across the smoky club during a gig, our mutual friend introduced us ..." I waved a hand and flashed her a grin. "It was lust at first sight."

"That's the version you want to go with?"

"What's wrong with it?" I quirked a brow.

"It's a bit ... well ... Hallmark Channel, isn't it?" She fished out a cherry sucker from her purse and unwrapped it.

"Hallmark Channel?" I repeated absently, my eyes tracking the sucker as she popped it into her mouth.

"Girl goes back home to her small town, finds a sweetheart and they live happily ever after ... sometimes one of them dies at the end."

"That's a happy ever after?"

"It's a tearful one."

"I thought Hallmark did feel-good movies."

"They do. They also do sad ones."

"Right," I said faintly.

She leaned back on the seat, and pushed the sucker against one cheek with her tongue while she thought. "No, I think..." She paused. "Okay, we met the night Harper was grabbed. You were there for me while she was missing. I needed the support."

"Because you were upset." I prompted.

"Yes."

A thought occurred to me. "*Were* you upset?"

She slanted a cross look at me. "Of course I was upset. My best friend was missing, feared dead. Why wouldn't I be upset?"

I shrugged one shoulder. "Who was there for you?"

CHAPTER 65

SEMI-CHARMED LIFE - THIRD EYE BLIND

Siobhan
PRESENT

"Who was there for you?" The question hung between us.

I opened my mouth to speak, then hesitated. *No one* had been there for me. I'd waited alone in the apartment for news, chewing my nails in fear and worry the entire time. When Gabe had called to say he'd found her, I'd cut the call and cried.

No one had known. No one had asked how I'd spent my time. Other than Harper, I had no one to lean on.

"I didn't need anyone," I told him, praying my voice stayed firm.

"Everybody needs *someone*, Red," he argued.

I ignored him. "We found ourselves getting closer after they found her and you took me to and from the hospital. It's a natural progression of events."

"Natural progression, right," he repeated. "I like my version better."

"Yours doesn't make sense. Mine has elements of truth in it." I took out my sucker and waved it at him. "Harper's disappearance was in the news, so my parents will accept that as the truth."

"Fine. If that's what you want to go with."

"I do."

We fell silent and the car slid through the traffic, taking us back to his home.

"You should have called me," he said abruptly after a few minutes.

"When?"

"When Harper was missing. We were dealing with Gabe and I didn't even think about what you must have been going through."

I frowned. "Why would I have called you? We weren't talking, remember?" I rolled the cherry sucker around my mouth, knowing his eyes were following the movement of my tongue.

He sighed and tipped his head back against the seat. "This is the problem with you. You give off this completely self-assured, capable persona." He smirked. "But you're a fucking hot mess just like the rest of us." He reached out and took my hand, raised it to his lips and kissed my palm. "It's okay to need to lean on someone else, you know."

"Learn that in your therapy sessions?" I asked, tugging my hand free and waving my sucker at him again. He plucked it out of my hand and tossed it out of the window.

"Maybe. Or maybe I learned it because I realized how much I need you." He leaned across and kissed my cheek, his fingers finding my jaw and turning my face so he could find my lips. "You're like this grounding force in my life, Red. When you're with me, everything makes sense. I don't need to get high with you around." His lips brushed over mine. "You're a drug that won't kill me and I'm not gonna lie, I *am* addicted to you."

His fingers slid into my hair so he could angle my head and parted my lips with his tongue. I lost myself in his kisses, his fingers on my skin, the taste of him on my tongue, and neither of us rose for air until the car parked outside his house and Diesel rapped on the privacy glass.

Dex threw open the car door, climbed out and then reached in for me. We were barely through the door before he turned and cupped my face between his palms.

"What do you say, Cherry Pie? Want to spend the next fifty years being my sole addiction?"

I looped my arms around his neck and leaned into him, breathing in his scent. "I am open to being convinced."

His blue eyes flared, and he reached back to unwind my hands and pinned them above my head, then leaned close so his mouth was almost touching mine.

"Tell me your safe word, Red," he whispered.

"Pineap—" I began to say, but he kissed me before I finished speaking.

Just like he always did.

EPILOGUE

LET THE BAND PLAY - BADFLOWER

TWO MONTHS LATER

Dex

We sat in the green room backstage of one of LA's biggest music shows on television, ready to perform our upcoming single release. Luca was twirling a drumstick between his fingers, Seth's fingers were flicking against his thigh—almost as though he was playing an invisible guitar—Gabe was pacing.

A year ago, I would have been hiding outside somewhere smoking a joint and watching people milling around. Now, though, I had my feet propped up on the table and was sipping a bottle of water.

Hardcore rock star living the dream, right here.

I didn't care, though. I felt better, both physically and mentally, than I had in a long time. The rest of the band had been great, none of them drinking whenever I was around. I knew, in time, I'd be fine being around alcohol but, for now, I was still being careful.

"Ready to go, guys?" A young woman popped her head around the door. "Courtney will be introducing you right after the ad break."

Seth and Luca rose to their feet while Gabe spun around, and he pulled the mantel of 'Gabe Mercer—ultimate fucking *rock star*' around him. He threw his head back, a teasing smile playing around his lips.

"Thanks, darlin'," he said and took the lead as she led us through the labyrinth toward the stage.

The curtain hid us from the live audience and we took our places. Gabe stood central in front of the microphone, Seth on his left and me on the right. Luca hopped up behind the drumkit.

No matter how many times we did this—performed in front of a crowd, large or small—there was always a certain amount of nervous anticipation which would drop the second we began to play. When we heard Courtney speak, Gabe took a step back, and the lights dimmed.

I hit my bass, feeling the notes vibrate through the floor, knowing the people in the crowd would feel it through the soles of their feet and up through their bodies until it synced with their heartbeats.

After a couple of beats, Luca joined in on the drums, and the curtains dropped. Gabe stepped forward and threw out his arms and the screen behind us lit up with the wings from our logo, turning him into a dark fallen angel.

He didn't speak, didn't move, waiting while Seth's guitar wove its magic in between my bass and Luca's drums, and then he grabbed the microphone and launched into "How Could I Forget You."

Through the flashes of lights hitting the audience, I could see they were all on their feet, screaming and shouting, but we couldn't hear them above our own instruments.

Gabe hit the high note, throwing his head back before bouncing forward and throwing his arms wide. He spun in a circle, singing the chorus, and came to a stop beside Seth. A grin spread across his face, and he nudged our guitarist, who ignored him, concentrating on the complicated guitar solo he was playing to a live audience for the first time.

Gabe nudged him again, and Seth's head came up, scowling. Gabe smirked and tapped his cheek with one finger. Seth shook his head. Gabe pouted—literally *pouted*—and elbowed him again.

Seth stopped playing, leaving me and Luca keeping the tune and slapped his palms against Gabe's chest to shove him backwards, lips moving furiously as he swore at our lead singer. Gabe rolled his eyes and tapped his cheek again. Seth shook his head and pushed past him, knocking him out of the way with his shoulder as he stalked to the far side of the stage.

Gabe jumped up onto one of the speakers and posed for the cell-wielding fans near the stage. Stripping off his t-shirt, he threw it into the audience, and pointed at his stomach. I snorted a laugh. Someone had written BITE ME and a downward arrow in black marker just above the waistline of his pants. He caught my eye and cocked an eyebrow, licked the tip of his finger and slid it down his ribs until he could pat the words. He blew me a kiss, back-flipped off the speaker and prowled across the stage to where Seth stood.

Grabbing our guitarist's face, he licked up the side of his neck and slapped an open-mouthed kiss to his cheek.

The crowd went wild.

Seth, as usual, took it in his stride, without dropping a note, and Gabe launched into the final verse, hooking an arm around our guitarist's neck and resting his head on Seth's shoulder. Seth, to the delight of the crowd, turned his head and pressed a kiss into Gabe's hair.

Then something changed. Gabe stiffened and he slowly lifted his head, brows pulling together. He stopped singing mid-verse and dropped the mic to the floor, took a slow look around the stage and walked off. I moved over to where Seth stood and leaned close.

"Where the fuck is he going?" I shouted above the music.

Seth shook his head. "Not sure. Keep playing. He'll be back."

And sure enough, Gabe reappeared moments later, a bottle of water in his hand, which he took a long swallow from and then tossed to one side. Hopping back up onto the speakers, he sung the final verse again, threw back his head and raised his arms.

Our logo flickered onto the screen, Seth's guitar fell silent, followed by Luca's drums. The lights pulsed along with my bass, then dropped, until it was just me, and then, I too fell silent.

I could almost hear the audience draw in a breath, then the applause started, and the lights flooded back on.

I took a second to cast my eye over the front row. Harper was there, with Riley, and there was Siobhan, jumping and clapping alongside everyone else. Gabe lifted his wrist to his lips, his eyes on Harper as she mouthed 'I love you' back to him.

And then we were being spoken to by Courtney Munroe, congratulated on our new single, and the usual round of interview questions began.

Seth

"We're here." Carter's voice jerked me out of my memories, and I blinked, refocusing on the car's interior.

If ever there was a time when I wished I was still a day-drinker, this was it, but I'd promised Riley I wouldn't go in there drunk.

"Seth?"

I jerked at the sound of my name. *Oh yeah, I still hadn't moved.*

"Wait out here," I said and threw open the car door. "I don't know how long I'll be."

"It's fine. I'll be here." Carter's voice gave away no indication of what he thought about what I was doing.

I nodded. "Right." I still didn't move. I should have let Riley come with me like she'd asked. Or Gabe. But Gabe had his own shit going on, and I hadn't wanted to cut into it.

"Do you want me to come in with you?" Carter asked.

"No. No, I'm good. I got this." I forced myself out of the car and up the steps of the private care facility.

The automatic doors slid open silently at my approach and I entered an air-conditioned reception area. A plush mauve carpet was the only splash of color in the otherwise white room. Even the woman manning the desk wore white. She looked up as I approached, her warm smile faltering when she took in the tattoos covering my arms and the skull piercing my eyebrow.

"I have an appointment with Dr. Grayson," I told her. "Regarding Marcie Enshaw."

She consulted the screen in front of her. "Mr. Hawkins?" She gave no sign of recognizing me or my name. "I'll let the doctor know you're here. If you'd like to take a seat …" She nodded the seats along one wall.

"Thank you."

I sat down and pulled out my cell to drop Riley a text telling her I'd arrived and that I'd call her once I was out, then switched it off so it wouldn't cause any disturbances while I was here.

"Mr. Hawkins?" I looked up to find a grey-haired fifty-something man in front of me, one hand outstretched. "I'm glad you decided to come."

I stood and shook his hand. "Have to admit it was touch and go for a minute there."

His smile was warm. "Understandable. Come through. I thought we could have a chat first, and then, if you're still comfortable, I'll take you through."

I nodded and followed him through a door, which had to be unlocked by an orderly and then into an office.

"Take a seat." He waved a hand toward a chair.

I sank into it, and he took the one opposite. "Can I get you anything? Something to drink?"

I bit back a laugh. I'd *kill* for a drink, but I doubted that was the kind he meant. "I'm good, thanks. I don't want to be rude, but I'd like to get it over with."

"No, I understand." He leaned back in his chair and eyed me. "Marcie has been doing really well. We've managed to find the perfect balance of medication to keep her calm and stable."

"Does she remember anything?"

"She's working through it. Her memory is intact. She simply doesn't like to think about it. It upsets her, for obvious reasons. But we have regular sessions and are working through everything."

"Does she know about Lex—Olivia," I corrected myself quickly. Marcie wouldn't know my sister by the name she'd picked out for herself.

"No. We felt that she wasn't quite ready to hear about what happened to your sister. For now, it's enough to know that you were willing to come and see her."

I licked dry lips. "I'm not—"

"I know you have reservations, Seth. But I honestly believe this will help *both* of you."

I gave a slow nod.

"Are you ready?"

"As I'll ever be."

The doctor smiled. "I'll go and ask someone to bring her through." He rose to his feet and walked across to the door. A short muted conversation later and he was back.

I shot to my feet, unable to sit still any longer, and paced the floor, gnawing on a thumbnail. When the door swung open a few minutes later, I froze and slowly turned to watch as my mother entered the room.

She looked much better than the last time I'd laid eyes on her. Her skin no longer had that unhealthy yellow pallor. Her hair was thicker and shiny, falling around her face in waves. She was still too thin, though.

She stopped just inside the doorway and stared at me. "Nate?"

I swallowed past the lump in my throat. "It's Seth now," I murmured.

"Oh ... yes, I'm sorry." Her eyes, dark and wide, tracked over me.

We met in the center of the room, and I folded her into my arms.

"My sweet boy," she whispered. "I'm so sorry. So so sorry."

My head bent of its own accord, and I buried my face into her hair. "Me too," I whispered.

Luca

The burn of overworked muscles was a welcome pain. With my earphones plugged into my ears, I followed the rhythm of the song, my fists connecting with the punchbag at every beat of the drum.

I could feel Dex's eyes on me, knew he was waiting for the right moment to raise whatever was bugging him. If it was what I thought it was, then there would *never* be a right time, but I was willing to wait and see.

The song came to an end, and I lifted my wrists so I could use my teeth to pull off the support wraps before turning to face him.

"Why are you watching me work out?"

Dex shrugged. "Got nothing else to do today."

"Nothing at all?" His shoulder lifted again and I scowled. "I don't need a babysitter."

"I'm not babysitting you."

I huffed. "What else would you call sitting here like a creeper watching me?" I threw my wrist wraps to one side and stretched, first one leg, then the other. "Why are you here, Dex?"

"Better question is, why *wouldn't* I be here?" He propped his feet up on my weights' bench.

"Unless you've developed an unhealthy interest in watching me sweat or you want my dick, I don't know why you'd spend so much time here."

"Rest assured, I have no interest in your dick." He smirked. "But since you brought it up, when did you last use it?"

"My dick?" I frowned. "Does jerking off in the shower count? If so, then a few hours ago."

"It would count if you were seventeen and an awkward virgin, but you're not. And I've never seen you go this long without a woman."

I arched a brow. "Are you worried about me? Or are you not getting enough pussy from Siobhan and need a helping hand? If that's the problem, just spit it out."

"Of course, I'm fucking worried about you. We *all* are."

"Seth isn't." I grabbed my water bottle and took a healthy swallow.

"Seth *is*. He wouldn't have dragged us all to London to bring you home if he didn't give a shit."

I pointed the bottle at him. "Seth is worried about the band, not me."

"*Everyone* is worried about the band. If your heart isn't in it, we're done."

"I'm the drummer. Easily replaceable."

"Fuck that. We're Forgotten Legacy, and that means you, me, Gabe, and Seth. Not some random stranger taking one of our places. One of us goes, we all go."

I rolled my eyes. "You're so fucking sentimental. What is this shit? Anyone can drop a drum beat."

"Bullshit," Dex snapped. "Why do you do that?"

I paused mid-stretch. "Do what?"

"Downplay your role in the band. You always do it."

A sneer twisted my lips. "You *really* think anyone gives a fuck about the drummer? Or even the bassist, for that matter. So long as Gabe and Seth are front and center, the fans are happy. Don't pretend like that's not the reality."

"That's *not* the reality."

I grunted. He wasn't going to convince me that wasn't the way of things, and he knew it. We'd had this argument a hundred times before. I had no idea why he was bringing it up again.

"Okay, if it's not my dick you're after, or my talent at finding willing pussy to share ... why *are* you here?"

"Because you're my *friend*, and you've been stuck inside this apartment for weeks. Ryder has been cooling his heels with fuck all to do."

"Ryder's been telling tales, huh?" Ryder had been my bodyguard for the last couple of months. The one before him had walked out after I punched him. Can't blame him for that, really. I couldn't even remember the guy's name or why I hit him.

"For fuck's sake, Luca!" my usually laid-back friend roared. "Get your head out of your fucking ass. This miserable pity party has to stop."

"Pity party?" Reaching back, I grabbed the neck of my t-shirt and dragged it over my head. "There is no pity party. I'm just not going to pretend everything is perfect."

"Seth was—"

"Fuck Seth. It's not about Seth!" I shouted. "Not everything is about fucking Seth!" I threw my t-shirt to the floor, battling to control my temper while Dex frowned at me.

"If all this shit isn't about Seth, then what's going on?"

"Leave it alone, D." I walked out of my gym and toward the bathroom to take a shower.

"I'll pick you up in the morning." He strode past me and continued down the hallway to my front door.

"Fuck you, Dex!"

The door slammed on his departing figure.

The silence left behind in his wake was heavy, and I briefly considered going after him. But given my state of mind and the clear anger he displayed, I decided against it. The last thing either of us needed was a public showdown, which is what would happen if I pushed it. Forgotten Legacy had had enough drama in the last few months without me adding even more to it.

Shaking my head, I took my after-workout shower, pulled on my favorite dark grey sweats, and dropped onto one of the oversized bean bags that worked as seating in my living room. A little green light was flashing on my cell, and I scooped it up from where I'd left it on the floor.

Unlocking the screen, I tapped the notification and vented a soft laugh when it opened. Looked like my Personal Conscience was checking in.

PC - I haven't heard from you for a couple of days. Are you okay?

ME - Don't panic. I haven't reached the point of offing myself quite yet.

The response was almost immediate.

PC - `Don't even joke about things like that. It's not funny.`

Whatever higher power had seen fit to cause me to send a text meant for a dead woman to the wrong number had done me a huge favor. The text conversations we'd had over the past few months, since I came home, had been a life-raft keeping me afloat when I was alone ... and I was alone a lot.

She had talked me off the ledge—or was that texted me off it?—the night I'd returned to LA, and we'd spoken via message almost every day since.

That first night, when I'd mistyped Lexi's cell number and sent a message meant for a ghost, a living, breathing person had replied and saved my life. Not that I'd told her that. We'd chatted for hours, her never pushing for answers, and the random anecdotes she shared about her daily life and family dramas had slowly drawn my mind away from the abyss I'd been staring down.

Since then, our conversations had covered all sorts of subjects, apart from three—her name, my name, and either of our occupations. I found it kinda liberating, in a way. She couldn't judge me based on my public reputation, only on the things I'd told her. She couldn't Google me because she didn't know my name, and that meant she was talking to me out of genuine interest in my well-being and *not* because of the fame and fortune I possessed.

It didn't stop me from thinking how sad it was that a stranger was more concerned about my mental health than my friends were.

A ding from my phone drew my attention back down to it.

PC - I need you to tell me you're not spiraling.

ME - I'm not spiraling.

Gabe

I stood in the doctor's reception room waiting for Harper. My lighter was in my left hand, and I absently flicked it open and closed, the soft repetitive click it made keeping my mind focused away from the things I had to tell her once we were out of here.

I'd wanted to go into the appointment with her, but she asked me not to. Had said that she didn't think she could do what she needed to do if I was in there, so I was stuck out here, waiting and thinking up the worst possible scenarios in my head.

When the door opened and Doctor Reynolds poked her head out, I closed my lighter, shoved it into my pocket and strode across the room.

"You can come in now. Harper is waiting for you, and then we can talk," she said. Her voice gave no indication on whether the news was good or bad.

My eyes immediately sought out Harper when I entered the room, and I found her sitting on a chair opposite a desk, bottom lip caught between her teeth. I dropped into the seat beside her and reached for her hand.

"You okay?" I asked in a low voice and she gave me a jerky nod, but her fingers trembled in mine.

"So, Harper … Gabe. I have the results from the tests." The doctor settled behind the desk and looked at us. "I'm afraid it's not good news."

I squeezed Harper's fingers.

"We think when you were in the car accident, there was some damage to your fallopian tubes. Because it was so long before you were able to get medical assistance, and due to the extent of your injuries once you were discovered, they went unnoticed as the focus was, at the time, on far more important things. The scarring caused by those injuries means there's a high likelihood that you will not be able to have children."

I closed my eyes, not wanting to see Harper's reaction. This was *my* fault. Once again, something I'd caused was hurting Harper.

"Not ever?" she asked, and the tremble in her voice sliced me in two.

"I wouldn't like to say that. There's always a tiny chance, but it's not something I would set my heart on. I'm sorry, Harper."

She sucked in a shaky breath and stood. "That's okay. Thank you."

The rest of the doctor's words faded under the ton of guilt I felt, and it was only Harper rising to her feet that forced me to bring my attention back to the room.

We both shook the doctor's hand and left. Remy was waiting with the car when we stepped outside, and I helped Harper inside.

"Talk to me, Frosty," I said softly, running my knuckles over her cheek. "Tell me what you're thinking."

"I think I knew before she told me. I must have, otherwise why would I have wanted to check and make sure?" she said and gave a little laugh. "It's not like we're planning on having kids any time soon, anyway, right? I wouldn't want to have them until we were married."

I nodded. "And there are other options we can explore, when the time is right. We're still young; we have time." I told her what I thought she needed to hear, but knew neither of us believed it. "We can get a second opinion. I bet there are specialists out there who can help." She gave me a wobbly smile, and I pulled her into my arms. "I love you, Harper. We'll get through this."

She rested her head against my shoulder and we drove back to the penthouse in silence.

Back home, Harper disappeared to take a bath and I let her go without argument. She needed time to digest what the doctor had said, to regroup and regain her balance. I knew she'd come out fighting. That was who Harper was. This wouldn't keep her down. I had to be patient. I couldn't make the same mistake I had when she first came home from hospital after Miles had taken her. I had to make sure she knew I was *here* for her.

I walked out onto the enclosed patio, which ran the length of the penthouse, and leaned against the railing which spanned one side. My lighter was back in my hand, and I flicked it open and closed as I stared out over the city.

There was a storm coming. I could feel it. And I wasn't sure what form it would take or where it would hit, but I knew it would be damaging to all of us. I felt powerless to stop it, yet I was wholly responsible for the path it was taking. All I could do was stand strong and hope I could repair the devastation it would undoubtedly leave behind.

L. Ann

AUTHOR NOTE

This book wouldn't have been possible without the support of a group of amazing people, so here's my thanks:-

My **admin team** - Tami, Tommie, Jen, Angela and Elise (who'll probably shout at me for putting her last).

To **Crystal** who has been my go-to person for all things drug-related for Dex's book. Without her, I probably would have got so many details wrong!

To my **Literati** - you guys keep me going with your enthusiasm and passion for the characters.

To **Aubrey** - words cannot express how much you blow me away with the covers and swag you design for me. Thanks for enabling my crazy ideas and coming up with just as many of your own. We need to figure out a way to make these guys really real!

To **Margot** - my editor - for understanding there are some things I just won't change no matter what.

To my **ARC team** - those final eyes on the book before it goes out to the world. You are an essential cog in the machine and you have no idea how nerve-racking it is sending a book out to you and waiting for your feedback. But you make it worthwhile every single time.

To **Lasairiona** - you're crazy and you feed into my crazy. Here's to Vegas 2022.

To **everyone** - when I first announced I was writing a

rockstar romance and taking a step away from paranormal, it was with a ton of nerves and questions on whether it was something I could do. Thank you for joining me on the ride and loving my broken rockstars as much as I do.

Luca's next - let's find out what mess he's getting himself into!

If you're not already a member, you can join me in my **Facebook Group**

https://facebook.com/groups/lannsliterati

I also have a **newsletter** where you get a free novella for signing up!

https://lannauthor.com/keep-in-touch

You can also find the playlist which goes along with this book on my **YouTube** channel.

FORGOTTEN LEGACY SERIES

Tattooed Memories - Book 1

Strawberry Delight - FREE Short Story

(available via my website)

Shattered Expectations - Book 2

Guarded Addiction - Book 3

Exquisite Scars - Book 4

(Coming September 2021)

MIDNIGHT PACK SERIES

Midnight Touch - Book 1

Midnight Temptation - Book 2

Midnight Torment - Book 3

Midnight Hunt Book 3.5

Midnight Fury - Book 4

Midnight Fire - Book 5

(coming October 2021)

Printed in Great Britain
by Amazon